HEIR

DEAD HOLLOW TRILOGY (BOOK THREE)

JUDY K. WALKER

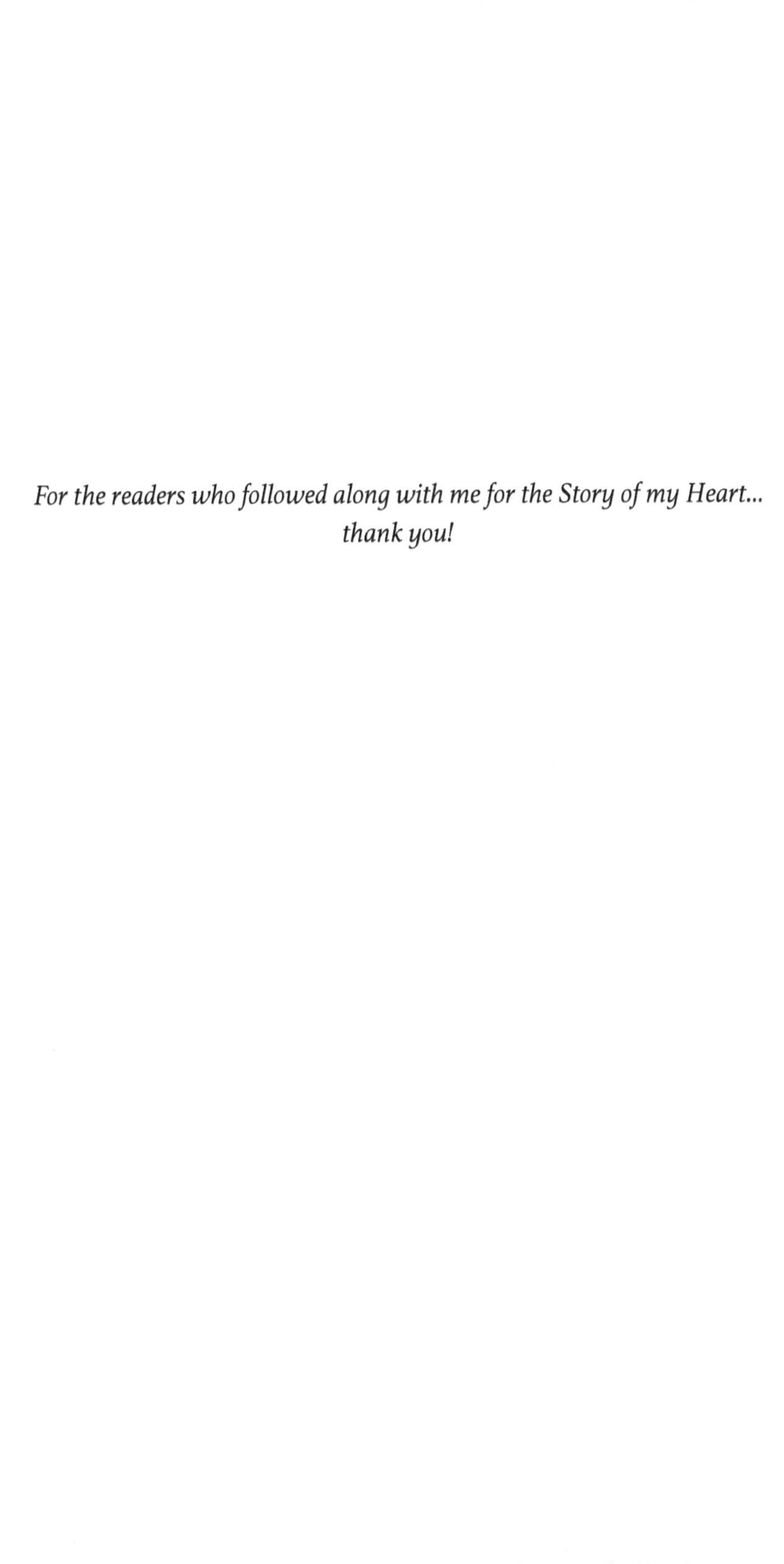

For the readers who followed along with me for the Story of my Heart...
thank you!

1

————

here am I?

Disoriented, Adam tried to turn and take in his surroundings, but he wasn't certain where he was. Not where he found himself in a geographic sense, but where *he* —whatever made *him* uniquely *him*—was. Adam wasn't in his own body. In someone else's? But he didn't have a sense of seeing through someone else's eyes, either; he just *saw*.

What did he see? It was dark, but not a void. He waited patiently for features to reveal themselves. Was he inside or outside? *Both. Or neither.* He smelled earth, damp stone and decomposition, and the lonely history of the world. He was drawn toward a charcoal grayness that was a cousin to light, and toward a small figure huddled within it. There was something else, something he recoiled from as he passed, but he couldn't stop. He was pulled to something else. To someone else.

Her face was a pale glow in the darkness, close to the ground. Too close to be standing. She was kneeling, or sitting on her heels. *She...* who was she? He couldn't speak to ask. Fear rolled from her like shock waves from an explosion. He could see the fear more clearly than he could see her. It pressed against him. More than a current—a tsunami in an ocean of fear.

He had a sense of movement, tiny ghost flashes—her hands? Why couldn't Adam see her hands? One of the flashes went to her face, and her face disappeared. Unnerved, he struggled to get closer, to comprehend.

Until he could distinguish a hint of color, a subtly shaded difference in the dark.

Blood.

Her hands were bathed in blood, and now her face—where her hands touched—had disappeared beneath it.

No... no, no, no—

She opened her mouth and screamed.

And he screamed with her.

Evie...

2

Adam fell through the grayness, flailing, hands catching at something... no, he was sliding. Sliding out of a chair. His back twisted painfully as his body torqued, one arm caught in the frame of a hospital bed, until he came to a stop in a half squat. His heart fluttered, and his returning vision grayed out again when he stood.

Come on, he thought, ignoring the tightness in his chest. *Come on...*

Breathing helped, once Adam remembered to do it.

Harlan's face swam into focus. Crisp, white sheet pulled up to his chin. Eyes closed, as they always were now. So it wasn't Harlan.

Evie. It all returned to him in a rush. Evie was in danger. Back in Cold Springs, a hundred or so miles away. He had to warn JJ that her daughter was in danger.

Adam's mind stumbled, sluggish. *Phone*. He needed a phone. He patted his pockets before remembering he still hadn't replaced the cell phone he'd trashed while trying to save Harlan. Of course Harlan didn't have a phone, and there was no landline in the hospital room. Adam staggered into the hallway toward the nurse's station. There was no one there, which was often the case this time of day. Night. Whatever.

He bumped the counter as he rounded it and grabbed the receiver from the desk. Silence. How was he supposed to get an outside line? He pushed a button and heard a clicking noise, but no dial tone. He punched another button. Still nothing.

"What are you doing?" a woman asked. Her dark hair was pulled back, and she wore blue scrubs and a frown.

Adam recognized her, but couldn't make out her name tag. His eyes still weren't quite focusing. "I—I'm sorry," he stuttered. "I have to make a call, and I can't figure out how to do it."

"This isn't a phone booth," she said.

"I know, but this is important. Please," he begged. "Please help me."

Her mouth twisted as she looked around. She took the receiver from his hand and sighed. "This one time," she said, punching buttons before handing the receiver back to Adam. "You can dial now. But make it quick."

"Thank you." Adam's fingers trembled as he dialed, and it took so long to go through, he feared he'd gotten the number wrong. Finally, it started ringing. "Come on, JJ, pick up. Come on—"

On the fourth ring, JJ's voice cut in. "What? Am I on?"

"JJ, it's Adam," he said, counting to three in his mind to give her a chance to wake up. He knew she was answering automatically, that she could make it through the shower and be parking at the Plattsville hospital for an emergency shift before realizing where she was.

"Adam? What's wrong?" Her mouth fumbled a bit with *wrong*, still trying to wake up. "Is Harlan okay?"

"He's fine. I need you to do something for me."

"Okay..." As she dragged out the word, her mind seemed to clear. "What is it that you need me to do at four a.m.?"

"Go check on Evie."

"Why?"

"Just do it!" Adam snapped, then pressed his cold hand against his warm forehead as he turned away from the nurse, who pretended not to watch him. "I'm sorry, JJ. Please do it now. I'll wait."

Adam rocked on his heels where he stood, back and forth, trying to cover the shimmy that encompassed his entire body. Trying to pretend he wasn't screaming inside. *Come on...*

An elderly man in pajamas approached the desk. He'd seen the man before, maybe roaming the halls. The nurse glanced at Adam, eyes narrowed, before reluctantly stepping away to assist the patient.

What's taking so long?

JJ's voice came over the line. "Adam, are you still there?"

He opened his mouth, but the sound that came out wasn't a word. "Yes," he said on his second try.

"She's fine," JJ said. "She's sleeping."

Adam dropped into one of the chairs, rested his head on his free hand, and whispered a prayer of thanks.

"And she's breathing," JJ added, "because I checked. I haven't done that since she had pneumonia when she was little. You want to tell me why you felt you had to scare the shit out of me?"

Short of breath, he didn't answer immediately.

"Adam? You there?"

"I had a dream," he whispered. "A very bad dream."

He could feel JJ on the other end, considering. "Like your 'dreams' before? When you saw things happening to people?"

People. To Rachel. And his mother and father. And him. "Not exactly. What if I saw something that's *going to* happen, that hasn't happened yet?"

JJ blew out her breath on the other end, and he could see her sinking back on her bed. But how? Was it his imagination? Intuition?

Her voice dropped. "Did you throw up?"

Leave it to JJ to get right to the point.

"No," he admitted. And that was unusual for his visions.

"Have you ever seen something like that before? Something... what's the word? Prescient?" she asked.

"No."

"So maybe that's all it was," she said gently. "A bad dream."

"Maybe," he said. Because he wanted to believe that. But he didn't. Not yet. "I'm sorry for waking you, JJ. Crap, you've got a hearing today, don't you? Is it for shooting the cop, or for the restraining order?"

"The protective order. But I'll have the same attorney with me."

"Will Marcus have a lawyer?"

"I don't know."

Adam waited—for her to say something else, for his anxiety to fade away. Neither happened. "How do you feel about seeing Marcus?"

"I feel like he's an asshole. How am I supposed to feel?" she asked. "Sorry. I don't want to talk about it."

"Would it help if I—"

"I said, I don't want to talk about it," JJ cut in. "How about we dig through your major life mistakes instead?"

Adam rubbed the building ache in his forehead. "I haven't taken enough chances to make major life mistakes. Not the kind that matter."

JJ sighed. "Aren't we a pair of pathetic turds?"

It was the language of their childhood. Adam could almost feel JJ's shoulder touching his while they leaned against the oak tree in her yard. He replied, "Except now we're old and crusty pathetic turds."

"Speak for yourself," JJ said, laughing softly. "Go back to sleep, Crusty."

"Okay," he said, though he knew he wouldn't. "You, too."

He set the phone down gently when he heard the line click, then went back to kneading his brows. The nurse hadn't returned. He wondered if she'd use a hand sanitizer on the phone when she did. Ear sanitizer? Was there such a thing?

"Adam?"

With his eyes closed and one ear still dodgy from its recent river injury, Iris's voice was almost unrecognizable. She sounded like an elderly woman—a grandmother—which Iris had never done. He almost dreaded opening his eyes and seeing how thin she'd gotten in the past weeks. How much she'd aged. When he did, he forced himself to smile.

"Is Harlan all right?" she asked.

He nodded, rose and put an arm around her bony shoulder. She'd said she was making a run to the twenty-four-hour Walmart to pick up some essentials, but Adam was pretty sure she'd lied. Iris had been spending a lot of time in the hospital chapel, more than she wanted to admit to. Or rather, she wouldn't want to admit why. Iris was a churchgoing woman, but she'd never had much truck with people who asked for intercessory prayer. Now, with Harlan's condition unchanging, that's all she had. And Iris didn't like to be a hypocrite.

"Why were you on the phone to JJ?" she asked.

"What makes you think—"

"Who else would you call at such a crazy hour?"

Days and weeks spent sitting, waiting, had not given her more patience for playing verbal games, either. Unless, of course, she was the one dodging.

"She has a hearing tomorrow on her restraining order," Adam said, not precisely answering because he'd learned from the best.

Iris wrapped her arm around his waist, and he hoped she couldn't pick up any physiological clues—sweating, heart pounding, shaking—that he was still upset. She had enough to worry about.

"She think it'll go okay?" Iris asked.

"Who knows?" he replied. "JJ is the Queen of Compartmentalization. And there are rooms in her mind that she never returns to."

"How is that different from locking yourself in a room you never leave?"

Adam stopped, and felt Iris stop next to him. Was that what he'd done, his entire adult life? Even beyond that, into childhood?

Iris had covered her mouth with her hand. "I'm sorry," she whispered.

The anxiety from his dream, the grief on her face—together they squeezed his chest up into his throat. He forced a smile that he doubted was convincing and pulled her back to his side. "You are a wicked old woman. The big bad wolf would've had his work cut out for him with you." Then he kissed the top of her head. Her long, white-gray hair smelled like vanilla. "Love you, Gram."

"Back at you, kiddo," she said.

Returning to the room, Iris took the chair closest to Harlan, pulled a shawl tight around her shoulders and tucked her chin to her chest, eyes closed as if she were going to nap. "I think you should take a break and stay in Cold Springs for a while."

Adam had started to slump in his own chair, but straightened. "How long is a while?"

"I'll be home in a day or two—I need to take care of some things that have piled up around the house—and we can talk about it then."

"Do you not want me here?" Adam asked.

Her eyes opened slowly, and she glared at him. "Don't even try it. I've spent decades resisting manipulation."

"Okay, okay," he said, raising his hands in surrender. He hadn't been trying to manipulate her—at least not consciously. He spent a moment or two feeling guilty, before he realized (it was a wee bit early to expect the synapses to be fully firing) *Iris* was manipulating *him*. She'd just won the argument, such as it was.

She is a wicked old woman.

Adam almost smiled. He would have, except he couldn't help feeling she'd done it because she was hiding something from him.

3

JJ tugged at her pantyhose, praying the run her thumbnail had started at her left butt cheek this morning didn't make a sudden break for her knee. Her skirt would cover it that far. Except for the walking slit in the back. God, she hated skirts. But that's what one wore when facing an asshole across the aisle, and hopefully not one behind the bench.

She glanced at her watch, a delicate gold timepiece she never wore. Had her ex-husband Marcus given it to her? JJ felt an instant's panic (Would he notice? Take it as some kind of signal?) before remembering it had been a gift from her mother. She should have known. It wasn't JJ's style, but it did *have a style*. Well-made and probably not cheap, it couldn't have come from Marcus.

The county courthouse was mostly empty. JJ didn't know if that was normal or not. Other than a field trip as a kid, she'd only ever spent any significant time in the hideous brick building when she'd gotten her divorce. (That may have colored her opinion of its architecture.)

Where the hell was Faith Callaway? The lawyer had asked to meet her at the courthouse before their hearing, and JJ had been watching the clock for hours, ever since Adam woke her. That is, when she wasn't watching her daughter.

She'd been doing that when Evie woke, but in a rare moment of mother-daughter rapprochement, Evie hadn't complained. JJ hadn't discussed the upcoming hearing with her daughter, but Evie knew it was happening today. Of course, JJ's wardrobe would have been a dead giveaway. And Evie must have felt JJ's anxiety. The child even said her mother looked pretty, when JJ knew she really wanted to tell her she looked "weird." She said that any time JJ wore anything other than jeans, sweatpants, or scrubs.

And there was her attorney, in a navy blue skirt suit, looking impatient with the elderly security guard who held her up. JJ rushed down the hall to meet Ms. Calloway, ankles wobbling the slightest bit in her unfamiliar heels. *Finally...*

She must have spoken her frustrated relief aloud. Ms. Callaway raised an indignant brow while adjusting the bag on her shoulder and tucking her bobbed, brown hair behind one ear.

"Sorry," JJ said, wiping her sweaty hands on her skirt. Fortunately, Ms. Callaway didn't offer to shake. "My nerves are a goddamn mess."

JJ regretted her words as soon as they'd left her mouth. Now she'd gone and taken the Lord's name in vain. Not that she thought the Lord cared, but plenty of his followers did, and having only met the woman once, she didn't know if her lawyer was one of them. "Sorry," JJ said again.

The woman's face softened and she said, "Let's go over there," pointing JJ to a bench.

Ms. Callaway settled her bag next to her and patted the hard wood for JJ to sit. JJ did so carefully, clutching her purse on her lap. Paranoia about her pantyhose, the zipper in her skirt, the buttons on her blouse, and any other potential wardrobe malfunction made it difficult to focus on her attorney's words.

"Normally you wouldn't have an attorney for this kind of

thing. Well, maybe from legal aid, but not from our office," the woman admitted.

"But Jeffrey appreciated everything I'd done for his mom while she was in the hospital," JJ said of the public defender.

"Mr. Lewis said that?" Her lawyer's mouth twitched. "Yeah, well, that might be true, but my boss also has his eyes on the cameras. And he doesn't want your case to blow up in our faces."

"Which case?" JJ asked.

"Excellent question," her lawyer acknowledged. "You know Sheriff Mason asked the State Police to take over the investigation into the officer-involved shooting."

JJ nodded, although "Sheriff Mason" always made her think of Grant's father Ulysses, the old Sheriff.

"You have not yet been charged, and you may not ever be. Here in West Virginia," the lawyer continued, "we have the Castle Doctrine. Broadly, that means you can use force to protect your-self or your family against an intruder, including deadly force."

"Sounds right," JJ said.

Ms. Callaway raised a finger. "Except, you have to have had a reasonable fear that you were in imminent peril of being killed or greatly harmed. That's when things get complicated, because the man you shot was on your property but not on your porch or in your home, and he was a law enforcement officer."

JJ squeezed her purse harder to keep her hands from shaking. "But I didn't know he was a cop."

Ms. Callaway rested her hand on JJ's arm. "None of this is insurmountable, and the fact that they didn't identify themselves works in your favor. If it comes to it, we'll also argue that they weren't acting in performance of their official duties, that they had no authority to be there—they weren't even Beecham County deputies—and we'll bring in the prisoner escape."

She paused, considering.

"Although if it gets to that point, they might try to remove me as your counsel, since I was Virgil Rutledge's lawyer, too." Ms.

Callaway waved a hand through the air dismissively. "Sorry. I'm just giving you the context. The fact that you'd been threatened and that you applied for a protective order the day of the shooting, these are all relevant to whether your actions were reasonably made in self-defense. That's why I'm here, to make sure nothing crazy happens with your protective order that could adversely affect your criminal case, if you're charged. Okay?"

JJ took a deep breath. "Clear as mud."

Her lawyer opened her mouth to follow up, until something behind JJ caught her eye. Ms. Callaway's mouth closed and hardened. JJ's neck twinged as she turned too quickly to look.

Marcus approached the door to the courtroom. Slicked back, his thick hair was closer to brown than blonde, heavy with some kind of gel but the right side of sleazy. He wore tan pants and a white Henley shirt, not quite snug across his broad shoulders. The least her ex could do was grow a beer gut. His eyes turned toward JJ, but a man in a suit stepped between them, cutting off her view.

"Looks like he got himself a lawyer," JJ said.

"That he did," Ms. Callaway said, rising and heading toward the courtroom, still looking as though (JJ's father would have said) someone had shit on her car seat. "Let's go."

"What does that mean, he's appealing the protective order?" JJ asked.

Her heel caught on the crappy carpet as they exited the courtroom. She had to hobble faster to catch up with her attorney as the woman took a hard right in the hallway, cell phone in hand, and veered into the ladies' bathroom. Ms. Callaway went straight to the stall and disappeared inside. JJ waited until the tinkling sound stopped, but found she still couldn't speak through the closed door. Soon Ms. Callaway emerged. Her bag slid from her shoulder and smacked against the sink while she was washing her hands. She shoved it back automatically.

"Sorry—should've peed before the hearing. I forgot how long-winded that jerk can be." She performed the same bag-shifting maneuver while scraping paper towels free from the dispenser. "Jerk being his attorney, not the judge. It means we're not done yet. It means he's trying to drag this out, hoping you'll be charged and he can use the shooting stuff against you. But in the meantime, he's agreed to abide by the order, so if he shows up, call the cops. And then call me."

"If he's fighting me in court, he won't come at me head-on. Not right now, anyway," JJ said, though she wasn't entirely convinced.

Her lawyer bent toward the mirror and pulled down on one cheek, examining her eye. Blinking, she said, "You're probably right. I didn't anticipate him fighting this, and it's been a while since I've done family law. I'll put my head together with Mr. Lewis, maybe have a friend drop by for a consult. There's some-body I can contact in the State Police today, see if he'll give me a hint of where their investigation is leaning. Call me this after-noon and we'll schedule something in the next few days. We should have notice of our next hearing by then, too."

JJ stood numbly, a sense of mild shock settling over her. "I thought we'd be done with this part."

"Me, too," Ms. Callaway admitted. "But it'll be okay. I'm sorry —I have to get upstairs to cover an arraignment."

JJ didn't immediately follow her attorney, but stood with her eyes closed, repeating *It'll be okay, It'll be okay...* It had to be. JJ couldn't imagine what Evie's life would be like if something happened to her. Who would raise her daughter? Her own mother? JJ opened her eyes and almost laughed, then finally headed for the door. *Mom raising Evie... that'd be almost as bad as—*

Marcus was waiting for her in the hallway.

He would definitely be worse.

She made herself look through him, as though he were nothing, before calmly turning in the other direction toward the exit.

"JJ!" he called out.

She ignored him. Halfway to the door.

"JJ!" Marcus said again. Then, "Janie, come on."

She stopped and turned on her heel. He nearly ran into her, but she leaned forward rather than backing up. "You didn't call me that when we were married. You sure as hell don't get to call me that now."

"Got you to stop though, didn't I?"

He grinned, and the secret curl of his mouth still threw her off-balance. It wasn't fair. Why would her body never learn what her mind had suspected from the start—that being with Marcus was a mistake?

"We're not supposed to be talking to each other," JJ said. Her arms were crossed. When had she crossed her arms?

"I know. I'm sorry," he said, almost convincingly. "I just want to know if you're okay."

"What the hell's that supposed to mean?" she asked, partly out of anger, partly because she knew Marcus liked to talk. Maybe he'd let something slip that would help her case.

He looked back down the hall, but there was no one in earshot, with the closest people gathered in a clump of suits and uniforms outside the courtroom door. Then he took a half step closer. "What did you get yourself mixed up in, JJ? It seems like every time I turn around, I hear something else crazy—kidnappings and murders and who knows what-all. Is this because your long-lost, best buddy is back? Is that it?"

JJ rolled her eyes. Of course he would latch onto that. Leave it to Marcus to be jealous of a memory he'd never met.

"Or maybe it's your new boyfriend, the Sheriff," his true colors slipping through with the edge in his voice. "Maybe he's behind all this. Or maybe he can't keep the populace in order because he can't drag himself out of your bed."

JJ gritted her teeth to keep her mouth shut (*motherfucker*, she thought), and turned and left him standing. When he got like this, all she could do was make things worse.

"Don't you walk away from me," Marcus growled.

His hand gripped her arm from behind, tugging, and she stopped—both breathing and walking—out of fear or prudence or some mix of the two.

"Was it the Sheriff's idea to say I poisoned my daughter's dog?" he asked.

JJ swung around and shoved him away. She registered a uniformed figure heading toward them, but her mind had stalled on her ex's accusation. "What the hell are you talking about, Marcus?"

His face flushed, Marcus said, "I did not poison Evie's dog, JJ. I would never do that to her. You know that."

JJ gave a short, harsh laugh. "Really? That's where you draw the line?"

He reached toward her.

"Sir!" It was Beecham County Deputy Beth Marshall, all five feet of her. She stood out of striking range, hand at the ready, though whether she'd pull a stun gun or one with bullets JJ couldn't say. "You need to step back now."

Marcus raised his hands and attempted his trademark charm, but he was too agitated to pull it off. "It's okay, Deputy. I'm just talking to my—"

"I know who you're talking to, sir. And I also know you shouldn't be. You can move along now, or you can head back to the station with me, give your attorney a call and see if we can straighten things out there. Your choice."

Marcus shook his head, but backed away. "Remember what I said, JJ," he said, before heading in the opposite direction. "It wasn't me."

The deputy still faced his retreating back as she asked, "You okay, Ms. Tulley?"

"JJ," she reminded the deputy. The petite woman had convinced her to file against Marcus, helped her with the paperwork, and directed her to the magistrate. "Yeah, I'm fine. Thanks."

"Did he threaten you?" Beth asked, in a voice JJ suspected—like many women in positions of authority—was deeper than came naturally to her. Her short hair barely peeked from beneath her campaign hat in the back, but there was no mistaking her for a man.

"No," JJ said. "Not this time."

He had, however, ensured she'd face another sleepless night.

Because if Marcus didn't poison Trooper, who did?

4

———

When did I get so goddamned old? Luther wondered, groaning as he rolled over to look at the clock. The red digital numbers blurred so much he couldn't even guess at their shapes.

I'm not that old. He slid a glass aside carefully, in case there was an eighty-proof residue in the bottom. *Just that stupid.*

11:52. He squinted at the glow of his bedroom window through the curtain. It must be a.m. Barely. That meant it was time to roll his sorry ass out of bed and get to work. Well, desk duty, if that qualified as work. That's what you got for decking another officer. Twice.

Luther switched off his bedside lamp. He didn't seem to be able to sleep without it on lately. He shuffled to the bathroom in his boxers, turned the shower as hot as it would go, and stepped in before it had a chance to get there. The initial chill helped clear his mind, before the hot water helped un-kink his muscles. And wash away the stink. Alcohol emanated from his pores. As it had pretty much since the day he'd planted his brother in the ground. Luther wasn't proud of it, but at this point it was a matter of whatever it took to get through the day.

He crawled out of the shower, put on his next-to-last pair of clean underwear, and ran a razor across his face without opening a vein. He'd given up on the beard, and it might be time to lose the mustache. It took a little more dexterity than he was capable of lately. He wandered around, looking for his phone, and finally found it on his nightstand. Next to the glass. Next to the bottle. Still a third full. Luther shook his head. If he didn't have his head on straight, or—God forbid—he got fired, he'd never find the bastard that killed Les.

LUTHER ADJUSTED the collar of his uniform before flipping the page on a crime scene report he'd read at least twice before. There had to be something he was missing. Whatever it was, no one else had found it, either. Or at least, no one had found the man who'd attacked Harlan Miller (and most likely killed Les), the man believed to be Daniel Carpenter. Nor had they found Adam's father, Virgil Rutledge, or his great-uncle Teddy, believed to have helped him escape. Beyond that, Luther couldn't say what anyone had found. There were multiple investigating agencies, most far afield of Beecham County, and they didn't exactly make an effort to keep Luther in the loop.

It had been quiet at the Sheriff's Department his whole shift. There weren't many calls, and that was good. There weren't many people passing by who felt compelled to talk at him, and that was even better. He figured most people just didn't know what to say to him. Of course, he'd never been the most popular guy in town, and with some people still clinging to the rumors about his dead brother's proclivities, Luther's reputation certainly hadn't improved.

Luther was supposed to have gone off shift a few minutes ago, but there was no one to send him home. Grant was long gone. The Sheriff knew what his deputy was doing: reviewing investigative files he had no business handling. He knew, and Luther knew he knew, but neither of them spoke of it. The way Luther saw it, Grant had enough boss-guy stress, what with Virgil's escape and the shooting and Luther decking Officer Kiss-Ass. The Sheriff wasn't about to volunteer for any more.

The sound of the front door brought Luther to attention. They didn't have enough personnel—or serve a large enough community—to keep the doors open twenty-four hours. There was always a dispatcher to handle emergencies, but often not much more. In other words, anyone who opened the door had a key.

A small woman with wet hair hunched over the lock, trying to disengage said key. It was Beth. Funny that he hadn't initially recognized her in civilian clothes. He couldn't decide if she looked bigger or smaller without the hat, but her head did look better proportioned to her body, and not quite as wide.

"Luther," she said, nodding as she helped the door on its way with her hip.

"Beth," he acknowledged. "What brings you back this time of night?"

"Forgot my phone," she said. "And you know how it is—it's got my life on it."

Luther didn't know. His phone was just that—a phone. Reception was so spotty it barely accomplished that function on a good day, and he didn't care for it to do anything else.

"What about you?" she asked. "Shouldn't you be gone by now?"

He shrugged. "There's nowhere else I need to be."

Beth's eyes went to the file in front of him, and he resisted the temptation to cover it with his arm. She might be the size of an eighth grader, but their newest deputy didn't miss much. "Want to get a drink?" she asked.

Luther thought of his worn recliner, the only thing waiting for him. Except the bottle, and the one he'd planned on picking up on the way home. His brother had had a recliner too. He'd been lying a few feet from it when Luther and JJ found him.

"Sure, why not?" he said, shaking his head free of the image. "We could go by Harry's."

The bar was a total dive, but had the advantage of being right around the corner, and someplace they'd never run into another LEO. Unless somebody was raiding the place.

He'd driven a cruiser home last night and back this afternoon, so Beth waited for Luther while he changed clothes, then gave him a ride in her compact car. It was a little too compact for Luther's tastes. He pushed the seat back far enough that his kneecaps didn't grind against the dash, but he still felt like he couldn't breathe, that there wasn't enough room for his chest to expand. Fortunately, the drive to Harry's took about as long as getting in and out of his seat belt.

Beth snickered as he struggled to get out. "I guess I don't get too many burly men in my car."

"Good thing," Luther said, unsure whether "burly" was an adjective he wanted or not. "If you did, you might never get them out again. You ever been here before?"

"No," she said. "Should I?"

"Not if you know what's good for you."

The nearest streetlight flashed against Beth's pale face as she looked at him askance, then locked up her car. Her breath puffed in the cold, November air.

"Keep your head down and you'll be fine. Besides," he said, dropping his deep voice even lower, "you're a trained poh-lice officer. What could go wrong?"

Light was apparently a valuable commodity not to be squandered at Harry's, because not much of it escaped from the bar. The simple, wood-framed building was dwarfed by its surrounding parking lot, packed with pickups. Inside, the smell was what you'd expect from an establishment with the sole purpose of getting people shitfaced as cheaply as possible.

There was no music, nothing but the murmuring rumble of conversations. The couple dozen people gathered around dim tables and on barstools wore a lot of flannel and denim and camouflage. In that sense, it wasn't all that different from most businesses in Beecham County, except for some indefinable bad vibe.

Luther pulled his baseball cap down lower. He could swear they'd been clocked as "the law" as soon as they stepped through the door. Then he almost laughed. Who was he kidding? They hadn't left Cold Springs, so undoubtedly they'd been recognized. But the ambient hostility was just as likely because he was Luther Beck as because he was a Sheriff's Deputy.

The bar was shaped like a reverse L. Luther strode casually to a pair of stools on the short end, out of the way of traffic and most prying eyes and ears. It was cool enough that he didn't bother removing his coat. If he did, he'd have to shove it under his ass anyway. There was no waitress, only a bartender with bushy, gray hair as dry as tinder. He didn't exactly look swamped, but when Luther nodded, the man took his time responding. He acted put out when Luther asked for a couple of beers, as though they'd stumbled into his living room and insisted on hospitality.

Beth stared at Luther, but he didn't know her well enough to interpret subtle expressions in the dim light. Had he already pissed her off by ordering for her?

"Sorry," Luther said. "I figured you wouldn't want to drink out of a glass, either."

She smiled. "Perceptive. So how you been doing, Luther?"

"I been doing just fine," he said, hoping that was the end of it. He gestured toward her wet hair. "I hope you didn't shower on my account, planning to whisk me away somewhere fancy."

"In case you haven't noticed, you're not exactly my type."

The bartender returned with their beers, and they lightly clinked the bottles.

Beth continued, "I was at the gym. Showered after."

"The one in Plattsville? How is that?" Luther asked, taking a big swig that half-emptied the bottle. He needed to pace himself.

Beth shrugged. "Mostly cardio. The pool reeks of chlorine, but somehow it's still skank, when it's open. But there is a decent little weight room."

Luther laughed before he could help himself.

"What?" Beth challenged.

Luther had another long pull from his beer before holding it up for another. Who knew how long it would take to get a second drink? Then he looked at Beth, top to bottom—which didn't take long—and let his eyes stop on her feet. Her toes stretched to rest on the stool's crossbar, and the floor was a world away. He shook his head, but didn't speak. There was nothing he could say that wouldn't sink his ass in a mess of trouble. Instead he grinned at Beth and watched and waited, as her mouth slowly curled to match.

"I will admit," she said, "the equipment is not always built for someone of my stature. But pound for pound, I can match anybody in there."

He raised his hands defensively and said, "I have no doubt!"

He'd forgotten how good it felt to smile. The bartender brought him another beer and he smiled even more.

"Did you eat anything today?" Beth asked, when he drained most of the bottle.

"Sure," he said, though he wasn't. Did toothpaste count? "You trying to take care of me, Ms. Marshall?"

"I told you, you're not my type," she said, pausing for a sip. She'd barely breached the label. "You know who did ask about you today... that lawyer."

Luther's brow wrinkled. "What lawyer?"

"You know, the one that represented Virgil Rutledge. Apparently she's helping JJ Tulley with her mess."

"JJ had a hearing today?"

Beth nodded, and Luther tried to remember the last time he'd seen JJ. When he'd decked Kilbourne and released her from her cell? No, JJ must have been at Les's funeral, but Luther didn't much remember it. Except that his asshole father Rudy hadn't shown. Not that he'd expected him to.

The bartender's protuberant belly reminded him of Rudy.

Beth was watching Luther.

He signaled for another beer and asked, "How'd it go? For JJ, I mean?"

"I'd guess not great, considering how she and her lawyer looked rolling out of the courtroom. Then the ex started bothering her, and I had to run him off."

Luther leaned in. "What do you mean, bothering her?"

"Nothing physical. Well, not while I was there, or I would've hauled his ass in. Maybe I should have anyway."

"He threaten her?"

"He was arguing with her. Something about her and the Sheriff. Oh, and he said he didn't poison her dog." Beth's brows raised, inviting him to comment.

Would the asswipe lie about that? Of course he would. He'd lie about anything. But not without a reason. And what would that be? Bearing in mind that he was an asswipe, so his reason might not make sense to a normal person.

"What did her attorney have to say?" Luther asked. *Faith Callaway.* Yes, Luther remembered the lovely Faith Callaway.

"About him or about you?" Beth grinned.

Luther pointed the next bottle at her as he asked, "You jealous, deputy?"

She snorted. "Hardly."

Luther made an *eh* sound of skepticism, although there truly had never been any chemistry between them.

"You really don't know, do you?" she asked.

He blinked. Maybe he'd gone through those first few bottles a little too fast. In fact, there was one more empty than he remembered ordering. "Know what?"

"I'm gay."

"Huh," was his eloquent reply. His facial muscles didn't want to respond, but whether that was shock or alcohol, he couldn't say. "I should've guessed."

"Why—because I didn't succumb to your charms? Or because I have short hair and lift weights? I play softball, too," she noted, more amused than angry. "We're not all butch, you know. Any more than all hetero females are delicate flowers."

Luther was uncomfortable with the direction the conversation had taken, though he couldn't have said why. He lowered his head, so he was almost speaking to his own shoulder. "Well, I know that."

"Uh-huh. My first serious girlfriend was gorgeous." She watched the remaining beer swirl as she rotated her nearly empty bottle. "Last one was damn attractive, too, if I do say so myself."

Luther stared at her. He'd passed from discomfort into the realm of No Words and took refuge in his bottle.

"You want to know how someone that looks like me could land a supermodel. I'll let you in on a little secret." She leaned forward and whispered, "I'm hung like a horse."

Luther jerked his head sideways to avoid her as he spewed his beer in a spit-take that would've made a teenager proud. Beth guffawed, and he alternately choked and heaved, joining her in a deep belly laugh that brought tears to his eyes.

Beth was still giggling, and he was wiping his eyes when the scowling bartender approached.

"Sorry about that," Luther said, coughing into his sleeve. Then he pulled out his wallet and set enough cash on the bar to cover their tab, plus some. A few men from a nearby table had stood and approached the bar, and Luther had a sense that something was in the air. "Mrs. Ed, as much as I'm enjoying this, maybe we should move on."

"Agreed," Beth said.

Luther grinned as she hopped down from the stool (*it was so far!*). Distracted, giving Luther a dirty look, Beth accidentally bumped one of the men heading for the bar. Or more likely, Luther thought, the man "accidentally" bumped her.

"Excuse me," she said, and tried to move around the man, who had a foot and a hundred pounds on her.

"No excuse for you," he said, then added, "dyke."

"Hey," Luther said, hands up. "We're leaving."

"That's right. And we don't want any trouble," Beth continued.

"A Beck that doesn't want trouble? Seems unlikely," said a second man who'd appeared next to Luther. About the same height but a little leaner. "'A' course, so does a Beck hanging out with a dyke."

"Keep walking," Luther told Beth. Even though every cell in his body screamed for a fight.

Luther had to hand it to her—she didn't challenge anyone directly, but she didn't cower, either. She pushed past the first man, then another, as they converged on Luther. One of the men put a hand on Luther's arm. Luther twisted, and the man immediately released him.

"Not tonight," Luther said, shoulder-bumping his way through.

"Makes sense, though. Him hanging out with a dyke," said the man he'd just passed. "You know his brother was a pervert, too. I guess that's better than diddling little kids."

Luther closed his eyes briefly.

A smile, the kind his mother always said meant no good, crossed Luther's face and lit up his eyes as he surrendered to the familiar, fiery buzz in his veins, opened his eyes, turned and threw the first punch.

5

————

ust once, I'd like to start the day not already late.

JJ gave Trooper a pat. The German shepherd mix had an iron bladder, and the girls could let him out if they beat her home, but she'd left a pee pad on the kitchen floor in an abundance of caution.

"Stay off the couch," she said, nearly slamming her toe in the door in her rush to lock up.

JJ tossed her bags in the back and patted her old Bronco's steering wheel superstitiously (*come on, baby*) before turning the ignition (*good job*). The tires caught a little gravel as she did a quick, swerving turn in her driveway. It was nice being mostly back on day shift at the hospital, but it definitely took some getting used to. Evie had spent the night with Rachel, so JJ made a hard left at the bottom of her driveway, then turned almost immediately onto the Nicholson's drive. It was her turn to drop the girls at school. Was she supposed to have made Evie lunch, too? Dammit, she couldn't remember. Too late now anyway.

JJ parked in front of the Nicholson house, leaving her SUV running. She wore a sweatshirt over her scrubs and pulled the hood up over her wet hair. It wasn't quite cold enough for her hair to freeze, but it sure did feel like it. After a quick, staccato knock (Otto had finally traded the screen in the storm door for a glass pane), she let herself in. Standing on the doormat, she glanced down to check her feet and heard something unexpected —raised voices.

Otto and Dorothy were arguing.

JJ pulled her hood down to eavesdrop.

Rachel's recent kidnapping had put a strain on the Nicholson marriage, but they'd seemed to have come through the rough patch. Some days their open affection was downright sickening, but she'd hate for them to swing in the other direction. JJ walked slowly (*sneaked* was such an ugly word) toward the kitchen.

"Our daughter is not a freak," Dorothy said, loudly. She tended to be the louder of the couple.

"I didn't say she was," came Otto's calm response.

"I'm done talking about this."

"Dorothy, be reasonable."

"Reasonable?" Dorothy's voice pitched even higher. "You're the one talking crazy, hocus-pocus crap."

"That *crap* is how Adam found our daughter. That crap is the only reason she's still—"

JJ couldn't make out the sound that interrupted Otto. Had Dorothy slapped him? She shook her head; it was time to make her presence known, before things got even more awkward. She pulled her hood back over her head.

"School bus is here!" JJ called out before barreling into the kitchen.

Otto held Dorothy's arm gently by the wrist. He released it as JJ entered, and Dorothy slowly tucked her arm behind her as she leaned against the counter.

"Sorry," JJ said, pulling her hood down. "I hope I didn't interrupt anything. I knocked, but with my hood on I wasn't sure if you'd heard me. Is everything okay?"

"Fine," Dorothy said.

Her dark hair hung limp around her face, gone pale with worry or exhaustion, and she wore what passed for pajamas (flannels and sweats) in a cold house in winter. JJ remembered today was Dorothy's off day at the diner.

"Everything's just fine," Otto agreed.

Neither of them was very convincing. JJ heard feet thundering down the stairs—her daughter at least was on her way.

"Rachel won't be going to school today. She's not feeling well," Dorothy said, glaring at her husband as if daring him to challenge her.

"I'm sorry to hear that," JJ said. "Do you want me to take a look at her?"

Dorothy's face softened. "No, thanks, JJ. She didn't sleep very well last night. She's been doing better with her asthma lately, but I know a lot of the kids are getting sick now. I just don't want to risk anything by sending her to school exhausted."

Evie stomped into the room. There hadn't been any significant snowfalls yet, but the child insisted on wearing her heavy boots. "Hey, Mom! I'm getting Rachel's homework, so I can't be late today."

"Subtle, kid," JJ said, rubbing her daughter's shoulder, which edged closer to her own every day. "Okay then, we're off. Let us know if you need anything."

Dorothy thanked her, and JJ headed for the front door almost as quickly as her hyper daughter, eager to leave someone else's marital dysfunction behind. But they'd barely made it off the porch when Otto emerged on their heels.

"Evie," he said, "why don't you run in and grab Rachel's lunch? Her mom packed it last night, but I'm sure she'll want to make her something special now. A hot lunch since she'll be home."

Evie looked to her mother. JJ waved her on, and Evie did her best Clydesdale impersonation clomping back in the house.

JJ's hand crept to her face, partly because she was embarrassed and partly because it was so damn cold. "How did you know I forgot to pack her lunch?"

"I didn't," Otto said. "Listen, there's something going on with Rachel."

"You mean she's really sick?" JJ asked.

"No." It was strange seeing the tall, broad man glance over his shoulder for his small-boned wife. "I mean, there's something going on in her head."

JJ shivered and put her hood back up. The temperature didn't seem to faze Otto, wearing only a long-sleeved T-shirt, but his ruddy beard probably helped.

"Isn't she seeing someone at the school? A counselor?" JJ asked.

Otto nodded impatiently. "Yeah, but that's not what I mean."

Otto stepped close enough that JJ imagined she could feel the heat from his body. Or maybe he was screening her from the wind. "She's been having these dreams," Otto said. "Dreams that wake her up at night."

"Like nightmares?"

"Not exactly."

JJ was getting impatient herself. "Then like what exactly? Come on—spit it out."

"I'm not sure, because she can't remember. But I think it's something..." Hands on his hips, Otto's gaze dropped to the ground. "I think it's something like Adam."

Suddenly what Dorothy had said as JJ walked in made perfect sense—*crazy, hocus-pocus crap.* "What do you mean, something like Adam? Visions?"

"I don't know."

JJ threw up her arms in frustration. "What do you mean, you don't know?"

"I don't know!" Otto yelled.

JJ took a micro step back, remembering the sensation of hanging on his back as he beat the crap out of Adam. Otto briefly closed his eyes and softly tapped his closed fist against his forehead. "I don't know. I can't explain it. But I know my daughter is seeing things the rest of us can't."

JJ shook her head. This couldn't be happening. Not to Rachel, too, on top of everything else. "Are you sure—"

Otto raised an eyebrow.

"Yeah, okay, we covered that," JJ conceded. "Obviously Dorothy disagrees."

Otto snorted. "Dorothy is still ready to hang Adam by his nut sack for no good reason. Rachel could be floating furniture around the room and Dorothy'd say, *Oh, isn't it breezy in here.*"

A short laugh escaped JJ at the thought.

"What about Harlan?" Otto asked. "Is he better yet?"

And any levity vanished instantly. JJ shook her head and mashed her lips together until she was able to say, "Harlan may never be better."

Otto let out a ragged sigh.

Harlan was the one who had truly set Adam on Rachel's path. And young Aaron Schofield's as well. It's unlikely either child— or Adam—would have survived without Harlan's guiding hand.

Evie came thumping out the front door as Otto asked, "And Adam?"

"What about Adam?" Evie asked. She had a soft spot for her mother's best childhood friend, since he had saved her own.

"I'll talk to him," JJ said. "But no promises. Let's go, kid."

JJ mentally kicked herself as she rolled down the gravel driveway. Marcus paid child support intermittently, if at all, and it was in the winter that JJ felt it most. How much gas had she wasted leaving her Bronco running? And for what, with its heater mostly on the fritz? The knowledge that she didn't have to worry about it starting?

She glanced over at her daughter as they approached the highway. Evie had been gung-ho about school a few minutes ago, but she was suspiciously silent now. JJ wondered if it was something Dorothy had said to her, or perhaps just the Nicholson marital dysfunction seeping in around the edges. Evie had been preschool age when JJ and Marcus had divorced, but it had still left an imprint on the child.

"So what's for lunch?" JJ asked.

"Sandwich," Evie said.

JJ didn't bother asking what kind; if her daughter couldn't be bothered with using an article, JJ wouldn't hold her breath for an adjective.

"You have your gym clothes or whatever you need for the workshop this evening?"

"Yeah," Evie said, but volunteered nothing more.

"Are you worried about Rachel?" JJ asked, thinking maybe that explained her daughter's funk. She glanced over to meet Evie's gaze.

"Why?"

Why indeed. Evie was hard to read, but maybe JJ was giving her credit for a little too much emotional maturity. Instead of answering, JJ asked, "Did y'all have a good time last night?"

"Yeah."

JJ sighed. Her child was suited for a life in espionage, with her natural resistance to interrogation. "You get your homework done?"

"Yes, Mom," Evie said, with a mild undertone of *how do you function on a daily basis?*

JJ finally took the hint and backed off. There'd be plenty of time for daydreaming about wringing her daughter's neck when she hit puberty. Instead, JJ kept recalculating her chances of making it to work on time (*the clock is four minutes fast, so if I hit the edge of Plattsville by...*) and reviewing the work schedule in her mind. How late she could be without pissing anyone off depended on who was working. And how crazy things were. Tuesdays usually weren't bad, but—

"Mom?" Evie said.

JJ held in a smile. Like any wild animal, the key was to leave her daughter alone and wait for the child to approach you. "Yeah, honey?"

"Where's Adam?"

JJ felt a chill, remembering her conversation with him yesterday. Should she have mentioned something to Otto? Rachel's father obviously believed in... whatever it was Adam was able to do. But maybe he believed in it too much. The man couldn't be objective.

"Mom!" Evie demanded.

JJ slowed down as she reached the Cold Springs town limits. "Adam is in Morgantown now. He and Miss Iris have a friend in the hospital there who's very sick."

Evie went quiet for a moment, then asked, "Is it someone I know?"

"No, sweetie, I don't believe you do." They approached the old brick schoolhouse now, the same one she and Adam had attended as kids. JJ lifted her butt and peered over the steering wheel, as if that would magically help her find a spot to pull over.

"Are you sure I don't know him?" Evie asked.

"Pretty sure," JJ said, whipping her Bronco into a clear section almost before the car in front of her had vacated it.

Evie grabbed her backpack from the footwell, threw the door open and hopped to the sidewalk.

"Hey! Don't forget your lunch," JJ shouted over the sound of her noisy engine. As Evie turned back for the bag, JJ found herself saying, "Why'd you ask if you know him?"

Evie jumped to adjust the pack's weight on her back. "I just figured if Rachel knows him, I might, too."

"What makes you think Rachel knows him?"

Evie looked at her mother as though she were an absolute idiot. "Well, Mom, I don't usually have dreams about people I don't know. Do you?"

And she slammed the door behind her.

What the hell? JJ pulled the parking brake and jumped out of the Bronco, engine still running. Someone behind her honked a horn in protest. "Evie!" she called out, rounding her vehicle. "Evelyn May!"

Evie stopped in her tracks and turned toward her mother with a look of outraged disbelief that JJ ignored to ask, "What did you mean about the dreams?"

Evie glanced—too casually—at the parents and students streaming by. Was her uncertainty simply social embarrassment, or something more?

"Sweetie, this is important," JJ said, resisting the urge to touch her daughter in public. It was bad enough she'd called her by her full name.

"Rachel's been having dreams about a man in a hospital," Evie said, hands tucked in her backpack straps as she stared at the ground.

"What man? What kind of dreams?" JJ asked, stepping closer and lowering her voice.

"Nothing weird," Evie said, mildly revolted. "Just some old guy. She sees him in a hospital bed. She thinks maybe he talks, but when she wakes up she can't remember what he said."

"What else?"

"That's all she told me. If you want to know more, ask Rachel." Evie looked over her shoulder. "I gotta go, Mom."

JJ watched Evie rush toward the white-painted, double doors, backpack bouncing. Horns blared again, insistent and angry, yet so distant to JJ's ears they could have been on another street. She ignored them as she walked slowly back to her Bronco.

She could ask Rachel.

I'd hoped Otto was wrong.

But she wasn't sure she wanted to hear her answer.

6

———

T*he world doesn't stop spinning just because you're a wanted man.*

Under other circumstances, Danny might have smiled at the thought. It sounded like a bad country song. His hands ached, so he consciously loosened his grip on the steering wheel. He felt a peculiar sensation—a kind of itching, just short of painful—under his skull. It was on top of his head, to the right of center. One hand crept over his scalp. *In there somewhere.* He pushed with two fingers. Nothing. Then he pressed his knuckles against his head and rubbed in circles. His car (purchased for a few hundred cash from an old associate) drifted to the shoulder, and he almost over-corrected with his left hand. But he kept rubbing his head, and gradually the sensation eased.

And people don't stop wanting to be paid.

The kind of people who don't bother telling you a second time. Danny wasn't some piss-ant mule or even a street corner hustler, but he wasn't a kingpin, either. He fell somewhere in the middle, and that was a dangerous place to be. He had the money. For now. But even though he didn't have any bad habits (he never sampled the product, for instance) and he always lived in shitholes, his emergency fund wouldn't last long. Maybe a couple of weeks. It would take a lot longer than that to get established somewhere new, especially somewhere that wasn't already spoken for. He could speed up the process, but he'd need somebody watching his back. Which meant getting the okay from higher up.

Danny wasn't worried. He'd been a solid performer for a bunch of years and never caused problems. Things would come together—they always did. Except, he still had to deal with the Rutledges. Especially Adam. He had a plan for that, too. But he couldn't quite remember it. Probably because the itching, tickling sensation in his head had returned, along with a droning buzz. Really, more of a hiss. And what was a hiss but a whisper?

He turned on the radio, hoping to drown out the sound. *Good luck with that.* He'd left West Virginia behind, but not the mountains. Well, these mountains were more like rural, rolling hills nobody had gotten around to clearcutting yet, but the end result was the same—shitty reception, whether cell phone or radio. Numbers scrolled by, with nothing but static to show for it. And instead of drowning out the whispers, the radio (*hissing, pulsing static*) seemed to amplify them. Not enough to make out the words, but enough to make conscious, sensible thought impossible.

"I guess I could sing," Danny said aloud, just to hear his own voice. Just to confirm that the other one he heard was not his.

"Except I can't fucking sing," he said.

What kind of attitude is that? the voice asked. The one that was not his.

Danny had heard whispers for as long as he could remember. Sometimes louder, more insistent, and sometimes far in the back of his mind. They tended to cycle, depending on what he'd been doing to keep them happy. Lately, the past few months, they were never happy. They—or was it *he*, a single voice? Voices were harder to recognize when you only heard them in your head—

they could never get enough. It wasn't fair. The whispers swirled and swelled, like a crowd in his head. A crowd he didn't invite.

"Leave me alone!" Danny screamed, loud enough to make his throat ache.

You know how to make that happen, came the whispered reply.

And that's when he saw him. Up ahead, on a straight stretch. By the side of the road.

A hitchhiker.

No, Danny thought. *I can't take the risk. Not now.*

And yet, he found himself pulling over ahead of the figure. He was a young man, mid-twenties, underdressed for November in jeans and a hooded sweatshirt, with a backpack slung over one shoulder. Danny watched him in the rearview mirror shuffling toward his car, not quite running but faster than a walk, as though he didn't trust a stranger to wait for him otherwise. The man approached the passenger side, and Danny found—to his surprise—that the power window worked on that side. Cold air rushed in.

"Where you headed?" Danny yelled over the roar of the wind.

The man leaned in, head stretching his hood. Dark hair escaped around the edges and his clean-shaven face had—*oh, too perfect*—a dimple.

"Wherever there's a roof," the man replied, grinning.

"All right, then," Danny said, stretching a hand down the side of his calf to feel the outline of the knife he kept there. He nodded toward the rear seat. "Toss your bag in the back and let's go."

"Great—thanks!"

While the man struggled with the rear passenger door in the wind, Danny reached beneath his seat and slipped a cord free, tucking it within range. Danny almost thought he saw snow in the air that blasted inside as the man dropped next to him. An echoing silence filled the car after the door slammed shut. Like a church. Danny stared at his passenger until the man became visibly uncomfortable, looking at the dashboard, the floor, the door handle.

"All right, then," Danny said brightly, wind buffeting his vehicle as he merged back onto the road. "Let's see what we can do about getting you somewhere more... hospitable."

7

____

Adam sat in his car, getting colder by the second. He rubbed the protruding bone of his wonky thumb and felt the chill on his skin. Still, it was hard to make himself move.

The parking lot was mostly empty, save for a couple of Beecham County Sheriff Department cruisers and three or four civilian cars that, like his, had seen better days. How long had it been since he'd been interrogated as a suspect inside that building, fled through the forest, and dodged roadblocks with Harlan... a couple of weeks? And how long since his father had escaped from custody? Even less. But upon returning to Iris's house last night, Adam had found a message from Grant, asking him to stop by as soon as possible. He figured when the Sheriff asks you to stop by, it was better to do so under your own power rather than waiting to be officially picked up.

The door of Adam's hatchback groaned as he opened it. *At least this time it's not me.* His hearing was still a little off, but the ear wasn't painful, and he felt mostly healed from last month's excursions. Healed, but exhausted. He didn't think he'd ever be not-tired again. Even sleeping in his familiar bed last night, rather than his car or a hospital chair, didn't help him rest. His mind wouldn't stop spinning, reminding him he should be doing something to help Harlan. Like tracking down his great-uncle Teddy.

Or tracking down Danny.

Except that wouldn't be to help Harlan; it would be to help Adam. To help the frustrated, impotent rage that lay waiting beneath all the exhaustion.

A woman deputy sat behind the front desk. Pen in one hand, the other cupped around her head as though to protect it, her eyes were so intent on the page in front of her she didn't initially see him. Adam couldn't remember her name, and even if he had it wouldn't have mattered. He'd forgotten he'd have to speak with someone other than Grant or Luther, someone who might still harbor suspicions about him, and it rendered him momentarily speechless.

Adam reluctantly cleared his throat. She lifted her face, and his twisted guts relaxed when she smiled.

"Good morning," she said, before picking up the phone. "Sheriff Mason, Adam Rutledge is here to see you…"

A man and a woman sat as far from each other as was possible in the small waiting area. Both glanced up sharply when the deputy said Adam's name.

"Mr. Rutledge, you can go on back," the deputy said. "Do you know the way?"

"I'll find it, thanks."

He'd noticed the Sheriff's door the last time he was in the office, not on his way to the interrogation room (he was in no condition to notice anything then), but on his way out. The door was wide open now, and Grant stood as Adam arrived, waving him to a chair.

"Thanks for coming in, Adam."

"Any word on Virgil? Or Teddy?" Adam asked, hoping that was why he was here.

"Nothing solid. But we're assuming they're still together," Grant admitted. "And Harlan?"

"Still no change," Adam said. He wished he'd worn a hat, just so he'd have something to do with his hands.

"I'm sorry to hear that. Is Iris still in Morgantown?"

"Yeah," Adam said, feeling briefly self-conscious for sounding like a teenager. "Yes, but she'll be back in a day or two to take care of some things."

"Good. Before I forget, Special Agent D'Antonio went back to Bethesda, but he left something for you." Grant handed Adam a flat object loosely wrapped in brown paper. "Once they finished processing the cabin, they didn't need this, and he thought you might like to have it."

It was Virgil's framed photo of Adam's mother. Adam's own copy was lost to him for now—stuffed in a duffel bag in a truck Teddy and Virgil had driven who-knew-where. Adam touched his mother's face before gently rewrapping the glass and setting it on Grant's desk. "I appreciate this. Would you thank him for me?"

"No problem." Grant leaned back in his chair. "While we're on the subject of photos, I don't suppose you have any pictures of yourself when you were younger—say early twenties?"

Adam grinned, trying not to appear as defensive as he suddenly felt. "Why, do you want to put me in a lineup for some ten-year-old cases?"

"Not exactly," Grant said. "Would Iris have any of you? Or would JJ?"

Adam crossed his foot over his knee, then straightened his leg again when it started to bounce. "JJ wouldn't. We never saw each other after I left Cold Springs, from the time I was maybe fourteen until last month. And Iris probably wouldn't either. She's not exactly camera-crazy. Sheriff, what's this about?"

Grant raked his hands through his auburn hair, and Adam noticed the man looked almost as tired as he felt. "I'm sorry; I wasn't thinking. I should have said right off the bat, you're not in any kind of trouble. Or at least, you're not a suspect." He pulled a folder from his desk drawer. "I need you to look at some pictures for me, if you don't mind."

He seemed to take Adam's silence as an affirmative response, flipping the folder open and sliding it around to face him. Adam scanned through the photos once, then slowly made his way through them a second time. There were eight, all black and white copies, with the quality varying from pixelated impressions to what resembled a model's portfolio pose. The three posed photos appeared to be of the same young man, but no one else was represented more than once. The subjects were in their late teens to mid-twenties. All had dark hair, no more than shoulder-length. From what he could tell, they were all of average height and build, though some were leaner than others. All wore casual clothing, but the photos were taken at different times of year, so the types of clothing varied. And there was no common denominator for setting, except none were taken in obviously urban areas.

Adam looked up to find Grant watching him closely.

"I don't recognize any of them," Adam said.

"You're sure?" Grant asked.

"Yes, I'm sure," Adam reiterated, although that wasn't entirely true. He didn't recognize any single man, but they were all vaguely familiar. "Should I?"

"How about these?" Grant slid a folder with another half dozen photos across the desk.

The second photo was a punch to the gut. Adam slid it to the side and reviewed the remaining photos before returning to the second one. "Maybe this one," he said. "Is he dead?"

"How do you recognize him?" Grant asked.

Adam rested his eyes on the heels of his hands. Whether to

block out what was in his mind—*freezing water, clawing arms, flashing images*—or make it more clear, he wasn't sure. "I told you I saw a flash of something while Danny and I were fighting in the river. This looks like the man Danny was choking."

"Okay," Grant said, as though victims were identified from near-death visions all the time. "And what about these names?"

Adam reluctantly removed his hands and blinked his eyes to clear them before skimming a typed list of a dozen names. "No. Nothing."

Grant nodded and ran his fingers over his mustache, perhaps trying to hide his disappointment. Then he spread the pictures like playing cards, until he found the one he was looking for. It was the youngest-looking of the bunch, and one of the slimmest. Adam had the impression he was basically still a kid, that the rest of his body hadn't yet caught up with his height. He wore a heavy metal T-shirt and jeans and was hamming it up for the camera, laying out his tongue and making devil horns with both hands. But he looked as though he were playing, laughing at the idea even as the picture was being taken.

Grant slid the list of names alongside the photo and pointed at one near the top. "As you know, we recovered two sets of remains from the mountain, near where you found Rachel. One was Sarah Edmunds. The other one, the body we initially thought was Danny, was this man."

Adam stared at the photo and thought "man" was being generous. "How old was he?"

"Seventeen," Grant said. "A runaway. He was the youngest."

"The youngest?" Adam asked, both knowing what Grant was saying and unable to comprehend it.

"Eight of these men were found murdered sometime in the past fifteen years. Well, nine now that we've identified him," Grant said, pointing at the goofy seventeen-year-old. "Three are still missing."

"What about him?" Adam asked, pointing to the lanky young man he'd seen dying by Danny's hands.

"One of the murdered."

Bile rose in Adam's throat. His esophagus burned as he swallowed it back down. "And you think—"

"We don't know what to think," Grant said.

But Adam could tell he was lying.

"I'll see if I can get another photo of the man you may have seen so we can firm up that ID. You said you don't recognize any of these other men..." Grant let his words hang in the air, obviously aware Adam wasn't being entirely truthful, either.

"I don't," Adam repeated. "Not specifically. But they all seem vaguely familiar."

"Uh-huh." Grant's tone walked the line between belief and disbelief. He pulled out a small notebook and flipped through its pages, then suddenly asked, "Were you in Chambersburg, January of 2004?"

Adam blinked. "I don't know where I was. I didn't exactly keep track. But I don't think I ever lived in Chambersburg."

"How about Waynesboro?"

Adam's breath caught. "Yeah, I might've been."

"And that's what—fifteen miles from Chambersburg, give or take?" Adam didn't respond, and Grant pointed at one of the photos, a man sliding from beneath a car, wearing a coverall. "He was murdered in Chambersburg then. Locals thought it was a robbery, but they never arrested anybody for it. How about Morgantown, August of 2010?"

"It's possible. I've spent a few summers there, but I usually bug out before classes start in the fall."

Grant pointed to another photo, so close-up it might have been taken at a correctional center. "That's when his girlfriend reported him missing. Although they thought maybe he was her pimp rather than her boyfriend, so I don't know how seriously they took the report. How about Johnstown, October of 2012?"

Adam couldn't help looking over his shoulder. D'Antonio had never liked him. The photo of his mother had been a ruse, a way to get Adam to trust them. Surely the FBI agent would appear in the doorway any moment with an arrest warrant.

"Pittsburgh, March of 2015?" Grant continued.

Adam turned back to face the Sheriff and asked, "Do I need a lawyer?"

Grant shook his head in—was it frustration? Disbelief? Adam wished he knew.

"Am I under arrest?"

"Adam, look at the pictures again."

"I didn't kill these men—"

"*Adam*," Grant cut in, "when we picked you up on the highway by the river, do you remember what you told me about the man you saw Danny choking?"

Adam's hands shook as he spread the pictures, trying to arrange them so he could see all of the men at once. Grant shifted a stack of paper to accommodate him. Adam's eyes flicked back and forth, back and forth. Some appeared happy; some appeared angry. Some he'd have a drink with; a couple he'd cross the street to avoid. They were all young, and they were dead. Or presumed dead. What else was there to see?

Grant slammed another framed picture down in the middle of the photos, and Adam flinched. No, it wasn't a glass photo frame. Adam bent forward. It was a mirror. Adam glanced at Grant, confused. "What do you want me..."

But then, catching sight of his own hollow eyes, he recognized what he'd been refusing to see. He remembered what he'd said.

Dark, mostly short hair.

Clean-shaven, or stubbly.

Average height or taller.

Lean, as he'd been in his teenage years and was tending toward now, stress having eaten his flesh down to the bare muscles.

The first boy, the youngest one, even had a dimple that helped his devil face look like a joke. So did three of the others.

Just like Adam.

Because that's what they had in common. The murdered men all looked like Adam.

8

Luther had struggled this morning to come up with a strategy. He needed to avoid attracting unwanted attention, so he couldn't be late to work. But he also shouldn't be too early, because that would be unusual as well. He made himself a sandwich and ate it standing at the counter while he watched the clock. Then his two and a half cups of coffee sent him to the bathroom, where he realized any attention-deflecting strategies were moot. The shower steam had finally cleared from his mirror (he'd skipped shaving), revealing that he had a helluva shiner.

He leaned in, painfully stretching the bruised skin around his left cheek. *Damn*, he thought. *I should've iced it.* But at least there was no damage to his eye. If Grant asked about it, he could always say he'd done it working on his car. Or he could say his old man gave it to him. That was probably more believable.

Harry's had erupted into an all-out brawl after Luther threw the first punch. He'd gotten in a few more good swings before Beth dragged him out the door. Boy, was she pissed! He'd told her no one would ever figure out who started it, and even if they did, their names would never come out. Harry's wasn't the kind of place where people told tales, even on the pigs. She'd driven Luther home and, after an initial ass-chewing, refused to speak to him the rest of the way. Which was too bad. Luther had actually enjoyed spending time with her. But she'd come around again. Eventually.

Luther couldn't remember the last time he'd driven his own vehicle, but it'd been long enough that his engine didn't immediately turn over. *Stupid*—it didn't do to leave a car sitting once the cold weather rolled in. And how had he not even run an errand, done anything not work-related (or accomplished on the way to or from work), in the past couple of months? He even parked in one of the department vehicle spots out of habit when he arrived at the Sheriff's Department, but realized his mistake before he cut the engine. He was five minutes early for his shift, which seemed about right. Grant's vehicle was in the lot. If Luther was very lucky, Grant would stay holed up in his office for the rest of the day, then rush out the door. Except Grant never rushed anywhere.

"Morning, Beth!" Luther said, bursting through the entrance.

Beth wouldn't meet his eyes as she said, "Sheriff wants you in his office."

"Oh, that sounds ominous," Luther said, in a light voice. When she didn't respond, he knew it was.

Well, shit.

Grant's door was closed, and Luther knocked twice before entering. "Morning, boss."

"It's afternoon," Grant said, head bowed over his desk as he scribbled his signature. "Close the door."

He looked up as Luther sat across from him, took in his deputy's shiner, and dropped his face to his hands. "Dammit, Luther."

Luther couldn't help grinning as he said, "You should see the other guy."

Grant's face flushed and he clenched his jaw before shaking

his head. "I did, Luther. I saw all the other guys. Or at least, the ones that were still hanging around by the time I got to Harry's from the restaurant."

Restaurant? What was Grant doing in a restaurant? His dad didn't do well eating out anymore, and old Sheriff Mason's wife wouldn't go out without him...

"Were you having a date? With JJ? Aw, shit, I'm sorry." And then Luther realized his mistake, the implicit admission. He tried to backtrack. "I mean, I know I'm on desk duty, but dispatch could have asked me to respond instead."

"Cut the bullshit, Luther."

Grant didn't often swear. Luther began to get an inkling that he was in worse trouble than he'd thought. "I don't know what you're talking about, sir."

"Really? You're suspended for a week, starting today. That ought to give you time to figure it out."

Luther's mouth dropped. "Suspended? Are you shitting me?"

Grant leaned across his desk, eyes hard. "You sure you want to use that kind of language with me right now?"

Luther squeezed his hands into tight fists and dug his knuckles into the seat of his chair. "I apologize. Are you shitting me, *sir*?"

The Sheriff stood, pressing his hands flat against his desk. They shook—vibrated, really—and Luther thought he heard something rattling in the drawer beneath them. Luther had never seen Grant so angry. Somehow it helped him rein in his own temper. After all, the Sheriff was not a vindictive man. Maybe, if he stopped provoking him for a minute, Luther could still talk his way out of this.

Grant picked his campaign hat up from his desk, almost crushing the crown, and for a moment Luther thought he would throw it. Instead, he set it back down and crossed to the window, saying, "Luther, why do you have to make everything so goddamned difficult?"

It was an excellent question, one Luther sometimes wondered as well. But he kept his thoughts on the answer—and anything else—to himself.

Grant stared out toward the little patch of grass that gave way to sidewalk, and then to the street that ran along the side of the building. The naked frame of a maple tree stood, leaves long gone. "I know you don't respect me the way you respected my father. I wouldn't expect you to. But I think you even hated me when I started. Well, resented me, at least. I figured you thought I didn't belong in this office. And maybe you were right."

Luther swallowed hard. Had he been that transparent? Apparently more transparent to his boss than he was to himself.

"But I do belong here now. I don't do the job the way my father did, but I do it better than anyone else could. And I thought, in the past few months, maybe you could see that. Maybe we were coming to some kind of understanding. That together, we could do some good."

Grant returned to his chair with a sigh. "Luther, it has to be tough for you, losing your brother the way you did. Having some psycho still out there. But you can't be around here now. You can't be part of this."

Luther bristled and, against his own advice, opened his mouth. "Did JJ tell you that, after the hearing yesterday, Marcus denied poisoning her dog?"

Irritation flashed across Grant's face before he could control it, which was not Luther's intent. He continued, "Probably didn't have a chance, before you got called away. Plus, I imagine it'd be awkward for her, talking about her ex with her date."

"Are you going somewhere with this, Luther?"

Grant must be supremely pissed off if he hadn't gotten there already on his own. Luther pressed on. "If Marcus didn't do it, maybe Danny Carpenter did. Maybe the dog was interfering with his surveillance of Rachel, or maybe he's got it in for JJ. Whatever the reason, if Danny Carpenter poisoned the dog..."

"Maybe he left fingerprints," Grant finished. "It's a long shot, but I'll check it out."

"I was also thinking—"

"Luther, no," Grant said firmly. "You're off the case. You need to go home, take some time to get your head on straight."

He was doing it. The Sheriff was really suspending him. *Shit.* Luther heard the desperation in his voice when he countered, "What if the girls are in danger? Rachel Nicholson and JJ's girl? What then?"

"Don't even try to pull that shit on me," Grant retorted. Then he paused and took a deep breath, words more measured when he continued. "I've made my decision, Luther. Give me a call in a day or two. We'll set something up for next week and see where you are then."

Luther closed his eyes against what was happening. "Please, Grant. I need this. What the hell else am I supposed to do?"

"Leave your duty weapon," Grant said, and waited, now seemingly calm. Patient, like some kind of priest. Luther wanted to wring his goddamned neck.

Luther stood, pushed his chair out of his way, unholstered his weapon and set it carefully on Grant's desk. The chair still bumped Luther's leg as he stepped around it, and his temper got the best of him. "Fuck!" he yelled, flipping the sturdy piece of furniture with one hand.

He didn't look back.

9

———

JJ smiled as she approached her driveway in full daylight. She'd gotten off work early. Everyone else was stuck at a mandatory training she'd already attended on night shift. And Evie would be staying at school for volleyball this evening. Volleyball wasn't even a thing when JJ was growing up. Now the high school team did a workshop a couple of times a year with the middle school girls. Early scouting for new talent, she assumed. The high school team was lousy enough that Evie probably could play for them already.

At liberty for once, JJ was looking forward to a few indulgent hours of—what? Vegging with a trashy book or movie? Laundry and cleaning were more likely. She should also check on Adam and Luther. *Yes, Luther.* They'd had their differences, and he could be an asshole, but Luther had done right by her and Adam lately. And she suspected he was taking his brother's death hard. She'd hate for the man to backslide while she wasn't looking.

Later. First she needed to follow up with someone else.

Trooper jumped down from the couch as JJ unlocked the front door. She shook her head at him, but he didn't even pretend contrition.

"All right, bad boy, can I trust you off leash?"

He grinned and thumped his tail in response. She didn't bother changing out of her scrubs (if she was doing laundry, a few extra twigs and leaves on them wouldn't matter), but she did switch out her work shoes for unlaced boots before setting off through the woods toward the Nicholson house. The air chilled her cheeks and shocked her throat and lungs when she breathed through her mouth. Still, it felt good to be outside and moving. She gave an appreciative tug at the ruff of Trooper's neck, walking next to her.

Dorothy's car was the sole vehicle in front of the Nicholson house, Otto presumably still at work. JJ trotted up the front steps. A breeze was picking up, and the metal railing didn't provide any cover for the entryway. She knocked on the cold glass of the storm door, then huddled close to the house and hugged the arms of her suddenly too-thin sweatshirt.

JJ was bouncing on her toes, about to try the door despite her earlier entry faux pas, when the main door swung open and Dorothy stared at her through glass.

"Hey!" JJ said. "How's Rachel doing?"

Instead of inviting her in, Dorothy edged outside, pulling the main door shut behind her and standing in the wedge of the half-open storm door. "Better. I think she'll be back in school tomorrow."

"Good," JJ said, still hugging herself, trying not to stare at Dorothy's socked feet on the freezing concrete slab. "Otto mentioned she's been having nightmares."

"Oh, he did, did he?" Dorothy leaned back against the door-frame, narrowing the wedge.

JJ had to shift sideways to speak directly to her, nearly tripping over Trooper. "Look, I'm not trying to overstep here, but I do have some training in this kind of thing."

That's exaggeration, JJ told herself. *Not complete fabrication.* "And Rachel knows me. I thought maybe if I talked to her—"

"No." Dorothy's mouth set, and she crossed her arms so the door rested against her elbow.

JJ hoped the pose was because she was cold. "If I could just—"

Dorothy straightened. "I said no. If you so much as say a word to my daughter—about what happened to her, about the dreams, about any of it—you won't be welcome in my home again." She backed inside. "And keep Adam Rutledge away from her, or Evie won't be welcome, either."

She closed the doors in JJ's face, hard enough that Trooper's ears flinched.

JJ stood, shivering. *What the hell?*

JJ WAS STRAIGHTENING the living room (how in God's name had Evie's smelly gym shirt made its way under the couch cushions?) when Trooper let out a single woof. A smile crossed JJ's face as she watched Grant's cruiser climb her driveway. She and Trooper went out to meet him, and she laughed when Grant got out of the car.

"How romantic," she said. "That's your apology for running out on our date last night?"

Grant held a nesting pair of large, aluminum dog bowls in his hands, as though they were a cake on a too-small platter. But he wasn't smiling. "I hear Mr. Brown denied poisoning your dog."

JJ snorted. "Yes, Marcus denied it. For what that's worth."

Grant continued, in lawman mode, "I don't have a warrant, but I'd like you to surrender the dog's bowls as potential evidence. I've brought these to replace them."

I don't have a warrant? Surrender potential evidence? His refusal to deal with her as a fellow human being, much less as a possible significant other, made her prickly. Well, pricklier. Dorothy had done a good job of setting her down that thorny road earlier.

"Why do you care who poisoned my dog?" JJ snapped.

Grant shifted the bowls to one hand and tucked them under his arm. "It's my job to care—"

"Oh, it's your job. Well, in that case..." JJ stomped around to the side of her house, as best she could through several inches of dead leaves. She heard Grant shushing on her heels.

"JJ," Grant barked, grabbing her arm, "I want to run the bowls for prints." She shook him off, but he continued, "Did it ever occur to you that Danny Carpenter might have tried to kill Trooper?"

Danny? *Shit,* that was a frightening thought. But why would Danny do that? And why couldn't Grant have just said that's why he was there in the first place? "You can keep your damn bowls, *Sheriff.* I threw the old ones in the trash—I didn't even bother cleaning them—but I haven't had a chance to take it to the dump yet."

JJ removed a rock from the lid of her second metal trashcan. The bowls (cast-off pots, really) sat near the top, in a plastic grocery bag tied closed.

"Here. Have at it." She handed the bag to Grant, bumping him as she moved back toward the driveway. She called over her shoulder, "You might want to see this, too."

JJ led him to the poplar tree she and Danny and Adam had carved their initials on as children. She pointed to where Adam's had been gouged out. "I don't know when this was done, but I noticed it after the Schofield boy was taken, and it was fresh then. Considering what's been going on with Marcus, at the time I wanted to lay this at his door, too. Unfortunately, Danny makes a helluva lot more sense than Marcus."

Grant traced the marks with his fingers, much as she had when she'd discovered it, violent Braille telling an inscrutable story. "What was their relationship like? Adam and Danny?"

JJ let out a harsh laugh. "What does that even mean? We were kids."

Grant leaned against the tree. "You were Evie's age, or older. Evie and Rachel have a relationship, with ups and downs. So what about Adam and Danny?"

JJ hadn't thought about it that way. Still, it was easier to remember personality snapshots of them as individuals than something so fluid as a relationship. "Adam was like he is now. He didn't like conflict, so when things got tense he'd either do something funny to defuse it, or he'd walk away."

"And Danny?" Grant asked.

"I don't know," JJ said. She realized she was resistant because she didn't want to think about him.

"Did either one of them *like* you?" Grant asked. "Did you date them?"

"No! Of course not," JJ said.

"Danny was twelve years old when he was taken," Grant reminded her. "Some twelve-year-olds are sexually active."

"We weren't!" JJ shouted, indignant.

Grant held up his hands. "I wasn't saying you were. I just meant... kids have feelings then. Whether they act on them or not."

JJ felt herself crossing her arms as tightly as Dorothy had earlier and blushing, though she couldn't imagine why. "Is this about *then*, or is this about *now*?"

Grant's face flushed to match JJ's.

"Do you really think that?" he demanded. When she didn't answer, he went on. "I'm trying to get a better picture of a dangerous man, from the people I thought knew him best."

Trooper appeared next to JJ and rested against her leg, as he often did when she was stressed. She rubbed between his ears and reminded herself that Grant was doing his job. But she still didn't like it.

"Fine," she said. "Sometimes Adam got us in trouble because he wanted to try something crazy he thought would be fun. But

Danny, every now and then I felt like he did things *for the sole purpose* of getting us in trouble. And he could be... resentful."

She felt guilty saying it, but it was the truth. Danny had trouble letting things go. And now, Danny had kidnapped her daughter's best friend for no reason that she could fathom. Only to lose her to Adam.

JJ remembered what Luther had said, the night he dropped her off after he released her from jail. He'd warned her that she and Otto should keep an eye on the girls. "Luther thinks—"

"I don't give a good goddamn what Luther thinks," Grant said. "Luther's been suspended."

Stunned by Grant's outburst, JJ finally managed, "Why?"

"Because he's a goddamn mess," Grant said, striding toward his cruiser, yelling the whole way. Or at least as close as JJ had seen him to yelling. "Now I'm down a deputy, I've got the State Police breathing down my neck about Luther's bullshit, and about you shooting a deputy from another county..."

JJ followed, and when Grant reached the driver's side, he turned on her. "Why did you tell Luther and not me about Marcus?"

JJ backed up a half step and nearly fell over Trooper, her silent shadow. "I didn't—"

"Why can't you ever confide in me?" Grant asked.

His voice had dropped, and he was almost pleading. But JJ was wired to be defensive, and it was a hard habit to break. "I don't need you—or anyone else—to protect me."

Grant shook his head and slammed a flattened palm against the window. When he faced her, he'd slipped back into his sheriff's mask. "It's my job to protect you and everyone else. What about Evie?"

"Do you think she's in danger?" JJ asked.

"No, I don't. But what if something happens to you?"

"I told you, I can take care of myself!"

Grant shook his head and got in his cruiser, slamming the door.

"Stupid man," she muttered, staring at the car, waiting for him to open the door and apologize.

Stupid me, she thought, when he didn't. *I should've known better than to try to have a relationship, with him or with anyone else.*

He started the engine, and JJ stood still as he reversed his cruiser, maneuvering to point downhill. *Let it go*, she thought.

But she couldn't.

She stalked to the driver's window and banged her hand against it once, but he didn't stop.

"I don't need you!" she yelled at the retreating car. When he was too far away to hear her, she added, "And I can take care of my daughter, too."

10

Adam stared at the photograph in his hands. What child didn't think his mother was beautiful? But Charlotte truly was, almost ethereal with her vivid eyes and hair cascading over her shoulders in dark waves. Harlan—and even Iris—had said his mother was a healer, but he wasn't sure what that meant. Was she like JJ, or was she something more... mystical? At the edge of his memories of the night she died, just beyond Adam's understanding, was a hint of the latter. Perhaps that was what she'd seen in his father. That beyond his madness, she and Virgil had something in common, a connection with the otherworldly.

He wished he could talk to Harlan, ask him about Charlotte and his dream of Evie and so many other things. It was his fault Harlan was wherever he was now, and Adam felt he should be doing more to bring him back. But he hadn't been able to heal Harlan on his own, and he'd come to understand he couldn't bring him back that way, either. Adam needed Teddy. His great-uncle would know how to reach Harlan.

And his father would know how to reach Teddy.

Adam sat on his bed and propped the pillows against the

headboard before leaning back and stretching his legs out long. Not quite comfortable, he raised his knees and rested the photo on his thighs like a table. Better. Adam relaxed, slowed his breathing, and let his eyes drift shut. He could almost feel Virgil's energy on the photo, a kind of heaviness in the physical space around it. Almost...

"I'M TELLING YOU, *there's something wrong. I can't get anything from him. It's like he's not even there...*"

Adam focused on the sound of the man's voice, using it as a guide wire, tracing it with his hands in the dark spaces of his mind.

"Tell me again why I'm supposed to care." Another voice. Virgil's voice.

Fuzzy white light, filtered through a cheap motel window in winter, began at the edges of Adam's vision and worked its way to the center. Teddy stood in front of the window, backlit by the thin, glowing curtain. Virgil had his back to Adam, shoving something into a duffel bag. Was it Adam's duffel bag?

Teddy's head swung suddenly in Adam's direction, as if he knew Adam was watching. But his focus returned to Virgil just as quickly. "You should care because Harlan wants this to stop as much as you do. And because the man nearly gave his life to make that happen."

Virgil zipped the duffel, and the buzzing, ripping sound echoed in Adam's ears. "Well, isn't that a shame."

Virgil circled the bed to the open bathroom and flipped on the light before entering. His movement within cast flickering shadows, but Adam couldn't figure out how to get closer for a better look. He was frozen in place.

With Virgil out of sight, Teddy stared in Adam's direction—no, *at Adam*—again as he spoke. "What do you think it'll do to Iris if Harlan dies? Or maybe even worse, if he doesn't? What if he lingers in between, and it's up to her to cut him loose and send him on his way?"

More banging in the bathroom. "She managed to go on after my father was killed, didn't she?"

Teddy's eyes faltered, perhaps unable to face Adam while asking the next question. "And what about Adam? What happens to him?"

Virgil stopped. "Why would you ask me that?" He threw a small bag from the bathroom onto the bed. "What we're doing is more important, to Adam and everyone else."

Teddy moved to the bathroom door, and Adam wondered if it was to shield him from his father's view. "I know you think that—"

"It is!" Virgil shouted. "Don't you understand how dangerous he is?"

"He who?" Teddy asked. "The kid?"

"Yes!" Virgil's hands went to his head and tangled in his shoulder-length hair. "Don't you see? It's both of them. Lawrence is behind all of this."

Teddy reached for Virgil's fingers, encouraging him to release the tearing grip on his skull. "Behind all of what? Virgil, please don't hurt yourself again. Behind what?"

"Behind everything," Virgil said. Teddy had succeeded in freeing one hand, and Adam could see strands of Virgil's hair clinging to his fingers. "All the way back to Dead Hollow. It's all part of his plan to come back."

"Virgil," Teddy said, pushing him gently to sit on the bed. He smoothed Virgil's hair back from his face. "It's okay. You know he can't really come back. Your father can never hurt you, or anyone else, again."

"Yes, he will. He's coming back through the boy. He—" Virgil twisted on the bed, so quickly his knees knocked Teddy to the floor. "Who is that?"

Virgil looked right at Adam, and his icy blue eyes stopped Adam's breath as he crossed the motel bed on his knees. Adam tried to pull back, to let go, but since he didn't understand how he'd gotten there in the first place, he sure couldn't find his way back.

"Aren't you full of surprises?" Virgil asked, a hint of admiration in his voice. "Maybe you can be of use after all."

His hand stretched toward Adam, past the motel room...

And then Virgil's head jerked sideways, much as it had when he'd become aware of Adam. Virgil looked toward the motel door, but—it was still in Adam's field of vision—there was no one there.

No, wait. There was no one *at the door*, but there was someone *beyond the door*.

"No," Virgil said, and continued, almost wailing, "No, no, no!"

Teddy stumbled toward them, but it was too late. Virgil was going somewhere—Virgil's *mind* was going somewhere—and he was taking Adam with him. He lurched, slipping sideways into darkness.

Someone pulled, harder and harder, against a desperate, animal thrashing, while hissing, "Shh."

Adam couldn't see, but he heard the familiar voice continue, "Shh, it's okay."

He could smell sweaty terror, hear a rasping whistle that spoke of dying, and feel...

An exploding heart, the slicing sensation of a constricted airway, his mind being ripped apart as it was pulled in infinite directions. And something else. Something so dark and malignant.

He felt the touch of death.

And then he felt another touch, yanking him from the outside. But it was too late.

11

Luther shut off his engine and stared at Iris Rutledge's house. He couldn't say why he'd come here. But, after heading home to change out of his uniform, it seemed like a reasonable alternative to getting completely shitfaced. Plus, he didn't have enough booze left in the house for that.

Adam's car was parked out front, but not Iris's. That was good. Luther wasn't sure he could face her right now. Luther was almost to the front steps when he heard a strange sound, like some crazy bird, or maybe a hog being butchered.

It stopped him in his tracks when he heard it again at the front door.

A person screaming.

Luther reached automatically for the duty weapon that was no longer there. *Shit.* And he'd forgotten his backup. He found the front door unlocked, and pushed it open carefully, mimicking the process he'd have used if he were still armed. He rotated, eyes taking in the kitchen, the front edge of the living room, the stairway. He believed the sounds had come from upstairs.

"Adam?" he called out. "You up there? It's Luther. I'm coming up."

He climbed the stairs cautiously. The treads creaked in half a dozen places, and Luther flinched every time they did. He paused, three stairs from the top, and listened. All of the doors on the second floor were closed except for two. He was guessing one was a bathroom. Low, whining sounds came from the other room.

Luther took a deep breath, then another for good measure. "Here goes nothing," he muttered.

He raised his legs so slowly ascending the last three steps, it made his hips ache. Luther hugged the wall as he approached the open door, then took a quick peek around. *Adam, no one but Adam lying on the bed.* Luther swung toward the closet as he entered. No door on it, and nothing inside but clothes and cardboard boxes. He turned to Adam, and his heart skipped a beat.

"Jesus Christ," he whispered.

Adam's eyelids were open, but his eyes were glassy, bulging and unseeing. His face was red, and his hands clutched at his throat while his legs dug against the mattress. A high, hollow whistle rang from his open mouth.

Luther felt a crunch beneath his foot (picture frame, some part of him registered) as he rushed to the side of the bed. Then he hesitated—*fucking crazy Exorcist shit*—but pushed the thought away.

"Adam!" he yelled, gripping his bicep.

He could swear he felt the cold of Adam's skin through his shirt. Was Adam choking himself? Or choking *on* something? Having a goddamn seizure? Luther grabbed Adam's hands. Adam feebly struggled against him, but still couldn't breathe, even with his hands away from his neck. The whistling sound faded away. His lips began turning blue, and his arms, pushing against Luther's, slowly relaxed.

"Shit!" With no clue what to do, Luther shook Adam, first by the arms and then by the shoulders. "Adam! Snap the fuck out of it! Come on, man! Adam! Adam!"

When Luther stopped shaking him, Adam flopped back to the bed like a doll. A trickle of blood beneath Adam's nose had smeared to his cheek. Luther raised his forearm to his face, covering his mouth and rocking slightly. *Jesus.* Was he dead? Tears prickled at Luther's eyes. *Oh, sweet Jesus. Not him, too.* He sighed a hitching breath and leaned forward to take Adam's carotid pulse.

Movement in the doorway snagged Luther's attention from the corner of his eye. He swung toward the door, reaching for his service weapon—

And grabbed air. Again. *Dammit.*

"Luther, what the hell is going on in here?" JJ asked. Her eyes grew wide at Adam's motionless body.

Luther opened his mouth, and a sucking sound emerged.

No, the noise came from Adam, a raw, rasping wheeze of a melody to Luther's ears. Adam rolled toward Luther and vomited on the bed. He gasped, coughing, and collapsed back on the mattress.

JJ tried to push Luther out of the way, but there wasn't enough room with the nightstand and the wall so close. "Keep him on his side," she said, racing around the bed for better access. "He'll choke to death."

Luther grabbed Adam's far shoulder and rolled Adam toward him, in time for the younger man to retch again. After the first round, there wasn't much left in his stomach—it was mostly bile, and maybe even a little blood—but he kept heaving. Luther turned his face away as the fermented, acidic odor made his own stomach lurch.

JJ climbed on the mattress behind Adam, supporting his back and uttering reassuring syllables more suited to a mother than a nurse. Finally, Adam stopped, eyes closed and curling an arm around his midsection. A bit of vomit had gathered in the corner of his mouth, and there was a suspicious smear on his temple. Leaning in, JJ whispered, "Shh, it's okay…"

Adam's eyes flew open wide, pink-rimmed and bloodshot and terrified. He crawled toward Luther as he twisted away from JJ.

"Easy, buddy," Luther said, pushing the weak, panicking man back to the mattress. "It's me and JJ. There's nobody else here. You're safe—I promise."

"He's right, Adam," JJ said. "It's just us. You're safe."

Adam looked at her, bucked up from the mattress to see past her, then fell back to the bed. It took Luther a moment to realize he'd passed out.

Luther waited, quiet, while JJ rested one hand on Adam's chest and the other sought out his pulse. When she shifted for a better angle, her posture triggered an image for Luther of her kneeling over Les's body, trying to save his brother. Luther staggered backward, and an object crunched under his feet again.

He bent to pick up a framed photo of a pretty young woman. He nearly fainted himself with sudden recognition—Adam's mother. The glass had cracked, but the photo appeared undamaged and, unlike his pants, had escaped the rain of puke.

"Here," JJ said, holding out a pillow. "Put this under his feet."

Luther set the frame gently on the nightstand, facedown, so he could take the pillow. Then he slid a forearm under Adam's ankles and tucked the pillow. "Is he gonna be okay? Do we need to take him somewhere?"

"His airway's clear," she said. "Let's give him a few minutes and see how he does. Do you know what happened?"

Luther leaned against the wall. His body was starting to shake, just a little, and he wished he had somewhere to sit. "I heard somebody screaming. The door was open. And I found him like this."

"Like what?"

Luther struggled to articulate what he'd seen. "Like somebody was choking him to death. Except nobody was there."

"Technically, choking is internal. Say, a foreign object lodged in your throat. Strangulation is external," she said, reluctantly easing away from the bed. "Keep an eye on him."

JJ stepped out of the bedroom. Luther heard water running, and before he had time to wonder what she was doing, JJ was back, carrying two wet washcloths. She handed one to Luther before she began gently wiping Adam's face.

"What's this for?" Luther asked.

"Back of your neck," she said. "And you might want to sit down. You're looking a little green around the gills. Last thing I need is you passing out, too."

Luther didn't argue, sitting on a hard, wooden chair. It was like something you'd find in a child's room. Wrapping the cool cloth around his neck, Luther looked around and realized it was a child's room. Complete with a baseball glove, skateboard, kid books and magazines... It must have been Adam's growing up. There was something almost spooky about the space, like time had stopped when Danny Carpenter was kidnapped.

But in a way it had. Being more than a decade older, Luther sometimes forgot that Adam hadn't been around much after that.

Luther hunched forward and got a strong whiff of nastiness. *Damn*. It was definitely on his pants. He lifted his head and wiped at a few pungent spots with the washcloth while he said, "Look, I know it sounds crazy, but I'm telling you it's like he was being choked—fine, *strangled*—to death."

"I know," JJ said.

The certainty in her voice made him realize she'd been doing more than simply cleaning vomit. Luther stood and examined Adam more closely. Two red, horizontal lines bisected his neck, low on his throat, maybe a quarter of an inch thick. One was darker, but both were already fading.

JJ wiped the cloth across Adam's face, and he began to stir. "See the way it looks as if he's been crying, that redness around his eyes? Classic sign of strangulation."

Luther glanced at JJ. "How do you know this shit?"

"DV training. Somebody finally figured out that if we know how to document evidence of strangulation at the ER, prosecutors have a better chance of getting convictions on serious domestic violence charges. And women are less likely to get murdered three months later." She brushed a bit of unruly dark hair back from Adam's forehead. "Adam, sweetie, can you hear me? We need you to let us know if you're okay, or we're taking you to the hospital."

Adam breathed deeply, winced, then fought a cough. He opened his eyes, and croaked, "M' okay."

"Can you sit up for me?" JJ asked. "Slowly."

Luther retrieved the pillow from the foot of the bed and helped JJ lift and support Adam until he was in standard sick-bed position. "Dizzy?" she asked.

Adam didn't speak, but shook his head no. His face was still pink, and Luther thought there might be a smattering of red pinpricks among the flush.

"I want you to just sit there for a while, let everything settle, before we get you cleaned up," JJ said. "I'm going downstairs for a minute. Let Luther know if something happens and you feel worse. Okay?"

Adam nodded, and let his eyes drift closed.

JJ's intense gaze locked on Luther before she left. He didn't need to be a psychic to figure out her warning. "I got it," Luther said.

Didn't need to be a psychic. Luther sat back heavily on the chair. He'd watched a man almost get choked to death by... what? Some kind of ghost? Or a boogeyman? *No.* This house might give him a little bit of heebie-jeebies, but he hadn't seen or felt anything else there but him and Adam. They'd definitely been alone. So what the hell had just happened?

Whatever it was, he had a cold feeling inside that what he'd witnessed was only the beginning.

12

———

JJ tried her best not to run down the stairs like a crazy woman. Because that must be what she was. Crazy. They were all fucking crazy.

She'd spent a fair amount of time in Iris's kitchen over the years, and most things were kept where JJ would have expected. She didn't dare use Iris's last onion, but she found plenty of potatoes and set a few on the counter. The milk in the fridge smelled okay, and there were even a few stalks of celery in the crisper that hadn't gone spongy. Plenty of butter, and the flour didn't have bugs. *Potato soup it is.*

JJ started a pot of water on the stove and dropped in a couple of rock-hard bouillon cubes that might have been left over from the Cold War. She quickly scrubbed lime and dirt from the potatoes, found a serviceable knife, and placed the first, large tuber on a cutting board. But she hadn't cleaned it as carefully as she'd thought. The drops of water pooling around it had a slightly muddy hue. JJ reached for the potato, to give it another rinse, and watched her hand shake. In her other hand, the forgotten knife rattled against the work surface.

JJ set the knife carefully on the cutting board and gripped the counter with both hands. When would the craziness stop? When could they have normal lives? She wiped a tear from her eye before it slid free. She couldn't shake the image of Adam, lying there. It wasn't the bloody nose, his just plain wrong color, or any of the other signs he'd been hurt that she couldn't let go. It was his stillness, the stillness of death that she'd seen on him before. The stillness that he seemed to seek out and, she feared, would eventually find for good.

She inhaled hard through her nose, almost honking, to get rid of a threatening sniffle. Then she washed her hands, diced the potatoes and celery and dumped them in the pot before heading back upstairs to Adam's room.

The men were much as she'd left them. Adam's eyes were closed, and Luther sat back on his unyielding chair as far as possible, a hand over his eyes. He was probably trying to avoid the sick stink.

"How's the patient?" JJ asked.

Adam didn't open his eyes, but raised a thumb. Luther didn't speak, either, but his color was now as good as it ever was, except for the purple bruise on his cheek. She squeezed by him for a better look at Adam. The marks on his neck had nearly faded, as had most of the redness across his face. His eyes were still red-ringed and bloodshot, but his pupils looked good and reacted normally to the flashlight on her cell phone.

"Any trouble breathing?" she asked. "Or speaking?"

He shook his head and held a hand in front of his throat. "It hurts," he said, voice a hoarse whisper, "but I can do it."

Satisfied, JJ went to the dresser and pulled out two pairs of sweatpants. She pointed at Luther. "I need your pants." Then she took a good, hard look at Adam. "And I need all your clothes."

They simply stared at her.

JJ said, "Adam might have brain damage, but you don't have an excuse. Do you want to keep wearing vomit?"

"No," Luther said, but didn't move.

"Can you help Adam get cleaned up?" JJ asked.

Luther nodded.

JJ held up the folded pants before placing them on the dresser. "I'll be in the kitchen. Here are your not-puke pants. When you're done, bring down the nasty clothes and the comforter and anything else that's been puked on and we'll throw them in the laundry. Got it?"

Luther nodded again, and JJ headed back downstairs.

There was something reassuring about hearing them move around above her in the old house. She was mixing butter and flour in a saucepan and about to add the milk when Luther joined her.

"Where's Adam?" she asked, stirring.

"Starting the laundry."

She raised her wooden spoon.

"He said he was okay to do it," Luther said, slowly backing away. "Actually, he didn't *say* anything. He just sorta shooed me away from the machine."

"Hunh," JJ grunted.

By the time Adam appeared, she was serving the soup. He walked up behind her, sniffed appreciatively, and whispered, "Thank you," in her ear.

JJ set the ladle back on its saucer but nearly knocked it to the floor, suddenly overcome. She turned and squeezed Adam to her. He was warm (maybe too warm) and solid, more muscled than she'd expected, but with too little padding atop it. "You have to be careful," she whispered. "Dumbass."

He was smiling when she released him.

"That wasn't your bad ear, was it?" she asked. "No excuses."

"I heard you," he croaked.

JJ gave Adam a plate of toast for the table and carried Luther's bowl with her own. He thanked her, and she replied, "You're welcome. You get that eye last night when you were ruining my date?"

Luther winced as he slurped a spoonful of soup. "Damn, that's hot." He blew on his spoon and took another sip. "It's good, though."

"Luther—"

"I might've done," he admitted.

She tasted her soup. Not bad, but it needed ham or bacon. She gestured with her spoon (a bad habit she always fell into when agitated) as she surmised, "So that's why you got suspended? For starting a brawl in a shithole bar?"

Adam's red eyes widened, but he didn't say anything.

Luther's spoon clanged against his bowl. "I didn't ask to be on the sideline while the sonuvabitch who killed my brother walks free."

JJ held her tongue.

They all sat, slurping in silence, until Adam asked about Evie. JJ said she was fine. She wasn't about to go down Adam's dream rabbit hole, but she did tell him what Otto had said about Rachel, and that he was hoping Adam could talk to her.

Adam shook his head. "No."

"Why not? He doesn't know what else to do." She hadn't initially been for the idea herself—and Dorothy certainly wasn't —but now JJ realized she'd changed her mind for some reason. Contrarianism? Being pissed at Dorothy for her ridiculous ultimatum?

"Speak with Harlan or Teddy," Adam said, pausing for a sip of water. His grating voice sounded painful. "Which at this point means Teddy."

"And where is he?" JJ asked.

"I wish I knew."

JJ pushed her chair back a bit and crossed her arms. "Is that what you were doing tonight? Trying to find him?"

"I might have done," Adam said, cracking a grin at Luther before being overcome by a coughing fit.

JJ got up and microwaved a cup of water. She watched Adam

hold his breath to keep the coughing at bay, and tracked down Iris's honey and a bottle of lemon juice while the water heated. Mixing it all together, she handed Adam the mug and sat in the chair next to him.

He drank about half of the concoction, face twisting at the sourness.

"Well?" Luther asked, leaning on the table.

"I was trying to connect with Virgil and Teddy. Something went wrong, and Virgil and I got pulled somewhere else." Adam closed his eyes and braced himself against the table. "I don't know where, but I think someone was dying."

JJ grabbed Adam's nearest hand, forcing him to look at her. "That someone was almost you. Again. You need to stop being a goddamn martyr. Finding Teddy is not your job." JJ glanced at Luther. "It's not *our* job. There are people trained to find Virgil and Teddy and bring them in."

Luther's eyes didn't waver. "They're doing a piss-poor job of it."

"Maybe," JJ said. "But do you think we'd do any better? We've all got our own shit going on. Luther, you're such a goddamned mess right now, if the Sheriff was anyone but Grant you'd probably have lost your job already. And you don't want that."

JJ placed a hand on Adam's shoulder. "He's got Harlan in the hospital to worry about. When he's not trying to put himself in there, too."

Adam stuck his tongue out at JJ, but not very far. Still, she appreciated the effort. She continued, "I've got Marcus breathing down my neck, fighting the protective order. Every day, I wonder if this is the day I'll be charged for shooting a cop, if this is the day my daughter's gonna end up God knows where, but hopefully not with my bastard ex-husband."

JJ paused, getting her emotions in check. "I understand that y'all want something to happen, that you want to *make* something happen. But I can't go sticking my nose where it doesn't belong, pissing off law enforcement while they're still investigating me for shooting one of their own."

"Grant wouldn't—" Luther started, but she cut him off.

"He won't even talk to me right now, so I won't hold my breath on him bailing me out." JJ stood and stretched impulsively across the table to squeeze Luther's hand. "Like you did a couple of weeks ago. Thank you for that."

JJ smiled. She'd finally said what she'd needed to say for a while, and she'd stunned him into silence in the bargain.

Her smile faded when she caught sight of Iris's wall clock, a cornucopia face surrounded by a faded yellow frame. "Shit. I gotta go get Evie."

Luther stood. "I can stick around for a while."

"Good, then I'll leave you the dishes," JJ said, setting her bowl in the sink and finding her purse near the door. "Call if you need anything. And Adam, don't try that stupid shit again. I mean it."

Adam nodded and managed an "Okay."

"Don't worry," Luther said. "I'll keep an eye on him."

"Well, gee, that's reassuring," JJ muttered, closing the door behind her.

13

———

"I**s it my imagination, or was JJ not so crazy about the idea of leaving us together?" Luther asked, mouth twisted in a smartass grin. "What'd she think we'd get up to without her?"

"Hookers and blow," Adam said.

"Ha!" Luther laughed, head thrown back. It was so incongruous, coming from the kid with the squeaky clean vocabulary in his now gravelly, Tom Waits voice. "We should be so lucky."

Adam rose, but Luther shook his head. "I'll clear the table. Just go sit."

It only took Luther a few minutes to stow the leftover soup in the fridge and wash the dishes. He tended to keep things neat in his own home, and no one could accuse him of having a sink full of dirty dishes. Of course, only using them once or twice a week helped.

Adam sat in a faded armchair. A brown and yellow afghan was arranged over its back, and Adam had folded it to prop his head upright.

"How's that neck?" Luther asked.

"Hurts pretty good," Adam admitted. "How's that face?"

"Only hurts when I smile," Luther said, and proceeded to do so. In fact, he had a powerful urge to rub the bruise with his knuckles, but he resisted it. "I guess JJ's in a tight spot now."

Adam nodded.

"You think that's it?" Luther asked. "Or you think there's something more? Something she's not saying?"

Adam raised his brows, and Luther said, "Yeah, I guess by definition if she's not saying, then you don't know."

It was dusky outside, with only a hint of light. Luther got up, knowing he was dangerously close to dozing if he stayed put. Too much adrenaline had left him too empty. That was the story of his life for the past month. He went to the front door and looked out at the driveway. The property was ringed by woods, but unlike at JJ's house, there wasn't much cover in front. Instead, a clearing that had once been a garden stood close.

Luther made his way from window to window, surveying. It was harder to get a sense of the back, but there were a couple of outbuildings, one tucked into the hillside, and then a whole lot of forest. He didn't see a back door, though presumably the house had one. Returning to the living room, he gazed up the stairs that had sent his heart to pumping not so long ago. He considered what he recalled of the layout.

Turning to Adam, he asked, "How the hell did you slip out of here when Kilbourne came to get you?"

Adam smiled. "Rutledge family secret."

Luther snorted. "And people say the Becks are sneaky fuckers."

Yep, there was more to Adam Rutledge than Luther had thought. He'd dodged the authorities for the better part of a week, not to mention tracking down Danny Carpenter. Or had Danny Carpenter tracked him down? It didn't matter. The result was the same—they'd ended up together, almost like they were meant to. Like something in the universe was pulling the two men together, then and maybe still.

The sonuvabitch had gotten away from Adam, but Luther had to admit it sounded like he'd done his best to stop him. Permanently. Now Luther recognized that as Adam's M.O., going until he dropped without holding anything back. That was something to keep in mind, but Luther's biggest concern was the weird shit he couldn't explain. He honestly didn't want to think about the unnatural or supernatural whatever it was, but it might be the key to getting what they both wanted.

"What's JJ think about all this..." Luther, at a loss for words, waved his hands around his head.

"I don't think she knows what to think," Adam said, coughing softly.

No shit, Luther thought. "Is it always like that?"

Adam swallowed so loudly Luther heard it—a hollow crackle —before wiping wetness from his red-rimmed eyes. "It only started when Rachel Nicholson was taken. It's always bad; I pretty much always puke. How bad depends on what I see. This was... more intense than usual."

Luther winced as Adam started hacking again. It sounded painful, and Luther went to the kitchen for a glass of tap water. "I wonder if an ice pack might help that," he said, handing the glass to a grateful Adam. "Or maybe some ibuprofen or something."

Adam didn't answer, but after a few sips he managed to stop coughing.

The man was coughing because he was nearly choked to death by someone who wasn't there. Luther shook his head. It was too crazy to believe. But the evidence was right in front of him. "So let me get this straight," Luther said. "You got choked because somebody else was being choked, and somehow you were there? In their head?"

Face pink, Adam gave an *I don't know* shrug. Or, Luther guessed it was more like, *I don't know and at the moment it's hard for me to give a shit*. If Adam used those kinds of words.

"Do you ever see things before they happen, or you just see them while they're happening?" Luther asked.

Adam paused, then made a rolling gesture with one hand.

"The latter?" Luther asked.

Adam nodded, but Luther felt his pause had been significant. "What else?"

Adam swallowed, then rasped, "Sometimes after."

"So sometimes you see things while they're happening, and sometimes you see things that have already happened?"

Adam nodded.

"Can you read minds? Look at somebody and know what they're thinking?"

Adam shook his head.

Luther wasn't sure if that was good or bad. He slumped in his chair. Last night's poor judgment, and everything he was reaping because of it, had started to catch up with him. "It's not often I find myself in agreement with JJ, but I honestly don't know what the hell to make of it, either."

"Tell me about it," Adam croaked.

Luther almost smiled. He had to admire the man's spirit. "Here's the thing," he said. "I may not be able to see the future, but I can't help thinking Rachel and JJ's girl—"

"Evie."

"That this asshole might still have some use for Rachel and Evie. We don't know why he took Rachel in the first place. Virgil might've been able to tell us something, if Kiss-Ass hadn't let him escape. And if Virgil weren't crazier than a shithouse rat. No offense."

Adam gave a single flick of his hand that Luther interpreted as, *None taken.*

"Anyway," Luther said, "I'm not convinced that he's done with them."

"Danny," Adam said.

The man was a regular name dictionary. Of course that's who

Luther meant. It was funny, though. On reflection, Luther realized he never said the asshole's name. A deputy was trained—even a suspended one—to speak carefully, to not make assumptions about a suspect's identity until he had convincing evidence of it.

Except Luther was never one to speak carefully. It drove Grant nuts. There was some other reason he was reluctant to name the man who killed his brother. Someday, when the asshole was dead and he had the time and inclination for navel-gazing, maybe Luther would figure it out.

"I disagree with JJ. I don't think we can wait for the law"—it felt weird to say that and know it didn't include him—"to find him. I don't think the girls can wait."

Adam stared at Luther. His blue irises stood out even more against the surrounding red, reminiscent of his father's spooky eyes. His intensity made Luther wonder if Adam had lied about being a mind-reader.

"This isn't about protecting the girls," Adam said.

"Not entirely," Luther admitted. "Look, we both want to protect the girls. But that's not all it is for either of us. You obviously want to find your uncle Teddy, I'm guessing to see if he can help Harlan Miller. And I want Danny Carpenter."

Luther waited for Adam to ask him why, but he didn't. Either Adam didn't know and didn't care why, or he *did* know, and *still* didn't care.

Which meant Adam wouldn't stop him.

"Virgil Rutledge is our best link to Teddy and Danny." Luther leaned forward and stretched a hand toward Adam. "We want the same thing—to find Virgil. I happen to think we can do that. If we work together. What do you say?"

There was no hesitation in his voice when Adam replied, "Okay."

14

———

Danny pulled over to the shoulder and cut his headlights before rolling down the windows.

The cold air blowing across the half-raised glass made a hollow sound, like a whisper. Or maybe the whisper had never really gone away. What the hell had happened, there at the end? At his moment of greatest triumph, someone else had been there. And yet, rather than spoiling his victory, it had tasted sweeter. That's why he was inclined to think Virgil or Adam—maybe both?—had been there. Observing. Not doing anything to interfere. Because he—or they—sanctioned his actions? No. Because they *couldn't* do anything. For whatever reason, they were powerless against him.

Just as he was powerless against the voice, the whisper that wouldn't leave him alone, even with the smell of his latest offering permeating the air.

If he wanted it to leave him alone, he supposed he'd have to do what it wanted. Again.

But first, business.

Danny stared down at his phone. A single bar. Good enough.

He dialed, confident. Some lackey answered on the other end. "Hey, it's Mitch," Danny said. "Let me talk to Victor."

SHIT. Danny tapped a finger against the steering wheel in the dark. He'd been naive. The price for Victor's help was more than he'd expected. Was he wrong about Victor's opinion of him? Was the man setting him up to fail? Or was Victor just being a greedy bastard? It didn't matter. Either way, Danny's cash reserves wouldn't cover it, and he couldn't raise that kind of money without doing something stupid that would attract attention.

Which left him one option. His nest egg. It wasn't without risk, either—he'd been an idiot, stashing it where he had—but it had some other potential rewards, too. Rewards that harked back to the Rutledges and the plan that had earlier slipped his mind. But first...

Danny released the seat belt on the body in the seat next to him before getting out of the car, taking the key with him. He walked around the rear, pausing at the trunk, and rested his hands briefly on its cold metal. There was a hint of gray light, once his eyes adjusted, but the sky above was a deep, dark gray-blue with indistinguishable high clouds that hid most of the stars. He wasn't sure if the moon was blocked by clouds or mountain, or hadn't risen yet. He took a deep breath; the frosty air felt good in his lungs, cleansing.

Invigorated, he opened the trunk and snapped on a pair of gloves. Next to the box of gloves was a small, hard-sided cooler, the kind that might carry someone's lunch. He didn't remember purchasing it, but had somehow known it was there and somehow, like a drunken memory, had known he'd find the knife inside. It was so long, its handle protruded from his jacket pocket, catching his elbow as he closed the trunk lid.

Danny set the cooler on the ground next to the car, then

opened the passenger door. He slid gloved hands beneath the body's armpits and pulled it free of the car. The body toppled forward like a drunk frat boy, and Danny bent his knees, maneuvering it into a better position. The man's head fell onto Danny's shoulder, as if to whisper a final secret.

It was so much easier like this, before rigor set in.

Danny knew he was isolated—he'd had to remove a chain to access this dead-end trail or whatever the hell it was—but he couldn't help looking around, for something other than trees. And listening for something other than the sound of the wind. Nothing on either count. Except the whispers, wriggling just inside his head. Like they wanted to crawl out his ears and be free.

He laid the man on his back, sat astride him, took out the knife...

Time was slippery, and it seemed only a moment had passed before he opened the cooler, having done something he'd never done before. What hand had guided his own through the motions in the darkness? Or had he done this before, and wiped it from his mind, like so many things?

Danny stood and slid his hands beneath the body's armpits again, trying to hold its back away from him as he lifted. The man's hood stuck out, tickling Danny's face. He wrinkled his nose and walked backward, dragging the man's feet on the gravel shoulder. The body jostled when Danny came to a sudden stop, calves striking something. *Damn guardrail.* But it was low, and it was there for good reason. The ground sloped abruptly on the other side, quickly disappearing into darkness.

Danny squatted, careful of his back, and flung the body forward. The upper torso settled on the other side of the guardrail, but the legs had hung up on it, as though the man were using the barrier to do his evening power sit-ups. Danny nudged the legs free, but the body clung to the shallow bit of level ground next to the guardrail. Danny stretched one leg over, hooked his foot beneath the body and gave it a little help, feeling the strain in his hip and calf. *Finally*. Then he heard debris crashing—that's all it was now, *debris*—rolling over the mountainside. He didn't bother getting a flashlight; it had gone far enough.

The gloves went in the cooler, and he returned the cooler to the trunk before getting back in the car. He'd left the windows open for fresh air. His activity had produced a light sweat, and once he'd stopped moving, the cold air chilled him. He started the vehicle, reached for the power window switch, and paused.

He could still smell the body. He might have to get a new vehicle. But to go where?

Cold Springs, of course.

He hesitated. Was he crazy to go back there? Maybe, but he didn't have a choice.

Fuck it, he thought, ping-ponging between the guardrails as he turned the car around on the narrow lane. Back toward Beecham County.

15

———

Adam sat in the living room, waiting for the dryer to finish. He gazed at his feet propped on the coffee table and felt absent Iris's disapproval. *JJ and I did jigsaw puzzles on that coffee table in winter,* he thought. *They were always missing a piece, and once she accused me of eating them.*

Luther had left an hour or so ago, probably tired of hearing himself speak since Adam's throat was too raw for chit-chat. Or maybe the man was just plain tired. He didn't look good, even if you ignored the black eye. Luther hadn't given many details on how he'd gotten his injuries, but Adam doubted Luther knew them. He'd logged enough hours as a bartender to recognize when alcohol and an explosive temper resulted in amnesia of one sort or another.

Was that why Adam hadn't told Luther about his dream of Evie covered in blood? Was it that he didn't entirely trust Luther's motives, or that sharing the details with another person would make it too real, one step closer to actually happening? Not that motives were ever an either-or proposition. Adam had generally found his to be a lengthy list of and-and.

The clothes dryer finally buzzed loudly. Adam shut off the

lights before slowly climbing the stairs with the warm comforter thrown awkwardly over his shoulder. Making the bed required more concentration than any mindless task should. *Is this really the short end of the fitted sheet?* He brushed his teeth. He didn't bother changing his sweatpants, but put on a different shirt before crawling into bed. Adjusting the comforter, he sniffed it surreptitiously, as though someone were watching. He knew the vomit smell wasn't in the fabric (it smelled of dryer sheets), but rather in his mind. Or maybe his nostril hairs.

Adam wasn't ready to turn out the light just yet. JJ would've said he wasn't done beating himself up. And maybe she was right.

I should try again. But did he really believe that? *I have to find Virgil. What if he can block me now? I need to know if he can.*

Did he? Or was he looking for an excuse? JJ was right. If he tried again, he wasn't sure he would live through it. And if something bad happened, she and Luther wouldn't serendipitously drop in again. So was he ready to die?

Adam reached for the light, then noticed the framed photo lying facedown on the nightstand and picked it up instead. The glass was cracked, but he could still feel the heaviness around the photo he associated with Virgil. It almost seemed that he could *see it* as well, a haze distorting the image like smog over a city. Adam set the picture back on his nightstand and turned out the light.

Pain shot up Adam's neck and into his skull as he lowered himself to his pillow and adjusted it. He thought about the pain meds in the bathroom cabinet, but was afraid if he got up, he'd never get back down to sleep. And the warm comforter felt so soothing. He tucked it around his neck to see if it would help the persistent ache. His face flushed with the sudden warmth, but it wasn't unpleasant. The muscles in his neck relaxed a bit, and he began to drift away.

Gradually the soft, drifting sensation transformed… and Adam found himself falling. Falling toward his mother's picture.

A tiny sliver of his mind said, *that makes no sense*, even as the rest of his mind kept falling and split in two. One part of him felt his old, worn mattress as he lay in bed. But the other felt a hard chair beneath him as he strove to stay awake. *I should get up and move around*, he thought, but he didn't. And soon, it was too late. His chin dropped toward his chest—

And that's when a man's voice, both familiar and not, whispered, *There you are. I've been waiting.*

Adam twitched, in the chair and in his bed, but was stuck, tethered to the voice.

You're not what I expected.

Was Adam supposed to respond? He couldn't, in either place, even if he'd known what to say.

But the question is, what will happen when I show you the things you can do?

Adam's neck screamed as he jerked himself free, out of a motel chair and back to his own bed. Heart pounding and throat throbbing, he switched on the light and rushed to the bathroom, falling to his knees in front of the toilet.

Please, please... The wave passed without him being sick. Adam breathed a cautious sigh of relief.

And a drop of blood fell on the toilet seat. Adam stared at it, transfixed by the bright red marring the white surface. Until another drop fell.

He grabbed the sink next to him for support as he stepped in front of the mirror. Nosebleed. Again. Not so bad this time. He pinched the bridge of his nose and held a wad of tissue beneath it. He waited a minute or two; it seemed to have stopped, so he tossed the tissue in the trash, on top of the roll or so of bloody toilet paper from earlier. He'd need to take that out before Iris returned home. It made the bathroom appear a mini slaughterhouse, or an off-the-books clinic for fugitives.

Adam gently washed his face and cleaned the toilet seat before returning to his bedroom. He stared at his bed.

No way. Not happening.

He grabbed his pillow (no blood) and yanked the comforter free of the mattress. He'd sleep downstairs on the couch tonight. Adam made it as far as the stairs, when he paused, head tilted as if hearing a siren in the distance. Shifting the comforter awkwardly onto his shoulder, he went back to his room.

"Sorry, Mom," he said, placing the framed photo facedown once again.

When he left, he closed the door behind him.

16

JJ had avoided Dorothy last night by waiting in the car while Evie delivered Rachel's homework assignments. This morning, she let Evie run inside (when in doubt, Evie always wanted to be in motion) to fetch Rachel so JJ could drop the girls at school. Dorothy had waved from the doorway, and JJ waved back, so maybe they'd already progressed to pretending nothing had ever happened. JJ hoped so. She didn't need additional drama in her life right now, and Evie and Rachel didn't deserve it, either.

To that end, she hadn't interrogated her daughter any more about Rachel's dreams and, playing it safe, she'd barely spoken to Rachel this morning except to ask how she was feeling. She didn't think the girls had noticed; Evie was good at taking up any conversational slack. JJ would respect Dorothy's wishes for now, but she wasn't happy about it. JJ may be taciturn with her own emotions (Marcus had preferred *secretive*), but she firmly believed nothing good could come from forcing a child to remain silent about her fears.

JJ would have to bide her time. She'd touch base with Otto again, too, but she'd have to be careful. Dorothy was the jealous type, and if she was looking for an excuse to push JJ away, that would be an excellent one.

Arriving at the hospital, JJ pulled out her cell phone, determined to take care of another item nagging at her before clocking in. A passing colleague pointed at her wrist, making a face. JJ knew it was evil, but she hoped the woman tripped over the curb in front of the hospital. Just a stubbed toe, nothing more.

He picked up on the fifth ring. And so did the ancient answering machine.

"Hello?" said an unfamiliar voice, as Iris spoke over him, "You've reached Iris Rutledge..."

"Crap," he said.

Yep, that's Adam.

"Hold on," he said, voice still ragged and deeper than usual. "I don't know how to shut this off."

JJ glanced at the clock on her phone. Two more minutes, and she'd be late. Actually, three minutes, because in two minutes she'd be exactly on time.

Clicking noises trailed off on the other end, followed by a dial tone. JJ shook her head and called back. This time, Adam picked up on the first ring. Before he had a chance to answer, JJ complained, "You could've just said if you didn't want to talk to me. You didn't have to hang up."

"Hello? JJ?"

"Who did that song, *Everybody Knows*?"

"I have no idea—"

"You know, the depressing one with the deep voice. It was in some 90s movie. Your voice could sing that song now, if you knew the words. How do you feel today?"

"Fine."

"You having any memory issues?"

"Other than remembering why we're friends?" he deadpanned.

"Ouch! Then I guess I shouldn't ask about pain in your neck. Did I wake you?"

"You might've done," he admitted.

"Sorry. Were you able to sleep? I mean, without anything else... crazy?" JJ asked. She glanced at the clock on the dash. She couldn't do the math while talking, but she was pretty sure she was crossing into late.

"I slept a little," Adam said.

Which in Adam-speak meant very damn little indeed. JJ braced herself, stepping out of her Bronco into the elements. "Damn, it's cold! Listen, I gotta go, but if you have any trouble today, promise me you'll go to the hospital. Have Luther take you. Whatever happened, if it was some kind of strangulation, that's not something to mess around with. Okay? Promise me."

"I promise," he said, then added, "Mom."

"Now see, why'd you have to go and ruin your sexy voice like that?" she asked, almost running into the automatic doors as she rushed through them.

He laughed and said, "Bye, JJ," before hanging up.

She tucked her phone away, smiling. What would it be like to have Adam around again, and the world back to normal? She would dearly like to find out.

MID-MORNING, JJ got a message that someone was waiting for her in the cafeteria. She took the elevator down on her break and glanced around, trying not to look too eager.

There was no auburn-haired man in uniform. Instead, a white-blonde head swung in her direction, and an elderly woman stood and waved her over.

"Iris, when did you get back?" JJ asked.

"About ten minutes ago," Iris said, handing JJ a coffee. "I came here first."

Her face was pale and her eyes and cheeks were sunken, as though the structure that held her together was eroding from within. It reminded JJ of Adam, even before yesterday's drama. He and his grandmother were traveling the same hard road, and the journey hadn't ended yet.

"I'm back because of Harlan," Iris said. "He's stable, but he's not improving. And they don't think he's going to."

"Have they actually said that?" JJ asked.

"Not in so many words," Iris admitted. "But they're transferring him back here from Morgantown. To me, that says they don't think he'll get better."

"Not necessarily. It could be admission policies, or an insurance mandate, or something else entirely," JJ said.

"It doesn't matter. It amounts to the same thing." Iris picked at the lid of her coffee. "I'm afraid they wouldn't tell me the truth anyway because I'm nothing to him."

JJ took the cup from Iris's hands and covered them with her own. "Iris, piece of paper or not, you're *everything* to him. Anyone can see that."

Iris looked away and pulled her hands free to swipe at her eyes. "Thank you, JJ."

"It'll be so much easier for you with him back in Beecham County. You and Adam both. You can sleep in your own bed, eat your own food. You know people, and you'll be able to tell if they're not being straight with you." JJ hesitated—was this what Iris needed to hear now? She wasn't certain, but felt it had to be said. "And even here, there are more long-term care options than you'd think."

"No," Iris said, voice firm. "That's not going to happen."

Iris was the last person JJ would accuse of being a Pollyanna, and she hadn't seemed naive about Harlan's condition. But everyone has blind spots, especially when he or she is under as much stress as Iris had been of late. JJ didn't want her to have false hope. "Iris—" she began.

"JJ," Iris interrupted, with a grim smile, "don't get the wrong idea. I haven't given up hope on Harlan. Not by a long shot. But he would not want to rot in a bed indefinitely, and I don't want him to."

"Does he have any kind of end of life directive on file?"

Iris snorted. "Of course not. This is Harlan we're talking about. But I swore to him that I will not let it happen. Do you understand me?"

Iris held JJ's eyes, waiting. Challenging.

"Yes, I understand." JJ hesitated. "Are you asking me for something..."

"No," Iris cut in. "I know how to take care of it."

If anyone could do it, Iris could. But then why was she risking whatever she might have planned by telling JJ? She certainly didn't need JJ's approval, and she hadn't asked for it. So she wanted something else from her. JJ raised an eyebrow at the older woman.

Iris sighed. "You always were too smart for your own good. All I want from you, dear child, is a promise: if something happens to me, you'll watch over Harlan and do whatever you think is right."

Whatever JJ thought was right... After Iris had already told her Harlan's wishes and her own. The devious old bitch.

"You don't ask much, do you?" JJ leaned back in her chair, coffee hovering in front of her face, considering. And then the question came to her that she should have asked long ago. "What about Adam?"

"I haven't told him yet that Harlan's being transferred."

JJ slammed the front legs of her chair back to the floor, sloshing her coffee. "That's not what I mean and you know it."

Iris hunched forward, voice low and eyes hard. "Do you really want Adam making that choice? Oh, he could do it. And he would. But it would break him. Utterly and completely break him. Like Charlotte broke his father."

JJ stared at her coffee, now churning acid in her stomach. Iris was right. Adam would always do whatever he felt was his duty, even if it killed him. And even if he hated himself for it. Whereas she... JJ lifted her eyes to Iris's scrutiny.

"You're more like me," Iris said, finishing JJ's thought.

JJ shook her head. "Are you sure you're not the psychic in the family?"

"Just an apt student of human nature," Iris said. "Do we have an understanding?"

The woman was asking JJ to risk her job—and criminal prosecution—by ending Harlan's life. But as appalled as she was by the prospect, JJ found she couldn't refuse.

JJ sighed, suddenly exhausted with her shift not half over. "Yes. But let's hope it doesn't come to that."

Iris let out a breath of her own, shoulders relaxing, lines around her eyes becoming less pinched. "Don't worry; it won't. But thank you for giving an old woman a little peace."

JJ's bones felt heavy in her chair, and her heart pressed against her chest. Iris, in contrast, popped up from the table with little apparent effort and gave JJ's shoulder a squeeze. "I'll see you again soon."

Was Iris born so masterfully manipulative, or did it come with decades of practice? JJ would probably never know. She and Iris were alike in some ways, but JJ didn't have the older woman's capacity for the long view. She slowly rose from her seat, leaning on the table as she watched Iris stride energetically out the door like a woman still decades from the grave.

Must be nice.

17

———

Adam took a long shower after JJ woke him, then surveyed the house to make sure nothing needed his attention before Iris returned. He hadn't been there long enough to mess anything up, not that he would have anyway. Adam had spent so many years living out of his car and a single bag that people he stayed with often didn't immediately notice when he'd left. Which reminded him...

He found an old duffel in his closet to replace the one he'd lost when Teddy took off in Jim Henderson's truck. Just in case. Adam could use another pair of jeans, too, but that would have to wait. Maybe he could pick up a pair at the Goodwill in Plattsville. Rummaging around the kitchen, he considered getting a few grocery staples, but he didn't know how long Iris would be back and she was particular about the things she kept on hand. He did stumble across a spare bulb for the porch light and replaced the one that had burned out.

With nothing else to occupy him in the house, Adam put on a pair of grungy sweats to tackle his ongoing project: restoring Iris's garden fence. It was chilly, so he wrapped a scarf loosely around his aching throat. The slight pressure felt reassuring against the sore flesh. The sun was out, and the gray-trunked, naked trees cast even grayer shadows in the glaring, white winter light. Adam was glad he'd worn a hat.

He'd decided about a half dozen fence posts could be salvaged and only had a few more rotten ones to pull out. Using a pick and a digging bar, he had to stop often to sip from his bottle of water to avoid being overcome by coughing fits. By the time Luther arrived, Adam had worked up a fine sweat beneath his layers, excavating posts and hauling stones.

Adam was used to Luther driving county vehicles and initially didn't recognize his car, some kind of big, blue SUV that was a short step from being a pickup. Luther rolled out of it, pulling a lined flannel shirt (not his heavy, deputy's coat) closer. He likewise pulled a squared-off trucker's cap low, practically recoiling from the sun as he crossed the yard. Add in the black eye that was now a purplish shade with a streak of red, and Luther looked like anything but a lawman.

"You hiding a hickey?" Luther asked.

Adam rested his pickaxe against a section of leaning fence. "What do you think?" he asked, unwinding his scarf for Luther to see.

"I think I don't see any bruises—" Luther tilted his head and reconsidered. "Well, maybe a little on that side. But in most nonlethal strangulations, you don't. Does it hurt as bad as you sound?"

"JJ called it my sexy voice."

Luther grunted. "No accounting for taste. Have you had anything to eat?"

Adam couldn't remember, which usually meant no.

"Come on, then," Luther said, looking at his watch. "Hopefully we'll hit Pete's ahead of the lunch crowd."

Adam didn't know who or what Pete's was, but he was content to ride along as soon as he slipped inside for his wallet and keys. His sleepless night (one in a long string of them) and the morning's exertion had caught up with him. Luther cranked the heat up high in his SUV. He was a conservative driver, and the seats were reasonably comfortable, so Adam was flirting with a doze almost before they made it to the main highway.

He couldn't stay awake, but Adam found he couldn't relax completely, either. Instead, he hovered in-between, aware of the engine's sound and the gentle sway of the road's curves, but unable or unwilling to open his eyes. Since sleep eluded him, he found himself reaching out, as he often did, for Harlan.

He hadn't realized how quickly he'd forged a connection with the man—not just an emotional one, but a pathway that his mind naturally followed on autopilot, like a commuter's muscle memory—until it was gone. Well, the path wasn't entirely gone, but it stopped, incomplete. End of the road. No chasm, no lake, no cliff face. Just no more pavement. Adam couldn't help but think there was still a way in, a way to find Harlan, if he went *off-road*.

But that's where Adam's metaphors failed him. He'd never seen a path and taken it; he'd always taken it and, in retrospect, seen the path by looking where he'd been.

He needed a guide.

With that thought, Adam felt himself sliding sideways—being *dragged* sideways—off the path and through the darkness, resistance tearing at his mind the whole way. He tried to relax, to push the panic away, because it hurt less when he stopped clinging to where he'd been. But who—or what—was dragging him? As he relaxed, he stretched tentatively, exploring the direction he was being pulled. But there was no sense of agency. It was an impersonal force, like opposite magnetic poles drawn toward a shattering collision. Panic dug its claws in again as he accelerated, then saw the opposite pole racing toward him... *was Virgil.*

Adam jerked awake, gasping so deeply it triggered a coughing fit that brought tears to his eyes.

"Easy there, Tex," Luther said. "You okay?"

Adam sipped slowly from his now ever-present bottle of water, careful not to inhale it. He couldn't speak, but gave Luther a thumbs-up when he was able. Then he dug his fingers into his scalp, rubbing away the tingling sensation that had settled there. And masking the trembling in his fingers.

ADAM RECOGNIZED Pete's when they arrived at the small, cinderblock structure. It sat in a low spot well back from the road, flanked by two tall pines and with weathered picnic benches in front. The restaurant had been around forever in one incarnation or another. Adam couldn't recall what it had been when he'd lived here. Soft serve, maybe?

Now it was barbecue, with a smoker out back releasing a pale, aromatic cloud that hung over the building like a good omen. Parking was along one side in the gravel and likely stretched into the grass when the lunch crowd hit. For now, Luther had gotten his wish; only a handful of vehicles sat in the lot. Luther pulled alongside the one on the nearest end and cut the engine.

"What do you recommend?" Adam asked.

Luther laughed. "Only thing to choose is half or full chicken, and with slaw or without. And it's not the tomatoey kind of barbecue sauce; it's the other kind."

Adam wasn't sure what the other kind was, but he was about to find out.

Inside, the laminate counter for orders and pick-ups was at one end, with a single bathroom door at the other. A handful of tables were scattered in between, all but two already occupied. It must get cozy come lunch, or maybe most of their business was take-out. A couple of guys stood in line together, wearing T-shirts with matching construction logos under their heavy work coats. Luther sidled up behind them, leaving plenty of space.

"I got this," Luther said. "Half or whole?"

"You sure?" Adam asked, and Luther nodded and gave him a move-it-along gesture. "Half's plenty. Thanks."

Adam strolled over to one of the empty tables to wait. They were the same cheap, white laminate as the counter. The plastic chairs weren't much to write home about either, but the chicken smelled mighty fine. Adam swallowed, for once because he was salivating rather than coughing. He pulled a chair from beneath the table and heard a man's voice behind him.

"No saving seats."

The man was dressed similarly to most of the men in the place (there were no women), in a hat, jeans, and a camouflage hunting coat over another layer or two.

Adam didn't recognize him, but smiled. "Why, is this ninth grade homeroom?"

The man didn't think it was funny, though when one of the other two sitting with him looked away, it might have been to hide a smile.

"You're not from around here, are you?" the man asked.

He was about Adam's height, carrying a few too many pounds, but not altogether fat. Honestly, Adam didn't care for his chances against him, not least of all because what kind of person tried to start something before lunch? And yet, he couldn't help replying.

"Actually, I—"

Adam started when someone smacked his shoulder.

Luther held a couple of stacked, flat Styrofoam containers. "Come on," he said, and strode to the exit without waiting for Adam to follow.

No one spoke at the table, but Adam had a feeling they would as soon as Luther was out of sight.

"You gentlemen enjoy your meal," Adam said, in part just to hear himself speak. He still didn't recognize his own voice.

Luther was sitting at a picnic table outside, the one that afforded the most unobstructed sun. Adam sat across from him, banging his knees in the process. Luther passed him a container and a pack with a plastic fork and napkins. Then he set another stack of napkins between them and weighed it down with a round rock apparently left for that very purpose.

"You sure you can handle the cold?" Adam asked. He'd noticed the bigger man seemed more sensitive to it than he was. Maybe because Adam had spent so much time sleeping rough.

"Fucking assholes," Luther said, popping open his container and stabbing the bird with his fork. "Last thing I need is to start the day with another fight."

Adam focused on his food rather than the stares they got as the lunch crowd began rolling in. The barbecue sauce was more like a clear glaze, with the color of the charred skin shining through. The flavor was intensely smoky, with a hint of lemon or vinegar. It tasted so good it brought tears to Adam's eyes. Or maybe that was the cold air.

Adam suddenly realized Luther was staring, and muttered appreciatively, "Amazing."

Luther grinned. "It's like watching a little kid eat. You know, the volunteer fire department used to sell this for fundraisers."

"Yes!" Adam said, pointing his plastic fork. "I remember. It was one of the only things Iris would eat that she hadn't cooked."

They ate in silence for a few more minutes (the coleslaw was pretty amazing, too), sipping water from plastic cups. Adam burped and took a moment to let his food settle. He hadn't been eating enough lately, and he was afraid he'd eaten too quickly.

Luther glanced at his watch, then tucked his Styrofoam container closed. "You ready?" he asked. "We can take our leftovers. They sure as hell won't go off in the car in this weather."

The two men tossed their water cups into a nearby trashcan as they rose. Someone had parked a little too close to Luther's SUV, and Luther, grumbling, nearly dropped his chicken while squeezing in the door.

Once they were moving, Adam asked, "Where we headed?"

Luther paused while he checked traffic in both directions before merging onto the highway. "I don't know if anyone told you this, but Danny was Les's dealer. All prescription stuff—he got hooked after a work injury."

"I'm sorry," Adam said.

Luther shrugged. The vehicle slowed as they crested a blind hill, dipping quickly before ascending the mountain again. "You know anything about my dad?"

"Can't say I do," Adam replied, though he recalled that Iris didn't approve of him.

"Lucky you," Luther said. "He's a right bastard. There's not much criminal around here he hasn't got a finger in. I'm hoping he can give us a lead on Danny."

"Makes sense," Adam said. The seat belt kept irritating his neck as they rounded curves. He yanked it back and forth to adjust it, the strap clicking and grinding in protest.

"You'll have to stay in the car," Luther said.

Adam glanced at him, but Luther's eyes were locked on the road. It wasn't an unreasonable request, but there was something off about it. Was Adam suspicious because of the way Luther'd said it, or was it just that he still didn't trust Luther?

Both, he decided.

18

Adam had gone quiet. Luther glanced over at him. He'd finally stopped fidgeting with his seat belt and gazed out the window, tracing patterns on the cold glass with his finger.

The bulk of the mountain was on Luther's side, blocking the direct sun, while it dropped away on Adam's side, revealing brighter valleys and east-facing mountainsides in the distance. A river ran somewhere below them, hidden now by topography and seemingly infinite, bunched-together trees. Their deadfall leaves, gray and brown trunks, and clumps of evergreen foliage dominated the mountain palette, but Luther still asked, "Any snow out there?"

"No."

Luther rubbed his cold hand across his face. He'd done a piss-poor job of shaving that morning. Or had he even bothered? He kicked the heat up a notch. "Weather's been so crazy the last few years, who knows? It might be a while. Or we might not get any more at all."

Adam didn't respond. Luther wasn't usually a chatterbox, talking for the sake of hearing his own voice. But the closer they got to Rudy's, the more unsettled Luther felt. He hadn't spoken to his father since Les died. Pop hadn't seen Les in the hospital, and he hadn't shown up for his son's funeral. *What kind of sorry excuse for a man would do that...*

Luther realized he was white-knuckling the steering wheel in lieu of his father's throat and stretched his cramping fingers before signaling for the back road that led to the man's property. This was not the time to lose his temper.

It occurred to Luther, when he reached Pop's driveway, that he still wasn't carrying. He hadn't gotten around to pulling out another gun since turning in his duty weapon. It was a pretty big oversight, considering the sort that hung out with Rudy Beck.

Fortunately, things seemed quiet as they approached the Beck estate. Only three functional cars were parked in front of the house, and all of those might belong to Pop. A few more were scattered around the yard like lawn ornaments in various states of decay. Of course, it wasn't even noon yet on a weekday. Some of the ne'er-do-wells Luther and Les had seen here last month might still hold down jobs. The rest were probably passed out elsewhere. Not that Luther could talk. Today could be the earliest he'd gotten out of bed since Les died. And, for this week at least, he was technically unemployed.

Luther stopped a good distance from the house, but it was still the closest he'd been to the two-story structure since his mother had died. The bones were holding, but it didn't look good, especially the deep front porch. The chain had broken on his mother's beloved swing, so one end of its seat rested on the warped porch. Luther remembered sitting on that swing next to his mom, snapping beans or shelling peas and tossing them in a bucket, while Les picked at his toes or whatever it was toddlers did in their playpens. Now a good chunk of one front step was missing, and it looked like a couple more were mostly rotted away. He wondered how long it would take some tweaker to call if they found Pop had stepped through one and broken his neck.

Maybe no one would call it in. At least, not before carting off everything Luther had seen stored in the two buildings on the far side of the property.

Before cutting the engine, Luther turned to Adam. "You want me to leave the heater running?"

"Nah, I'll be fine," Adam said, leaning his seat back a notch.

Luther got out of his vehicle and waited, forearms resting on its warm hood. Still no crazy dogs, so that was something. Luther had sworn he'd never set foot in that damn house again, and he was a stubborn sonuvagun. That wasn't the only reason he couldn't bring himself to knock on the front door, but it was the only one he could articulate. The simple truth was, the idea of doing so actually made him physically ill. He wished he'd stopped eating the chicken sooner. A bit of gas rumbled in his belly and snuck out as a nasty burp.

Finally, he saw Pop walking toward him. He'd been so focused on the house, he wasn't sure if the man had come from behind it or from his buildings full of contraband. It was cold enough that Pop was wearing a navy button-down shirt over his usual white undershirt, but it hung open, framing his bulging belly. Luther didn't want to talk too close to his vehicle, so he walked to meet him.

As soon as Luther started walking, Pop stopped, hands in his pockets, and waited for Luther to come to him.

"I wondered when I'd be seeing you here," he said.

"House needs painting," Luther said, thumbing at the structure. Somehow, walking across the dead grass in the cold, he'd lost some of his usual anger at his father. Or maybe it had transformed into something else. What exactly that was remained to be seen.

"You volunteering?" Pop asked. When Luther didn't reply, he said, "That's what I thought. Then why are you here? To borrow an icepack?"

He pointed at his cheek and grinned, but his expression

lacked its usual edge as well. Maybe they were both tired of putting on a show, now that there was nobody left in the audience.

"Little late for that," Luther said, rubbing around the edges of the bruise. "Little late for a lot of things. I came here for some information."

And quicker than a snap of his fat fingers, the old Rudy was back. He swiveled his head, the better to see Luther through his dominant, truth-telling eye. "Really? That's funny, 'cause I heard you got fired."

"Suspended," Luther said, pulling his collar closer against the wind and marveling inside that Pop hadn't triggered his temper, as had doubtless been his intent. "The last time we spoke, you gave me a name that would get me to your buddy—what did you call him? Mitch? I need another name."

Rudy's mini pompadour flipped over in the breeze in one big chunk, like some little yippy dog's tail. "The last time we spoke, you had me in a goddamned interrogation room. In case *you* haven't noticed, now you're on my property."

And there it was, that warmth in Luther's chest, a growing hum in his ears. It seemed he wasn't immune after all. *Dammit.* "In case you haven't noticed, this isn't about the law."

"Then what is it about?" Rudy crossed his arms.

Luther shook his head, his temper already making him a little dizzy.

"Let me guess," Rudy continued. "Handing my head to your Sheriff on a platter so you can get a gold star? Kissing his ass so he'll let you back on the force?"

Luther stepped so close he almost spit on his father as he shouted in his face, "You selfish bastard! Everything revolves around you. What the fuck do you think? It's about finding the sonuvabitch that murdered Les."

Luther's fists were clenched by his sides, but he wasn't sure they'd stay there. He and Pop had been building toward an adult, knock-down, drag-out fight for decades. But for once, his father didn't take the bait.

Rudy simply asked, "Why? What are you gonna do?"

Luther spoke through jaws clenched almost as tightly as his fists. "What do you think?" he said again.

Pop dug a toe into ground barely clinging to its thin, brown grass, helping it on its way to becoming bare dirt. "A'right. I might be able to get you the names of a couple of guys he worked with from time to time. Muscle mostly. I'll give you a call."

"When?" Luther asked.

"Later tonight."

"Okay," Luther said. He'd learned growing up that when his father gave his word, he meant it. Though it was generally a promise to beat somebody's ass, and more often than not, his or his brother's.

Luther flexed his hands, trying to release the muscle memory of his fists. He'd be freezing again in a few minutes, but until then, he wished the wind could cool his temper. He needed to get away from his father.

He walked back to his vehicle, eyes avoiding the house. Pop followed. When Luther's hand was on his door, Pop said to his back, "I saw you put him next to your momma."

Luther didn't have to ask how he knew. Rudy's visits to his wife's grave were the closest thing Luther had ever seen to religion in his father. "That's what she would have wanted," Luther said, without turning.

"And what about this? What you're thinking to do... would she have wanted that?" Rudy asked.

Luther swung around, grabbed the collar of his father's shirt, pushed him away from the car and got in his face. "Seriously? Now that she's dead, you care what she'd want? You think she wanted your crazy, criminal bullshit swirling around her, all the time? Always wondering what you'd bring home to her doorstep." Luther edged so close his belly brushed against his father's. "Or how about you beating the shit out of her, you think she wanted that? I remember—"

Luther turned his head and bit his lip so he could go on. "I remember her being pregnant, between me and Les. Trying to hide it. And then sitting outside the bathroom while she cried after you beat it out of her. So don't talk to me about what she'd want, because you sure as hell didn't give a shit while she was alive."

"Fine," Rudy said, taking a step back. His face was flushed, and Luther braced himself for his father to either take a swing at him or have a heart attack. Instead, Rudy asked, "Is that Adam Rutledge in the car?"

Luther glanced inside at Adam's closed eyes but didn't answer.

"That's okay," Rudy said. "I know it is. You left him in there like a hunting dog because you didn't trust me not to say something, didn't you?"

Luther still didn't speak. Pop turned so he was facing away from the vehicle. "Son, you ought to know by now, I can keep your goddamn secrets. No matter how dirty they are."

The door handle felt cool beneath Luther's hand. "I'll be waiting for your call," he said.

19

———

Come on, Adam thought, eyes closed, slouched in the truck seat, drifting but not quite falling through darkness. *I know you're there.*

He had a notion that Virgil was almost within reach, but where? Adam sank deeper, but the strain intensified, like he'd left a piece of himself behind as an anchor and that piece was about to snap.

But instead of Virgil, Adam found the voice. Or rather, the voice found him, as it had last night.

You sure you want to be here? 'Cause you're playing with the big boys now.

The space around Adam grew warm, and his throat throbbed.

What is it you're looking for? Or better yet, WHY are you looking? That's what makes all the difference. Do you want to know my why?

A sudden tug in his chest, like his heart was being threaded through the eye of a needle, took Adam's breath away. Now he *was* falling, faster and faster—

The driver's door slammed shut and Adam flinched upright. He couldn't see clearly, with the edges of the world blurred by glaring winter light, but Luther's shape had settled next to him and was starting the SUV. Adam fastened his seat belt, fumbling a bit with the catch, and stared out his window. He rubbed his chest, still aching where he'd felt the tug, and tried to pass it off as adjusting his seat belt in case Luther was watching. They turned from Rudy's property onto the single-lane back road, and gradually the passing trees came into focus.

Adam noticed a tickle on his lip, and his hand brushed across it before thinking. Blood smeared his finger. *Frick.* He must have spoken out loud, because Luther glanced over at him.

"You okay?" Luther asked.

"Yeah. You have any tissues?"

Luther pointed to a pack resting at an angle in the passenger side cupholder. Adam took one and held it to his nose for a few seconds, but the bleeding seemed to be nearly spent. He flipped the visor down and used its mirror to wipe his upper lip and around his nostrils. Then he flipped it back up and pressed the tissue to his nose again.

There was a pullout ahead, barely wide enough to get off the road, frequented by hunters and those looking for privacy. Adam checked the tissue again as Luther swung into it. Just a drop or two of blood. Not seeing an obvious place for trash, he crumpled the tissue and shoved it in his pocket.

"You sure you're okay?" Luther asked.

"Fine," Adam said. Though Luther's features still swam a bit in his vision.

"Did you do that?"

"You mean, did I punch myself in the face at Rudy's?"

"Don't fuck with me, Adam. I'm not in the mood. What the hell's going on?"

Looking out the window, Adam's eyes were drawn to the way the ground dropped precipitously a couple of feet from their vehicle, then leveled out briefly before rising again as a tree-studded, leaf-strewn mosaic. It gave him a hint of vertigo.

It was force of habit for Adam to make something up, to fudge. He didn't always blatantly lie well, but he was good at fudging. But why should he? Luther wasn't on the clock—he wasn't even on the force now. They were supposed to be working together. And Luther may be the only person who could help him find Teddy. It's true that he didn't fully trust Luther, but he wasn't exactly giving Luther good reason to trust him, either.

"I was trying to get through to Virgil," Adam admitted. "I know I can—I did it yesterday."

"And almost died," Luther added, but without heat.

"Yeah, well, I wasn't planning on doing that this time," Adam said, and felt the corner of his mouth twinge in an unlikely smile.

Luther shook his head. "Dumbass. You get anything?"

Adam thought about the voice. He couldn't have said why, but he wasn't ready to share that just yet. He wasn't ready to think about it at all. "Only a bloody nose."

Luther's response was interrupted when his phone rang. "How the hell do we have reception here?" he muttered, before answering, "Yeah."

Adam heard a man's voice echo from the other end, but couldn't make out the words. Luther leaned across him and opened the glovebox.

"Hold on," Luther said, shoving aside legal paperwork and the owner's manual to retrieve a small notebook. He struggled to pull a teeny pen free from the top spiral. "Go ahead."

Resting the notebook on the steering wheel, Luther scratched down a few words. "Okay. Is that it?" he asked. Then he hung up without saying goodbye, and turned to Adam. "I appreciate the investigative effort, but I'd rather not have to clean your brains off my seat when they leak out your ears."

The image made Adam shudder. Or maybe it was the cold. When they left his father's place, Luther had—for once—neglected to turn on the heat.

Luther tapped his notebook against the steering wheel.

"Besides," he said, "Pop gave me a couple of names that might help us find Danny. And if we find Danny, chances are we'll find everybody."

Maybe. Adam wasn't sure. Day by day, Adam was becoming less sure of everything.

Luther continued. "I think I can get Beth to run them for me, see if we can get addresses, but I probably shouldn't use my own phone to ask her. If she helps, I don't want it to blow back on her."

"I still don't have a cell phone," Adam said. "But you're welcome to use Iris's landline."

"Sounds like a plan," Luther said. He pulled back onto the empty road and finally flipped on the heat. "Damn, it got cold in here."

It was a twenty-minute drive to Iris's house. Adam leaned back, but the head rest angle was all wrong. His throat stretched too far, and he started to cough.

"There's a case of water in the back, if you need it. I can try and pull over somewhere again..."

Adam waved a hand and held his breath, waiting for the coughing to subside. He'd overdone it already today. Worse, he had nothing to show for it. Maybe JJ was right about him being a martyr. But a martyr for what?

"Was your dad always crazy?"

Luther's question jarred Adam out of his useless introspection. "Was Virgil always crazy?" Adam repeated, trying to ground himself in the question. "I asked Iris about that. She didn't much care for the word—*crazy*—but said he'd always had issues. Why do you ask?"

"I don't know," Luther said. "I guess I was thinking about how people get to where they end up. Like Rudy, wondering if he was always an asshole. My momma saw something in him once upon a time, but I'll be damned if I know what."

Luther stretched a hand toward a hazy film on the windshield; when it wiped off, he turned on the defrost as well. "Whatever it was she saw in him that was good, it must've died with her."

Adam couldn't argue. It was more than he could do to figure out his own father.

They spent the rest of the drive in silence.

Adam's head hurt, a lopsided pain that ran across the front from temple to temple but afflicted the left side worse. He was awake, but had closed his eyes against the gray sky when Luther said, "Is that Iris's car?"

In fact it was, parked in front of her house next to Adam's hatchback, and there was a faint glow of artificial light from the kitchen. Adam straightened in his seat and adjusted his scarf where a wrinkled section had irritated his neck. "Huh. She said she'd be home soon, but I was thinking it'd be tomorrow. Will she see the bruise?"

Luther parked behind Adam's car and spun around for a better look at his throat. "You might want to keep the scarf on. And not speak."

Adam tossed the scarf loosely around his neck as he got out of Luther's vehicle. Luther lagged behind him as they entered the house. A couple of paper bags sat on the counter, and Iris was putting groceries away, head in the refrigerator. Adam hugged her shoulders from behind.

"Hello, darling boy," she said. Closing the fridge door and swiveling to the counter, she added, "And Luther."

"Ms. Rutledge," Luther acknowledged.

"Luther needs to use the phone," Adam said.

"It's in the living room," she said. "Help yourself."

"Thank you, ma'am," Luther said, and headed in that direction.

"What's wrong with your voice?" Iris asked Adam.

"Just a little sore throat. There's potato soup in the fridge that JJ made, if you're hungry," Adam said, leaning against the counter while Iris shelved pasta and other dry goods in her cabinets. "Looks like you're staying for a while."

"Well, I do live here," she said, continuing to organize her pantry rather than look at him.

Adam blinked. Despite her warm greeting, there was a strange undercurrent in the room. He even wondered if she was trying to provoke him. "Is something wrong?" he asked. "Is Harlan okay?"

"Is Harlan okay?" she repeated. "Well, that's always the question, isn't it?"

"Fine. How about, are *you* okay? Iris, what's wrong?" Adam gently removed a box of macaroni from her hand and set it back on the counter. "Iris…"

She sighed and leaned against the counter as he had, except with her arms crossed. "Harlan is being transferred to the Plattsville hospital."

"Is that good or bad?"

"Good in the sense that we can both be here instead of Morgantown," she said, but sounded unconvinced.

"And for Harlan? Does this mean there's been a change?"

"No change," she said.

If he hadn't improved, but they were transferring him anyway… it took a moment for the implications to sink in. "So they're giving up on him?" Adam asked.

"I don't know. They're not saying much."

Adam stared at a chip in the beige floor tile. Had he done that as a kid? Or maybe even his father or grandfather? How had Iris kept it clean, free of funk in the cracks for so many years?

He kept his eyes locked on that spot as he asked, "And what about you? Have you given up on him?"

"I'm not even going to answer that," she said, and went back to stowing her purchases.

Adam's mind stalled, with no useful forward motion but thoughts continuing to spin inside. He didn't even look up when Luther returned to the kitchen.

"Thank you, ma'am," he said. "All done."

"Luther, what in heaven's name happened to your eye?" Iris asked.

"Well, I, uh—"

"And you need a haircut, too," she continued, before Luther could finish stuttering an answer. "When's the last time you had your hair cut?"

"I'm afraid I couldn't say, ma'am."

"If you stop by—"

But Adam interrupted his grandmother. "When?"

"Whenever I'm here and he's free."

"No," Adam clarified, though he suspected she knew his meaning, "when are they transferring Harlan?"

"In the next day or two."

I shouldn't ask; nothing good will come of asking. I should just walk away. And yet, Adam couldn't help himself. "How long have you known?"

"A little while," she said, folding the paper bags and stacking them in a bin beneath the kitchen sink.

"How long?" Adam repeated, voice rising.

"It doesn't matter how long," Iris said, in her end-of-discussion tone.

He should be used to it. After all, she hadn't bothered to tell him his father was alive for decades, not until Rachel Nicholson's kidnapping forced her hand. She hadn't shared anything about Virgil's certifiable craziness that was Adam's inheritance. Or anything about what Adam might see—*had seen* as a child, though she tried to bury it—that could make him believe he was crazy. So what else was she not telling him?

Adam vaguely registered Iris saying his name, and Luther standing awkwardly at the edge of the kitchen as Adam passed by on his way to the stairs. He got the old duffel bag from his room with a few changes of clothes and toiletries, and after a moment's debate put Virgil's picture of Adam's mother in the bag as well.

Carrying his bag to the stairs, Adam experienced a sense of déjà vu. At least this time he wasn't running from the cops.

He passed Luther and Iris again at the bottom of the stairs and grabbed his keys on the way out the door.

"Adam—where are you going?" Iris shouted.

Ignoring her, Adam went straight to his car. There wasn't room to back around; he'd have to wait for Luther to move his SUV to leave. Still, Adam turned his key. Nothing. Not even a click. And again, the same. *Damn battery.* He rested his head on top of the steering wheel. Iris banged on his window.

"Adam!"

Still ignoring her, he glanced toward the house, where Luther was tromping down the front steps. Adam slid across his passenger seat and exited from that door. "Can I catch a ride with you?" he asked.

"Sure," Luther said, and motioned toward his SUV.

"Adam, stop acting like a child," Iris said, circling his car. "What are you doing?"

Adam fumbled getting his bag inside, and Iris caught up to him. He finally faced her, unwilling to slam the door in his grand-mother's face. "Do you have any idea..." he began, but couldn't finish.

Hands on her hips, Iris said, "Don't you dare presume to tell me what I do and do not know, what I do and do not understand, young man."

"No, because you know everything. But it's all in your vault of secrets." Adam shook his head in disbelief. Poor Rachel, and Aaron Schofield. And all of those young men in the pictures in Grant's office. Gone. Would any of it have been different if he'd known more? Known sooner? Maybe. "You ever stop to think about the damage your secrets have caused?"

Lips pressed shut, she didn't answer.

Adam's voice was calm but sober when he did. "Of course not. We're talking about people's lives, Iris. Your secrets kill people." He stepped into the vehicle, closed the door in a careful, deliberate motion, and told Luther, "Let's go."

20

Luther waited until he reached the bottom of Iris's driveway to ask, "Where to?"

"I don't know," Adam said.

Luther drove down the highway, content to fill his vehicle with gas at the first station they passed and see where they ended up. After all, he had nowhere he had to be. He wasn't welcome at his job. In the past few hours, he and Adam had both fought with their nearest living relatives, so that was off the table. He supposed he shouldn't have been surprised when Adam pointed at Harry's Bar and said, "Let's go there."

"No," Luther said. "I just got kicked out of Harry's. We'll find a better place."

Luther lived closer to Plattsville than to Cold Springs, and fewer people knew him there. He got gas first (you never knew what would happen to the rest of your day once you set foot in a bar), then took Adam to an establishment on the outskirts of the larger town.

"You sure you want to stop here?" Luther asked. "I'll be honest. I've spent a helluva lot of my off hours drunk since Les died, and I'd be hard-pressed to say it was an improvement."

Adam's only answer was to get out of the car and head inside.

"Well, shit," Luther said, but followed. Inside, it was definitely a step above Harry's. The room was more spacious, and being mid-afternoon, it was relatively empty with only two other patrons, each a man occupying his own booth. Adam was already seated on a stool at the bar. Luther crossed the open area to join him, noting his feet didn't stick to the floor here, either.

"But the smell's always the same," he muttered, sitting next to Adam.

"Not really," Adam said. The bartender, a man about Luther's age, ambled over and Adam said, "I'll have a bourbon. And don't waste your top shelf."

"Have you done a study of bar stink?" Luther asked. "Because you don't strike me as the hanging out in bars type."

The bartender returned with a short glass. Adam drank it without flourish before setting it down and requesting, "A double." While the bartender stepped away to retrieve the bottle, Adam told Luther, "I've made money a lot of ways over the years. But bartending is probably what I've done most. You want anything?"

"It depends how long we're going to be here," Luther replied.

"Not long," Adam said. He thanked the bartender as he poured him another.

"In that case, I'm good," Luther said.

Adam drank down the amber liquid, not like he was doing shots, but in a series of measured swallows, like medication. He set down his empty glass, took a deep breath, and said, "I'll have one more double and a glass of water, and then you can close me out."

The bartender did as he asked, then told Adam the final tally. It was the first time he'd spoken. Adam pulled out his wallet and handed him enough cash to include a generous tip. The bartender nodded, said thanks, and strode to the other end of the bar to watch TV until the next customer arrived.

Adam took his time with the last bourbon, relatively speaking. "A lot of bars have the same beer miasma. But if you can get past that layer, there are other, different layers. Working nights doesn't exactly do wonders for your sense of time—you're out of sync with everybody—but at a lot of bars, I could tell what night it was by the smell."

Luther looked at Adam, unsure whether he was being serious. "You mean, like a..." His voice dropped, even though they were practically alone. "Like a psychic thing?"

Adam laughed, then finished his bourbon in one last toss. "No. Drink specials." Then he drank his glass of water, like a kid chugging fluorescent Gatorade, before adding, "There's no way you're going to mistake a bar full of whiskey sours with a bar full of piña coladas."

He stood, hands sensibly braced on the bar until his legs were solidly under him. Not that anyone sensible would drink that quantity of bourbon in five minutes. Luther gave the bartender a wave and followed Adam out. He walked about a step and a half behind him, the perfect distance to help Adam if need be, but not inadvertently get tangled in his feet. Especially since one was dragging a little.

Luther got in the car and put his seat belt on. He could smell the alcohol on Adam's breath in the next seat. "You want to talk about it?"

"No," Adam said.

"Good, because I'm shitty at that sort of thing," Luther replied.

Adam's face wrinkled. "Only tastes good while you're drinking it. Got any gum?"

"Afraid not," Luther said.

"I was living in the back room of a bar right before all this crap started," Adam admitted. "Probably still have a paycheck waiting. I wouldn't say I like bars, but they're familiar. Sometimes you need a dose of the familiar."

"Is that what you were dosing?" Luther asked. Adam shot him a look, and Luther added, "Sorry. Told you I'm shitty at that kind of thing."

"Well, then, you'd make a lousy bartender," Adam said, leaning back. "Woo, okay. That didn't take long to kick in."

"You're not gonna barf in my car, are you?" Luther demanded.

"No. Just taking the edge off."

Luther swung by a convenience store for some orange juice and milk (Adam waited in the car) before heading toward home. Home was a simple, one-story, two-bedroom house with a carport, built in the 1970s like the other four houses on his mini street. The landscaping was even simpler than the architecture, a lawn with a single tree. The lots weren't huge, but they'd offset the structures so no one had a view into anyone else's windows. Luther rarely saw his neighbors, and hadn't spoken with any of them in a blue moon. He wasn't even sure he remembered their names. Hell, that's what the mailboxes were for.

A Beecham County Sheriff's cruiser was parked in Luther's driveway when they arrived. Luther probably could have gotten around it into the carport, but it would have been a tight squeeze, so he parked alongside it instead. Grant's head popped out of his car as Luther cut the engine. The Sheriff walked around to their side of the cruiser and leaned against its hood, waiting.

"Adam," he said, tipping his hat. "Didn't expect to see you here. What's wrong with your leg?"

Of course Grant would notice. Although, on reflection, Luther decided he'd seen the limp earlier today, even before Adam started drinking. But he didn't argue when Adam said, "Kicked a bar stool."

"Unprovoked, I might add," Luther said. "Since I was driving, I didn't imbibe. You come all the way out here to beg me to come back, Sheriff? Couldn't make it twenty-four hours without me?"

Luther had forgotten he'd overturned the Sheriff's chair the previous day, until the hard set of Grant's jaw reminded him. "No,

Luther. I'm here to tell you to keep your damn nose out of where it doesn't belong."

Adam made some sort of hiccup or burp, distracting Luther for a moment as he wondered if he'd have to hose down his carport. Adam raised an apologetic brow as he covered his mouth, and Luther turned his attention back to Grant.

"Sheriff, I'm afraid I don't know what you're talking about."

"She denies it, but I know you've got Beth helping you, too. Just stay out of it."

Luther tugged on his cap. "I don't know what the hell there is to stay out of. Are you telling me you're any closer to finding Les's killer?"

Grant stepped toward Luther, his face coloring. "What do you think? I've got a shitty sketch and a theory about who the guy might've been twenty years ago."

"Well, then," Luther said, tucking his hands into his pockets. "Doesn't sound like there's anything I can do to mess that up."

The Sheriff's toes bumped Luther's as he edged into his personal space. "And you damn well better not be getting JJ mixed up in it."

Ahh, so that was it. Luther should have known. He took a deep breath, in through his nose, to calm himself. Luther hadn't crossed any lines yet, and if he didn't want Grant sticking to him like white on rice, standing over him when he did cross said lines, for once Luther would have to be the more even-tempered man.

"Grant, there's nothing for JJ to get mixed up in. In fact, Adam and I won't be around for a few days. Now that deer season's in, I thought I'd take him hunting, maybe hit some of Les's favorite spots," Luther said. Even though he was lying, he still got choked up a little at the end.

"Really?" Grant asked. He obviously didn't believe him, but Luther had given him time for his equanimity to get a foothold again.

Luther nodded. "I imagine it's been a while since Adam's been out, so there is a chance he might shoot me. Other than that, you got nothing to worry about." Luther felt his phone ring in his pocket and twisted to pull it free—Beth. He held the phone high. "So if that's all, Sheriff, I gotta talk to somebody about getting on their property to kill us some deer."

Grant shook his head and pointed his campaign hat at Adam as he got back in his cruiser. "I expect you at least to show some sense."

Adam saluted.

Smartass.

Luther answered the phone before Grant had even cleared his driveway. "Good timing," he said. "You got something for me?"

Beth's voice was low and muffled, like she was holding the receiver too close to her mouth. "Luther, the Sheriff's on to you. He asked me—"

"Yeah, I know. Do you have something for me or not?"

A frustrated huff rattled in Luther's ear. "Luther, I don't think you understand. The Sheriff is pissed. I could get in serious trouble over this."

The cold wind picked up, and Luther covered his naked ears so he could hear better while walking to the carport. "You mean, like I did over what happened at Harry's?"

"You started that!" Beth said indignantly.

"You're the one who invited me out for a beer," Luther said, feeling like a shit as he said it. "Does he even know you were there?"

Silence on the other end. Luther watched Adam shove his hands in his jacket pockets, pirouetting and scanning as if he'd never been to Luther's house. Probably because he hadn't.

"Look, I'm not trying to get you in trouble. I just want to know, did you get me those addresses or not?" Luther pulled his little notebook from his coat pocket in anticipation.

"You're an asshole," Beth said. "But I got a couple of possibles for each. You ready?"

Luther trotted back to his car, fighting the wind that kept snatching his pages as he scribbled in his pad on the hood. He read each of them back to her, then said, "Okay, got it. Thanks, Beth."

"Yeah," she said. "Don't bother calling back again."

And she hung up.

Adam joined Luther, shoulders hunched against the cold. "What are we really doing?" he asked.

Luther held up his notepad. "Oh, we're going hunting all right. But not for deer."

And this time, he'd remember his goddamn gun.

21

Adam shifted in his seat.

"You need anything to eat?" Luther asked.

"No, I'm okay," Adam said. They were back in Luther's car, and Luther's packed bag had joined Adam's in the back. Sometimes Adam wondered what proportion of the past twenty years of his life had been spent in cars. More than most people, he'd wager.

"I guess we've still got that chicken if we want it," Luther said. "You're not going to get sick in my car on these mountain roads, are you?"

"Not as slow as you drive," Adam said. He traced the edge of his hairline with two fingers. His skull felt bruised. And it did feel a little hollowed out from the whiskey, but he'd been drinking a lot of water, so he wasn't too worried about ill effects.

"Can I ask you something?" Luther adjusted his visor as they crested a hill, facing into the sun.

"Can I stop you?" Adam covered his eyes, then traced the other side of his head as they descended again. It was even worse.

"What's with the limp?" Luther asked.

Adam glanced at Luther in surprise. "I guess I can't hold my liquor," he said, sticking with his previous lie.

"Bullshit," Luther said, eyes never leaving the road. "You were limping at Pete's this morning too. Almost busted your ass sitting down."

Adam rested the heels of his hands against his eye sockets. He wished he'd brought the bottle from the bar with him. Although, come to think of it, some of the sharper curves in the road were not altogether pleasant with his current level of intoxication. He opened his eyes wide and, jaw dropping, stretched his face.

"Look, man," Luther continued. "You're a shitty liar. And we're supposed to be working together. So why don't you save yourself the effort and be straight with me? It's not like I'm asking who you lost your virginity with."

"Becky Newcomb. In the back seat of her dad's car," Adam said, earning a smile. But Luther was right, and he was for all intents and purposes trapped with the man for an indeterminate period of time. Plus picking and choosing the truth was downright exhausting. "I'll try, but it's tricky to explain what I don't entirely understand."

Luther risked a quick glance at him. "That's okay. We give points for effort."

"When we were back at the cabin—Harlan, Teddy, and I—" Adam paused, but it was too late to fix his slip.

"Let me guess," Luther said. "You used some prevarication in your official statement. Well, in case you haven't noticed, I'm not exactly an acting officer of the law at the moment. So don't stop on my account."

Adam sighed. It was getting so hard to keep everything straight. "Okay. I know I said he left us, but Teddy stayed with Harlan and me the whole time. He's the one who connected us with Virgil—remember, Virgil was still in jail at the time."

"Go on," Luther said.

"So after we did... *whatever we did* to stop Danny, none of us were in great shape. Teddy went to get something from the truck, and he left us. Just drove off. Said he didn't want us involved in what he had to do."

"Which was presumably breaking your dad out of jail," Luther snapped.

"If it was, Harlan and I didn't know anything about it. Not that it would've mattered. We were stranded," Adam reminded him. "Anyway, I noticed when Teddy took off that he was limping."

Luther slowed to a crawl for a particularly sharp turn before commenting, "My recollection is Teddy isn't exactly a spring chick."

"True," Adam admitted. "But as you know, lately I've been trying to get in Virgil's head, see if I get some clue to his and Teddy's whereabouts. And every time I do, I feel like…"

"You feel like what?" Luther asked, impatient.

Adam shivered, then tried to articulate the thoughts that had caused his shiver. "The more time I spend in Virgil's head, the more of him sticks to me."

Luther glanced over sharply, drifting onto the shoulder in the process. Once he was back on the pavement, he asked, "And Virgil has a limp? So you think that's where you and Teddy got it?"

"Yes," Adam said. "And I don't have to try to reach Virgil anymore. It's like his head is a vortex, and I keep getting sucked in."

Luther shuddered next to him. "Jesus."

"Yeah," Adam agreed. "The loss of control is pretty spooky."

Luther suddenly laughed. "And you thought alcohol would help with that?"

Adam shrugged. "Not really with the loss of control. More like, muddying the water. Making the path into my head a little less obvious."

And he feared Virgil wasn't the only one blazing a trail into his mind.

Teddy's crazy potions had the same purpose, taking away the signposts so the path was harder to find. The whiskey—even cheap whiskey—was more palatable, but he doubted it worked as well. But who knew? Look at the way Harlan drank to block out the constant assaults on his mind.

"I know it's not a long-term solution," Adam said. "But I just needed a break, before I do go crazy. Not that taking a break does anything to find Virgil."

Luther slowed and signaled to turn onto the interstate merge. "Well, I don't know about Virgil, but I've got the addresses on those associates of Danny's over in Virginia. That's where we're headed now. It'll be a while though, if you want to try to catch some sleep."

"Yeah, maybe I'll do that," Adam muttered, whiskey and exhaustion overtaking him.

22

JJ scrubbed the sides of her kitchen sink. How could a place dedicated to washing dishes get so scuzzy?

She knew she was procrastinating. Dorothy was working this evening, and the girls both had a rare evening at home. JJ had volunteered for dinner duty, but was blanking on what she could fix without making a trip to the supermarket. Maybe if she swore the kids to secrecy, they could feast on macaroni and cheese and microwave popcorn. They wouldn't mind.

She and Otto had already sworn them to secrecy when they told the girls they could play outside. Dorothy was in another of her overprotective phases, afraid all the dead leaves would trigger Rachel's asthma. That was a possibility, but Rachel—and her mother—needed to learn to deal with her attacks. Prevention could only do so much, including breed panic when it failed.

JJ had finished up the sink and stepped over Trooper to stand in front of the open refrigerator when the girls burst through the front door. "Easy on the hinges, ladies—"

"Mom!" Evie shrieked. "Come quick! Rachel's dad cut his leg off!"

"What?" JJ asked, whirling toward the door. Both girls were panting, and Rachel wheezed slightly, shaking hand held to her chest. "What are you talking about?"

But now Evie was unable to catch her breath. JJ ran for the door as Rachel managed a single word... "Chainsaw."

"Shit!" JJ pushed past the girls and ran down the front steps and into the woods that buffered their properties, not waiting for them to follow. She recalled now Otto saying he'd be clearing some deadfall this afternoon, and hearing the machine's intermittent roar. When was the last time she'd heard it? With the girls playing in the woods, had they seen the accident immediately? Or had Otto been bleeding alone?

She saw the flash of his white undershirt ahead, his body lying on the ground. His ear protection and the chainsaw lay nearby. The engine wasn't running, but JJ double-checked that the switch was off. Otto's head lifted as she approached, his face nearly as pale as his shirt.

"Thank God it's you and not Dorothy," he said.

"I won't tell her you said that," JJ replied, kneeling next to him.

He hadn't cut his leg off, as Evie had said, but JJ could see why the girls had been upset. Chainsaw wounds were nasty, more chewing than slicing, and there was blood everywhere—crimson splatter on his T-shirt and arms, and soaking through the right leg of his jeans. A long-sleeved, button-down shirt was tied around his thigh, between his heart and the wound, but blood still seeped from it.

"How long has it been since you tied the tourniquet?" JJ asked.

"I don't know," Otto groaned. "But it hasn't been long. I sent the girls for help almost as soon as it happened. Damn thing just kicked, and there was nothing I could do."

JJ took a deep breath. *Remain calm.* Otto wasn't going to bleed out in the next few minutes, but she'd be a helluva lot faster than the rescue squad. She glanced back toward her own house and her Bronco. She'd need it rather than Otto's truck to safely fit the kids inside. But Otto had injured himself much closer to the Nicholson house. And he outweighed JJ by a good hundred pounds. *Think, dammit, think.*

The girls finally caught up with her, leaning with their hands on their thighs. "Evie, help me move this," JJ said.

Together they shifted one of the thick chunks of wood Otto had been working on. "Girls, I need your help now. Rachel, can you get me a jug of water from your house? And Evie, I need my first aid kit from the pantry. The big one in the green bag. Okay?"

JJ waited until the girls took off on their respective assignments to start with Otto. She'd wanted to avoid upsetting them if she could.

"Otto, I can tell you now, this is not gonna be fun. We need to elevate your leg, so I'll lift it up on this log, but you'll need to shift your ass a little. Are you ready?"

"Yeah," he said, but roared as she moved his bloody leg.

JJ had a fleeting fancy that the wound on his thigh, gaping like a mouth, had produced the inhuman noise. She moved closer to his face, unsure if he could hear her now. "Otto, you still with me?"

He grunted.

Rachel approached, bouncing a gallon jug against every part of her body as she awkwardly ran. JJ leaned in and said, "Don't tell Dorothy, but I've always wanted to make you scream."

Otto laughed, a painful, gasping noise, but exactly what JJ had been hoping for. JJ took the jug from Rachel and peeled the cap away, but waited a moment because Evie was nearly back as well. First aid kit in hand (*I should've brought the damn thing to begin with*), JJ cut away Otto's pants leg.

"Girls, I don't want you to watch," she said, before pouring the water over his leg. Her kit had a real tourniquet, but although Otto's bleeding was bad, she didn't think it was immediately life-threatening and decided to go with pressure instead. "Let's see how well this puppy works," she said, applying a clotting sponge, then securing it with a compression bandage before slowly releasing the shirt tied around Otto's leg.

JJ watched for the better part of a minute, then said, "So far so good. You might get away from this without me putting my hand on your groin after all. Rachel, do you still have a wagon around here somewhere?"

She nodded, and Evie said, "I know where it is, mom."

"Excellent," JJ said. "I need you to get it and bring it back here. I'll go get my truck and drive it around. Rachel, do you have your inhaler?"

The poor child was still too winded to speak, nodding again and patting her jacket pocket.

"Good girl. I want you to stay here with your dad until I get back, and use your inhaler if you need to." JJ turned her attention to Otto, squeezing his hand. His skin was cool. "You okay until I get back?"

"Yeah, I'm good."

"You're something," JJ said, then raced back through the woods to her house.

JJ stumbled, trying to take her front steps at a curving run, but didn't fall. *Cell phone. Wallet. Car keys.* Pause. Breathe. *Okay, that's it.* On second thought, she grabbed a spare pillow while she was at it. She locked the door, ignoring Trooper's whines inside.

JJ caught some gravel turning around in the driveway. *Don't drive in the ditch*, she reminded herself, making a hard left onto the road and again into the Nicholson driveway.

She almost left her car running, but didn't want to push her luck. On a day when Otto had succeeded in taking a chunk out of his leg, the Bronco could roll down the hill or through the Nicholson house. She was short of breath herself by the time she reached Otto and the girls. Otto was still conscious and the only person not panting.

"Here's the plan," she said. "Otto, we'll see how much of you we can get in here. The pillow goes under your leg, wherever you are—on the ground, in the wagon, in the car—we want to try to keep that leg raised. Rachel, you do what you can to keep your dad from bouncing out, and Evie, you try to keep us a clear path. Got it?"

"Got it," the girls said.

"Otto, I'll get this as close to you as I can. What are the chances of you climbing in?" JJ asked.

He was so pale and drawn, JJ imagined she could see his teeth through his cheeks. "If I don't, the guys at work will never let me live it down."

JJ picked up the wagon and set it next to Otto (easier than pushing it), then got behind him. She held his shoulders, and Otto put his weight on his good leg and against JJ until he was far enough from the ground to get in the wagon. JJ grunted. She was used to moving patients, but usually she had help. Evie grabbed the wagon when it started to roll. Otto wound up sitting mostly upright, clutching the sides, legs extended one on either side of the handle. JJ doubled the pillow and tucked it beneath his knee. Obviously she'd wanted him prone, but he was simply too tall. They didn't have far to go, and this would have to do.

JJ felt like she was moving blocks to build the pyramids, dragging the child's toy with huge Otto atop it, wheels churning in several inches of leaves and snagging the occasional branch that Evie had missed. They nearly lost him in a rut at the edge of the woods, but finally made it to the driveway and her Bronco.

"Girls, you'll have to share a seat in the front with me. We're giving Otto the back." She helped him stand, and now was grateful the man was so tall. It made it easier for him to get into her SUV. This time, he didn't complain of the pain or say anything at all, which worried her. He was probably in shock.

"Mom, what about the seat belt?" Evie asked. She and Rachel had squished into the passenger's seat together.

Don't you dare, JJ thought, turning her key in the ignition a second time. "Just put it over both of you, sweetie, and click it in."

"I don't think they're supposed to work that way," Rachel whispered.

JJ checked her rearview mirror. Otto was as horizontal as possible, and she couldn't tell if he was still conscious. "That's okay. It's just one more thing we won't tell your mom."

When they hit the highway, JJ handed her cell phone to her daughter. "Sweetie, do you know how to go through my phone numbers and call Miss Iris?"

"Of course." Evie adjusted the shoulder strap so both arms were free, nearly strangling Rachel.

"You might have to wait until we get to the straight stretch up here for a signal," JJ added.

Within a few seconds, Evie said, "It's ringing."

JJ held out her hand for the phone. "Iris, it's JJ. Otto Nicholson had an accident, and I'm taking him to the hospital. I have the girls with me. Is there any chance you could pick them up and keep an eye on them for a few hours?"

"I'd be happy to. Did you tell Dorothy yet?" Iris asked.

JJ sighed, then cringed as she took a curve a little too fast, eliciting a gasp from Rachel. "I have not. I don't suppose you'd do it? She's at work at the diner."

"Now you are asking for a big favor," Iris said, tone dry. JJ let out a single laugh, and Iris said, "I'll call her. But you'll owe me."

Approaching the outskirts of Cold Springs, JJ resisted the temptation to blaze through town. She did maintain a solid ten miles an hour over the limit all the way, a good way to get a ticket depending on who was on duty. They also liked to patrol the stretch on the far side of town, so JJ kept her lead foot in check until she saw the official town limits sign. By then, the ground was climbing again toward the next set of mountains, so her accelerator could only do so much.

"You okay in the back?" she asked, searching her mirrors fruitlessly.

"Jim Dandy," Otto said, voice rough.

"We're almost there," JJ said, which was true. In ten or fifteen minutes, she'd be at the front entrance. She should've called ahead, but forgot. She handed her phone to Evie again. "See if you can get the hospital for me."

Evie held the phone in both hands, staring. "There's no signal."

"That's okay," JJ said. "Keep trying."

They probably wouldn't have reception before they hit Plattsville, but it was worth a shot.

"I don't want to go with Miss Iris," Rachel said, her voice so soft JJ could barely hear her.

"It's okay, sweetie," JJ said. "Your dad will be okay. He just needs more help than I can give him."

"No," Rachel said, voice shaking, leaning out around Evie and fighting the shoulder harness. "We need to all stay together."

JJ glanced over at the girl. "I promise, either your mom or I will pick you up as soon as we can. You've stayed with Miss Iris before. You'll be safe with her."

"Not this time," she whimpered, and turned to face the window.

Poor child, JJ thought. But there was nothing else she could do.

23

___

Luther sat, waiting. It had been about fifteen minutes, so he was due...

"How much longer are we gonna sit here?" Adam asked.

Luther looked at his watch. Right on cue. "As long as it takes. Which means until the next shift of bouncers shows up. Which should be any minute."

Which was, in fact, a complete fabrication. Luther had no idea when they'd switch over, but it sounded reasonable. They'd been sitting across the street from *Foxy's*, a dive bar with scantily dressed waitstaff, for going on three hours. Time enough for it to have gone dark on them, and time enough to freeze their asses off. One of Danny's associates worked there as a bouncer, but hadn't shown yet.

"What makes you think Danny'll get in contact with this guy?" Adam asked.

Because I need him to, Luther thought. Out loud, he said, "He and Danny have a long history. Rudy said the guy sells drugs out of the club, and Danny is his primary supplier. Danny had to pull up stakes in West Virginia. He'll have commitments of his own, farther up the supply chain, so he's not gonna abandon somebody he thinks is safe."

"What if he knows Rudy knows about this guy?"

The million-dollar question. "Rudy didn't think he did. And Rudy is a pretty sneaky fucker."

"You do many stakeouts?" Adam asked. "As a deputy, I mean."

Luther stretched his head and dropped his shoulders until he heard a satisfying pop. "Not that many. Especially if you don't count speed traps. Usually they came up as part of some task force, working with the Staties or the Feds."

"You ever pee in a cup?"

Luther laughed. "Not on the clock. But one time, I almost got my ass shot with my pants down. I snuck over to the vacant lot next door, whipped it out, and the next thing I know, all hell's breaking loose. Before I can get my zipper up, one of our suspects comes flying around the corner and slams right into me. We both go down, but I managed to roll over on top and get the cuffs on him. We were working with the Kirby County Sheriff's Department, but Grant was the next man on the scene. He stood behind me and blocked everyone else's view until I could get my pants fixed. Thank God I didn't have a patrolman's belt to deal with, or I'd still have been putting my pecker away."

Adam shook his head.

"Sorry," Luther said grinning. Though he doubted Adam could see it. "My language tends to degenerate in the field."

"Your language is pretty degenerate all the time," Adam said, pulling his cap tighter on his head, tucking his hands into his coat sleeves, and propping a knee on the dash.

Luther still smiled, remembering. Afterward, he'd thought Grant was prissy when Luther offered to shake his hand, and Grant had refused. *Wash it first.* But now he knew it was the man's dry humor. He'd been blind to a lot of things, wrapped up in his own petty brain chatter, including how much slack the new Sheriff had given him. Though he still didn't consider the man completely blameless in his current suspension. It didn't help that Grant's head was all twisted up around JJ.

Adam suddenly made a noise from the seat next to him.

"What's that?" Luther asked. He leaned around, trying to get a better look at Adam by the single distant streetlight. His eyes were closed. *That asshole just snored.*

"Hey!" Luther said, nudging Adam with an elbow. "Wake up, you wuss."

Adam snorted, sat up straight, and said, "Sorry," that way you say *sorry* when you know you're supposed to be, but you're not yet sure why.

"Why don't you stretch your legs?" Luther suggested. "There's a convenience store down the street."

Adam rubbed his face. "Good idea. I can hit the head while I'm there. You want anything?"

"Only if you wash your hands first," Luther said, but the inside joke was lost on Adam.

Luther wasn't about to admit it to Adam, but he was struggling to stay awake himself. The long drive, the inconsistent schedule of late, the drinking as though he were twenty years younger—it was all catching up with him. Luther wasn't the most reflective person, but he knew he'd been seized up inside since Les's death, wound tighter than the packing in a baseball. Now that he and Adam were doing something, gathering some forward momentum, he felt as though that packing had started to loosen. That loosening was another reason he found his eyelids drifting in the cold car, even though he'd had to drink himself into oblivion in his own bed. Maybe it was a good thing.

Then again, a loosely packed baseball was one that didn't serve its purpose and got tossed out of the game.

He stared at the strip club, willing himself to stay awake. Foxy's was an old, brown brick building that could have been a restaurant or realtor or just about anything in a previous life. The main entrance had a single, standard door, and people weren't exactly lining up to get in. Luther had done some quick recon when they arrived. Neither of the two bouncers matched Luther's description of Danny's associate. One bouncer remained near the door, and another acted as a floater, cruising the space to deter any trouble. They'd been working hard to look busy while Luther sipped at his overpriced, watered-down beer, but it'd been early. It still was, but there were enough people coming and going that the floater occasionally wandered outside in his coat to make sure no one was getting up to no good.

Luther wondered how much longer Adam would be. He could use the conversation. And some goddamn warmth. Luther made sure his headlights were switched off, then started the engine to let the heat run for a few minutes. He adjusted the vents that blew on his face. Lately it seemed like the ones by his feet didn't work at all, and he had to endure an upper body sauna to be able to move his toes. But for the moment, a sauna didn't feel so bad...

A car door opening startled Luther. He sat up, blinking dry eyes. "All right, you caught me. I shouldn't have turned the damn heat on—"

Luther felt a sudden pressure across his throat, while an arm encircled his chest from the seat behind him. The pressure increased slightly, with a piercing sensation at one end. A knife.

His chest tightened as Luther held his breath, afraid inhaling would push the knife deeper. But breath-holding led to panic, and as much as his reptile brain wanted to take over, Luther's training told him he couldn't panic. His eyes strayed to the rearview mirror, but he'd switched off the dome light for surveillance, and the angle was all wrong anyway. He couldn't see a thing.

He swallowed, throat suddenly dry. "I don't have much cash, but you're welcome to what there is of it. And I can't identify you, so all you have to do is take it and walk away. Just leave me with a story to tell my friends about the time I fell asleep outside a titty bar —"

"What are you doing here, Deputy Beck?" The man's voice was rough, hoarse. Not like Adam's, but like it didn't get much use. And yet it was vaguely familiar.

"You know who I am?" Luther asked, maybe stalling for time, or maybe scared shitless and trying to find his way.

"Who's with you?" The pressure on his neck changed, the blade rotating so it was less flat against his throat and more ready to slice through it. "Is Adam Rutledge here?"

Luther's mind struggled to outrace his tripping heart. How could he have been so stupid? He'd said he hoped to catch a glimpse of Danny, but he never really believed he'd show. Now he sat with a knife at his throat. Luther had to do something before Danny killed him, or Adam got back and Danny pulled a gun or something crazy and killed them both. Luther's weapon was tucked in a mounted vehicle holster, on his right side but just out of reach so long as his back was stuck to the seat. And then he'd have to twist pretty significantly to fire. The SUV's engine was still running. He could knock it out of park, maybe hit the car in front of them. But he didn't have room to build up much speed for impact.

"Listen, Danny—"

The passenger door suddenly swung open. It was too late. There was no way Adam, carrying a paper bag of goodies, could have seen the man in the back seat. He climbed in, shoulder first and averting his head in a tall-ish man's habit.

"I wasn't sure what kind of soda you drink, so I got you a…"

Adam's voice trailed off and his eyes widened. He stared at the spot behind Luther's head, blinked and squinted in the dark. Then he slowly lowered his bag to the floor in front of his seat, his door still open. Instead of fleeing, Adam said, "Virgil, I'd advise you against killing a Beecham County deputy. Even one that's been suspended."

24

Adam was amazed how calm his voice sounded, at least to his own ears. Maybe there was an advantage to having to work so hard to force speech from his aching throat. He couldn't really see the knife—not to make out any details—but in his mind he could see Luther's blood, bathing the vehicle. And him helpless to stop it.

He pushed the gruesome image away and continued, "You should put the knife down. This may not be the best neighborhood, but they are coming up on their busy time across the street. And I'd think the last thing a fugitive would want is attention."

Dark as it was in the car, the whites of Luther's eyes still showed over-large, and Adam bet he was sweating. The dry heat blowing from the vents against his own face made his skin crawl. "Virgil," Adam said, his voice a low warning.

An exhalation, a visceral sound of disgust, came from the back seat before Virgil lowered his knife. "You just couldn't leave it alone. I had this under control!"

Anger instantly replaced Adam's relief. "You mean like you had it under control when Danny took Rachel Nicholson. And Aaron Schofield."

Luther rotated in the driver's seat before Virgil had a chance to respond. Adam was pretty sure he'd drawn a gun, although he couldn't imagine how he intended to use it in the vehicle. Shoot through the seat?

"And like you had the fucker under control when he killed my brother," Luther growled.

He'd shoot through the seat all right. Or the door, or Adam, or anything else that got in his way. And that would be the end of it. Or at least, the end of finding Danny. Adam was convinced they had no chance of doing so without Virgil, and at that moment he acknowledged finding Danny was almost as important to him as it was to Luther. But Luther was in no condition to think straight now, and he suspected Virgil never was.

"So where's Teddy?" Adam asked, finally pulling his door shut. "Is he your getaway driver? I didn't see him at the convenience store—maybe he's parked on the next street?"

Virgil and Luther continued staring at each other, though Adam wasn't sure what they could see in the dim car. Finally, Virgil turned toward Adam and said, "Uncle Teddy isn't exactly cut out for this kind of stuff."

Adam waited while Luther slowly stowed his gun in its holster. But how long would it stay there? Adam needed someone to help him maintain calm. And the only man who could do that was the same man he was here to find. "I have to see Teddy," he said.

"About Harlan?" Virgil asked.

"Why, do you know something about him? Does Teddy?" Adam demanded.

A car's headlights swept across them, coming from the other direction, and Adam saw his father's face twist, as though he'd tasted something that might kill him. "No. But you can talk to Teddy later tonight."

Adam clenched his jaws in frustration. He worked to keep his voice even as he said, "I need to speak with him now. And it's not only about Harlan. I need his help."

Virgil shook his head and settled back against his seat. "A couple of hours isn't going to make a difference. And I'm not going anywhere until I see if *he* shows."

The way Virgil had emphasized he made the back of Adam's neck tingle. "Who is *he*?"

"Don't be coy," Virgil said. "I have a feeling your deputy friend isn't leaving either."

Luther didn't say anything, but he did shut off the engine. Great. Just great. Adam couldn't wait to see Teddy, so he wouldn't be the sole voice of reason.

In the meantime, Adam had so many questions for Virgil. He wasn't sure where to start, especially since he doubted the man would answer any of them. He decided to begin with the least charged issues and work his way up to the ones that mattered most. "Why did Danny take Rachel Nicholson?" Adam asked.

Virgil slid toward the middle of the back seat, for an unobstructed view of the club. "Was that the girl's name? I don't know. He didn't tell me he was going to do it, or I would've stopped him."

"And how exactly would you have done that?" Luther asked, adjusting the rearview mirror.

Virgil didn't answer.

"Maybe he didn't tell you beforehand, but I'll bet you can take a wild guess why he kidnapped her," Adam pressed.

"To punish you," Virgil said. "And probably me."

Something about Virgil's proximity, his matter-of-fact way of saying the most disturbing things, made it hard for Adam to breathe. His hand strayed to his throat, but he gripped the door handle instead. He wasn't ready for that question yet.

"Why does he want to punish me?" Adam asked.

"I don't know." Virgil's voice was flat, missing any inflection.

"Are you on medication?" Adam asked.

"Just Teddy's," he replied.

Adam gripped the door more tightly, suddenly feeling claustrophobic too. The darkness pressing against the window felt like a wall. He wondered if Luther would yell at him if he rolled down the glass and stuck his head out.

"Have you seen this guy?" Luther asked. "Danny's friend?"

"The boy doesn't have friends. But I've seen the man he meets here," Virgil said.

Luther said, "Then maybe you should be sitting in the front instead of Adam, since you're the only one who's ever seen him."

Adam couldn't make out Luther's expression, but he had pitched his voice as though to communicate something of significance. Too bad Adam had no idea what that was.

"You mean sit in the front where you can keep an eye on me?" Virgil asked, a hint of amusement coloring his speech. "Sure, we can do that."

Adam looked at Luther, and the man gave him a *move along* motion with his hand. It was the only clear communication he'd had in the past five surreal minutes. Adam knocked over the forgotten bag by his feet as he got out of the car, and paused to gather the rolling drinks and spilled snacks. He picked up the bag, then nearly dropped it again as he stood.

Virgil blocked his way.

It was the first time they'd stood toe to toe... well, maybe ever.

The last time Adam had set eyes on his father was the night he and JJ had rescued Rachel Nicholson, and Luther had rescued Adam. Or at least, kept him from freezing to death until help arrived. The only thing Adam remembered about Virgil from that night was nearly killing him, and nearly being killed *by* him. Adam was surprised to learn he was slightly taller than his father, but his father's shoulders (hidden beneath multiple layers, including a hooded sweatshirt) appeared slightly broader than his own. Virgil had gotten rid of his heavy beard, but the dim light cast shadows across his features. The shape of his face seemed familiar, especially the jutting cheekbones and cleft chin.

Virgil stepped back to let Adam pass and said, "You're getting skinny again."

Adam bumped his head getting in the back seat. He still couldn't fathom the sudden turn of events. His fugitive father was sitting next to a deputy, not in restraints, but watching a seedy bar to catch another fugitive. It was too bizarre.

"Did you say you brought me something to drink?" Luther asked.

Adam fumbled in the bag. He couldn't imagine Luther needing caffeine to stay awake now. He certainly didn't. He handed Luther a Coke between the seats, wondering where he'd stowed his gun and whether it would come out again anytime soon.

"I don't suppose you have a spare," Virgil said.

Adam did, and he handed it to his father, careful not to touch his fingers as he passed it off. He listened to the fooshing sound of the bottles being opened in companionable succession.

The world had gone crazy.

25

———

"I've never made potato candy before, Miss Iris," Evie said, mashing potatoes in a bowl by hand. She looked at the bag of powdered sugar on the counter. "I'll bet Rachel's never done it either, have you? Her mom doesn't let her eat candy."

Rachel sat quietly at the kitchen table, ignoring her friend, fidgeting with the cuff of her shirtsleeve. Her long, dark hair hung to her shoulders, having escaped its tie, and fell across her alabaster cheeks. Evie thought she resembled a lost princess, definitely someone who needed to be saved. And that's usually where Evie came in.

Since Rachel wasn't listening, Evie whispered to Iris, "I've never seen so much blood in my life. She was really scared."

Her palm dusted with flour, Iris rubbed between Evie's shoulder blades with the back of her hand. "Blood is not something anyone likes to see. And it's always scary when someone we care about is hurt."

Iris rinsed her hands in the sink before going to sit next to Rachel. "I know how your mom feels about candy, but I'll bet your dad isn't so strict. In fact, I'll bet I know his favorite candy."

Rachel lifted her head. "Dad isn't as strict about a lot of stuff."

Iris smiled, an adult kind of smile that meant something was funnier than what was being said. "Every time I make a batch of this, I set aside a few pieces and put them in a little bag. And I take that little bag to the feed store—you know who works there, right?"

Rachel nodded.

"It's a little secret your dad and I have. And now you know too," Iris said, taking one of Rachel's hands in hers. "Would you like to roll out the potato mush with the rolling pin, or do you want to be the peanut butter spreader?"

"I'll do the rolling pin," Rachel said in a small voice.

"Good girl," Iris said, kissing the top of her head and rising with a groan. "How about you, Evie? Can I trust you to do the peanut butter, or will you lick it from the spatula?"

Before Evie could answer, Iris's phone rang, one of the old, loud kinds like Evie had at her own house. Iris walked to the living room to answer it, the girls on her heels. "Yes," Iris said.

Iris didn't say much after that, and Evie had trouble focusing on all of the uh-huhs. She stepped closer to Rachel and seized her hand. It was so quiet, Evie heard the buzzing of a voice on the other end, and some rhythmic noise that may have been the kitchen clock.

Finally, Iris said, "Okay then, we'll see you soon." She hung up and turned to the girls. "Rachel, your dad's going to be fine, and his leg's going to be fine. They're keeping him in the hospital tonight, just to make sure he doesn't have any problems, and your mom's going to stay with him. She'll call you later. And you'll spend the night at Evie's house. Evie's mom will be here in half an hour or so, which gives us about enough time to finish and clean up."

Evie squeezed her friend's hand and said, "Told you," then danced ahead of her to the kitchen. Iris floured the rolling pin and got a spatula for the peanut butter. "The part where you roll it all up and slice it," Evie said, "that's my favorite part."

"I thought you'd never made potato candy before," Iris said.

"Mom must have told me about it," Evie said, looking around for Rachel. She was still trailing behind. "I'll bet if you wanted, you could write secret messages in the peanut butter. No one would ever know."

Rachel stood next to her, and the girls watched Iris's knotted fingers adjusting, arranging, giving the potato-sugar mixture a last stir in the mixing bowl.

"But how would anyone read your messages?" Rachel asked.

"Good point," Evie conceded.

Iris looked past them, where headlights were sweeping across the windows, illuminating her front curtains. "That can't be JJ already," she said, wiping her hands.

The girls followed her to the window when she peeked out. A car door opened, triggering the flash of the motion light by the porch. A moment later, Iris said, "Of all the nerve…"

Evie wasn't sure what that meant, but Iris did not sound happy. She turned off a lamp in the front room, sending them into relative darkness.

"You girls stay inside," she said firmly. "Don't stand by the windows, and don't come out, no matter what. Got it?"

"Yes, ma'am," Evie and Rachel said in unison, more afraid of disobeying Iris than they were of anyone outside.

Iris grabbed a heavy cardigan from the back of a chair, slipped it on, stepped out on the porch, and pulled the front door closed behind her. Evie and Rachel crept to the window, carefully peeking around the edge of the curtain before jerking their heads back.

"Isn't that your dad?" Rachel whispered.

"How do you know that's my dad?" Evie's parents had been divorced longer than she had lived next to Rachel, and her dad didn't come around much.

"I saw him at school one time, sitting in his truck. He said who he was and asked about you, but I just kept walking," Rachel admitted.

"When?" Evie demanded.

"I don't know," Rachel said, tiny index finger to her lip. "But it was before... you know. All the bad stuff."

Meaning when Rachel disappeared. They never talked about it, but Evie knew.

"Marcus, what brings you around this time of evening?" Iris's voice rang out from the porch; she must not have closed the door all the way. The girls crowded behind it to better hear.

"Oh, I'm sure you can guess," Evie's father said. "You usually know everything that's going on around here."

His voice sounded calm and reasonable, but that didn't mean anything. Evie loved her father and was pretty sure he'd never hurt her, but she also knew he had a temper. And sometimes his mood changed so fast, it made her think she was the crazy one. That's when her mom would send her inside or next door or just somewhere else. And she didn't want to leave, but she was scared not to. Plus, her mom was tough—she figured tougher than a lot of dads she knew. (Maybe not tougher than Rachel's dad; he was huge, and even though he'd practically cut his leg off today, he hadn't cried.) Still, one of these times, her mom was going to tell her to leave, and she wouldn't. Evie was going to stay, no matter what her mom said. And then she'd see what happened.

If Miss Iris had spoken, Evie didn't hear her. Her father continued, "How's Evie doing?"

Rachel gazed at Evie, eyes big, but Evie held a finger to her lips.

"I'm sure she's doing fine," Miss Iris said. "JJ takes good care of her. What do you want, Marcus?"

"Funny you should mention JJ. I know she thinks a lot of you. I was hoping you could talk to her, put in a good word for me," he said.

"And why would I do that?"

His voice sounded almost like he was laughing. "Because I'm a good man. Don't you ever miss having a good man around, Iris?"

"You mean a bully who thinks it's okay to strike a woman? No, I don't miss it a bit," she said.

The girls jumped as the doorknob moved and the door edged open a smidge.

"And let me tell you," she continued, "bullies always get what's coming to them. Good night, Marcus."

Evie and Rachel stepped back quickly, flush against the wall. Evie saw the same cringe on Rachel's face she felt on her own; hopefully they wouldn't get smushed.

"Iris!" Marcus's voice rose. "You need to tell JJ to back off."

The door had swung open a foot, but paused. "You need to get off my property. If you come around here drunk again, I'm not calling the Sheriff. I'll take care of you myself."

Iris came through the door quickly, and this time closed it securely behind her. She stood, back against the door, staring at the girls without speaking, until they heard Marcus's truck start and watched the headlights swing around as he retreated down the driveway.

"Some people like to cause a scene," Iris said. "Come on, ladies, we have some candy to finish."

Rachel slipped off to use the restroom while, back in the kitchen, Iris and Evie attempted to pick up where they'd left off. "I need some coffee," Iris said, starting a new pot. "Did you hear all of that?"

Evie didn't answer. Iris dumped the bowl of potato mush onto the clean counter. She seemed to have forgotten rolling was supposed to be Rachel's job, or maybe she was getting it started for her.

"Your father isn't—" Iris paused, brushing a strand of white hair out of her face with her wrist. "Your father loves you. But he's a very confused man."

"Mom's not confused," Evie said.

Iris smiled. "Very rarely. Especially now that she's divorced. Some people love their children, but just don't belong together."

"Like my parents," Evie said, tapping the spatula against her palm.

Iris looked past her where Rachel stood uncertainly at the edge of the kitchen. "What's wrong, sweetie?"

"I don't know," Rachel said, hands fluttering around the hem of her shirt, across her forearms, like a moth in its last moments of life.

Iris went to Rachel and took her hands, but the girl's head began swiveling, looking over one shoulder and the other, without really seeing.

"Do you feel sick?" Iris asked.

Rachel whimpered. "I feel bad. I feel—"

Evie found herself shaking, too, though she didn't know why. She tried to stop as Iris kneeled in front of Rachel, held her face still and repeated, more firmly this time, "What's wrong?"

"I'm scared," Rachel whispered.

Iris didn't dismiss Rachel's fear or talk down to her, instead calmly asking, "What are you afraid of, Rachel?"

The girl's eyes filled with tears, one finally spilling over as she said, "I don't know. But it's coming."

Iris pulled Rachel to her, and Rachel began crying in earnest. Evie thought she heard Iris mutter something about Adam, but it was hard to hear over Rachel's soft sobs. Evie began pacing, as she usually did when she didn't know what to do to help. Her mother said she was—

Something flashed against the front windows.

Headlights. Again.

"Miss Iris," Evie said, voice quivering, "there's someone coming."

Iris stood, and Rachel clung to her. "It's okay, girls, it's probably Evie's dad again."

Rachel pulled desperately on Iris's pants. "No, we have to hide. We have to hide *now*!"

"Rachel, calm down—"

"Please!" Rachel wailed.

Evie could see the vehicle was almost to the top of the drive, but she couldn't make out any details beyond the headlights in the dark.

"Okay, fine," Iris said, grabbing a flashlight from the junky bit of her counter and heading toward the stairs. "Come with me."

Evie watched, dumbfounded, as the wall beneath the stairs moved. *Disappeared.* To reveal a secret room. As scared as she was, Evie couldn't help saying, "That is *so* cool."

"I'm glad you think so, dear," Iris said, handing Evie the flashlight and pushing Rachel toward her. "I need you girls to stay quiet in here, and stay put, no matter what. Got it?"

"No," Rachel said, nose pink and snotty with tears. "You have to hide with us."

Iris smiled and pushed Rachel's hair away from her face. "Everything's going to be fine, and we'll have a funny story to tell your mom when she calls. I promise."

But when Iris met Evie's eyes, she nodded and stared at her hard. Evie knew what Iris was saying. That she was lying, and it was Evie's job to take care of Rachel. Evie nodded back, and Iris smiled, but it was a scary smile. Like she was ready to do battle. Evie thought Iris might be the bravest old person she knew.

And then Iris made the wall move back into place, and the world turned black. But Evie wouldn't turn her flashlight on. Not yet. Instead she squeezed Rachel's hand in the dark. And waited.

26

He blinked in the glare of the porch light. It felt weird, knocking on Iris's door after so many years. Not that he'd knocked on it much as a child. Mostly he'd just burst through, following on Adam's heels.

When Iris finally answered the door, she seemed confused. She didn't recognize him, and she may have even been expecting someone else.

"Yes?" she said.

He smiled his most charming smile, waiting for her to open the storm door and pull the main door to, keeping the heat inside (and for his purposes, making her escape less likely). Then he responded, "Hello, Iris."

"I'm sorry…" Her voice trailed off, but she still wasn't there yet.

"You mean you don't recognize your favorite peanut butter thief?" he asked. "Iris, I'm hurt."

He watched her face (now wrinkled, but not bad for as old as she was) transform through nanoseconds of recognition, then fear, then what? Acceptance? Resignation? Or maybe he was projecting, and that was a dangerous thing to do with someone like Iris. "Aren't you going to invite me in?"

"Of course, Danny," she said, stepping calmly back into the house and waiting for him to follow.

It was a peculiar feeling hearing his old name—he'd gone by so many over the years—but it also seemed appropriate in a house that hadn't changed much since his childhood. They made their way to the kitchen, where he sat at the familiar table.

He laughed. "Funny how the table doesn't seem as far away now." He stretched his arms out, getting reacquainted with its— and his—dimensions. Iris stood next to the sink, staring at a coffee pot that was finishing its cycle. "I ate a lot of meals here. Probably more meals than I ate at home. Your pork chops—" He laughed again. "My God, how I've missed your pork chops. Maybe because they were a special treat, you know? Something we didn't get every day."

Suddenly, instantly, he felt the warmth leave his body, as if it were on a switch, leaving him icy inside. He'd been like that for a long time, but the switch seemed to be on a hair trigger of late. "I guess you never taught Virgil how to make pork chops. Or much of anything."

Iris turned to face him, arms crossed. "What made you think I wouldn't answer the door with a gun?"

He shrugged. "I know you don't like them. Never did when we were kids." He paused, preparing himself for her reaction. "Do you still keep that rifle in the back room?"

And there it was, an involuntary flick of the eyes that told him everything he needed to know. Yes, she did, and she'd never make it there in time.

Danny's hand strayed to his scalp, and he realized his head felt strange, as it had done more often lately. He scratched at his temple and continued, "Virgil mentioned it from time to time, the gun that killed his father."

"Did he?" Iris said, with no emotion whatsoever. "You didn't cut yourself, did you, Danny?"

He removed his hand from his hair—had he scratched

himself bloody? No, his hands were mostly clean, but there was some blood spattered on his sleeves. He avoided the temptation to look at his jacket front, not wanting to get distracted. Instead, he leaned back in the hard, wooden chair and clasped his hands in front of his flat stomach. "I'm fine, Iris, thanks for asking. But Virgil never knew the truth, did he? About how his daddy died?"

Something about his words or his manner caused Iris's calm façade to slip. In fact, Danny felt a bit disoriented himself, not entirely sure what he'd just said, or why he'd said it. He shook his head to clear it, sat up, and rested his elbows on the table. "Did you know your son took me?"

"No," Iris said.

"Don't you lie to me," Danny said, voice deceptively mild.

Iris retrieved a couple of coffee mugs from the cabinet. They were simple, cream-colored ceramic. The coffeemaker had stopped sputtering, so she poured a cup and set it on the table in front of him. She didn't offer milk or sugar.

"I didn't know. But at some point, I suspected," she admitted. She turned her back to him and leaned against the sink, apparently staring out the black window.

"Why didn't you say anything then?" he asked.

Her voice dropped, almost to a whisper. "Because I thought he was dead. I thought you were both dead."

He wrapped his hands around the hot mug. "Sometimes, so did I."

What was he doing here? Suddenly he couldn't remember. What had he hoped to accomplish? And how could he possibly leave her behind now?

Danny heard a gunning engine in the distance, an instant before headlights flashed across the front room. Someone raced up the driveway. "Were you expecting anyone?" he asked.

"No," Iris said, "but I wasn't expecting you."

This could be a complication.

Danny stood and glanced over his shoulder at the

approaching lights as Iris calmly poured herself a cup of coffee... Except, her hand gripped the carafe handle tightly.

Too late, he watched her arm swing in an arc, flinging the pot of hot liquid at him. He ducked, averting his face, and screamed in pain and anger as the coffee scalded his side and one cheek. He toppled sideways, falling over his chair as Iris slammed into him, running for the front.

Danny scrambled after her, hitting his stride as he reached her, just steps from the door. She yelled for help, but her voice was lost in the roaring that filled his ears. Instead of tackling her, he grabbed one arm and swung her in a half circle, sending her flying away from the door. She landed hard. He stood over her, catching his breath, as she crawled away from him toward the wall, covering her head with her arms.

A banging noise signaled someone struggling with the storm door, moments before he burst into the room. It was a man around Danny's age and build, handsome, with a flushed face. His eyes flew to Iris, then back to Danny.

Danny smiled as the man raised his hand, which held a pistol.

27

JJ could smell blood, but she wasn't sure if it was on her clothes or in her car. Hopefully the former. She'd have to wait until daylight to clean her Bronco. She'd call tonight as soon as she got home and see if someone could cover the first couple hours of her shift tomorrow. The girls would need a decent breakfast and as normal a morning as possible after what they'd experienced today. What if they couldn't face school? She doubted she could get the full day off, but maybe Iris would be willing to watch them. Unless, of course, Harlan was being transferred tomorrow.

At least Iris had already fed the girls dinner. All JJ had to do was get them home and get them to bed. She couldn't remember the last time she'd changed Evie's sheets, but she wasn't going to worry about it. Dorothy might notice, but the kids wouldn't. Nor would they care.

Turning onto Iris's driveway, her headlights revealed an extra vehicle. It looked suspiciously like a red pickup. *Shit*. Was it better to park behind Marcus and block him in, or give him an easy escape? JJ leaned toward easy escape; she didn't know if she had it in her to deal with that asshole tonight on top of everything else.

Parking next to his truck, JJ pulled out her cell phone and dialed 911. She was tired, but not stupid. Her luck was holding for once; Deputy Beth was working the switchboard.

"Beth, this is JJ Tulley. I'm at Iris Rutledge's house to pick up my girl, and Marcus's truck is here."

"Ms. Tulley, do you want me to send someone over?" Beth asked. "JJ?"

Something wasn't right. *The lighting.* Any other day, she'd have noticed it right away. The front door was open, and she was seeing light from an interior room. *Shit.* She nearly dropped the phone, fumbling to get her glovebox open. No gun. Of course there was no gun in her car. They'd confiscated it when she shot a cop. *Shit.*

"JJ? Are you there?" Beth repeated.

"Something's going on here. Please send someone, but I can't wait. Evie and Rachel are inside," JJ said, getting out of her car.

"JJ, no. We'll be —"

"I'll leave the line open," JJ said, dropping her phone on her seat and walking slowly toward the front door.

The front porch motion light flashed on when she got closer, briefly blinding JJ. Marcus must've heard her car, and there was no sneaking up on him now. "Marcus? It's JJ. I'm here to pick up the girls."

Front steps now, and she could see light from the kitchen through the ajar front door. JJ strained to hear something—anything—other than her breath wheezing in and out her open mouth. "Iris? Are you there? Iris?"

No answer, but there was a soft noise nearby. A moan... She crossed the wooden porch, her forward motion making one of the chairs rock in her peripheral vision. Then she was across the threshold...

And there was Marcus, facedown on the floor in the front room, blood spreading from beneath him.

"Iris!" JJ screamed, running to her ex-husband. "Iris!"

She rolled him over for a better look. His shoulder was bleeding, not as badly as Otto had been, but bad enough. Gunshot? He moaned, not quite conscious but not quite completely gone, either.

"Marcus! Marcus," she said, patting his face and smearing blood on it in the process. "You need to talk to me, Marcus. Where are the girls? Marcus, where's Evie?"

He moaned again. "Come on, Marcus. Where are the girls?"

His eyes fluttered, and he began muttering, "What girls? Evie? Where's Evie?"

JJ pressed against his shoulder. She needed to stop the bleeding, but all she could think of was her daughter. "Evie!" she screamed. "Evie! Where are you?"

She paused, throat raw. There was no answer, but there was something... a thumping. "Girls, where are you?" she yelled.

The thumping continued, and JJ followed it to the stairs. The bolthole. Iris had mentioned it once, but JJ was sure she was joking. Now how the hell did she get the damn thing open?

"It's okay, girls. I'm here."

She left bloody smears on the wall, tracing the joinery, pressing fruitlessly, until finally she felt something release. The wall swung open and Evie and Rachel fell against her, sobbing. JJ hugged them tightly, struggling to say, "Easy, it's okay. You're both safe now."

But were they? JJ's gaze flew to the ceiling. She hadn't checked upstairs, hadn't even checked the rest of the rooms down here. And where was Iris?

The stress of the situation had triggered Rachel's asthma, and JJ heard her wheezing. "Easy, baby. Remember to breathe. Remember to count." She peeled Evie's face away from her chest. "Evie, you're okay now. But I need to know, where's Miss Iris?"

Evie's face was streaked with tears. "I don't know, mom. I don't know. She put us in there, and then—" Evie's wide eyes drifted toward the front room. "Daddy?"

Maybe Iris had gone for help. JJ had almost forgotten about her bleeding ex. Evie tore from her and ran to her father, stopping a few feet away. "Is he dead?" she asked.

JJ quickly herded the two girls to the front door. "No, sweetie, he's not dead. He'll be fine. Both of your dads will be fine. But I need you to wait for me in the car."

She gave them a nudge, then remembered her phone. "Evie, your friend Deputy Beth is on the phone, waiting to hear if we're okay. Will you please tell her to send an ambulance?"

Evie nodded and ran toward the Bronco, dragging Rachel with her. Now that she had a mission, her daughter would be fine. JJ turned back to Marcus, kneeling beside him on the floor. She applied pressure to his wound with one hand, and brushed his wavy hair back with the other. His eyes opened, and his heavy lashes made him look angelic. An angelic asshole. She spoke slowly and clearly, as she would with any other patient. "Marcus, you're going to be okay. There's an ambulance on the way, and I'll take care of you until they get here."

He opened his mouth to speak, and she smelled alcohol on his breath. Typical Marcus. He'd probably accuse her of violating her own protective order.

"What's that?" she asked, and bent closer.

"Came back... Don't know why," he muttered. "Tried to stop him... He's got my gun."

"Who, Marcus?" JJ asked. "Who did you try to stop? Who's got your gun?"

He focused on JJ's face as he said, "The man who took Iris."

28

Wednesday was apparently not a very exciting night at the strip club. Adam had dozed off in the back, and Luther couldn't remember the last time he'd heard a sound in the vehicle beyond his occasional soft snore. Luther was in no danger of falling asleep himself. He had never been comfortable in Virgil Rutledge's presence. But now, seated next to him in the dark, Virgil in no way restrained, Luther realized he'd burned through a great deal of his fear of the man.

"How did you know about this place?" Luther asked. "What made you think Danny might come here?"

Virgil didn't answer, but Luther hadn't really expected him to. The man wasn't exactly a team player, which was why, regardless of his biological relationship to Adam, Luther didn't trust him. He needed to figure out the man's endgame if he was going to have any chance of predicting what he might do. So Luther answered for him.

"You've been checking up on him for a while, haven't you?" Luther didn't bother looking at Virgil. It was too dark to see his expression, and he wouldn't have been able to read it anyway. Virgil seemed to have some blown circuits that made interpreting anything he said or did difficult. "So why have you been watching him? What did he do that you couldn't abide? I find it hard to believe it was the drug dealing."

Luther angled across his steering wheel with interest when someone exited the club. False alarm, a college kid trying to make a call on his cell phone. "Come on, Virgil. You sure you don't want to tell me what else he was up to, this adopted—I mean, kidnapped—son of yours?"

Virgil's head swung toward him in the dark. Luther had touched a nerve. But before Virgil could answer, Adam shuddered awake in the back seat, drawing their attention.

"Did you feel that?" Adam asked.

Luther wasn't sure which of them he was speaking to, and he wished Adam's throat would heal. His words sounded downright spooky.

"No," Virgil said. "Who was it?"

"I don't know," Adam admitted. "I just—I don't know. You're sure you didn't feel anything?"

"I'm sure," Virgil said.

"I don't suppose Teddy has a phone," Adam said. Virgil didn't bother to reply. Perhaps he'd hit his word quota. Luther decided to test his theory.

"Whatever happened to Sarah Edmunds? You know, the girl you kidnapped after Danny." When Virgil didn't reply, Luther added, "The dead girl."

He'd expected Virgil to ignore him, or maybe even get angry, attack him in the front seat. At least it would add a little excitement to their surveillance. Instead he said, "I don't know."

Adam bent forward, head between the seats and the two men sitting in them.

"What do you mean, you don't know?" Luther demanded. "You don't remember what you did to her?"

Luther vividly remembered the meticulous, painstaking work the techs had done, combing the mountain to make sure they recovered all that remained of the girl, every pitiful piece. Adam's outrage quickly joined Luther's.

"You're the one who buried her!" Adam said. "You were going to bury Rachel next to her. She wasn't even dead, and you were going to—"

Adam threw himself back against the seat, hands to his head. Luther had started something now. He hadn't meant to, but by peeling back the first layer, he'd just shoved them under a bushel of onions. And of course it would be overwhelming for Adam. Where the hell do you start, once you start questioning your psychopath father? And how do you stop?

"I didn't kill her," Virgil said. "Sarah. Not directly. I thought I was doing the right thing for him."

Adam began to rock in the back seat, and somehow that gave Luther enough distance to put the pieces together. "You didn't want Danny to be alone. She was supposed to be..." Luther struggled for the right concept, but the only one he could find seemed so wrong, like a toddler holding a rifle. "She was supposed to be his playmate."

Virgil pointed at Luther, excited. "Yes! Exactly."

The convenience store snacks roiled in Luther's belly, threatening to rise. It didn't help when he remembered he was the one who'd started them down this road.

Luther's phone rang—JJ—and he swallowed hard before answering. "Yeah, JJ?"

"Is Adam with you?" she asked.

Adam lurched forward, as if he'd heard his name. "Are the girls all right?" he asked.

JJ must've heard him, too. "The girls are fine," she said. "It's Iris."

"At least JJ doesn't have to worry about Marcus while he's in the hospital," Luther said. No one commented. "Is this it up here?"

"No," Virgil said. "You'll make a right at the next big light."

They were on their way to Virgil's motel room to meet with Teddy. If they hadn't known Danny was in Cold Springs an hour ago, grabbing Iris, Virgil would've insisted on sticking to the surveillance instead. Which was pretty messed up, since Iris was his mother. Once again, Luther was reminded that he didn't trust the fugitive asshole as far as he could throw him.

A few minutes later, Luther was parking in front of a rundown, two-story motel that would only look worse in daylight. Virgil pulled a heavy plastic key card from his pocket as he limped toward a room on the ground level. The man had barely gotten the door open when Adam pushed past him.

"Teddy?" Adam called out. "Teddy!"

But no one answered. A lamp illuminated the full size bed, but no one was lying in it, nor was anyone sitting in either of the two chairs. Adam headed for the bathroom, even though it was obvious no one was there. He even looked in the shower and checked behind the door.

"Where is he?" Adam demanded.

Virgil shrugged. "I guess he didn't come back."

Luther stepped out of Adam's way as he crossed the small room to confront Virgil.

"What do you mean he didn't come back?" Adam asked.

"Uncle Teddy and I had a… difference of opinion," Virgil said.

Adam turned his back on his father, clenching his hands into fists at his side.

"A difference of opinion about what?" Luther asked.

"Does it matter?" Virgil said.

Luther was starting to feel Adam's frustration. "Yes, it fucking well matters."

"About Harlan. And the boy," Virgil said.

"You mean Carpenter?" Luther clarified. In his early thirties, the man was hardly a boy.

"Teddy was concerned because he couldn't reach Harlan." Virgil thumbed toward his son. "Especially after Adam showed up in our heads. But I thought it was more important to track down..."

He paused, and Luther watched him struggle to utter the name, "Danny."

"So when's the last time you saw Teddy?" Luther asked.

"Teddy left this afternoon," Virgil admitted. "He dropped me off at the club on the way."

Adam was a blur of motion, slamming Virgil backward against the nearest wall so hard Luther was surprised they didn't fall through into the next room. Adam pinned his father, forearm against his throat. "You stupid sonuvabitch! And you didn't even tell us he was gone."

"I thought Teddy would come back," Virgil said. "I don't know where he could've gone."

Adam drew his arm back, hesitated, then punched the wall next to his father, leaving a dent. He stormed out the door into the night.

"And I thought Pop was bad," Luther muttered.

29

———

Adam tripped over a curb in the dark, rubbing his aching hand. He didn't know where he was going. But as he covered step after step of pavement (one leg still aching), he realized he desperately needed something natural, something alive. And then he saw it, the tiniest square of grassy lawn still hanging on against the advance of winter, with a leafless tree in the center. It would have to do.

The yard was fenced, but he scaled it easily now that he had a destination in mind. Sitting beneath the tree on the cold ground, he looked up at the house. Two stories, dark inside, with its exterior pale against the night sky, it seemed its occupants were tucked in for the night.

Good. Someone in this awful world should be able to sleep.

Would Danny hurt Iris?

Once when they were little—they couldn't have been more than six or seven—Iris had caught Danny in her kitchen, eating peanut butter from the jar with a spoon. She'd swatted his hand, but instead of kicking him out, she made him sit at the table while she fixed him a peanut butter sandwich. She'd realized, as Adam hadn't until years later, that Danny was hungry and used to fending for himself. After that, she'd always made them lunch when they were at the Rutledge home. But Danny never stopped sneaking into the kitchen and stealing peanut butter. He did it as a game, just to prove he could, often leaving the jar or even the spoon out on the counter for Iris to see. She became so attuned to the sound of the cabinet doors opening that she would yell from the laundry room or one of the bedrooms upstairs, stopping him in his tracks. He'd laugh and scamper back outside, biding his time until he tried again.

So would Danny hurt Iris? Not the Danny Adam knew, but the Danny he'd known was gone. Grant had even hinted—okay, more than hinted—the adult Danny was a serial killer. But could the man actually harm someone he knew? Someone he'd loved?

Adam leaned back against the tree trunk, took a deep breath, and closed his eyes. He ignored the throbbing in his knuckles and pulled his mother's key from beneath his shirt, rubbing it between cold fingers before reaching out to Iris. Nothing. But then, he'd never been able to reach her. No one could. So what had woken him in Luther's car? Harlan would know. Had he felt it when Iris was taken? Adam tried to find the path to Harlan, to find his way to him without thinking. But again, he came up blank. Maybe he was just too upset. Iris was everything, all the family he had, and the way they'd left things...

To his surprise, shoulders hitching, Adam began to cry. He was so exhausted, and no one could help him. Gasping for breath, he realized, *I don't think I can go on.*

But then, through his tears, movement caught his eye. He blinked, swiped at his face, and saw a small figure in an upstairs window. Watching him. He thought it was a little girl—the pale shape gave the impression of lace. Perhaps he should have panicked, afraid she'd summon an adult to get rid of the intruder in their backyard, but instead he felt comforted. As if she was reminding him, *Of course you'll go on. You have to.*

Adam sighed, wiped his face on his sleeve, and stood. Was she really there? He supposed it didn't matter. Like the times he'd seen his mother in his dreams, he thought, tucking her key back in his shirt. He walked to the fence, then turned back and gave a quick wave before jumping over it again and following his footsteps back to the motel.

30

Evie woke, disoriented. She was in her own bed, but squished over to one side, clutching Bearington Bear. She hadn't taken him to bed with her since she was little.

Then she remembered—Miss Iris was gone. And her dad was in the hospital. She squeezed Bearington tightly.

Rachel's dad was in the hospital, too. Rachel was staying with her; that's why she was sleeping funny. Evie stretched out her arm. Then where was Rachel?

Evie sat up, heart racing. Had the man taken Rachel again? She tried not to panic, scanning her dark room. And then she saw her, standing by the window. Rachel's pale nightgown made her look like a ghost.

"Rachel?" Evie whispered.

Her friend didn't respond.

"Rachel?" she repeated.

This time, Rachel glanced over her shoulder at Evie. The girl lifted her hand at the window, then walked carefully back to Evie's bed, trying not to stub her toes. The mattress sank as she climbed in, and Evie waited for Rachel to settle before yanking the blankets back toward her own side. Then Evie lay, staring at the ceiling, wondering what time it was, and whether her mom would make them go to school tomorrow. Did she even want to go? She wasn't sure. Finally, Evie asked, "Who were you waving at?"

"No one," Rachel said. "Go back to sleep."

31

Danny sat on the edge of the sagging motel bed, elbows on his knees, and stared at the partially open bathroom door.

Soon. Soon he'd have the help he'd asked for from Victor. But he didn't know if he could hold it together that long. He wasn't sure how he'd gotten here—not the driving part, but the decisions that led to the destination. And he had a sneaking suspicion that however it had happened, he'd forgotten something important along the way.

Danny felt like his skin was crawling off his flesh. Except it was also in his brain, the crawling feeling tingling with a million slithering feet. Was this what methamphetamine was like? He laughed and for a moment almost felt sorry for his customers. But they chose their path. And what was his?

He could make out her shape on the bathroom floor. In the shadows, next to the bathtub and the toilet. The gag was a darker slash across her face and her white hair. Which could so easily slide down, around her neck.

He'd never killed a woman before. Had he? Well, maybe. Unintentionally perhaps, with bad product. Or really good product. And then there was Sarah. She had been at least female and on the cusp of womanhood when he'd stopped her. He hardly felt she should count, though. This... this was different. Something wanted him to kill Iris, and he wasn't sure it was something within him. Except what else would it be?

He scratched at his scalp, harder and deeper. He shouldn't be hearing the voice again. Even if the man he'd shot at Iris's was basically self-defense, there was the hitchhiker yesterday. That should have kept him safe for at least weeks, if not months. And yet, he sat on the bed, knowing that if he got any closer to Iris, he might not be able to control the urge to harm her. And he wasn't sure he wanted to do that. He certainly didn't want to be a slave to the voice, but he also felt there had to be something more for Iris.

The whispers chanted, *sacrifice*.

He didn't let himself look at her when he slammed the bathroom door shut. By the time he reached his car, he wasn't thinking of her, either. He was thinking of the next one.

32

Luther leaned against a piece of furniture he didn't have the name for. Fiberboard Piece of Shit, how was that? He'd quickly learned that the size and layout of the motel room made pacing damn near impossible, and he wasn't about to go outside in the cold. Unless Adam didn't show up soon. That's why Luther avoided looking at his watch. If he did, he'd have to set a solid deadline for venturing out to find him.

Virgil sat in a chair, at an angle so they weren't exactly facing each other, but each knew what the other was up to. There was just enough light in the room to highlight Virgil's spooky, glacier ice eyes, so Luther tried not to catch his attention. Except talking made Virgil uncomfortable, so that might deflect his attention even more than being quiet.

"What can you tell me about Danny?" Luther asked.

Virgil didn't turn, but he did say, "Nothing that will help you."

"Really? How about where the man might take Iris?"

"I don't know," Virgil said. "With the exception of the club where I found you, I don't know where he would have gone without Iris, much less with her."

There was a noise behind Luther, and Virgil glanced at the door as it opened to admit Adam. Luther pretended he hadn't been about to hunt the man down and continued questioning Virgil. "Can you track Danny, get in his head somehow?"

"No," Virgil said, averting his eyes from his son when Adam stood next to Luther.

It was strange, Danny taking Iris. He'd taken a couple of kids before, but never an adult. Well, Luther shouldn't say never. It's hard to say what the man had been doing over the past fifteen years. But presumably most of that had been under the radar, people who wouldn't be missed. The children had attracted attention. So did taking Iris. Was he trying to get attention?

"Why would he take your mother?" Luther asked. When Virgil didn't respond, Luther took a chance on provoking him. "You pass on some kind of mommy issues?"

Virgil slowly turned, and Luther told himself it was like facing down a big dog—never let him see your fear.

Virgil said, "He did it to punish us."

Us. Meaning him and Adam? But why? Luther still didn't understand.

"I agree that's Danny's ultimate goal," Adam said, "but the punishment is more satisfying if we know what he's doing, and if he can see us knowing. He wants us—at least one of us—to find him. So whether we can or not, he thinks we can. You said you can't track Danny, but can we get through to Iris?"

"No," Virgil said. "Not with her shields. Dad was always trying to get through, to understand what she was doing, because she sure as hell didn't know, but I imagine that just made her walls stronger."

It took Luther a moment to connect "dad" with Lawrence Rutledge. He hadn't known the man, but he'd heard enough stories to not regret the omission.

"He didn't even have any theories?" Adam asked.

Virgil shrugged. "She does it naturally, unconsciously. That made him think maybe something happened when she was very young that triggered her to shield. Then someone forced her to cover up what she'd done, push it away and pretend it wasn't part of her. But that was all speculation, and it doesn't help us anyway."

Adam rubbed his wall-striking knuckles absently. "So if we can't get to her, what do we do now? Look for Danny directly, or for Teddy because he might know something we don't?"

Virgil shook his head. "Like I said, Teddy doesn't have the stomach for this."

"Then Danny it is," Adam said.

Whatever issues Adam had with his father, he seemed to have buried them, at least long enough to recover his grandmother. Luther hoped. He wasn't used to being the coolest head in the room.

Luther's phone rang—*Grant*. Could any good come of talking to the Sheriff right now? Best case scenario, he'd ask Luther to return and help them find Iris. Which is what he hoped to do here with Adam and Virgil. Except here, his options weren't limited by being a deputy. Worst case scenario... well, it didn't really matter since the Best Case didn't compel him to answer. He pressed a button and sent the call to voicemail.

Luther waited, but Grant didn't leave a message.

He wasn't the only one waiting. Adam watched Luther, but he shook his head and tucked his cell phone back in his pocket.

"We've been on the road a lot," Adam said. "Even if we weren't dead on our feet, we don't know where to go next. We need a few hours of sleep before we try to figure out our next move."

Luther glanced over at the side of Virgil's head. Virgil was ignoring him, or maybe he was avoiding looking at his son. "You really think you can sleep in the same room with him?"

"Good point. We'll take turns sleeping," Adam said. "If Virgil tries to run away, shoot him."

Luther didn't think Adam was joking, and he didn't find

permission to shoot Virgil very reassuring. After all, Virgil running away wasn't what threatened to keep Luther awake.

LUTHER MUST HAVE BEEN MORE EXHAUSTED than he'd realized, because he managed an hour or so of sleep before Adam woke him for his shift. He felt better now, though he could use a cup of coffee and his stomach was devouring itself. He was supposed to wake Adam in a few minutes, but he might let him sleep a little longer. He knew Adam needed the rest, and yet his sleep didn't look all that restful, fists clenched next to him on the bed, one swollen from hitting the wall. His head jerked in micro-movements and he murmured occasionally. Nothing Luther could make sense of, just sounds at the bottom edge of his hearing.

Virgil didn't look much better. The man had dozed off sitting in one of the chairs, easily enough that Luther suspected he was an old hand at it. He hadn't moved a muscle for hours, but he was also beginning to stir. Luther glanced from one man to the other. They had similar heights and builds, but awake, he wouldn't have assumed they were related. In sleep, with their expressions unguarded, the comparable shape of their faces was apparent, especially the echo of their distinctive cleft and dimple chins. What else did they share? What that you couldn't see on the surface? For Adam's sake, Luther hoped it wasn't the crazy gene.

At the moment, it looked like they were sharing the same nightmare.

Virgil shuddered, and Adam's movements on the bed became more dramatic. Could they be... *seeing something? Together?* Luther had no idea how that would work. He leaned toward the older man, and Virgil's eyes suddenly flew open. Luther bolted upright, toppling his chair as he backed away from Virgil. But Virgil wasn't awake; his spooky eyes were open, but unseeing. Meanwhile, Adam's head and arms thrashed from side to side.

Luther's knees trembled as he inched toward the men. "This is entirely too fucking weird."

33

Adam was in that place again, the place he'd never wanted to return to, but somehow he'd gotten sucked back in. And he didn't know how to get out.

It was dark, but he assumed that was a matter of acclimating. *Patience.* Or maybe it's because he wasn't attached to anyone, *inside* anyone.

No, that wasn't it. It was dark because *someone was making it dark*, like throwing a hood over a falcon.

Once Adam realized that, the all-enveloping blackness disappeared, like shedding the hood. It was night, and he was outside, so it was still dark. But there was enough residual light—from the moon? the surrounding buildings?—to watch two men stumble into an alley, their breath clouding as they laughed and bumped shoulders. They continued past a dumpster, then huddled close to one wall. As they moved, so did Adam, as if tethered to them but free-floating.

"Goddamn, if it ain't cold as shit out here!" said a voice that was becoming familiar. Danny wore a trucker hat and a denim jacket with a sheepskin collar that stood out in the dim light.

"I can't feel a thing," said the other man in a vague, singsong voice. An inch or two shorter, he also wore a denim jacket, but no hat.

"You sure about that?" Danny asked. "Bringing me out here like this, you better make it worth my while."

"Why, Mr.—" the smaller man said, grabbing Danny's collar. "What did you say your name was again?"

"Mister'll be just fine," Danny said.

Danny quickly spun them around. The other man still clutched Danny's collar, but now found his back was against the brick wall. His head wobbled a moment before he recovered. He slowly pulled Danny toward him, until the warm vapor of their breathing mixed. Danny's hand came to rest on the man's shoulder, then slid up to the side of his throat. The man giggled and gave a small shudder.

"You are cold," he said. "I thought you said you were a businessman—cash only—but I'm willing to trade for more of what you got there in your pocket…"

Adam felt himself getting drawn closer. He couldn't see it, but he could feel Danny's smile in the dark.

"I appreciate the offer, Adam," he began.

"My name's not Adam," the man said, voice flattening, as though some primal instinct was desperately fighting to get through the intoxicants in his system.

But it was too late.

"I do appreciate it," Danny continued, "but I had something else in mind."

Danny squeezed the man's throat one-handed, pressing him against the wall. His other hand rose and covered the man's mouth and nose. The man clawed ineffectually at Danny's arms.

No. Adam advanced on Danny, but something blocked him. A veil of darkness—the hood—threatened again, and Adam shook himself free. As he did, the choked man finally broke through his own paralysis, kicking frantically. Danny grunted and slammed the man's head against the wall. His knees buckled, but before he could crumple, Danny seized him by the shoulders, then pinned him against the building with a forearm.

Adam had to stop Danny. He smashed against the barrier between them, but found himself sliding toward the struggling man instead. The victim's mind sucked at Adam's like a gravitational field, just as his lungs gasped desperately for air. Fluttering, feathered tendrils thrust into Adam's skull. His stomach lurched as though he were falling from a second-story roof, and then Adam landed inside someone else. He felt Danny's forearm against his chest, bruising bone on bone. Adam tried to move his arms, to fight back, but they were dead to him. The body had nothing left to respond.

Danny leaned in, chin almost resting on his shoulder, and whispered in his ear, "It's okay."

Adam was suddenly aware of Virgil next to him as Danny jerked his arm back. The dying man's mind clung feebly to Adam, and Adam wasn't sure which of them screamed when Virgil ripped Adam free. He and Virgil lingered in the alley, and Adam saw that Danny now held a knife. He watched, helpless, as Danny's arm flashed forward and up, the blade entering the man's midsection.

"Shh," Danny whispered, twisting the knife in the groaning man's guts. Unable to hold his victim upright anymore, Danny dropped with him, kneeling and still clutching the knife. The man gurgled, and Danny's free hand went to his temple, stroking the dark hair there. "Shh... It's okay, Adam. Just let go."

... JUST LET GO, Adam.

He could feel hands on him, Danny's hands, and Danny was going to kill him again. Over and over. Adam struck out blindly, and the hands seized his arms. Adam scuttled backward, stopping only when his back hit the wall. But it wasn't a brick wall in an alley. He flailed desperately, even as he realized, *those aren't Danny's hands*. Adam's vision went from black to gray, then added a pinhole of brightness in the center.

"Adam! It's okay," a man said.

It's okay.

Adam swung wildly at the voice, fist going wide and catching nothing but air. His effort knocked him off-balance, and he fell forward (*I'm on a bed*). Landing on his face, Adam twisted, thrust a knee into someone and heard a satisfying grunt, followed by, "Goddammit!"

"Just back off," another man said. *Virgil.* It was Virgil. "Give him a chance to get his bearings."

Adam rolled onto his knees, curled into a ball, and waited for the pinhole of light to spread. As it did, a wall of sickness slammed into him. Through him. He scrambled to the edge of the bed on instinct, and by the time he hit the floor, his vision had cleared enough to make out the entrance to the bathroom. He barely made it to the toilet in time, retching before he could even lift the seat.

His lungs felt ready to burst, but Adam held his breath, afraid of inhaling the next round of vomit. Holding his breath made it somehow hard to distinguish words, but he recognized Luther's voice and his stout legs standing next to him. Or maybe his head made it hard to hear—*my God, my head hurts*. Adam feared the force of heaving would kill him, squeeze his skull into oblivion.

He lifted his head, far enough to see past Luther to where Virgil stood.

"Adam, man, are you okay?" Luther asked.

Adam ignored him. "Was that happening now?"

"What?" Luther asked. "Was what happening now?"

"I think so," Virgil said.

This time, the vomit burst from Adam so forcefully and so unexpectedly, it hit the seat. At least, it would have done, if there'd been enough substance to do so. Stomach acid burned Adam's throat, and his airway threatened to lock in protest.

Luther stepped over Adam's legs, and a moment later handed him a cool, wet cloth. "What the hell is going on here?" Luther asked, stepping back over Adam toward his father.

"He killed Adam," Virgil said.

Luther's mouth dropped open as he looked back at Adam. "What the hell's that supposed to mean?"

"That's what he does," Virgil said. "He kills Adam over and over."

Luther rubbed a hand over his face and paced back and forth alongside the bed. "You mean, Danny..." But his voice trailed off and he sat on the mattress.

Adam clutched the washcloth and felt the heat of his forehead through the scratchy fabric. Virgil kneeled next to him at the bathroom threshold.

"I'm sorry," he said. "I tried to keep you out."

The dark veil. The barrier. But Adam shook his head, immediately regretting it. "No. You don't get to apologize."

"I did try—"

"No!" Adam shouted, evoking pained tears with the effort. He swallowed and closed his eyes, but found being unable to see still made him uneasy. "What did you do to him, to make him like that?"

Virgil reached toward him, but let his hand drop to the dirty brown carpet at an angry look from Adam. They both stared down at Virgil's palm, with its deep creases and pale scars. Adam's eyes were drawn to one long, heavy scar that eclipsed the rest as Virgil said simply, "It wasn't me."

34

Ninety minutes later, hundreds of miles away, Danny's hands shook as he entered his own motel room. He slammed the door behind him, then slumped against it. What the hell was he thinking? They'd find the body by morning. Okay, so there was nothing to connect him to the guy, and his motel room was sixty miles away. It was still stupid. Now he'd have to leave. He pulled off his jacket and threw it on the bed. He hadn't seen any blood, but he'd probably have to get a new coat just to be safe. *Fuck.* No, wait—there was blood on the sleeves, but it didn't look wet.

He done it enough times that his cleanup ought to be on autopilot, but he struggled to make himself move, to figure out the next step. *That's okay*, he told himself, *when you're on autopilot is when you screw things up.*

Danny wedged a chair under the door handle, then kicked off his shoes. Would he need new shoes, too? *What a cluster fuck.* He headed for the bathroom. He'd strip in the shower, and—

"Jesus Christ!" Danny staggered backwards, falling onto his ass. There was a woman in his bathroom.

She lifted her white head to look at him. At least she wasn't dead. And then he recognized her. Iris Rutledge... *What the hell is Iris Rutledge doing here?* He clutched his head with shaking hands.

I'm losing it. I'm fucking losing it. How can I not remember something like this?

Deep breath. Stay calm.

Concussion. He hadn't been right since he'd killed the old man and fought Adam in the river. Probably hit his head on one of those rocks harder than he thought. Concussions did all kinds of crazy things to your brain.

Okay, so he wasn't crazy. He just had to be wary about the head injury. Obviously he had taken Iris—she lay bound on his bathroom floor. The question was why. She was never the most affectionate person, but she'd treated Danny well and he had nothing against her. But she was Virgil's mother, Adam's grandmother. Adam had it coming, and Virgil... Virgil had betrayed him, chosen his first son over Danny. So what better way to get to them than through her?

Then he started to remember. Sitting in Iris's kitchen, blood on his sleeves (*what had he done before that?*), Iris throwing the coffee... Danny felt heat along the edge of his jaw from a mild burn. Then that asshole with the gun. An obvious throwaway, Danny had kept it afterwards.

Danny got to his feet and returned to the bathroom. Iris flinched as he flipped on the light. He had no idea how long she'd been there, but she'd wet herself, so it must have been a good long time. That meant she'd be numb and aching—not to mention elderly—and so long as he wasn't stupid, she shouldn't be capable of putting up much of a fight.

He went to his bag and got a pair of sweats and some scissors. He wasn't sure he trusted himself with a knife. Back in the tiny bathroom, he stood over Iris.

"I'm going to cut you loose. Then I'll pull the door closed—but not all the way—and you'll have exactly two minutes to get cleaned up and put on the sweats. At two minutes and one second, I'm opening the door. Got it?"

She nodded, and he cut through the duct tape that circled her ankles and wrists. "And when you get that tape off your mouth, don't even think about screaming for help. Even if someone hears you, they won't give a shit. They'll just think your John is giving you a little more than you bargained for. And I'll kill you. Except not right away."

One big step backwards took him out of the bathroom, and he pulled the door shut, leaving a crack. "The clock starts now," he said.

His hand hovered by the doorknob and his ear by the door. There was no way for her to escape, and no weapon short of breaking the bathroom mirror, but he wasn't about to underestimate the woman. Within seconds, he heard the low sounds of suppressed groans. He heard her pants fall to the floor, and a moment after that running water. The water stopped around the two-minute mark, and he gave her an extra fifteen seconds to get into his sweats. "I'm opening the door," he said.

Iris stood, hands on the sink, staring at her reflection. Glancing at him, she pointed at the tape over her mouth. Her eyes watered as she slowly peeled it away, then bent over the sink and washed the pink skin around her mouth.

"I don't suppose you have any—" Iris's voice cracked. She swallowed hard, coughed, then drank water from the sink in her cupped hand.

"Aloe vera?" he asked. It was out of his mouth before he was even sure why, before he remembered how she used to keep a plant by the kitchen window and put it on everything. "I don't."

She shook her head. "Toothpaste," she said.

He kept an eye on her while rummaging in the bag on his bed, then handed her the tube. She used her index finger to rub the paste over her teeth, then rinsed her mouth. "That's a little better," she said.

"Good," he said. Again, before he knew he would. He suddenly realized he had to be careful; he had an inexplicable desire to please her, probably a relic of his childhood.

"You're a bit of a mess yourself," Iris said, trying to be casual but not quite pulling it off.

Dammit. He hadn't cleaned up yet. "No one you know," he said. "Get in the bathtub."

She stared at him, as if trying to choose her words strategically. That's when he noticed her posture was lopsided and one hand still rested on the sink, supporting her. Her limbs were probably still recovering their circulation.

"You don't have to sit in it," he said. "You can stand, or you can sit on the edge. But I need you *in the tub.*" He stepped toward her with his last few words, and Iris flinched before she could stop herself.

"Okay," she said, grabbing the towel rack to support herself as she inched painfully toward the tub. She nearly fell stepping into it, but he didn't move to help her. She slowly lowered herself to sit on the edge, knees pointed so she faced the shower walls as much as she faced Danny.

"Stay there," he said. He started by washing his hands, then his face. He wasn't going to be able to take a shower, so he peeled off his cotton shirt and began scrubbing his arms, starting at the wrists and working his way up. When he reached his elbows, he decided he'd gone far enough and moved on to his neck.

"Did Virgil do that?" Iris asked.

She'd been so quiet, he'd almost forgotten she was there.

"The scar," she said.

"I've got a lot of scars," Danny said.

"The one on your side," she said, pointing on herself.

"No," he said, scrubbing at a spot on his neck that may or may not have been blood.

"And the others?" she asked.

He patted himself dry with a hand towel. "Isn't it a little late to care?"

She didn't answer.

He looked down at his jeans. They'd do for now. Whether his pants could tie him to a murder wouldn't matter until he got caught, which he didn't intend on doing. Especially with a kidnapped grandmother in tow.

"Stay," he told Iris, leaving the door open.

Danny removed the plastic liner from the trashcan in the bedroom and shoved his coat and shirt inside, tying a tiny knot in the top. Then he threw on another T-shirt and a hooded sweatshirt. He was going to freeze his ass off, but it couldn't be helped. Finally, he turned to Iris, still sitting on the edge of the tub.

"We're leaving," he said. "If you want to pee, do it now. But don't close the door all the way."

Iris climbed awkwardly out of the shower and pushed the door mostly closed. A few seconds later, he heard her urinate. Then she washed her hands and opened the door again.

"You're not going to be stupid, are you? Because you know what'll happen if you're stupid. Don't you, Iris?" he asked.

"I think I can guess," she said, voice weary.

"And what would that be?"

"You'll harm someone else instead. Someone I care about."

"And there are so many people who fall into that category," he said. "Young people, with their whole lives ahead of them. Unlike you. So I think we have an understanding."

Danny zipped up the main part of his bag and dug into a side pocket to pull out a pair of fuzzy handcuffs suitable for a bachelor party. "Of course, the human will to live, the instinct of self-preservation, can be overpowering. With you wearing these, I think we'll both be able to relax better."

He tossed them to her. Iris missed and had to squat to pick them up. She sat on the mattress and rested one hand on her lap to attach the first cuff. The second was easier.

"I guess we should've put your coat on first," he said, realizing he still wasn't thinking straight. As opposed to when he'd apparently grabbed her coat and scarf after shooting a man, he thought, settling the coat around her shoulders and draping her scarf over her neck before retrieving his own bag.

Danny went to the door and looked outside. There was one other car in the lot, parked in front of a dark room. The manager was at the far end, with no view of their room unless he was standing outside. Which no one would be doing at four a.m. in this temperature.

He turned to Iris. He'd been almost afraid of her as a child, but she seemed so small now. Danny leaned down into her space. "Remember, cross me, and I will cut Adam into little pieces while you watch. Got it?"

She nodded, spine straight but lip trembling.

Of course, he planned to do that anyway.

"Okay. Let's go," Danny said, and led Iris out into the cold.

35

———

I know I'm going to regret this.

JJ stood outside the door to her ex-husband's hospital room. She had some pretty compelling reasons not to enter: 1) it could confuse the issue of the protective order, and 2) being shot wouldn't change the fact that the man was an asshole. Her sole reason for going in: the asshole was Evie's father. And no matter how much of an asshole he was, she would always owe him for that.

She sighed; hopefully he'd be heavily medicated.

Marcus opened his eyes as she entered and gave her a slightly dazed smile. "JJ," he said. "Nice of you to stop by."

"Well, don't get used to it," she said. "Do you need anything?"

"No," he said, raising his hand with its IV. "I got everything I need right here."

"I'll bet you do," JJ said, shaking her head. Against her better judgment, she took the seat next to his bed. "They haven't found Iris yet."

His smile faded. "I'm sorry to hear that. I did everything I could."

"I know. And I appreciate it." She believed him, but she also had to remind herself that she'd believed his bullshit for years before she'd finally wised up.

Marcus reached for her hand and she didn't pull away, ostensibly to avoid tangling his lines. *Yeah, right.*

"You know it's not too late for us," he said.

And that's when she pulled her hand away. "You do know we're divorced, right?"

"That's just a piece of paper."

True, and JJ knew how much respect he had for pieces of paper. That's why instead of arguing, she got straight to the point. "Marcus, doing the right thing once doesn't magically change who you are."

He turned his head away, and it was everything she could do to resist pushing his hair back from his bruised face. She wondered if she'd been too harsh with the father of her child. After all, he had been shot. "That's not to say you can't change," she added. "You can, every day with every choice."

"Really, JJ? Because I don't think my choices have a whole helluva lot to do with where we ended up," he snapped.

"Or you can stay a dick," she muttered, shaking her head. But he wasn't finished.

"You know, you've put Evie in a lot of danger," he said.

"And how the hell do you think I did that?" she demanded.

"I don't know yet. But I'll bet we could find out in court. How you've managed to get her connected to all these kidnappings, and get me shot."

"You're fucking crazy," JJ said. She took a deep breath. He was baiting her. One of his favorite pastimes. Instead of reacting, she thought critically about what he'd said, and what had happened over the past twenty-four hours. "Where did the gun come from?"

"What do you mean?" Marcus asked, confused and wary, perhaps finally realizing being doped to the gills in a hospital room wasn't the best time and place to challenge his ex-wife.

JJ should have followed this train of thought before, but she'd been focused on the girls. (Girls he hadn't even asked about, she noted, except as a bargaining chip.) "Why did you take a gun to Iris's house? Are you even supposed to have a gun?"

She stopped. There was no good reason (being pissed off was a poor reason for doing most things) to highlight the holes in the man's story and help him write a new one. She left without another word, ignoring whatever nonsense Marcus spouted at her back.

JJ nearly ran into Grant in the hallway and burst out, "How my daughter can have half that dumbass's genes is beyond me."

A smile flashed across his face. Then he must have remembered this wasn't the time for smiling. Or possibly that they were supposed to be mad at each other, although they'd both behaved like adults when she'd given her statement the night before.

"How are the girls doing?" he asked.

"Surprisingly well," JJ said. "More inseparable than ever. They decided to stay home today. Otto is stuck in here a little longer, so Dorothy is watching them."

"I'll probably drop by later to speak with them again. You have any objection as far as Evie goes?"

"Not so long as it's you, and Dorothy is present," JJ said. "Any news on Iris?"

He shook his head. "Just doing some follow-up interviews."

JJ thumbed toward the door. "He's full of shit. I'll bet he had his gun on him when he came back because he was going to threaten Iris, about me or Evie or whatever his scrambled brain had come up with. I told you he was drunk when I found him, didn't I?"

"Yes, you did. And believe it or not, it had occurred to me that he wasn't telling us the entire truth," Grant said, voice twisting with sarcasm. He removed his hat and ran a hand over his head. "Sorry, JJ. I've got a lot of balls in the air right now, and Luther picked a lousy time to run off the rails. He said he took Adam hunting."

JJ snorted with disbelief.

"My thought exactly," Grant said. "I called him so he could get word to Adam about Iris, but Luther didn't answer."

"He knows," JJ said. "I didn't speak with Adam, but I did tell Luther, and Adam was there. Wherever *there* was—Luther wouldn't say."

Grant's mouth pursed, and he looked up at the ceiling. "So once again, he'll talk to you—"

"Don't even start," JJ snapped. "There's enough crazy shit going on already without adding our dysfunction."

Grant nodded, but JJ wasn't sure if he agreed with her or was just acknowledging she'd spoken. He set his hat back on his head and tapped it down. "Take care, JJ."

She shook her head as she watched him walk toward the elevator. *Stupid damn man.*

36

Adam fought to keep his eyes on the road, to not look every time Virgil moved in the passenger seat. But his head kept twitching in Virgil's direction. Adam wanted to understand what had happened with Danny, what Virgil had done to try to keep Adam away from him. But every time he started to think about it, Adam's hands shook so much it became difficult to hold the steering wheel. Driving Luther's vehicle, a veritable tank compared to Adam's hatchback, was challenging enough on an hour or two of fitful sleep. He didn't need to be swerving all over the interstate and waking Luther in the back seat.

His mind jumped haphazardly, from uncomfortable subject to uncomfortable subject, finally settling on the last time he'd seen Danny in the flesh, when they'd nearly killed each other. That night, after riding home to Cold Springs with Grant, Adam had dreamed of his mother's death. Virgil had been present, and together they watched the grieving husband nearly kill his son. But Virgil couldn't do it. What had he said when he'd called Adam at Iris's house? *Not even with him whispering in my ear...*

"Who was whispering in your ear?" Adam asked.

"When?"

"When mom died, in Dead Hollow."

"You know who," Virgil said.

He did know. *Lawrence.* But Adam didn't know why he'd wanted Virgil to say it out loud, any more than he knew why Virgil didn't want to. So he moved on, surprising himself by asking, "Are you ever prescient? Do you ever see things that are going to happen, or might happen?"

"I know what prescient is," Virgil observed.

Adam glanced over, and Virgil briefly met his eyes. Virgil could use a shave (they all could), and he could use a haircut, but for the moment he looked relatively normal. The three men could have been going on Luther's fabled hunting trip.

"Sometimes, I get hints. Especially right before something big happens. But it's nothing like Harlan," he said, a hard edge in his voice at the other man's name. "Same way with seeing things by touch. It happens, but rarely—there's got to be some powerful energy with that person."

Virgil glanced over his shoulder. Luther was still sleeping. "It's hard for me. Even when I see something, I don't always know what's real."

Adam was surprised by his father's admission. And he was curious about when he knew and how he knew something was only in his mind. Was it only in hindsight? Or were there clues, signs something wasn't real that were easy to ignore? But now that his father had started talking, Adam was wary of interrupting him, lest he not begin again.

Virgil rested his head against the seat, and his Adam's apple stuck out of his throat like a chunk of bone. He sighed and said, "Your mom was good at that, helping me figure out what was real. But then, I stopped telling her about things."

"What kind of things?" Adam asked softly.

Virgil shrugged. "I don't remember. But I always told myself I did it to protect her. Now I think maybe I just didn't want her to tell me it wasn't real. Because then, maybe she didn't need to be protected. And if she didn't need to be protected, why would she need me at all?"

Adam glanced at the gas gauge. Luther's tank went through fuel a lot faster than his little car did, and they'd need to stop soon. Preferably where they could get breakfast, too. He hadn't seen any exits for a while, only relentless open fields that hurt his eyes with their glare, broken by the occasional hill or pine corridor.

"Tell me about her," Adam said, struggling to keep his voice matter-of-fact rather than pleading.

Virgil smiled, a rare sight Adam was grateful to witness. "She was like Iris in some ways. Strong-willed, hardheaded, someone you did not want to cross. But she was fair, and she wasn't hard like Iris. You know what I mean?"

Adam considered his experience growing up with Iris. She'd loved him unconditionally, but he knew she was capable of completely cutting someone off, seemingly without regret, if that's what she felt she had to do. "Yes," he said, "I think I do."

"Charlotte was good for me, but I think she was also good for Iris. She helped her bend a little, see possibilities..." Virgil's voice trailed off, and he began picking at his thumb. "When Charlotte died, I ran away. No doubt about that. But Iris, in her own way, she retreated as much as I did. Became hard again."

Adam felt Virgil's eyes on him as his father continued, "Me, I'm like Iris. But you, I think you took more after your mother empathy-wise. So maybe you softened Iris a little, too."

"Why do you think Danny took her?" Adam asked.

"I told you. To punish us."

"Do you think..." Adam paused, unsure if he wanted the answer. But he cleared his throat and continued. "Do you think he'll kill her?"

"Probably," Virgil said, then added cryptically, "It depends on who he is."

A groaning sound, barely recognizable as human, emanated from the back seat as Luther stirred and pulled himself upright. "Where are we?" he asked.

Never quite sure how to answer that question on an interstate, Adam didn't bother.

Luther leaned between the seats as a big green exit sign came into view. "That looks promising," he said. About half a minute later, the smaller signs advertising gas stations and restaurants came into view. "Hot damn—Waffle House. Let's get off here."

Adam took the exit and pulled into the first gas station between them and the beckoning yellow sign. His stomach growled. Not even the nasty, lingering scent of old barbecued chicken could curb his appetite. He drew alongside the pumps, careful of the SUV's large bulk. Adam killed the engine and released his seat belt, ready to jump out, but Luther beat him to it.

"I got it," Luther said. "Just pop that thing there left of the steering wheel."

There was a clicking sound as Adam pulled the lever. He wondered if Luther was being paid while he was suspended. He felt a little guilty, but he didn't argue since he was getting pretty cash poor himself. Adam decided he'd pay for breakfast instead. He glanced over at Virgil, who'd been quiet since Luther woke. The man was still fidgeting with his thumb.

"You okay over there?" Adam asked.

Virgil didn't respond, but he wasn't shaking or screaming, so Adam assumed the answer was yes.

The vehicle shifted slightly when Luther climbed back inside, and Adam glanced at him in the rearview mirror. Luther nodded, and Adam started the car, waiting for the various bings and bongs to quiet before moving. The Waffle House was a couple hundred yards ahead, and traffic was light. Adam made an easy right turn onto the highway. As he did, a smear of red caught his eye.

Fresh blood. On Virgil's thumb.

Adam pulled one of the last tissues from Luther's pack and held it out to Virgil. "Here. You might want to wipe that off before we go in the restaurant."

Luther could understand Adam not wanting to sit next to his father. He wouldn't want to sit next to the crazy bastard either. But goddamn, he could use some elbow room. Restaurant booths were not made to accommodate more than two adult males. He shoveled down his remaining eggs and cheesy hash browns, dabbed his face with a napkin, and said, "Excuse me."

Adam moved, and Luther slid awkwardly down the length of the brown leather bench, banging his leg as he stood. "I'll be back. Don't let her take my coffee cup."

Luther stepped outside. The building's funky, bottom-flaring shape provided no cover whatsoever, and there was no landscaping, either. Luther headed toward his SUV, then remembered Adam still had his keys. At least standing next to it would block the wind. He called Beth direct, before he remembered he wasn't supposed to.

She answered after a single ring. "Luther, where the hell are you?" she asked.

"Getting breakfast," he said. "What did Grant want last night?"

"Well, I reckon he thought we could use some help with Iris," she said. "Obviously he was wrong, since you didn't even bother calling back."

"Y'all got anything yet?"

"What do you think?" she snapped. She was silent for a moment, then asked, "Luther, what are you really up to out there?"

"You sure you want to know?" he said. She didn't answer. "That's what I thought. Listen, I'm sorry about what I said yesterday. I'd never try to get you in trouble."

"Then you shouldn't have said it."

Luther rested his shoulder against his car, cupping his ear to hear her over the wind. "You're right. But it was reflex. I'm not used to people actually helping me."

"Ha! That's the most ass backwards, woe-is-me thank you I've ever received," Beth said.

"It's a gift," Luther acknowledged, then barreled on. "Did Danny Carpenter take Iris?"

"You know I can't discuss—"

"Beth," he cut in, "I can help."

He waited, long enough to double-check that his car doors were locked. Finally, Beth said, "Iris hid the girls, so they never saw him, but Rachel Nicholson swears it's the man who took her."

They had assumed as much, from the time JJ had given him the news. Danny taking Iris made no sense, and yet it made the only sense. What the hell was the man's endgame?

"Okay. Thanks, Beth." He sighed, about to crush his chances for more coffee. "You know those names you ran for me?"

"Yes..." she said. He could feel her making the intuitive leap as she dragged out the single syllable.

"Those are known associates of Danny Carpenter. Well, not Danny exactly, but Mitch... whatever the hell his alias was," Luther said.

"Where'd you get that information?" she asked.

"An anonymous tip," he said. Grant would realize immediately that it had come from Rudy. "And between you and me, we didn't get anything from the strip club in Woodbridge. Maybe you'll have better luck."

"Luther!" Beth said, her voice like a whispering yell. "What the hell do you think you're playing at? You're already suspended. Are you hoping to get fired, too?"

"No, Beth. I'm hoping to help save a woman's life." He kept the part about *maybe killing a sonuvabitch while I'm at it* to himself. "If I get anything else, I'll be in touch."

He hung up before she could tell him what he already knew, that he was being an idiot. What he'd pay money to know instead was whether he was being the right kind of idiot, and for the right reasons.

Luther went inside and found Adam and Virgil still in the booth. Adam looked up and said, "I got the check."

"Thanks," Luther said, holding out a hand for his keys. "Let's go then. We need to be scooting."

Luther crossed the brisk parking lot and made a beeline for the driver's side. Virgil got in the back seat, leaving Adam shotgun.

"What's going on?" Adam asked.

"The Sheriff doesn't have shit on Iris yet, so I gave them the names," Luther said, cold hands fumbling with the key in the ignition.

Virgil gripped Luther's shoulder from behind, rigid fingers like an overtightened C-clamp. "What if they find him before we do?"

Luther jerked himself free and twisted in his seat to face the man. "Then they'll find Iris, hopefully safe and sound. Listen, I want this motherfucker as much as you do, but I won't risk Iris's life to get him. I wouldn't think you would, either."

Virgil shook his head back and forth quickly, like an animal trying to rid itself of parasites. "You don't understand."

Luther let out an exasperated sound. "You're right, I don't." He bit his tongue to prevent him saying more while he drove across the parking lot and signaled, heading back toward the interstate.

"Besides," Luther continued, as though they'd been having a civilized conversation, "we're only twenty minutes from the second guy. The Sheriff won't beat us there from another state."

WITH THE LAST few miles on a rutted, semi-paved road, their destination ended up being more like thirty minutes than twenty. But Luther was right—they were way ahead of any investigators. And it didn't matter anyway. The guy was a dead end.

Luther had told Adam and Virgil to stay in the car so he'd feel comfortable availing himself of all the tools at his disposal, including some he'd never have used as a deputy. For instance, he might tell an untruth from time to time, but he didn't offer bribes while interrogating witnesses at the Sheriff's Department. And he didn't wear his sidearm. But Luther hadn't bothered getting stupid this time; he believed the guy when he said he hadn't heard from "Mitch" in months. They stood on the man's porch, freezing their asses off, which was fine with Luther. If the rest of the dilapidated house matched the leaning roof, he'd rather be within jumping distance of getting clear. Heavy clouds hung in the overcast sky, and Lord help the tenants if they brought snow.

Danny's former associate stood with his gray camouflage hat pulled low and hands shoved deep in his pockets, rocking slightly to cover the shakes. His skin was bad, starting to show sores. Luther couldn't smell anything, but he wondered if they cooked meth inside.

"I heard maybe Mitch got hisself in some trouble, over in

West Virginia or Kentucky somewhere. Can't say for sure, though. Past few months, we sorta... shifted our revenue streams, if you know what I mean. Mitch is more of a pharmaceuticals man."

Which is the reason Luther had given for wanting to see him. "A'right," Luther nodded and backed down the porch. A cool mist had begun to precipitate from the sky.

"You sure I can't interest you in something else?" the man said. "It's a helluva lot cheaper, and no supply side worries. Know what I mean?"

The longer he spoke, the faster his words tumbled free, but Luther still found it unlikely anyone was ever in doubt of the numbnut's meaning.

"No, thanks. I'll stick with what I know."

Luther was about to step on solid ground when his vehicle's back door flew open and Virgil rolled out, heading toward them fast enough that Luther hoped the tweaker behind him didn't pull a gun. When he didn't, Luther decided he was used to crazies.

"What about her?" Virgil demanded, pointing at one of the windows in the front where a young woman's face was pressed against the glass. Virgil pulled a few bills from his back pocket and held them in the air. "I got fifty bucks if either one of y'all can tell me something to help find him."

Virgil pointed at the woman again and crooked a finger. She backed out of view, but to Luther's surprise appeared in the doorway a few moments later, staring through a door with a tattered screen, as though it still posed a barrier to the cold or anything else.

"Aw, hell, she don't know nothing," the man said.

Virgil walked up the steps, past Luther and the man of the house as if they didn't exist. "You've seen him, haven't you? You see everything. You know Mitch. Dark hair, kinda intense. When he looks at you, you know it. Soulful, some people'd say." Virgil's mouth curled as he raised an eyebrow. "He ain't hard on the eyes, is he, sweetheart?"

She smiled a secret smile, shoving the ends of her pale hair in her mouth and dropping her gaze to her dirty, socked feet toeing the floor. Her skinny legs were bare, with a faded bruise visible on one thigh. She wore a stained, pale blue T-shirt with a cartoon character over what appeared to be men's boxer shorts, and was somewhere between twelve and twenty. *Dear God, please be at least eighteen*, Luther thought, while he wondered how she wasn't shivering in the cold.

And also wondered who this coherent man was inhabiting Virgil's body.

"I said, she don't know nothing," Danny's associate crabbed, with a little heat this time.

Virgil continued to ignore him, and Adam apparently decided that was his cue to leave the vehicle as well. *Great, the whole goddamn Rutledge clan.*

Luther shook his head, and Adam stopped, leaning against the bumper. Luther hoped tweakers didn't start pouring from the house. A beater pickup was the only other vehicle in the driveway, but that didn't necessarily mean anything. He'd seen people piled in like tweaker clown cars at Rudy's.

The man's nasty face was flushing even deeper, so Luther held his hands high, palms flat. "Easy, friend."

"I ain't your fucking friend, and I sure as hell ain't his," the man said, nodding toward Virgil. "Who the hell's he think he is?"

Depends on the day, Luther was tempted to say, but kept to himself.

Virgil still turned a deaf ear to the man he'd pissed off, but seemed to have captivated the young woman.

"Is Mitch your boy? He looks like you," the girl said, in a soft, slightly vacant voice that made Luther uneasy. Virgil stood a few feet away, but she reached through a gap in the screen toward his eyes, fingers tickling the air as though she was touching them. Then she looked past Virgil at Adam. "So does he."

"You ever see anybody else with Mitch?" Virgil asked. One hand crept behind his back, tucking the cash in his pocket. His hand remained there, the fingers digging into each other his only outward sign of stress. "Or did he ever have somebody else in his car, like we did tonight?"

The tweaker's hands also left his pockets and balled into fists at his side as he told Virgil, "It's time for you to get off my fucking porch."

"That big black guy," the girl said.

The man's eyes swung toward her, until Virgil's hand tugged the cash free from his pocket again and held it high.

"Which one?" the man asked. "Nicky? With the dreadlocks?" He gestured at his shoulders with his hands.

"No, the tall one," she said, gesturing herself with one hand on her tiptoes. "With super short hair. And the..." She pointed at her chin and cheek, then twisted her finger.

"The dimple?" Virgil asked, then pointed at Adam. "Like him?"

Adam stepped forward to accommodate them.

"Yes! The dimple," she said, smiling wide enough that if she'd had any, hers would be in evidence. She pointed at Virgil's chin, but it edged more toward cleft than discrete dimple.

"That's, uh..." The man tapped a finger against his forehead and Luther imagined he could hear it ring. "Rashid! That's who that is."

He grabbed for Virgil's cash, but Virgil held it out of range.

"We're gonna need more than a first name," Luther said, hoping to move things along before all hell broke loose.

"That's all I got!" the man protested. "Like she said, he's a big guy. Maybe six-four? He, uh, he's mostly muscle for uh, you know, those guys with Detroit connections."

"Who else does he hang with?" Luther asked.

"Nobody," the man said. "He is one stone cold motherfucker. If he's with somebody, it's 'cause he's working with them, and even then it ain't for long."

Luther glanced up at the girl, but she seemed tapped out at one epiphany. "A'right," he said. "I guess that's it. Let's go, buddy."

They hadn't gotten much, but Virgil offered the cash to the girl anyway.

"Hey!" the man protested, before she could take it.

Virgil swung around, and whatever the man saw on Virgil's face made him back up so quickly he nearly fell. "Okay, okay," he said.

The girl didn't seem frightened at all, of Virgil towering over her or the tweaker on the porch, but Luther wasn't sure she had the capacity for fear. Virgil handed her the money and muttered something as his hand lingered on hers. Luther couldn't tell if she responded, but a moment later Virgil was brushing past him on his way back to the vehicle.

Adam and Virgil were already in their seats by the time Luther got behind the wheel. Luther wasted no time pointing them in the direction of the main highway, noting as he did that the front door of the house was closed and the girl wasn't watching from the window. The SUV lurched over a culvert at the end of the driveway, and he resisted looking back again. He wondered if she'd be okay.

"She's fourteen," Virgil said.

"What? Jesus." Although Luther had lapsed into thinking of her as a "girl," he'd hoped that was just sexist habit. He couldn't be sure, with his head turned away, but Adam didn't seem surprised. Luther glanced at Virgil in the rearview mirror. "How do you know?"

Virgil didn't answer, except to say, "I offered, but she didn't want to come with us."

The mist had become real rain, and any other time Luther would have been venting about the shitty wiper blades he still hadn't replaced. Instead, the whole way back to the main road, Luther racked his brain, trying to think of someone he knew in Virginia law enforcement that could check in on the girl. Hell, he wasn't even sure what county they were in now.

He pulled over at the first convenience store. He needed coffee. He left the engine and heat on and called Beth. No answer. And neither Rutledge had spoken yet.

What the hell was he thinking? How was he supposed to find Danny or Iris or this Rashid guy or anyone else? He had no intel, no tech support, nothing but his mouth and a tank of gas, and neither of those would get him far.

His cell phone rang, still in his hand. Beth.

"What do you got?" she asked, right to the point.

"Not a goddamn thing," he said. "You?"

"Not much more. Couple of sightings that didn't pan out. I assume the other name was a bust."

Luther almost smiled. They'd gone from barely speaking to her knowing him far too well over the past month. "Close to it," he said. "Hasn't seen Danny for months because he's too busy cooking crank. The only other associate he could give us was a 'Rashid,' last name unknown. Big, black guy, he said maybe six-four, and tied in with the folks out of Detroit."

"Makes sense," Beth said. "If prescription drugs are Carpenter's bread-and-butter, that's where most of them are coming from."

"Along with heroin and just about everything else but meth and pot," Luther agreed. Those tended to be sourced locally or from Mexico. "I got the impression Rashid isn't based here, but I don't think he's in transport, either. But that's me pulling shit out of my ass."

"Are you fishing for an ass compliment?" Beth asked. "Because you're not going to get one from me."

This time, Luther did smile. "Thanks, Beth."

"Always happy to be your reality check," she said. She

dropped the forced light tone as she continued, "You know, Luther, it's time to come in."

"Soon," he said. And he was thinking about it. "Listen, when they hit this place, there's a girl they need to run through the system. I don't know what all she's on, but if she's not underage I'll eat the Sheriff's hat. And odds are good the tweaker motherfucker running the place has been selling her."

"Shit," Beth said. "You telling me this as a mandated reporter, or an anonymous source?"

"I'm telling you as whatever the hell it takes to get her out of there," he said.

Then maybe it wasn't for nothing after all, Luther told himself as he hung up. The Rutledges, still quiet, were both watching him. It was a little spooky, like some kind of sci-fi movie where he was the only one who didn't know what was going on, the only one who couldn't hear the voices. He took a deep breath, shaking off his exhaustion-born paranoia.

"I'm sorry, Adam," Luther said. "This isn't working. We hit a dead end my way, and we're no closer to finding Carpenter or Iris. I think it's time for me to go back to Beecham County and beg the Sheriff's forgiveness. And Virgil... hell, I don't know what to do about you. I guess drop you off somewhere. I won't take you in, but—"

Virgil gently, almost tentatively, put his hand on Luther's arm. "It's okay, Luther. We'll find them. The three of us together."

Luther nearly touched Virgil's hand, but stopped, unsure why. Instead he simply asked, "Really, Virgil? How's that?"

"He has a plan," Adam said.

But from the expression on his face, Luther didn't think Adam was happy about it.

38

____

"You really think this is going to work?" Iris asked.

She'd been quiet for hours, though not sleeping, at least not since daylight. Danny checked periodically, not that he expected her to leap from the moving car while handcuffed.

"What?" he asked.

"Whatever this is," Iris said.

He didn't answer, but he'd certainly been thinking about it. He wasn't sure what Iris's role would be, but he knew he needed her alive for now, that she would be a crucial element in the resolution. Beyond that, he no longer felt stressed trying to figure it out. He trusted the process.

They were headed to a safe house, a place he'd used before. He didn't feel comfortable leaving her there alone, but soon he wouldn't have to. He hoped. Not for the first time, Danny reflected that there were a lot of moving parts in what lay ahead.

"Can they track you?" Danny asked.

Iris stared at him, her face almost as gray as the overcast November sky. "Who? The police?"

Danny focused on the highway. The turn had to be close

—*there*. He swung right, hitting the unpaved surface a little too fast, the front bumper scraping as it bounced off the incline.

"Sorry," he said.

The land around them was heavily forested, but brush, now mostly brown and curling, grew to the edges of the road. He continued until he arrived at a wide spot and pulled over, leaving the engine running. They had plenty of gas. He'd stashed a can in the back when he filled up a few hours ago before returning to the motel, along with a bag of convenience store provisions. Danny leaned over the seat for the paper sack. He hadn't recalled his passenger at the time, but he tended to load up on the road so he didn't have to stop as often.

He unscrewed the cap of a water bottle before handing it to Iris. She lifted it awkwardly with her cuffed hands to drink.

"It'll be another hour before we stop, and I'm afraid if you need a bathroom before then, you'll be peeing your pants again," he said. "Well, my pants this time."

Iris took another small sip of water, swished it around her mouth, and handed the bottle back to him.

"Wise choice," Danny said, then peeled the wrapper from the end of a granola bar and passed that to her. Once Iris started chewing, he drank from another water bottle and opened a bar for himself.

"Not the cops," he said.

Iris looked at him, confused. She had a small smear of chocolate on the corner of her mouth. He didn't bother pointing it out.

"Can Virgil and Adam track you?" he finally clarified.

Her brows wrinkled, whether at the overwhelming sugar in the granola bar or the idea he'd presented, Danny wasn't sure.

"I wasn't aware I'd given birth to a bloodhound," Iris said.

Danny laughed. "A litter of Rutledges. Now that's a frightening thought. No, Iris, if only it were that simple. You know what I'm asking, darling." She went rigid but didn't flinch as he reached toward her, tapping her temple with his index finger. "Can your boys get *in here* to figure out where you are?"

She tilted her head away and gave it a slight shake when he stopped poking her, but it wasn't a timid retreat. Instead, she glared, creases deepening around scornful eyes as she replied, "So you believe in that hocus-pocus garbage, too. I guess I shouldn't be surprised, since Virgil raised you."

He found himself laughing again. My God, the woman had balls. More than most men he'd met. Finishing the last bite of his granola bar, Danny crumpled the wrapper and tossed it in the paper sack, then carefully turned his car around on the tiny lane. Back on the highway, he said, "I used to be like you. I thought he was crazy, too. Well, I mean, he is. Obviously. No news flash for you there—he's your son. But the hocus-pocus garbage? I believe him now. You do, too. You just don't want to admit it. Why is that?"

He tapped a finger against the steering wheel, eyes on the rearview mirror and a vehicle behind them that was accelerating to pass. He heard himself say, "Your people didn't go for such notions, did they? Spooky powers, I mean. They were too fire and brimstone." He glanced over at her and caught her with her lips slightly parted, face uncertain. "You did something and they said you were going to hell, didn't they? I'll bet they even beat you for it."

She turned away without answering, and Danny set aside his pop psychology speculation. (*Was that all it was? Because it had felt a lot more certain than that.*) He returned to the problem at hand. Honestly, he couldn't decide if he wanted the Rutledges to find Iris or not, but he was pretty sure they would. One way or another.

Iris continued staring out the window at the world passing by. Danny saw lifeless gray trees, a shuttered shack that once housed a fishing supply store, a skunk carcass along the side of the road that had left a bloody smear in its path. In short, he saw a world where everything was dead and dying. But what did Iris see? He'd known her to be a tough, no-nonsense woman. Tougher than Virgil, although in his defense she was better equipped for it, having lost a child (some would argue two) and endured decades with Lawrence Rutledge. Now she was old, which was yet another reason mortality would come as no surprise to her. But after so many decades of fighting it, would she dig in or give up?

Danny was inclined to think the former, and that his decision to leave her handcuffed was a prudent one. Keeping Iris alive and close fulfilled some need in him, some desire for completion. But if things got too complicated, the cuffs would make her easier to kill.

39

Breath shallow, Adam opened his mouth to compensate as he tried to catch up with his father. He still wasn't sure where they were—some kind of state park—and Virgil had outpaced him from the moment they'd left the vehicle and entered the woods. Luther brought up the rear.

"The last time we went after Danny, you got us in the door. But Teddy's the one who brought me in and held us all together," Virgil called over his shoulder at Adam. "Without Teddy's help, the two of us have to do exactly the same thing, the same way, and at the same time."

Virgil paused in a clear patch, turning in a slow circle as he gazed up at the surrounding canopy. His eyes glittered like ice-flecked clouds beneath the metallic sky. The ground blanketed with pine needles reminded Adam of the house by the river, and of the place where Harlan had introduced him to proper healing techniques. For all the good it had done.

"It's like two people getting through a door with one big battering ram versus two people with—I don't know. Two smaller battering rams," Virgil continued. "They have the same amount of strength either way, but using two rams, their forces are separate, and they might work at cross-purposes."

Virgil's gaze fell from the sky and came to rest on Adam.

"We'll need to concentrate," he said, bony fingers digging into Adam's equally bony clavicle to compel Adam's attention.

Adam felt like he was coming down with something, all clammy and hot and cold at once. It was hard enough to stand, and enduring Virgil's intense stare made it even more difficult. But Adam's eyes grew dry and achy from not blinking; looking away was impossible.

"Sounds to me like a good way to get crushed," Luther said, as short of breath as Adam was.

Virgil's nostrils flared wide as he released Adam.

"Fine, crush a hand, or whatever the hell would happen in your analogy. You're talking about using brute force, when before you made it sound like you had a key," Luther added. "Explain to me what it is you hope to accomplish."

Virgil sat on the ground. Adam joined him, moving more slowly than his father had, and he still nearly fell. He was having trouble judging distances in three dimensions.

"We'll get inside Danny's head and try to come by some clue to where he is now," Adam answered, since Virgil held his tongue. "The way we did with the boy."

Adam couldn't remember the boy's name. How could he not remember that? The child had nearly died, and it was just a few weeks ago. Two weeks, maybe? He wasn't sure about that either.

"Are you ready?" Virgil asked.

Was Adam ready? *No.* But did he have a choice? *Also no.* Finger in its chain, he gently slid his mother's key free from his shirt.

Virgil's breath hissed. "You still have it."

"Of course I do," Adam said. It was almost all he had of his mother, and he always wore it. "Harlan said it's a good focus."

Virgil's gaze narrowed, with a paranoid wariness Adam recognized but had hoped was gone. "Did he try to take it from you?" Virgil asked.

"No! Why would he do that?" Adam demanded, suddenly energized by anxiety. This was why he couldn't trust Virgil; the man's crazy prejudices blinded him. "And Harlan didn't kill Lawrence, either."

"I was there, and I know what I saw," Virgil said.

"I'm telling you, Harlan didn't kill him."

Virgil dropped his head, and Adam thought that was the end of it.

Adam was wrong.

Virgil snarled, and pine needles and dark, moist earth flew through the air as his feet dug deep for traction. He lunged so quickly, Adam couldn't do more than blink before his father's head struck his midsection, slamming Adam onto his back hard enough to knock the air from his lungs. Pain shot through Adam's ribs as they impacted the exposed edge of a root. He struggled to breathe, but couldn't with Virgil atop him.

"Hey!" Luther yelled.

Virgil's face swam into view over Adam's. His features were indistinct as Adam's vision wavered and grayed, but his hair hanging down gave him the semblance of a madman.

"You don't know," Virgil growled, face ruddy with rage.

Adam's already abused muscles seized, and a hollow, stuttering rasp escaped his throat.

Virgil stared down at him, and his face collapsed, along with the bloody temper that had filled it. He climbed off his son, and Adam finally managed a deep, wheezing inhale that raked across his raw windpipe.

"Easy," Virgil said. He laid a hand lightly across Adam's chest and repeated, "Easy."

Adam swatted Virgil's arm away and rolled over on his side, gasping and panting until he felt merely short of breath instead of dying. He extended one hand up his back, but couldn't reach the aching spot where the root had jabbed him. The funk of the decomposing needles and leaves on the ground irritated his throat and lungs even more. He lurched onto all fours, but couldn't make it higher than knees and elbows.

"Adam," Virgil said, "I'm sorry. I was trying to push him out, but he got in my head—"

"Back the fuck off!" Luther said, moving between the two men. "Give Adam some space."

Adam crawled to the nearest tree trunk and tumbled into a seated position, back against the tree. Luther slowly followed, side-stepping to keep watching Virgil, ultimately positioning himself slightly behind Adam so he could see both men.

"Y'alright?" Luther asked.

Adam nodded.

"Anytime you mess up your ribs like you did—well, like Otto and JJ did—you gotta be careful," Luther said. "You'll think you're healed, but they're still just looking for an excuse."

Adam removed his jacket, cringing with the motion, and laid it over his crossed legs. His mind felt the clearest it had all day, so maybe some good had come of the pain. He closed his eyes, trying to calm himself. Instead of the hitch that came with every measured breath, he turned his attention to the pressure of the trunk and the roughness of its bark against his back. He placed his palms against the earth and searched for center.

Iris's face flashed in his mind, angry, the time he'd last seen her. He pushed that image away and chose another. The guileless instant of pleasure he'd seen on her face when she'd set a plate in front of him (deer tenderloin), feeding him his first night back in Cold Springs. He focused on that, rather than his guilt for visiting her so rarely. That's what was important, finding Iris. For now, everything else had to fall away.

And it did.

"Are you ready?" he asked Virgil, without opening his eyes.

"You want to—"

"We're going to find Iris," Adam said. He had no room in his mind, nor time, for anything else.

"Adam, are you sure about this?" Luther asked.

Adam ignored him.

Working with Harlan and Teddy at the house by the river, Adam had contacted Danny through a shared memory from their childhood. Adam wasn't sure how—or even *if*—he'd chosen the swimming hole, but he suspected it had some resonance for Danny at the time. He also suspected it worked to their advantage that Danny hadn't known such interference was possible, and that he was distracted, about to kill Aaron Schofield. (*That was the boy's name.*) They wouldn't be taking Danny by surprise this time, and Adam prayed he wouldn't be distracted by homicidal intent. They'd also be acting without Harlan and Teddy, the men who best understood the theory behind what they were attempting. So how could he and Virgil surmount these hurdles, these barriers to Danny's mind and Iris's safety?

They needed a more powerful memory.

One that incorporated all three of them.

"No," Virgil said.

Adam didn't ask how he knew what Adam had in mind. "You have a better idea?"

"Don't do something rash because you're angry at me."

Adam opened his eyes and met Virgil's. They didn't seem as frightening as they had just moments ago. "I take it that's a *no*, you don't have a better idea," Adam said.

Virgil's scruffy jaws clenched, and he looked away. "I don't like going back there."

"Believe it or not, neither do I," Adam said.

"Y'all gonna share with the man who doesn't have a decoder ring?" Luther asked, hands on his hips. "What are you doing? Is there gonna be seizures or puking or speaking in tongues? And what the hell am I supposed to do?"

Adam met his father's grim expression. *What is going to*

happen? They both shrugged at the same time, not mirror images, but remarkably similar across the distance of a couple of decades. The corner of Virgil's mouth curled in something akin to a smile, and Adam's answered.

He and his father may have had an understanding, but Luther appeared spooked, eyes a little too wide as they passed from one man to the other.

"Luther," Adam said, and waited for the man's attention to stop skittering back and forth and settle on him. "We don't know what's going to happen. Are you armed?"

The deputy patted the holster at his side.

"Good. Then all you need to do is make sure nobody kills us while we're... otherwise engaged," Adam said. He closed his eyes, then added, "And don't let us kill anybody else."

He wasn't sure how Luther was supposed to accomplish that, to even know what was going on in places he couldn't see, so he was glad Luther didn't ask.

Adam took his mother's key between his fingers again, half-bracing himself for another attack by Virgil. *He'll do what he does; I can't change that.* Adam breathed deeply, the way Harlan had told him, listening to his exhales echo through his nostrils, the resonance reminding him of breathing while wearing head-phones. *Sound...* Adam didn't need visuals. This time sounds would take him where he wanted to go.

He went deeper and let everything fall away—the traffic in the distance, Luther's breathing, the rustle of a foraging bird, the chill breeze teasing the pines. What sound would take him back in time, to a night twenty years ago?

The campfire... wouldn't its warmth feel good right now? Adam heard it crackling in the distance, then drew closer, until his closed lids glowed orange. Such a reassuring sound, although he almost jumped when a bit of burning sap popped like a small gun.

But if he jumped, one of the other scouts would make fun of

him. So he remained still, eyes closed, and let the crackling surround him. A single voice rose and fell, telling stories to the hushed boys. He focused on its cadence, ignoring the words.

Eventually the campfire lost its hold, and there was another, different crackling. The plastic tarp beneath Adam's sleeping bag, shielding him from the damp and cold of the ground, crackled as he rolled over.

The tarp crackled as he got out of his sleeping bag. Adam clung to the sound, remained with it when all he wanted to do was open his eyes and follow his mother into the woods as he had so many years ago.

Then there was a gap, a hole in time, until Virgil arrived. The tarp crackled again as he snatched Adam's sleeping bag and the boy within it.

Before the sounds of his flight could take hold, Adam felt himself falling, Virgil next to him. Until another crackling snagged at their minds. The crackling of...

40

———

The car's tires crackled on the gravel road.

Danny's head almost dipped into a doze with the repetitive, hypnotic sound.

"Are we nearly there?" Iris asked. She stretched her cuffed hands toward the door, bracing herself against the rocking motion.

"Little old to be asking that, aren't you?" Danny said. In fairness, it had taken longer than he'd thought it would. "Don't worry—you can pee soon."

A big rock popped against one of their tires as they drove over it. Except it didn't sound quite right. More like the snap of a wet pocket in burning wood. For an instant, he could almost smell the smoke. The scent was gone just as quickly.

Danny stuck a finger in his ear and wiggled it back and forth.

Now the crackling sounded more like the crinkle of heavy plastic.

Like unfolding a dry, plastic tarp.

Danny's mind began to slip, to slide backwards...

To a milky-colored, translucent plastic, spread out on the floor, doubled over, as if in preparation for painting. But instead of rollers and trays, a body lay facedown upon it. A man's body, with a slender, athletic build, the dark hair on the back of his head sticky with blood. Danny pulled the plastic over him from one side, lifting his far arm to edge the plastic beneath it. His hand was still warm, still pliant.

It was easiest to roll him now, like a human burrito—

"The road!" Iris yelled. "Danny, stay on the road!"

Danny blinked hard, until he saw the shoulder ragged with high, brown grass. He turned the wheel gently back toward the center of the lane, gravel crackling, crackling beneath the tires...

The tarp crackled beneath him as he crawled from his sleeping bag and slipped into Adam's. He snugged down until his head was hidden from view, breathing in Iris's fabric softener. He knew Adam would leave him be when he returned, unwilling to cause any trouble. He grinned. The question was how to keep the sleeping bag for good. Maybe if he said it was his... No, that wouldn't work. No one would believe him over Adam, with that angelic face. He and Adam had both ridden with Mr. Henderson. What if, at the last minute, he decided to ride home with someone else? And when he grabbed his sleeping bag from Mr. Henderson's trunk to change cars, he'd just take Adam's instead.

Danny heard footsteps; Adam must be coming back. He held perfectly still, almost not breathing, afraid if he did he'd start laughing. Except he'd probably start laughing anyway. Danny guessed he didn't really need to keep the Batman sleeping bag forever, but he couldn't wait to see Adam's face when he said he'd farted in it. A little giggle snuck out.

Someone smooshed the top of the sleeping bag, mashing Danny's head. He grunted—he hadn't counted on Adam sitting on him, but he didn't dare yell and draw attention. Except suddenly he was rising from the ground! His body lurched—

"Danny!" Iris yelled. "Wake up!"

Her cuffed hands fumbled with the steering wheel. But she couldn't stretch far enough to turn it, and it was too late.

Dead grass slapped against the windshield as the car dropped off the edge of the road, and Iris screamed.

41

———

Adam rolled over to his knees, vomiting on the forest floor. His skull split like two earthen plates were colliding to form a mountain in the center of his forehead.

Somewhere, Luther's voice said, "Guess I was right about the puking."

Adam couldn't see. He fell forward, palms out, and one landed in warm, stinking chunks. His head was so full, bursting with what he'd witnessed. And experienced. He retched again, certain that this time his eyeballs would pop. *Oh, God.*

"Adam?" Luther said. "Are you done? Shit. Virgil, get his other side."

A pair of hands gripped Adam's right arm, and then a few seconds later, his left. Adam's legs trailed behind, scraping dark tracks in the moist soil as the two men dragged him. His left side suddenly dropped, his thigh striking something solid when the man carrying it stumbled.

"What the hell did I get myself into?" Luther muttered, before Adam's right side was lowered to the ground. "Virgil, you still with me?"

Adam curled into a ball, hands clutching his head, thinking surely he could detach it from his neck. If only he pulled hard enough.

"Adam." This time it was Virgil's voice, weak but unmistakable, next to his ear. Virgil gripped one of Adam's hands and pulled it away from his head. He pressed the hand against the ground, peeling Adam's fingers open until his palm was flat against the earth. "Remember where you are."

Luther did the same thing on Adam's other side, mashing his hand to the ground. Lying on his belly, pine needles scratched Adam's cheek as Virgil repeated, "Adam, remember where you are. Feel where you are. Just breathe."

So he did, though the breathing wasn't easy. The ground still made him want to cough. He thought of Harlan, of sitting with him and feeling the hum of the earth beneath them. The resonance that was always there. And it was here, too.

His vision started to clear. Virgil, kneeling next to him, nodded, and Luther released Adam's hand. Virgil still held the other one, gazing down at Adam with glistening eyes. His expression was so familiar, it triggered an impossible flash of memory. For a moment, lost in time, Adam was peering at his father through the bars of a crib.

"What have we done?" Adam whispered, voice hoarse.

"Shh," Virgil said. "She's okay. We'd know if she wasn't okay."

"Would we?"

A tear streaked down Virgil's face, past his silent mouth.

42

———

There was a ringing in Danny's ears. And something else, mechanical maybe. His neck protested as he lifted his head from where it rested against the seat. His head —*Jesus!* It hadn't hurt this bad since...

Danny opened his eyes, to see a world swimming as though he were underwater. *Motherfucker.* They'd done it to him again, Virgil and Adam. How? And why? He put the car in park and switched off the ignition, hoping that would stop some of the noise. Danny felt like shit, but nothing like the last time, so either they couldn't do that kind of damage without help, or they weren't trying to kill him now. His head drifted back against the seat and his eyes closed. *Just a minute.* He just needed a minute to rest, to get his head on straight.

But a sharp sound cut through the droning. The clicking of a seat belt. *Not his.*

Danny lifted his boulder of a head again, in time to see the passenger door open and Iris stumble out.

Sonuvabitch!

The car was on a slight incline, with the driver's side sitting higher. Danny fought his seat belt, then kicked the door so hard as he opened it that it nearly slammed back shut on his leg. Crispy, brown blades of grass approached his chest. He waded awkwardly around the back, falling against the trunk. His elbow skimmed over its now buckled corner, and he slid to his shins beneath the car.

Shorter, slighter, forty years older and wearing handcuffs, Iris hadn't made it far. He found her crawling on knees and elbows through a flattened patch of grass a few yards away.

"Iris, just stop!" Danny yelled. "Where do you think you'll get to?"

She kept crawling, so he grabbed one of her feet and yanked backwards. Iris rolled over on her back and her slip-on sneaker came off in his hand. Still hunched forward, he stared at it, as she lifted her other leg and kicked him in the nuts. It was a glancing blow, but enough to make his stomach cramp as he tucked instinctively.

Iris tried to stand, making it as far as her knees. Danny untucked long enough to punch her once, a hard right hook to her jaw. Iris was out before her body hit the ground. Danny dropped to his knees, squeezing himself tight, until he could raise his head without puking.

He stood, groaning, and nudged the elderly woman with his toe. She didn't stir, but she was breathing. Stupid damn woman. He'd hit her harder than he'd intended, but she was lucky he hadn't killed her. Control wasn't one of Danny's strengths lately. He walked back to the car, leaning across the passenger side to get his cell phone.

Danny gazed across the grassy field, a single gnarled oak in the distance, as he waited for the call to go through. They'd been so goddamned close. The old house was maybe a tenth of a mile away. Less than that. But even if everything still functioned, he couldn't get the car back on the road without a tow winch, and Danny wasn't about to carry Iris that far. She'd have to walk it when she woke up.

"Yeah," came a deep voice on the other end of the line.

"Rashid, it's Mitch," Danny said. "Here's the address I need you to meet me, as soon as possible. And be prepared to stay a few days."

"Does it need to be a defensible position?" Rashid asked.

"Yes," Danny replied. "I think it does."

43

"He needs a few more minutes," Virgil said. "Then maybe something to eat. No wonder he's getting so damn skinny."

"No kidding," Luther said.

Adam lay, apparently asleep, jacket tucked beneath his head and curled on his side on the ground like a child. Maybe a child with pneumonia. Luther had seen Adam looking pretty rough over the past month, but, with the exception of hallucinating and hypothermic on the mountain, this was about as bad as he'd seen him.

Virgil, on the other hand, leaving aside his temper tantrum a little while ago, appeared as sane as Luther had ever seen him. The removal of his scraggly mountain man beard helped. But the sideways, paranoid glances from the jail were gone. When he spoke to Luther, he looked at him directly, but not so intently you thought he was trying to fry your brain with a laser beam. His hands still shook some, but the fidgeting to the point of self-harm (they thought Luther hadn't noticed that) had stopped. Maybe Virgil was rising to the occasion, under the pressure of his missing mother and unraveling son, rather than crumbling beneath it.

But he was still a fugitive.

And Luther still didn't trust him.

"You can't even tell me what kind of car he was driving?" Luther asked.

Virgil shrugged. "It was a car. How do you identify a car from the inside?"

The sound of Luther's phone ringing seemed incongruous in the forest, his vehicle only visible if Luther leaned and squinted at the parking lot. He stepped away from Virgil after checking the screen.

"Hey, Beth," Luther said. "Something up, or did you call to insult my ass again?"

"Aren't we touchy," Beth said. "Just checking in. You got anything for show and tell?"

Luther thought about what he'd witnessed over the past couple of days, about what Virgil had told him while Adam dozed that, even when the man was coherent, sounded crazy. Maybe Danny and Iris had wrecked. Somewhere. Because Adam and Virgil had fucked with Danny's mind. Yeah, that was helpful.

"Sorry, Beth, I got nothing. You?"

"Your favorite Fed is back. And D'Antonio says this Rashid guy, if he's who we think, is somebody you don't want to be messing with. DEA has a Rashid on their radar that fits the profile, a real pro. The good news is, he doesn't cause a lot of collateral damage."

"And the bad news?" Luther asked, because there always was some.

"He gets the job done."

Luther hung up, feeling no wiser. What would the job be in this case? Why would Danny hire him? Not to go after Adam— he'd do that himself. And there was no indication Rashid was involved with snatching Iris (whatever crazy-ass reason Danny had for that, because Luther still didn't buy what Adam and Virgil were selling).

Virgil walked toward Luther. His limp was less pronounced than it had been, now nothing more than an intermittent, mild drag.

Luther pointed, not caring if he was being rude. "What'd you do to that leg?" he asked.

"It doesn't matter," Virgil said.

"I've seen Adam with that same limp," Luther said.

"When?" Virgil asked, face blanching.

"A few days ago."

Virgil glanced over his shoulder at his son, then said, "I broke it. Years ago. Never got it set right."

Never got it set right? Luther wondered if he'd even gone to a doctor. Probably fell over something, out in the woods.

Or *off* something.

Luther thought back to the promontory where they'd found Rachel and Virgil and Adam. And the remains of Sarah Edmunds, the child whose injuries had been consistent with falling. "What happened to Sarah Edmunds?"

Virgil shut his eyes and shook his head. Luther felt a tickle of temper in his guts; the man was going to dodge him again. But to Luther's surprise, he didn't.

His icy eyes were frank when he answered. "I wasn't lying when I said I don't know. I buried her close to where I found her —at the bottom of that rock pinnacle. I didn't see what happened."

Luther had a pretty good eye for untruth. Virgil wasn't lying. But he wasn't telling everything. Luther rubbed his scruffy chin, considering. "There was a seed planted that day that you never forgot. You think Danny did it."

Virgil's gaze dropped, just for a moment, before he admitted, "I have my suspicions."

"Why?"

"Their relationship wasn't... what I would have hoped," Virgil said. "And Danny was standing near the top when I found her."

Luther shook his head. What ever happened to starting with torturing your neighbors' pets? Of course, here he stood talking to Virgil like the man hadn't played any role in the little monster's psychosis. Like Virgil hadn't kidnapped Danny and the first person Danny had likely killed.

"You were right about me keeping tabs on Danny," Virgil said. "I followed him sometimes, when I'd seen him and he felt particularly... ripe for doing something that couldn't be undone. I've been thinking about what Adam and I saw, the gravel road and the high grasses. It reminds me of a place he went once, over by Kirkville. I could see a house in the distance, but I didn't follow him all the way in. He was meeting somebody else and I didn't want to risk being seen."

"You think you could find it again?" Luther asked.

Virgil's face twisted in a grimace. "Probably not without a map, and I don't know where we'd get one that's got that much detail."

Luther didn't have a smartphone, and he didn't fancy squinting at one for something like this anyway. "We can look it up online, maybe a library, or somewhere when we get some food. He gonna be okay?" Luther asked, nodding at Adam, who still hadn't stirred.

"Fine," Virgil said.

"Really?" Luther challenged, dropping his voice. "Because from where I'm standing, he doesn't look so fine."

"I can protect my son—I *am* protecting my son," Virgil said.

"Who's protecting him from you?" Luther asked.

"I told you—" But Virgil stopped, apparently unwilling to say whatever it was again. His glare would have spooked Luther a few days ago; he must be building up a tolerance to the man.

"It won't happen again. And Adam will be fine," Virgil

repeated, sitting against a tree where he could watch over his son. His finger rubbed roughly below his nose, over an almost indistinguishable spot of dried blood.

Fine, huh? Luther thought. *Bullshit.*

44

———

J couldn't put it off anymore. She told herself she'd been busy, but she was always busy, and she could always make time for something so important. She kept finding something else she had to do instead.

It was time to see Harlan.

He'd arrived hours ago, but she was afraid to see him. There, she'd admitted it. She hadn't seen him since... well, since he'd stopped by this very hospital to see Iris, before he and Adam fled the authorities. Before he and Adam saved Aaron Schofield, and Harlan was nearly killed in the process.

JJ pushed his door open, but didn't turn on the light. Late afternoon sun filtered through the partially open blinds. Harlan's body was still, the way she'd seen patients be still before, patients who would never leave the hospital under their own power. She walked to the chair someone had pulled next to his bed and sat.

She hadn't known Harlan long, but he'd been such a vibrant, sharp-witted man. His eyes had perpetually sparkled under his dark brows, as though with the knowledge of a naughty joke that, against your better judgment, you were suddenly sure you needed to hear. Those eyes were shut now, the lids that covered them nearly as dark as his brows. His tanned face had faded to a shade more pale than the white hair sticking to one side of his head. His lips were chapped, but his mustache looked trimmed. She felt certain Iris had been tending to him, but Iris hadn't seen him for a day or two. JJ made a mental note to get him some lip balm. Just until Iris returned.

The natural tendency when someone was in a sickbed was to hold that person's hand. It was as if, once the eyes were closed, our hands were the back door to the soul. But JJ paused, recalling how contact had caused him actual physical discomfort when she'd tended to Harlan in his cabin. She didn't know what she believed about what he—or Adam, for that matter—could do or see. But she did know Harlan was... *sensitive*, for lack of a better word, and being in a hospital must be torture for him, subject to all the poking and prodding and bombarded by sounds and smells. Assuming he was still in there somewhere.

She rose from her chair, leaned over him, and after a moment's hesitation, kissed his brow. "I think you're still in there," she whispered.

"Good. So do I." The man's slightly nasal voice startled her, coming from behind.

JJ fixed her standard nurse's smile on her face before turning to greet an elderly man. His white-blonde hair had gone slightly wispy and receded from a peak in front, and the bump on his narrow nose was vaguely familiar. He wore a flannel shirt and work pants, and although she couldn't smell him, she was sure they'd been worn more than once.

"Can I help you, Mr...." she prompted.

He squinted as he looked at her chest. No, at her name tag. "Tulley," he said. "You must be Max's daughter."

He didn't volunteer a name of his own. Instead, he walked casually past her to Harlan. The gloves sticking out of his back pocket resembled a mini rooster's tail. JJ thought back to when she'd entered the room. The bathroom door hadn't been fully shut, and if it had, she would have heard him open it. Which led her to believe this man had hidden in Harlan's bathroom, waiting. But waiting for what?

"Who are you?" she asked.

He placed a hand on Harlan's arm, over the sheet, not on bare skin. Then he closed his eyes, and JJ wondered how long she was supposed to stand by for a response before fetching security. Finally, he released Harlan's arm and turned to her, smiling faintly, almost apologetically. "You've been mixed up in all of this too, haven't you?"

"I'm afraid I don't know what you mean," JJ said, but she did. She didn't know who this man was, but she knew *exactly* what he meant.

"Harlan doesn't want to be here," he said. "He wants to find Iris."

"Really? And I suppose Harlan told you that."

"No," he admitted. "But he doesn't have to. I know him."

"If you don't give me a name, I'm calling security," JJ said. And she meant it, even though—frustrating as the man was—she hated the thought of him being manhandled out of the building.

"I'm sorry," the man said, chin dropping. He almost looked embarrassed. "I don't know why I thought you knew. I'm Teddy Rutledge."

That was not the answer JJ was expecting, and her brain fumbled. "Does—" Who? Adam? Iris? Grant, and whichever agencies had the man on their Most Wanted list? She tried again. "Does anyone know you're here?"

"I'm not sure if Harlan does or not," Teddy said, not entirely answering her question. "It's very difficult to read him right now. Tell me, what do you think they'll do for Harlan in this place? You think they've got some sort of magic wand?"

"Of course not," JJ said. His question mirrored her own thoughts so closely, she found herself being defensive. "I suppose you do. Have a magic wand."

"No, I don't," he said, lowering himself slowly into the chair. "But I can reach him. And he can bring himself back. In fact, he's the only one who can."

Maybe. JJ squeezed her hand into a fist and rubbed it against her hipbone to help her focus. Because this wasn't just about Harlan. "Where's Virgil?" she asked.

Teddy shrugged and said, "I don't know."

She thought he was lying, or at least holding something back. "Did you help him escape?"

He grinned, and JJ recognized a hint of Adam. "Are you a prosecutor? I don't know anything about anybody escaping. I just gave a relative a ride."

JJ went to the closed door and peered out through its narrow window. Moments ago, she'd threatened to call security herself, but now she half-feared seeing a SWAT team in the hallway. "Adam took off somewhere, I'm pretty sure looking for Virgil. Along with everybody else. But the only reason Adam wants Virgil is to find you. Well, at least that was the case before last night."

Teddy propped his elbows on the chair's arms and lifted himself straighter. "Look, all kidding aside, I know the law's looking for me. And I know I don't have much time to do what I came for."

JJ almost asked what that was, until it suddenly became obvious. She stepped back involuntarily, flush against the door. "Oh, no. You are not kidnapping Harlan."

Teddy stood, more quickly than she'd have thought possible, and said, "You and I both know the only kidnapping victim around here was poor Iris." He pointed at Harlan in the bed. "And that man is the only chance we have of getting her back alive."

JJ kept shaking her head, arms tucked across her scrub shirt.

"And we both know, if Harlan stays in here, he'll die. Him, and Iris, and who knows who else before this crazy damn drama is over. This Danny, or whoever the hell he is, he's not gonna stop. He's gonna have to *be* stopped."

Teddy was right. She knew he was right. But life was never about being right. It was never that simple, or there wouldn't be so damn many lawyers. "You can't just roll Harlan out the front door," she said. "It's not your choice to make."

Teddy's voice remained calm and, if anything, became more reasonable. "Do you think he wants to be here? If Harlan could speak, if he could tell us *his* choice, what do you think it would be?"

"It doesn't matter. There are procedures, liability waivers," she protested.

"Good thing he gave one of those whadyacallit directives to Iris," Teddy said.

Once again, she didn't need to see his impish grin to know he was lying. But maybe he did have enough of something—besides bold self-assurance—to get Harlan out of the hospital before anyone caught on. Even so, removing Harlan from his regular care at the hospital could make his condition deteriorate. Although breathing on his own, he was being fed and hydrated intravenously, and monitored for nutritional issues and bedsores and pneumonia and everything in between.

JJ gestured at the equipment—monitors, IV lines, catheters and various tubes. "What about all this? You have a medical degree I don't know about? You can't do this by yourself."

"Of course I can't," he said, as if it was a ludicrous suggestion and he didn't know where she'd gotten it. "I'm also aware Harlan is not a light man. That's why you're going to help me."

                                45
                          ———————

Between sleeping late, Rachel's mom constantly hovering, and the Sheriff questioning them again, Evie and Rachel hadn't had a moment alone all day. Now, sitting cross-legged on the floor of Rachel's room, Evie couldn't help looking over her shoulder at the door. She felt trapped. They might as well be in school.

Evie walked to Rachel's window and peered around its edges. Second story, no close trees, no overhang, no ladder. *Wait a minute...* Rachel's mom was paranoid (that's what Evie's mom said; Rachel's mom called it "safety conscious"). Every few months, she made the whole house do a fire drill. Evie had stayed over during one. She walked to Rachel's dresser and reached behind it where she found—*yes*—a ladder. It was a folding kind that hooked under the interior windowsill, then dangled to the ground. Rachel's eyes goggled.

"Have you ever used this?" Evie asked.

Rachel shook her head, speechless at the magnitude of Evie's proposition.

"Well, then," Evie said, so giddy she was on the verge of laughing, "I think it's time for a fire drill."

"YOU'RE sure the man who took Miss Iris is the same man who took you?" Evie asked, setting off on a looping route to avoid the spot where Rachel's dad had sliced up his leg.

Rachel glanced back at her house, where the ladder hung from her window like a neon sign. Evie was frankly amazed she'd talked her friend into using it. Then Rachel tugged at her ponytail, pushing the elastic band closer to her skull.

Finally, she sighed and said, "Yes. I'd explain it if I could. All I can say is, I knew it was him. Every time he's around, I get this nasty, sick feeling in my stomach. The same thing happened when he showed up at the diner."

"Okay. I believe you," Evie said. She wasn't sure she did, but that wasn't something you told your best friend the day after your babysitter was kidnapped. "I wonder why he took Miss Iris."

"I don't even know why he took me," Rachel said.

Evie was surprised; Rachel didn't say much about what had happened to her, and she never volunteered anything. "Yeah, but you're a kid. People take kids. Miss Iris is old, like older than our parents. By a lot."

"That's true," Rachel said, thoughtful.

"I know she's not related or anything, but Miss Iris protected us," Evie said. "I feel like we should be doing something to help her."

"Adam will save her," Rachel said, as assuredly as she might say Friday meant apple crisp in school lunches.

"Just because he and Mom saved you?" Evie scoffed. "What if Adam doesn't even know she's gone?"

"He knows."

"How do you know he knows?" Evie challenged.

Evie didn't have a lot of patience for things she couldn't see or prove. But Rachel didn't tell stories that weren't true to get attention like some kids did, and she didn't make things up. So how could she know?

Evie's eyes widened as she remembered Rachel standing at the window the night before, waving. She'd said at no one. "You saw Adam last night!"

Rachel's face flushed. "Maybe."

Evie grabbed Rachel's shoulders and stared at her. "You did! Why didn't you tell me?"

Rachel shrugged her off. "I don't know. It's like all this other stuff I don't understand. I can't explain it, and I didn't want you to think I was crazy."

Evie fixed her eyes on the shape of her own house, barely distinguishable through the leafless trees, to work out the view from her bedroom window. "I don't get it. Was he standing in our yard?"

"When I looked outside," Rachel said, "I didn't see your yard. I saw somebody else's, fenced-in dead grass with a tree in the middle, and Adam was sitting under the tree. And there was someone else, too. An old man was standing over his shoulder, but faded, like he was a ghost or he wasn't really there. But I know Adam really was. Somewhere."

"So what do you see now?" Evie asked, gesturing toward her house.

"I see the trees, and the squirrels, and the sky, and the same things you see," Rachel said. "It was just that one time."

Evie picked up a small, dead branch, smacking it against her palm. "But you said you've had weird dreams lately, too. Can you see other stuff? Or do other stuff?"

"I don't know," Rachel admitted. "I've never really tried, because I was afraid somehow it would connect me to... you know."

"The man who took you and Iris?"

Rachel nodded, obviously still uncomfortable speaking about

him. "And the other man, too. The one who chased me in the woods."

"But you felt safe with Adam," Evie pointed out.

"So?" Rachel asked, but like she had to ask. Not because she really wanted to know what Evie was getting at.

"What if you tried to see Adam? Or tried things that didn't have to do with anybody in particular? How would you do that?" Evie asked.

Rachel pulled her ponytail around and chewed on the end. Evie found herself bouncing on her heels, trying not to smack Rachel's hair out of her mouth. But it seemed to help her friend think.

"Well," Rachel said, "when I saw Adam last night, he was sitting under a tree. And I feel like most of the other times we connected, at least one of us was outside. So I think it might work better—if we wanted to experiment—if we sat in the dirt."

Evie grinned. "Okay." She bounded over and grabbed Rachel's hand, leading her to what looked like a more comfortable spot and dropping to the ground. "This'll be so cool."

NOTHING, Evie thought, *was ever the way books and TV made you think it would be.*

"Are you sure you can't make this rock float?" Evie demanded, holding the mostly round chunk of sandstone on her palm, fingers free to avoid any interference. She imagined all the tiny grains—colored tan and white and rusty and quartz-sparkly— blowing apart.

"No, I can't make rocks fly. How much longer do we have to keep doing this?" Rachel groused.

The seat of Evie's pants felt damp, and leaves had crept into her socks and the cuffs and waist of her pants. She let the rock fall to the ground and picked up a crispy, reddish-brown oak leaf, admiring all of its intact fingers. She held it up by the little stem and said, "Have you ever tried to make the wind blow?"

"Don't be stupid, Evie. What do you think I am, one of the X-Men?" Rachel snapped.

Evie rolled her eyes, then stared at the ground where she set the oak leaf. "Fine," she pouted.

She wiped bits of dirt from her hand onto her pants before spinning her friendship bracelet around her wrist, picking half-heartedly at its knot. They'd made the bracelets after Rachel's escape from the crazy guy. Actually, Rachel had done most of the making, but it was Evie's idea. She'd thought it would take Rachel's mind off whatever scary things made her so quiet, even when she was safe at home.

Evie snuck a glance at her friend. Dark smears beneath her eyes and lips pale, Rachel looked tired. Rachel always looked tired, with her asthma and whatever other medical excuses her mom used to keep her indoors. But she looked more tired today.

"I'm not tired. I just don't want to do this anymore," Rachel said.

Evie protested automatically, "Who said anything about you being tired?"

"You did," Rachel said. "Just now."

Had she?

She'd thought it, but had she said it out loud? She didn't believe she had. Her brows wrinkled as she stared at Rachel—was she messing with Evie? Or had she somehow read Evie's mind?

Evie's pondering was interrupted by the sound of her mother's Bronco racing up their driveway. Her mom always took the driveway fast (she said it was to keep from sliding). To be fair, it may have seemed faster than usual because of the pickup, right on her tail. The girls looked at each other and rose, not bothering to brush off the leaves before running the rest of the way through the woods to Evie's house.

46

JJ rushed from her Bronco to the passenger side of Teddy's pickup. Or was it Jim Henderson's pickup? Whatever the hell vehicle she'd thought was going to ram into her bumper multiple times on the way home. Of course, Teddy's lousy driving wasn't what upset her; it was wondering why it was lousy. Was he distracted by Harlan dying next to him, racing to get somewhere they could attend to him? Or was Teddy just a shitty driver?

She breathed a sigh of relief as she threw open the truck door. Harlan looked okay. At least, no worse than he had in the hospital. A moment later, Teddy stood next to her, carrying a folded sheet. She wasn't sure he'd recovered from the last time they carried Harlan. His belly pushed out the front of his flannel shirt more, like maybe he was favoring his back.

"I can't believe I let you talk me into this," she said.

He didn't respond, but went to work with JJ to slide Harlan, unconscious, out of the truck. Grunting and groaning, they maneuvered Harlan free without dropping him, carrying him parallel to the ground on top of the sheet. JJ had the foot end, and when she swiveled toward the house, she came up short.

"We're taking him in the house," she said, glaring.

"Soon, JJ, but this is where he needs to be now," Teddy said. "You have to trust me."

"Trust you!" Exasperated, JJ tried not to shout. "I could lose my job. And I'm not about to let Harlan get sick—or worse—because you've got some damn fool ideas."

"Mom," Evie called out.

JJ's head swung around to see her daughter and Rachel standing at the edge of the woods. Rachel was panting, and when Evie spoke her voice sounded young, uncertain. "Mom, what's going on?"

Teddy took advantage of the distraction, saying, "We'll put him over there," and proceeded toward the edge of the woods with their cargo.

Face flushing with anger and frustration and fear, JJ had no choice but to stagger after Teddy. "Don't ask, honey," JJ told her daughter, voice strained with the exertion. "It's nothing you need to worry about. I'll explain later."

The girls appeared unconvinced.

"Right here," Teddy said.

They lowered Harlan to the ground beneath the big poplar tree. Teddy jogged back to his truck while JJ knelt beside Harlan, assessing his status. Pulse and skin seemed good, and pupils were equal and reactive as they had been since his admission. JJ glanced up at Teddy's return to see him carrying a glass jar. He didn't shake it, but swirled it in a vigorous circle before kneeling on Harlan's other side and lifting the man's head.

"What the hell are you doing?" JJ demanded.

"What?" Teddy protested. "You told me he could drink."

"I said *in theory* he could drink, but that it's dangerous, and you have to be very careful." She stared at the jar in his hand. "Especially if you're trying to force-feed him that nasty shit—"

"Mom!" Evie said.

JJ looked up guiltily, having forgotten the girls were there. "Sorry, sweetie."

Once again, Teddy took advantage of JJ's distraction, pouring the tiniest bit from the jar into Harlan's mouth. JJ held her breath, afraid the unconscious man would aspirate the liquid. She watched a subtle motion in his throat as the swallowing reflex kicked in. Teddy poured a few more small sips, and each time he swallowed, but Harlan never opened his eyes.

JJ sat on her heels as Teddy screwed the lid back on his jar and set it next to him. Placing a gloved hand across Harlan's forehead, Teddy closed his eyes. After a few moments that felt like more, he shook his head, removed his gloves, and took one of Harlan's hands between his. Teddy bowed his head and sighed.

"I can't reach him," Teddy admitted, "but he's there. He'll come back to us."

JJ wasn't so sure, but since the girls were watching, she held her tongue and tried to look positive. She and Teddy hefted Harlan toward the house while Evie raced to get JJ's keys from the Bronco. Trooper exited the front door as soon as Evie opened it, calmly sniffing Teddy and then Harlan before trotting off to do his business.

Evie held the door as JJ and Teddy squeezed past with the unconscious man between them. Her daughter's face went so still, JJ could tell it was the first time she'd gotten a good look at Harlan. His mouth was gaping slightly beneath his silver mustache, as though he'd forgotten his words in the midst of saying them. He didn't look dead, but he didn't look wholly alive, either.

"He'll be okay," JJ said, because she had to.

But when Evie met her mother's eyes, JJ could tell she didn't believe her.

The poor man looked as lost as Iris.

~

"I HOPE he doesn't asphyxiate. Lord knows the last time I changed these sheets," JJ said. Hands still full with Harlan, she nodded to Evie. "Sweetie, would you peel back the comforter and the top sheet? Thanks."

Teddy grunted, and Harlan's careful descent to the guest bed became more of a controlled fall. Harlan was wearing a pair of navy pajamas Iris had brought to the hospital. JJ adjusted the pillow under his head and raised the covers to his chest, smoothing them like a wrinkled shirt. Now what? She couldn't remember what kind of mattress protector was on the bed, but it might not be totally waterproof.

She chastised herself, *Who gives a shit about the mattress*? But JJ knew it wasn't about the mattress; it was about focusing on the things she could control in a situation where so much was out of her hands. She could feel the children standing behind her, and suddenly realized their presence alone kept her from laying her head next to Harlan and crying. The sight of him in the bed where her father had died last year was too much. That, and everything else.

You did your best to protect your child from the world…

"JJ," Teddy said softly, interrupting her dark thoughts. "Do you mind if I sit with him?"

"Of course not," JJ said, voice breaking. She cleared her throat and said, more strongly, "You're welcome to stay here. As long as it takes."

Though she didn't know if she could stand to watch another man she loved die in this room.

Because it had been a sickroom, two chairs still stood alongside the bed where she'd left them. She and Teddy each took one, and the girls sat cross-legged on a rug on the floor next to a bookshelf still packed with her father's paperbacks (Tom Clancy and Robert Ludlum and John Le Carré). Trooper settled in front of them, and the girls stroked the dog's back.

"So you're..." It took JJ a moment to remember Adam's grand-father's name. "Lawrence's brother?"

Teddy nodded.

"Who's Lawrence?" Evie asked.

JJ cringed. She'd hoped the girls were either young enough or old enough to ignore the adult talk, but they were in that bridge age where they listened if something was actually interesting.

"I'm Adam's great-uncle," Teddy said.

Both girls' eyebrows raised theatrically before they shared a look. *Great,* JJ thought. *Now he's really got an audience.*

"Girls," she said, "everything going on in this room is a secret. If anyone asks..."

She stalled out. What lie did you teach your child and her best friend to hide a fugitive?

"You can be *my* great-uncle," Evie volunteered, then pointed at the bed. "And he's your brother, and we're all taking care of him because his insurance ran out."

JJ could tell Teddy was trying not to smile, but she felt a pres-sure against her chest, the pressure of the Future Evie. Her child's facility with fabrication did not bode well for JJ emerging from her teenaged years mentally competent. She turned her attention to Rachel instead.

"Does your mom know you girls are over here?" JJ asked.

Rachel's open-mouthed blush was answer enough.

"Go call her now and let her know," JJ said, and watched the girls scramble out the door to the living room, racing with eleven-year-old drama. Trooper followed at a more reasonable pace. Turning back to Teddy, JJ chose her words carefully. "So you know Virgil?"

Teddy leaned back and rested his hands on his little belly pooch. "As well as anyone does."

"Including Iris?" JJ asked.

"Oh, yeah. Definitely better than Iris. I understand the parts of Virgil she won't acknowledge," Teddy said, without rancor.

"The same parts she denies in Adam, and apparently did throughout his childhood."

"Because you... share those parts?" JJ asked.

"Yes."

So Teddy was some kind of psychic, too. Adam had alluded to that when he talked about tracking down his uncle, but he hadn't been explicit. Or maybe she hadn't listened. She was no Iris, but JJ was certainly uncomfortable with all of this stuff and waded into that Egyptian river from time to time herself.

"Adam won't talk about what they did in Watkins County, but you were there, weren't you?" JJ asked.

Teddy looked away as he nodded, clenching his jaw. It didn't take a degree in psychology to recognize the man had a lot of issues around Harlan, not least of which was blaming himself for Harlan nearly dying. "How much do you know about what happened after you left? About how Harlan ended up this way?"

"Almost nothing," Teddy admitted. "But I've seen the things Adam can do—and what's even scarier, the things he *thinks* he can do—without having had any training. I have no doubt that he saved Harlan's life."

JJ stretched her legs straight and covered her eyes with a groan. She considered Teddy's words carefully, then sat up too quickly, feeling a twinge in her back. "You know *almost* nothing?" she pressed.

He sighed. "I was afraid you caught that. Okay, between you and me and these four walls, I was absconding with Virgil in yonder pickup when all that craziness was happening. Virgil was supposedly sleeping, but I felt something. It's hard to explain..." Teddy tipped toward JJ and stared at her so intently it actually made her queasy, like she was moving in her chair. "You've worked in the ER, haven't you?"

"Yes."

He continued, "I'll bet you've worked with some people where you don't even have to speak. You anticipate each other—" He snapped his fingers. "Just like that, you know what to do next. It's a combination of habits and patterns and natural inclinations and something inexplicable."

"Woo-woo," JJ volunteered.

Teddy touched his nose in acknowledgment.

"Well, that's Virgil and me, but more so. We always had a connection, from the time he was a kid." He gestured toward the bed. "Harlan and Adam are the same way."

"You were talking about what happened to Harlan that day, while you were in the truck," JJ prompted.

Teddy sighed. "It wasn't what I felt, it was what I *didn't* feel. Like Virgil was hiding what he was doing. Before I left Virgil yesterday, we were arguing—not for the first time—and he told me what Adam had done, trying to heal Harlan and then chasing that man down. Now, don't get me wrong, Adam's got a lot of raw power, but doing all that should've killed him."

JJ rubbed the headache that was coming awake in the middle of her forehead. "Are you saying Adam didn't do it?"

"No, I'm saying he had help. From Virgil. That Virgil was feeding him energy."

"He can do that?" she asked, incredulous.

"Among other things."

JJ sat up. "Among *what* other things?"

Teddy shrugged. "I don't know. There's no handbook for this shit, no Grand Poobah who calls a meeting to order and tells us how it works. We don't know what can be done until somebody does it."

"But you know something else. Dammit, Teddy, stop dicking me around!"

"You kiss your daughter with that mouth?" he asked.

JJ glared, sure the man said far worse himself on a regular basis, and Teddy relented.

"Okay, but I don't want you getting ahead of yourself," he warned. "You know how Virgil's not the most stable person."

"Yes," JJ said, motioning for him to talk faster.

"He used to come see me when things got real bad, and I have some herbal remedies, like what I gave to Harlan. But that wasn't the only thing that helped him get his head on straight." Teddy paused.

"What?" JJ demanded. "You'd sacrifice a goat?"

"That's not a joke!"

Teddy yelled so close to her face that JJ jerked backward, nearly tipping her chair. His chest heaved with every wheezing breath, his eyes popped, and his face was flushed and sweaty. JJ was afraid she'd given the man a heart attack, though she couldn't imagine why.

"Easy, Teddy," she said. "You're right; it's not a joke. I'm sorry."

Teddy put a shaking hand to his face and said, "It doesn't matter. Look, the point is, it wasn't just the potions. *I* helped balance Virgil. He took from me—or I gave to him, I don't know which—*the ability to be sane.*"

Now JJ was the one having trouble breathing. "Explain."

"It took me years to figure out that's what was happening. It's similar to the energy thing I was telling you about with Adam and Virgil. Whatever it was Virgil took from me, I could eventually replenish. Restore. But—"

"You have to know how," JJ said. "And you have to know you're being drained."

"Exactly."

"Does Virgil know he's doing it?"

"I don't think so," Teddy said. His face had gone from flushed to pale, with two rosy spots on his cheeks. "And I don't know for sure that he can do it with Adam. But if he can share energy like that, over distance..."

JJ's face tingled, lips numb, as she flashed back to Virgil trying to kill his own son with a shovel, each of them thinking they were saving Rachel. And each of them, in his own way, right.

If they were together, Virgil would make Adam insane.

Thank God Adam hadn't found his father yet.

JJ put her head in her hands. Suddenly a coma didn't sound so bad. Except of course, it was. It was fucking awful. How could she even think such a thing in jest? So much rested on Harlan's shoulders. Could he feel it, even now, wherever he was?

"Are you sure we can bring him back?" JJ asked.

Teddy's heavy, calloused hand came to rest on the back of her head, stroking JJ's long hair. She'd known the man for less than an afternoon. It should've felt weird, or too familiar, but it didn't.

"What would your daddy have said?" he asked.

Somehow she was never surprised by someone knowing—or knowing of—her father. "He'd have said that was a stupid goddamn question."

Teddy gave a soft laugh. "He might at that. But he also might surprise you with words a little more tender for his only daughter."

Teddy's hand paused with the sound of a commotion in the front of the house.

What now? JJ stood reluctantly to see what the girls had gotten into and heard a car engine approaching.

"Shit," JJ said. "Just stay here with Harlan. Whoever it is, I'll get rid of them."

Trooper barked. Once. *No, not now. Not with a fugitive in the house,* JJ prayed. But too late.

The girls ran into the bedroom, hair streaming behind them, with Evie in the lead.

"Mom," she panted, "the Sheriff's here."

47

———

"**S**onuvabitch!" JJ said.

But Evie pretended like she didn't hear. She'd have asked what they were supposed to do, but her mom, pacing to the threshold of the bedroom before staring at the two old men, obviously didn't know yet. Evie bounced from one foot to the other, apologizing for stepping on Rachel's. When she did, she saw poor Rachel's eyes bugging out.

"You," JJ finally said, pointing at Adam's uncle, "stay out of sight. I don't know if there's a warrant out for you, but I'd prefer not to find out. Girls, come with me and just... I don't know. Act natural, but keep your mouths shut."

She ushered the girls out, saying as she closed the bedroom door, "We'll get through this, one way or another."

Evie understood enough of what was happening to feel excited and scared at the same time, and the energy inside her was bubbling over. *Act natural*, her mom had said. So what did Evie normally do when the Sheriff came over? That was easy.

She ran ahead of Rachel and her mom to the front door, where Trooper waited patiently. Evie caught a glimpse of her mother's stricken face as she threw the door open and wanted to say, "It's okay, Mom; I've got this." But she didn't have time.

Trooper loped down the steps ahead of her. The Sheriff was already out of his parked cruiser and halfway to the front steps. She raced toward him, heart pounding. "Hey, Sheriff!" she called out. "Are you here to teach me those rope tricks?"

"Afraid not, Evie," he said.

He smiled, but it was a small one, the kind you give a kid when you don't want them to know bad things are afoot in the adult world. Except Evie never understood that way of doing things, because kids always find out. And it sucks being the last one to know.

"Remember, you promised. At Halloween. And that's been..." Evie paused, unsure exactly how long it had been. She settled on, "A long time."

"I know, Evie," he said, inching carefully toward the steps she blocked. "And I want you to hold me to that. But not today. I need to talk to your mom."

Evie slipped an arm through the Sheriff's and said, "Why don't you ever come around anymore?"

It was the perfect thing to ask, because he stopped and stared down at her, speechless. But she'd actually asked because she wanted to know. She just didn't realize it until she'd said it. His mouth opened and closed, a little like Fat Justin when the new kid hit him in the gut next to the swings. The Sheriff looked up, saw her mom standing on the steps, and removed his hat, sputtering, "I'm sorry. I've been busy."

"Mom, he wants to talk to you," Evie said, stating the obvious because her body was still vibrating and talking helped her settle down, feel more in control.

"Grant, come on in. Can I offer you some coffee?" JJ said.

"That'd be good, JJ. Thanks. Hey, Rachel. How you doing?" he asked.

Rachel seemed ready to hide behind JJ's leg like a little kid, but she mumbled, "Good, Sheriff."

Evie took her friend by the arm and was clomping toward the front door when she heard the Sheriff behind her ask, "Whose truck is that?"

Evie caught her toe on the top step.

"Careful, Evie," JJ said. "A friend left it here."

Evie breathed a sigh of relief and continued inside with Rachel, where she gestured toward some coloring books on the coffee table. Evie didn't feel like coloring, but if they kept their heads down and looked occupied, the Sheriff would probably ignore them and keep talking to her mom. She and Rachel sat on the floor, and she slid one of the books toward Rachel. Then Evie grabbed a crayon and began filling in between the lines while surreptitiously watching her mom pour two mugs of coffee.

"Thanks, JJ," the Sheriff said, then dropped his voice. "Listen, there are a couple of things I need to talk to you about."

"Go ahead," JJ said, before taking a long sip of coffee. "Oh, sorry, this needs cream. You want any?"

"No," he replied, and waited for her to finish messing around in the fridge, to face him head-on, before continuing. He set his mug on the counter. "I was over at the hospital. We have to talk about Harlan. "

Poop, Evie thought. That was the name they'd used for the unconscious man. She had to warn Adam's uncle.

Evie nudged Rachel and nodded toward the back rooms. Rachel glanced toward the adults in the kitchen, then back at Evie, obviously uncertain.

"Come on," Evie whispered.

She tried to be quiet, slipping out of the living room, but there was nothing suspicious about kids escaping adult conversation anyway. Evie paused outside the bedroom door, listening, though she couldn't have said for what. Then she yanked it open, shoved

Rachel in ahead of her, and pulled the door carefully shut behind them, waiting for the metallic click of the latch.

Adam's uncle, sitting next to the unconscious man, looked at her expectantly, but didn't seem that worried. Maybe because he was so old.

"The Sheriff knows about him," Evie said, pointing at the motionless man in her grandfather's bed. "You have to hide."

Adam's uncle gestured down at his large body. "Honey, do I look like the hiding type?"

Growling with frustration, Evie took him by the hand, dragging him around the bed to the closet. It was big, taking up most of the wall, and had plenty of room since they'd gotten rid of a lot of her grandfather's clothes after he died. She shoved aside a couple of hanging jackets, and thought she smelled her grandfather again, just for a second. But that was stupid. Smells couldn't last that long.

"Get in," she said, stepping aside to give him easier access, though the closet doors were louvered accordion panels, so he had plenty of room. She spied a folding stool at the far end and scooted that to him as well.

"Thank you," he said, and she waited for him to figure out how to lock it in a standing position before closing the door and plunging him into semi-darkness.

"Now be quiet," she said.

Evie peered at the closet door from various angles—standing normally, squatting, standing on tiptoes. She didn't think it was possible to see him from outside, but she'd try to remember to stand in front of it to be safe.

Rachel sat in the chair next to the bed that Adam's uncle had vacated. Her sneakered feet didn't quite touch the floor, not that Evie's would have either.

"He looks familiar," Rachel said, staring down at the unconscious man.

"Maybe because he's related to Adam," Evie suggested.

"*He's* not related to Adam," said a voice from the closet. "I am."

"Shh," Evie hissed. It bothered her that they hadn't heard anything from her mom and the Sheriff. Were they on their way to the bedroom? Maybe he'd left after all.

Rachel slid off the chair and stood over the unconscious man. Evie thought he was less pale than he had been when they'd carried him in, more like he was sleeping than dead. Rachel leaned over him, staring down at his face.

"Why doesn't he wake up?" she asked.

"Because he needs to heal," said the voice in the closet, but more softly this time.

"The first time I saw Adam," Evie said, "I didn't think he'd wake up. But he did, and he thought I was my mom, even though we don't look alike at all."

"Hello?" Rachel whispered into his face.

She climbed on the mattress next to him. Her hand looked so small reaching for one of his.

"Sweetie, you shouldn't do that," the voice said from the closet, louder now.

"Shh," Evie spat, exasperated. But she couldn't help asking, "Why not?"

Before he could answer, she heard footsteps in the hallway and her mother's voice, "He's in my dad's old room."

The feet paused outside. "I don't know what the hell you were thinking, JJ. I saw Harlan today! And the man does not belong outside of a hospital."

The doorknob twisted, and the door shuddered an inch or two before stopping. Rachel sat calmly on the bed with her eyes shut, while Evie held her breath. Waiting.

"This is what he wanted," JJ said.

It was weird for the Sheriff to sound so angry while Evie's mom sounded so calm. Usually it was the other way around.

JJ continued, "I promised Iris that if anything happened to her, I would take care of him."

The door swung open slowly, and JJ and the Sheriff hovered at the threshold, as though reluctant to disturb the quiet space. Evie looked at her mom. She was pressing a knuckle against her lip so hard that her lip turned colors. JJ blinked, shook her head slightly, and inched toward the bed.

"Rachel, sweetie," she said, "you probably shouldn't do that. Harlan doesn't really like to be touched."

Eyes still closed, Rachel smiled slightly, but if she heard anything, Evie didn't think it was her mom's voice.

"Rachel," JJ said, and touched her shoulder gently.

Rachel opened her eyes, but again, Evie doubted her mother had prompted the action. Rachel wrapped both of her tiny hands around Harlan's, his slightly darker, rougher skin showing between her almost fluorescent fingers.

"I know you," Rachel said to him. "You helped find me."

Evie gasped—the man's bruised-looking eyelids fluttered, and he opened his eyes. The silver hairs of his mustache quivered as his lips curled in a smile beneath them.

48

J J knew what she'd seen, and yet she couldn't believe it.

Oh, my God.

His eyes were open, and Harlan was staring back at her. Right at her.

JJ squeezed around Rachel, who was still holding his hand, and rested her fingers on top of his head. His eyes were good. Pupils reactive. Tracking her as she moved. Even now, she hesitated to touch his bare skin without gloves. Instead, she looked him in the eyes (*he's in there, I swear to Christ he's in there*) and spoke to him.

"Harlan, can you hear me? Do you know who I am? If you do, blink twice," she said.

She heard the painful crackling of his sticky, dry throat as Harlan swallowed. His tongue snuck out to wet his lips—just a tiny bit, at the center—and she realized, *he's going to try to speak.* A moaning sound came from his mouth, a little like warming up a piece of machinery. She turned her cheek and leaned closer, until she could feel his breath against it.

"What's that, Harlan?" she asked.

"Don't be a dumbass, JJ," he whispered.

Tears sprang to her eyes as her hand flew to her mouth. Her breath caught in her throat, but she managed, "That's Nurse Dumbass to you."

His smile was stronger this time, deepening the creases in his face, and JJ almost kissed him on the lips.

Harlan and Rachel were the only calm people in the room. Evie was wide-eyed with wonder, and Grant, stunned, had dropped his hat on the floor, where it remained, forgotten. JJ smiled at her daughter. It struck her that here, in the very room where they'd helped Maxwell Tulley endure the worst days of his life and ultimately pass on, they were sharing something miraculous, the likes of which they would probably never see again. JJ held out her arm, inviting Evie to join them. Evie pushed eagerly past Grant—

And the closet exploded.

The louvered doors burst out on the far end, popping completely off their track. Their top edge caught the corner of the bed, and she heard a *snap!* as Teddy's massive body fell on top of them. She hoped the noise was only the doors.

"Still there?" she asked Harlan.

"Yeah," he whispered.

His eyes closed—but briefly, she suspected in his best approximation of an eye roll.

Grant hadn't moved except to pull Evie clear (which JJ appreciated). Evie opened her mouth to say something—undoubtedly an elaborate cover story—but JJ shook her head firmly as she maneuvered around her daughter and the Sheriff to reach the downed man. Teddy was lying awkwardly on his belly, slightly hyperextending his back.

"You okay?" she asked. "Don't move until you tell me what hurts."

"Just my pride," he said. "I didn't realize my leg had fallen asleep, so when I moved... well, my leg didn't, but the rest of me did."

Teddy tried to roll over, but with the doors crushed beneath him, there was no solid surface to rest his knees. JJ struggled to move a big piece, hanging together only by the tilt rod.

"Here, let me help," Grant said.

But there wasn't really enough room for the three of them between the bed and the closet.

"Teddy, I mean it, stop moving," JJ warned. "You're making it worse."

Grant glanced at her, face pink with effort beneath his auburn hair. "Did you say Teddy?"

She grunted, lifting one of Teddy's legs. "Yes, *Teddy*. And yes, *that* Teddy. What do you say we untangle him from my closet doors before you run him in?"

JJ was joking, but she had no idea what Grant would do, either what he was authorized to do or what he'd feel obligated to do. She hadn't wanted to be found harboring a fugitive (that was a crime, too, wasn't it?), but part of her motivation for secrecy was to avoid putting Grant in this awkward position. A tear dripped from the end of her inverted nose, a tear that two minutes ago was pure happiness but was now anxious and muddled.

Teddy's chubby, slightly fuzzy, large hand dwarfed JJ's as she helped him to stand. After a wheeze of exertion, he said softly, "It'll be okay, JJ. Don't worry. Just let me talk for myself."

For both of us, he meant.

They'd see about that.

Once he was steady on his feet, Teddy held a hand out to Grant. "Theodore Rutledge, son. I expect you have some questions for me, and I'll be happy to answer them all if you can give me a few minutes with Harlan to make sure he's on solid ground."

"I understand your inclination, sir, but I've got some time pressure here myself. I've got a woman missing—"

Grant paused, glancing over at Harlan, probably wondering

whether he knew about Iris. If he didn't, JJ figured Harlan would soon enough.

Teddy cut in. "Let me stop you right there, Sheriff. You have my word that I don't know—" he counted off each item on a thick finger, "where Virgil Rutledge is, where Danny whatever-the-hell-his-name is, or where Iris Rutledge is."

"How about Adam Rutledge?" Grant asked.

Teddy shook his head. "Him, neither. Sorry, Sheriff."

Grant exhaled heavily and rubbed his hand over his hair, before retrieving his hat and setting it on one of the free chairs. "In that case," he said, and raised his brows significantly at JJ.

"Girls," she said, "why don't you go fix yourselves a snack? You can even watch TV, if you don't tell Dorothy."

Rachel gave Harlan's hand one last pat before joining Evie by the door.

"Mom," Evie drawled, playing at her teenaged self, "don't you think we have enough secrets already?"

"Go," JJ said, glaring at her daughter's back as she shuffled down the hall, feet apparently too heavy to lift from the ground.

"Precocious is the word you're looking for," Teddy said, distracted. He pulled his gloves from his back pocket and slipped them on before sitting next to Harlan. He didn't touch Harlan, but his voice quivered slightly as he said, "You gave me a scare there, old buddy."

"That's 'cause you always wanted to kill me yourself."

Teddy snorted a laugh and quickly wiped his eyes. "JJ, you want to get me that jar of nastiness I had earlier? I might have left it outside."

"No. But I'll send Evie to get it," JJ said, stepping out into the hallway to yell her daughter's errand.

Once she'd done that, she joined Grant, standing against the wall next to the door. Their shoulders touched, and she found herself leaning into him, more and more, until somehow the fingers of one hand had found his.

While they waited, Teddy examined Harlan, much as JJ would have done, from crown to toes. He pressed gently at various spots, though nowhere on his skull except the center of his forehead. JJ couldn't recognize a pattern in his movements. Some points were large muscles while others were bony or connective. Sometimes he used a few fingers, and sometimes a palm. Teddy peeled back the bedding at Harlan's feet, massaging from toes to balls of the feet to arches. He was tugging gently on his feet, extending Harlan's legs, when Evie returned with the jar. The girl's nose wrinkled as she handed it to him.

"Thank you, Evie," JJ said, in a *you can leave now* tone.

And she did, reluctantly.

Teddy sat next to Harlan, unscrewed the jar lid and placed it on the neighboring nightstand.

Harlan's nose wrinkled, reminiscent of Evie's. "My favorite," he croaked.

"Shh," Teddy said, cupping a hand beneath Harlan's head to lift it. He shook his other hand free of its glove, and JJ handed him his jar. Teddy continued, "We already know you're a goddamn Superman. Now shut the hell up, drink this, and get some sleep."

Harlan drank carefully, taking multiple, shallow sips to keep from choking. JJ could see his body relax as he did, as if gravity was pulling him into the depths of the mattress. The liquid level had dropped an inch or so when Teddy stuck out his arm, handing her the jar. Harlan's eyes drifted shut as Teddy lowered his head to the pillow.

"Iris," Harlan whispered.

"That's right," Teddy said. "We've got a lot of shit to take care of, and we need you in tip-top shape to do it. That's the way it works. Remember when we knocked out Adam?"

Harlan smiled and mumbled something. The words got lost in his whiskers, but JJ was pretty sure he said "feisty fucker."

She choked on a laugh, nearly spilling the nasty liquid all

over her scrubs. *Scrubs*? Why the hell was she still wearing her work clothes? She laughed at herself again, and again, before she realized she wasn't laughing.

Grant took the jar from JJ and handed it back to Teddy before wrapping his arms around her. And then she dissolved in tears, Grant lowering her to the floor as her knees buckled. He sat next to JJ and tucked her against him, head beneath his chin, their backs resting against the bed. The world swayed gently, and JJ couldn't decide if he was rocking her or she was rocking him.

"I've got the kids," Teddy said, slipping past them and closing the door behind him.

Her father's room was always the darkest in the house. The day's light was fading already, and the bed cast a shadow tunnel over them. She didn't know how long they stayed there, but eventually her sobbing quieted enough that she could hear Grant's heart beat, feel it through her chest as though it were her own. And then he shifted the slightest bit next to her, and she knew he had to leave. Be the Sheriff. She patted his chest and nodded.

"I want to stay here," she said. "Just a little longer."

Grant somehow stood without kneeing her, clasped her face in his hands and kissed the top of her head firmly. He breathed in the smell of her hair like Trooper did scents he wanted to roll in. She squeezed Grant's hand, then smoothed her fuzzy hair, feeling a dampness she suspected was his tears.

Still sitting on the floor, JJ turned from the door and curled into a ball. The bed felt as solidly reassuring next to her as it had those last nights with her father. And she could feel Harlan's presence upon it, as she'd felt her father's.

She heard Teddy in the doorway, come to check on them, as Grant was leaving. Grant murmured something unintelligible.

"Leave her be, son," Teddy said. "I'm afraid Harlan's not the only one who needs to be ready for what's to come."

49

———

JJ rallied a few minutes later and nearly ran into Teddy in the hallway. Exiting the bathroom, he looked a little worse for wear. His face and hair were damp, and there were water spatters on the front of his shirt. She tried to recall what he'd said about leaving Virgil. "When's the last time you slept?"

"I could ask you the same thing," he said, smiling and stepping aside so she could take a turn at the sink.

JJ washed the itchy tear tracks from her face as quickly as she could. Now that she'd left Harlan, she didn't want to miss anything.

Apparently neither did Evie. Both girls sat ostensibly watching cartoons, but JJ was under no illusions about the object of her daughter's attention. Sitting on the couch, legs tucked beneath one of her grandmother's afghans, Evie rested her head on her hand. Her chin pointed approximately at the TV, but when JJ sat next to her daughter, she noted she also had a decent view of the two men seated at the dining table.

"You know you've put me in an awkward position," Grant said.

"Is there a warrant for my arrest?" Teddy asked. "And if so, on what charge?"

"How about aiding an escape? Or at least harboring a fugitive." Grant shook his head. "I don't want to arrest you any more than you want to be arrested. Where is Virgil Rutledge?"

"I told you, I don't know," Teddy said, leaning back in his chair.

"When did you last see him?"

"Yesterday morning. I left him in a motel in Woodbridge, Virginia. But I can pretty much guarantee he's not there anymore."

"Why is that?" Grant asked.

Teddy sighed. "Because he couldn't have found what he was looking for. Not if his boy was here in Beecham County kidnapping Iris."

"You mean Danny Carpenter?"

Teddy nodded.

"What can you tell me about him?" Grant asked.

"Very little," Teddy said. "I only met him face-to-face once when he was a kid, not realizing at the time that he wasn't Adam. But I can tell you he scares Virgil. And anything that scares Virgil, scares me."

The Sheriff tilted his head back and rested his palms on the table. JJ recognized it as one of his thinking poses. "So Virgil was looking for Carpenter before Iris was taken?"

"He feels like it's his responsibility to stop him," Teddy confirmed. "And I assume you know, Adam's trying to find Virgil."

"What makes you think that?"

Teddy tapped a finger against his temple. "Adam was in here. I tried to hide him from Virgil, but..." He shrugged.

JJ wasn't sure if Grant understood—or believed—what the old man had said any more than she did. The Sheriff's head tilted, and he stared at Teddy askance from beneath one raised brow. Then he jerked his head, as if to clear it, before picking his hat off the table and slamming it back down again with frustration. "Adam and Luther. Those sneaky sonuva—"

"Little pitchers have big ears," JJ warned.

Grant turned toward her guiltily; not only had he forgotten about the children, she was pretty sure he hadn't seen her enter the living room.

"How long will he sleep?" JJ asked, since she'd already interrupted them.

"Maybe an hour," Teddy said. "He needs a lot more, but I promised him we'd find Iris."

"And how do you plan on going about that?" Grant asked.

"I don't know," Teddy admitted, rubbing his hands over tired eyes. "I truly don't. But having Adam would help."

Grant met JJ's eyes, and she shifted next to Evie, reaching around her. "Sweetpea, you want to hand me the phone?"

Evie grabbed the receiver from the table, dodging its cords as she passed it to JJ, before snuggling in next to her. JJ chose to think affection was her motivation rather than nosiness.

JJ dialed, then shook her head. "Luther's not answering."

"Of course he's not." Grant sighed. "I need to talk to Harlan as soon as he wakes. And I'll need to talk to you again, Mr. Rutledge. If I leave for an hour, will you be here when I come back?"

That was just stupid. JJ wriggled free of Evie and headed for the kitchen, calling out, "Why don't you radio in and make any calls you need to from here? I'll fix a little something. By the time you eat, Harlan'll be awake and he can answer whatever questions you want."

Grant glanced toward the windows at the fading light, obviously torn. Finally he said, "Thanks, JJ."

JJ pulled a couple of pizzas from the freezer and cringed at her baking sheets banging as she pulled them from the cabinet. Then she started a salad, timing her chopping so she didn't miss anything the men said.

"Mr. Rutledge," Grant continued, "I was hoping to talk to

Harlan about this, but I'd forgotten—you used to live in Cold Springs, didn't you?"

"Yes, sir," Teddy said.

"What can you tell me about Dead Hollow?" Grant asked.

JJ nearly diced her finger, watching in her peripheral vision as her daughter's head swung toward the Sheriff. "Evie, why don't you and Rachel go to your room and do some homework?"

"I don't have any—"

"Now, Evie," JJ said firmly.

JJ knew she'd made the right decision when Evie didn't even roll her eyes. If anything, she looked relieved. As did Grant, for that matter.

"Dead Hollow," Grant repeated, once the girls had left the living room.

"You want to be a little more specific?" Teddy asked, voice sharp.

JJ gave up on the salad and any pretense she wasn't eavesdropping, moving to sit at the far end of the dining table to give them space if not privacy. After all, it was her house.

"The Rutledge family has a unique relationship with Dead Hollow, don't they?" Grant asked.

"You mean because Adam's mother died there?" the older man said.

"I mean because of what your brother Lawrence used to do there. Your brother, and the rest of his... followers."

Teddy's chair squawked as he scooted it closer to the table, and his voice was low and rough when he asked, "What do you know about that?"

Seated at the head of the table, Grant leaned until his chest nearly touched its surface. His voice dropped as he replied, "Don't forget, Ulysses Mason was my father. You wouldn't expect him to swear his son in without giving him the lay of the land, would you?"

Grant—and his father, but especially Grant—had always

seemed so distant from the darkness of their occupation. JJ supposed she had been naive to think that was the case. She tried to hold still through a little shiver, not wanting to draw the attention of the silent men. She may not know precisely what they were talking about, but she was glad she'd sent the children away.

"This isn't idle curiosity, Mr. Rutledge," Grant said, finally breaking their silence. "I've got a forensic team heading out there right now. A couple of hunters stumbled across something disturbing this afternoon."

Biting her tongue to keep from speaking, JJ could barely make out Teddy's hoarse whisper, "Was it at the altar?"

"Pile of stones, with a bigger, flatter one on top?" Grant asked. "There wasn't a ton of blood, but someone had left what looked like a pig's heart. That sound familiar?"

"Shit," Teddy said, hand pressing to his face.

"I need to know if there's any chance this could be related to what's going on with Danny Carpenter," Grant said.

Perched on the edge of her chair, JJ caught a whiff of pizza, almost entering too-done territory. But she waited for Teddy's reply.

"I'm afraid so," he said, "but I don't know what it means. Let me think on it."

JJ BROUGHT THE GIRLS IN, and everyone (except Harlan, who was still sleeping) ate pizza and salad, with JJ and Grant sitting at the two ends. A cloud seemed to hang over the dining table, with eyes mostly focused on plates. Evie and Rachel peeked surreptitiously around the table and at each other when they thought no one was looking. Still, it was the quietest meal JJ had ever sat through with the girls.

"Thanks, JJ. I needed that," Grant said. He glanced toward the bedrooms at the back of the house. "But I really should be—"

He was interrupted by his phone ringing.

"Excuse me," Grant said, stepping away as he answered. "Yeah, go ahead, Beth."

JJ had thought the table was quiet before, but now the entire house was silent, even the wind that had been brushing the eaves. Silent and waiting. She watched Teddy squeeze his water glass tightly as Grant said, "Jesus. Okay, I'm on my way."

Teddy pushed his chair back from the table and stood.

"It wasn't a pig," the Sheriff said.

JJ stifled a gasp, aspiring to remain at least outwardly calm as the girls' faces swung toward her for reassurance. But she had to ask. "Who is it?"

"We don't know," Grant admitted.

The girls' eyes went wide, confused and scared. Rachel began rocking slightly in her chair, and Evie asked, "What wasn't a pig, Mom?"

JJ took her hand and made a shushing sound that was supposed to comfort her. She could tell it didn't.

"I'm going with you," Teddy said.

"What about Harlan?" JJ asked.

Grant reached for his hat, resting on an empty chair. But it was Rachel who answered, in a small voice, "He wants to come, too."

All attention turned to the silver-haired man who appeared in the hallway. Harlan stood, bracing himself against the walls but still quivering like a blade of grass against a child's breath. "Someone gonna give an old man a hand?"

50

"**S**it there," Danny said, pointing to a chair by the dark wood kitchen table. "And if you move, I promise I'll fucking kill you."

Iris's left eye was nearly swollen shut, and her face had the unhealthy hue of uncooked sausage, the homemade kind in links. She asked, "Aren't you going to do that anyway?"

Danny sighed and leaned against the table. It was heavy, sturdy. "It is looking that way," he admitted. "But you and I both know, another minute alive is another chance to live."

He removed the cuff from her right hand and attached it to one of the table's legs, above a decorative support that ran from the leg to the tabletop, forming an equilateral triangle. Even if Iris flipped the table over, she'd have to break off that support before she could slide her cuff down the table leg to get free.

"Sorry I can't offer you something more comfortable," he said, "but you'd stink up the upholstery."

"And whose fault is that?" she asked.

His balls still ached, but he was mildly impressed that she showed no shame or embarrassment whatsoever for wetting herself again when he'd struck her. It had to be uncomfortable, though, sitting in urine-stained pants. "If it's any consolation, I doubt the plumbing works anyway. It didn't the last time I was here."

That wasn't quite true. Someone had stopped up the toilet bad enough that Danny had chosen to go outside, but the water was otherwise working, as was the electricity. Still, the place was a shithole.

The lighting—where there were bulbs—had an unnerving tendency to hum and pulse. Torn patches in the kitchen's discolored, vinyl flooring exposed the subfloor. The living room, a broad, open space that was the first room you entered from the front door, had a similar flaw half-covered by a rug so nasty a stray dog wouldn't lie on it. The broken springs of its sagging sofa would send you running for a chiropractor, but only after you'd checked that all of your shots were current. A gaping hole in one plaster wall revealed the electrical wiring within, if you were unwise enough to peek inside. (One glimpse of vigorous, scuttling movement had been enough for Danny.)

Iris's head twisted ever so slightly toward the front, as though she tried to hide the movement, but it was hard to miss with the bright, striped scarf hanging around her neck. There was nothing wrong with the woman's hearing. Danny removed her jacket from her shoulders and draped it over another chair, then, on a whim, removed her scarf as well. He might need it later, to keep him warm while he got another vehicle. He strode to the living room to watch Rashid's approach through a grimy, narrow window next to the front door.

Rashid drove an enormous, black SUV, like an Expedition or Navigator, and probably wasn't happy about the road dust turning it gray. Danny peered back toward Iris in the kitchen and was satisfied he could leave her for a moment. He did, however, leave the front door open. The temperature inside was freezing anyway, and maybe fresh air would help clear out the funky smell.

The vehicle came to a stop, then rocked slightly as Rashid engaged the parking brake. The whole property had a mild downhill slope from the house out the driveway. The majority had been engulfed by high grass, with Danny's abandoned car and a single, dead oak tree providing the only vertical relief.

Danny descended the rotting front steps carefully as Rashid exited the SUV. "I don't suppose you have a tow winch on that."

"Do I look like your fucking greasy overalls, day-laboring lackey?" Rashid asked. He wore dark jeans and a rich, charcoal sweater, Danny suspected the cost of which could have gotten him a tow to the state capital. Lest there be any doubt, Rashid added, "No, I don't have a damn tow winch."

"God, I've missed your sunny disposition," Danny said. "Is it any wonder nobody else around here wants to work with you?"

"Here I thought it was because they were a bunch of racist rednecks," Rashid said, strolling around to the back of the SUV. The hatch swung up to reveal a variety of hard, plastic cases, secured along the side and floor of the cargo area.

"Well, that's possible, too. Listen, before we get down to the nitty gritty, I need to run something by you."

Danny explained that he needed to return to West Virginia to retrieve a cache of product. "Mostly oxy, eighty milligram. And a key of heroin."

"Is it that blue shit?" Rashid asked.

"It came from Victor—what do you think?" Danny said. Most of the heroin Victor sent him was laced with fentanyl. Not that Danny cared. He wasn't stupid enough to use it, though he wondered if Rashid didn't dabble on occasion.

"What's my cut?" Rashid asked.

"The usual. And I can be back in a few hours, tomorrow at the outside if I run into complications. There's just one thing."

Rashid looked toward the house. "I'm guessing that one thing would be the reason you wanted me to stay for a while. You got somebody in there you want me to babysit?"

"On the money as always," Danny said, not entirely happy. Danny liked working with Rashid because he was quick, but it was also why he didn't work with him more. Sometimes, Rashid was a little too quick.

Rashid left Danny standing, walking toward the house. His long legs casually ate the distance like candy, up the steps and into the living room. But he was always looking, always aware of his surroundings without seeming to be. Another reason Danny liked working with him. He followed.

Finally, Rashid saw Iris in the kitchen, sitting quietly, shoulders slumped, handcuffed to the table. Her long, white-blonde hair had gone fuzzy with neglect, and the bruise on her face stood out all the more next to it. Rashid leaned in, without touching the doorframe or anything else, scanned the space for other occupants and didn't see any. "Are you fucking with me?" he asked. "Your grandma?"

"She's not—"

But Rashid held up a hand, interrupting him. "No, I don't want to know who she is. Doesn't matter. I'll do it. Add my daily rate on top of my cut."

Danny had expected as much. "Depending on how long it takes me to get back, there's a slight chance someone might come for her."

"Define slight," Rashid said.

Danny shrugged.

"Uh-huh. Not so slight that you didn't want me to bring an arsenal. Fine, but you just doubled my rate." He walked past Danny, back outside to the SUV. Danny caught up with him as he opened the rear hatch and Rashid asked, "We have a backup location?"

Danny pulled a folded piece of notebook paper from his jeans pocket. Rashid took it and shook his head, Danny guessed because of the state of the directions or the quality of his penmanship. Either way, he thought, gritting his teeth, he didn't appreciate the condescension.

Rashid grunted. "Helluva drive." He tucked the paper in his back pocket, then nodded toward the house while reaching for a hard-sided rifle case. "Change her pissy pants before you leave. I can't have that in my car if we have to move out in a hurry."

51

———

Adam found the pervasive scent of coffee beverages both reassuring and mildly revolting.

After leaving the state park and making their way to the highway, the men had found an Internet café at the next reasonably sized town. Adam and Virgil sat at a table, sipping coffee and waiting for their food, while Luther used one of the computers in the back. They'd decided they'd attract less attention if Luther did most of the internet digging himself. Once he'd checked out a few things and narrowed down Danny's possible location, Virgil would join him for a final consult.

"Try not to look so nervous," Adam said. The nap outside after... *whatever* (he really needed some terminology for this crazy crap) had helped him feel almost human, but not for long. He hoped the caffeine in front of him would nudge him further in the right direction.

"I don't go to these kind of places," Virgil said. "The tables are always too small."

Adam almost laughed. They had stopped in a small college town, and the vibe was definitely more hipster than redneck. But

Virgil was a fugitive from the law, an escaped prisoner; you'd think social awkwardness would take a back seat.

When he woke—or rather, when Virgil woke him—Adam's thinking had been clearer. He'd gained some emotional distance from what was happening, enough to wonder about the past. "How much does Iris know about the night mom died?"

"What do you mean?" Virgil asked.

"Well, Iris wasn't there. You never came back, so presumably someone in law enforcement informed her what happened."

"Okay," Virgil nodded, and Adam was thankful he didn't take the observation as a criticism.

"So all she knows about that night is what they told her?" Adam asked.

"I guess." Virgil winced as he took a sip of the latte Adam had ordered for him. "Do they not sell a regular cup of black coffee?"

Adam didn't usually drink lattes, either, but his thinking was still a little sluggish. He wasn't sure his stomach could handle straight coffee, and a latte was the only drink with milk he could think of while standing at the counter. Of course, he'd felt a fool when he passed the condiment station with unlimited access to five kinds of milk.

"What about me?" Adam asked. "Wouldn't I have told her about it?"

"Probably not," Virgil said, braving another sip. "I imagine it's common for a child to not speak after something like that. And you weren't really talking yet anyway."

"Really?" Adam asked, taken aback.

Virgil's mouth crooked in an almost-smile. "You were a late talker. Hell, I don't even know when you started in earnest. It must've been after I was gone. Everyone was afraid there was something wrong with you. Everyone except me and Charlotte. We knew you weren't speaking yet because you didn't have to."

"What do you mean I didn't have to?"

They were interrupted when the server arrived with their burgers. Adam smiled and waited for her to leave, ready to push Virgil if need be, but his father answered while pouring an obscene amount of ketchup on his bread.

"You were an only child, no cousins, no other kids," Virgil said. He paused to shake his head and mutter over a sweet potato fry. "You never had to interact with anyone but us and Iris, and we always knew what you wanted. Especially Charlotte."

Adam's stomach growled, but he hesitated to eat, afraid of missing a single word about his mother. "Was she..."

He didn't finish, but he didn't have to. Virgil raised his eyebrows. "You mean you don't know?"

When Adam didn't answer, Virgil said, around a mouthful of meat, "I should've figured Iris wouldn't tell you anything."

"Harlan said she was a healer," Adam said.

Virgil's eyes narrowed, but he grudgingly admitted Harlan was right. "She was a lot of things, things I don't even think she knew about, and who knows what else she would have become, in time. Maybe she was a psychic, maybe she was a witch—"

"A witch!" Adam said, too loud, and looked around to see if he'd drawn any attention.

"I didn't say she was. Really, I don't even know what that means. They're just words. Labels. I know she was exceptional, that she knew and could do things that weren't easily explained. That she was fierce and forgiving and..." Virgil paused, hand shaking as he reached for his latte. "And I know only someone like her could have loved someone like me."

Adam stared down at his untouched food, to give his father a moment. But that moment was brief. Luther approached, winding his way through the poorly arranged, mostly empty tables.

"Why didn't you tell me the food was here?" he said, and lifted the top piece of bread on his burger, scraping off a pile of sprouts. His disdainful expression reminded Adam of Virgil sampling his latte. "Since when do cheeseburgers grow in gardens?"

"Any luck?" Adam asked.

"I think so," Luther said. "Virgil, would you come check real quick so we can eat and hit the road?"

Virgil grabbed a couple more fries and wiped his hands on a napkin before rising to follow Luther, leaving Adam to eat his own food in peace. He'd been hungry a few minutes ago, but now Adam barely tasted what passed his lips.

The talk of Adam's mother had distracted him from his original purpose in asking his father about that night. His mind kept returning to the place where his mother had died. What was it Iris had told Adam about Dead Hollow, when she visited Adam in the hospital after the craziness with Rachel? That his grandfather Lawrence had taken his followers there... snake-handling in the *Valley of Death*. That was it. Virgil had also mentioned Dead Hollow when Adam had "dropped in" on him and Teddy in the motel room a couple of days ago. Adam wasn't certain of Virgil's exact words—he'd sounded crazy, and Adam had been worried about getting caught—but something about it all going back to Dead Hollow and being part of Lawrence's plan.

The final connection: Dead Hollow was where Virgil had kidnapped Danny. Surely it wasn't a coincidence, but Adam couldn't imagine what it all meant. He also couldn't imagine Virgil explaining it to him. Virgil might not be a passenger on the crazy train at this instant, but Adam feared anything could send him hopping on the next car. Luther was no help—he seemed uncomfortable with all the mystical crap (Luther's words). Adam needed someone grounded but open-minded to talk to. Someone like Harlan. With Iris gone, Adam hoped someone checked on him after he was transferred. *JJ*, he thought, relieved. She'd keep an eye on Harlan.

Adam had no recollection of eating his food, but he found his fingers grasping absently at phantom fries on an empty plate. He couldn't see Luther and Virgil over a low wall that partitioned the space, but he assumed they still had their heads together over a monitor. Adam decided to bus his portion of the table before checking in with them.

He must have stood too quickly. Adam's heavy plate clattered against the table as he found himself sitting again, hard. The young woman who'd brought their food (tiny, with a pink-streaked pixie cut) was passing by from another table.

"Are you okay?" she asked, touching his arm gently.

Adam's lips were numb, but he forced a smile. "Fine, thanks. Pulled a couple of all-nighters on my thesis, and I guess I need more coffee. Or maybe more sleep."

She looked at Adam. *Really* looked at him, like he was a human being instead of just a guy who nearly dropped a dish. "Not that we can't use the business, but I think you'd better choose sleep for a while. And leave the plate."

Adam waited a minute or two, then attempted standing, hands on the table and the back of the chair. *So far, so good.* He walked carefully past the over-bright local art and the coffee and ceramic displays, past the half wall, to the three public computer terminals and bathroom access in the back. Luther had already printed a couple of pages and was zoomed in on another. Virgil pointed tentatively at the screen, showing the combination of fascination and ill-at-ease Adam usually associated with older people confronting unfamiliar technology.

"How's it going?" Adam asked.

"Almost done," Luther said. "You mind seeing if they'll box up my food?"

"No problem," Adam said. "Then I thought I'd get some fresh air."

Luther pulled his keys from his pocket and started to toss

them, but stopped mid-swing, handing them to Adam instead. "Here—we shouldn't be more than a few minutes, but feel free to curl up in the back."

Am I that transparent? Adam wondered, trying to recall how much of the parking lot he'd have to cross before he could crash.

52

———

Standing, Luther watched Adam talk to their server. By the look on her face and the way she fidgeted with her half apron, the young woman also wondered if she'd have to pick him up off the floor.

"I said, I think that's the place," Virgil said, finger hovering less than an inch from the screen, as though afraid to touch it but figuring Luther was blind as a bat.

Luther sat back down, made sure everything was lined up on the screen, gave the command to print, and waited for the sound of the little zipping jets. It was his first time paying for internet in a public place, but it hadn't been as painful as he'd expected. When he rose from his seat and scanned the front, Adam had left.

"Okay, let's go," Virgil said, as soon as the printer stopped.

"Wait." Luther put a hand on Virgil's elbow. Virgil stared like he'd put his dick on his arm, but Luther didn't budge. The other computers weren't being used, and Luther slid a chair from the nearest one, motioning Virgil to sit.

"What's wrong with Adam?" Luther asked.

"He's sensitive."

Luther shook his head. "Hunh-unh. Sensitive is a kid that cries because you said his choo-choo train picture looks like a doghouse. Sensitive is not..."

His voice trailed off because he didn't really want to say the things he was thinking out loud, didn't want to make them any more real.

"What I meant by sensitive is, Adam is like a sponge. His mind absorbs everything," Virgil explained. "He needs someone, someone like Uncle Teddy, to teach him how to filter what's coming in."

"Why can't you do that?"

Virgil shrugged. "I don't know how to teach anyone—it just came naturally for me. But I have been blocking some of it for him."

Luther was trying not to get hung up on the whos and hows and what-fors of a world he couldn't have admitted existed a month ago. But that didn't mean he'd thrown his critical thinking out the window. "You don't understand how you protect yourself, and yet you think you can use that same mechanism to protect someone else. It ever occur to you that maybe what you're doing is making Adam worse?"

Virgil's mouth stretched thin, immobile as a line on their maps, while his eyes regained the jumpiness that had been mostly absent of late. Luther leaned forward, elbows on his knees, and lowered his voice.

"What do you think's gonna happen if we do find Danny and Iris, and Adam's in this kind of shape? Huh?" Luther waited, but Virgil still wouldn't answer, so Luther did, as uneasy as it made him to do so. "Somebody's gonna end up hurt, or worse. Somebody meaning Adam, and probably Iris, too."

Virgil looked away, and Luther heard the irritating, nails-on-a-chalkboard quality sound of his teeth grinding against each other.

"Your son is gonna end up dead, Virgil. Is that what you want?" Luther asked.

But the man had completely shut down.

Luther wanted Danny—he wanted to wring his goddamn neck for what he'd done to Les. Not just in his final hours, but in the final months of Les's life, when Danny had isolated his brother by feeding his addiction. Luther wanted it so badly he could almost feel the man's throat in his hands. He wanted Danny to beg for mercy, so he could choose not to give it. He wanted him to suffer. He wanted to watch the life drain out of the man, to witness the moment Danny's soul crossed over into hell. No matter what it might mean for Luther's own.

But he'd also made promises to old Sheriff Mason, to uphold the law (which he'd mostly done over the years) and to watch over Adam Rutledge. The latter was more important—maybe even more important than the promise he'd made to Les before pulling the plug—and Luther couldn't help but think he'd done a piss-poor job of keeping it.

"Fuck this," Luther said, extending past Virgil toward the printer. "I'm calling it in. If Danny and Iris are there, law enforcement should be the ones going in."

"No," Virgil said, swatting his arm away like a child.

Luther patted at his pockets and realized he'd left his cell phone in the car. He wasn't sure how to share the map with Grant anyway. He doubted the cafe had a fax machine, and the camera on his cheap phone didn't work for shit.

"Fine," Luther said, straightening in his chair and grabbing the mouse. "I'm sure I can figure out how to email the goddamn map."

"No! You have to be there in the end," Virgil said, eyes glittering.

Great, Luther thought. *The bastard's crossed back over into Loopy Land.* He tried to ignore Virgil and the familiar tingling the man brought out on the back of Luther's neck. But it wasn't easy, nor did it make figuring out the tech bit any easier. *Right-click? Shift-click? Maybe a dropdown menu?*

Suddenly Virgil squeezed the webbing of Luther's thumb and the outside of his hand, forcing Luther to drop the mouse.

"Ouch!" Luther shook his hand, trying to release the cramping muscles. "Motherfucker! What was that for?"

"I said, no. You're going with us."

The computer mouse swung below the desk, dangling by its cord. Luther reached for it, even though he wasn't sure he could hold it. Virgil grabbed his hand again. But this time, this time his touch changed everything.

A jolt ran through Luther that made his chest ache, and he watched Virgil's pupils blow out like he'd been hit by a massive dose of amphetamines. Luther flashed back to seeing Adam, lying on the ground on the mountain, hypothermic and incoherent, the darkness in his eyes swallowing all but the barest sliver of blue. And then Luther flashed back—*fell* back—even further.

The car had been parked next to the barn, a little automatic piece of shit Escort with the keys in the ignition. Luther didn't know who it belonged to. Some asshole too smashed to know any better. Or maybe they figured no one would mess with it at Rudy Beck's house. He hoped it was somebody bad-ass. If they blamed Rudy, maybe they'd do something about it. About Rudy. Because if they didn't, someday Luther was going to have to.

Luther didn't have a license yet, but he'd been driving around their property since he was tall enough to reach the pedals and see over the steering wheel. Before that, really. He used to sit on Rudy's lap and steer while Rudy worked the pedals. Once Luther had run them into the ditch and the steering wheel bloodied his nose on impact. Of course, that was nothing to the ass-whooping Rudy had given him. Luther had slept on his belly for days afterward.

He'd never driven alone at night before. Colors looked weird, washed out. The trees felt closer—looming—and keeping track of the headlights was more challenging than he'd have thought. Luther was pretty confident in his abilities behind the wheel, but the deer were thick this time of evening and unpredictable, so when he finally found the high beam switch he left them on. He'd seen three deer so far, faces mildly curious and eyes glowing on a bank above the road, but he'd only met one vehicle. It was a pickup, and he doubted his headlights were set high enough or bright enough to have caused the driver much bother.

Luther didn't know where he was headed. He just had to get out. His mother wouldn't go with him, but she wasn't in too bad of shape this time and he'd convinced her to lock herself in little Les's room with him. Luther often thought he'd end up killing Rudy. Have to shoot him, he guessed—there was no other way he could think of to get rid of the man. Unless he killed him while he was sleeping, but Luther knew he couldn't do that, no matter how much of a mean old bastard his father was. He also knew if he did shoot Rudy, he'd have to make it count. Son or not, Rudy wouldn't hesitate to kill Luther in retaliation.

The bad turn before Dead Hollow was coming up, and the one at Dead Hollow itself was even worse, so Luther slowed a little. He knew the key on those steep curves was to brake beforehand—don't ride your brakes as you're turning—and pick your path and keep to it, not futz around making little adjustments back and forth. But his hands shook on the wheel; he kept seeing the bruise rising on his mother's cheek as he handed her an ice pack. Sonuvabitch.

Distracted, Luther didn't slow quite enough before the first curve. A mild panic fluttered in his chest as he did his best to control the car, fighting the ton-plus of inertia that wanted to keep going straight. He made it through the first turn, but when the next one swung even more sharply in the opposite direction, Luther overcorrected. He drifted across the center line, just as a foggy glow breached the side of the mountain, heralding an oncoming car.

Luther whipped the wheel back, but it was too late. The other car's headlights flashed as it swerved. Brakes screamed on the asphalt, but the car slammed into the guardrail anyway. And kept going, rocketing off the road and into the trees...

LUTHER JERKED his hand free from Virgil, heart pounding and lungs bursting as though he'd been underwater. Sweat drenched his armpits and ran down the sides of his face. Maybe he was having a heart attack.

He deserved one.

Virgil's lips had paled to a putrid shade of lavender, and his glistening eyes were so red Luther expected him to blink bloody tears.

Luther didn't know what to say. He had no words.

Not that it mattered. Virgil wasn't giving him a chance to speak.

"Sonuvabitch!" Virgil screamed, lunging at him.

Luther's chair flipped and the back of his head smacked the floor hard enough to feel concrete beneath thin carpet. Virgil climbed on top of him, as he had Adam mere hours ago. He wrapped a hand around Luther's throat, lifted it an inch or two, then pressed down. Luther felt a small pop in the soft tissue of his throat, like a kneecap sliding in and out of place.

"I should kill you," Virgil said.

Luther smelled mustard and meat and milky coffee and saw a small speck of lettuce in his teeth. Virgil adjusted his arm—and Luther's throat—maneuvering closer, until his forehead came to rest on Luther's. His skull grinding into Luther's, Virgil continued, "Kill you, the way you killed her."

Luther shut his eyes, motionless and calm. All the strands, all the could-have-beens in the universe had finally coalesced into the moment he'd anticipated for thirty years. And yet, the grief still felt so heavy on him. Heavier than Virgil. Heavier than the weight of the world. It pressed down, found its way into the crooks and crevices to fill Luther up inside until it leaked out the corners of his eyes.

"Yes," Luther whispered, voice creeping higher from the pressure of Virgil's hand. "You should. Just kill me."

And he waited for the end.

53

"What the hell!" demanded a female voice.

Luther opened his eyes, straining them toward the top of his skull until his brain ached. The pink-haired server hovered at the red edges of his vision.

"I'm calling the cops," she said.

"No," Luther said, trying to sit and lifting Virgil with him.

The pounding pulse and squeezing pressure in Luther's head eased as Virgil released his throat, and the gray slowly faded from his vision. Luther grunted when Virgil kneed him in the thigh while climbing off.

"Wait," Luther said, swallowing hard and raising a single hand until he could gather his strength to hoist the rest of his body. "No cops. It's a misunderstanding. I was having a seizure—"

"Bullshit!" the young woman said.

"Okay, fine," Luther said, getting to his feet slowly with the aid of the nearest chair. His throat was fine but everything else ached. Luther gave the young woman his most agreeable, sheepish smile. "You're right—that was bullshit. But he and his son have been going through a rough time, and I said something I shouldn't have. We weren't fightin'; he just reacted. And I'm fine. So there's nothing to gain by calling the cops."

She stepped behind the half wall barrier while crossing her arms and scowling, clearly trying to look as though she weren't intimidated.

"I'm very sorry, miss," Luther said. He pulled a twenty from his wallet and set it next to the unharmed computer. "To cover any inconvenience. And we're leaving right now. We're truly sorry."

He motioned Virgil to turn and walk around the partition on the end farthest from the server, to avoid threatening her with their proximity. Nothing was broken, most of the other customers had already turned their attention back to their laptops, and filing a complaint was a time-consuming pain in the ass. Luther doubted she'd do it. So long as he and Virgil-the-fugitive made it out of sight with no further incidents.

Luther lumbered to the door and paused outside, scanning the parking lot. Adam's dark head rested, motionless, against the rear passenger window of Luther's SUV. Luther headed left, toward a recessed, open air seating area that no one else was stupid enough to use in November. He'd barely turned the corner, out of view of the parking lot, when Virgil shoved him from behind.

"I saw you that night," Virgil said. "Standing above us on the road. Don't try to pretend you didn't see me."

Luther had seen him. Heard him, too. And not just that night. At least a year's full of nights in the decades since. Begging for help, and threatening to find him if he left. And now he had. Found him.

Luther stood his ground while Virgil got in his face. "How could you leave her to die?" he demanded.

Virgil suddenly slammed his forehead against Luther's, hard enough that his world briefly went dark with the pain. Luther's law enforcement training kicked in, and he grabbed Virgil's wrist almost before he could see it. Then he yanked Virgil toward him, spinning him around and twisting Virgil's arm up behind his back before pinning his other arm as well.

"I was fifteen!" Luther protested, applying more pressure than he'd intended. "I couldn't save her any more than you could."

"You could have tried."

Yes, he could have. He needn't have climbed down the bank to the wreck—he could've simply gotten help. Faster. Luther had stopped at the nearest payphone and called it in anonymously, but that was in town. What if he'd stopped at someone's house instead of waiting? What if he'd prioritized their safety over his own fear?

It didn't matter, because he hadn't, and he couldn't change that. So he'd told himself. But it had never brought him comfort or closure or any of that other bullshit, even when Charlotte Rutledge's widower and abandoned son were still abstracts.

Luther stepped back as he released the man, but Virgil's initial fury seemed spent. He was thankful no one had emerged from the corner health food store at an inopportune time. Still, their business wasn't finished. Luther stared at the shop as he parked himself at the nearest cheap, plastic table, remembering he'd never gotten his burger from the cafe.

Virgil sat silently across from him.

Yelling at Virgil had snapped Luther out of his existential fog. For now. No doubt it would return at night, as it usually did. These days, Les's face often joined Charlotte Rutledge's in Luther's dark hours of recriminations. Still, Luther waited for Virgil to speak because Virgil would determine what happened next. But Luther soon found himself unwilling to wait any longer.

"Will you tell Adam?" Luther asked.

Virgil clasped his hands together, as though praying. "I can't. You have to be there at the end."

Luther ignored the batshit crazy aspect of Virgil's premise in favor of analyzing the attendant logic. "Does that mean you won't... send me away?" he asked, not even sure how that would work since they were traveling together in *his* vehicle.

Virgil shut his eyes and squeezed his hands together more tightly, tapping them against his forehead, harder and harder. "You do realize, you broke everything. Right?"

When Luther didn't answer, Virgil opened his spooky eyes and boomed like Satan's evangelist, "Do you know this? Do you know what you've done?"

"Yes, sir," Luther said, and meant it to the marrow of his bones. "Yes, I do."

"That's why you have to fix it. Why you have to be there." Virgil pinched his own face with the hands that had gripped Luther's throat, and his eyes filled with revelatory tears.

"I finally see it. You'll be there for both endings. No matter how much I want to kill you, or how much you deserve to die. It's your turn to watch over Adam. To protect him." Virgil sighed and brushed away the wetness. "You know, that's the second time Adam saved your life."

"When was the first time?" Luther asked, his skin puckering into a familiar creepy crawl from the fleshy bits of his arms to his neck and back down his spine.

Virgil stood and tugged the front of his jacket straight. "Danny wanted to kill you on the mountain, when you apprehended me and sent the girl for help. I am glad she didn't die, by the way."

"Danny? He was there?" Luther sputtered.

"Of course he was. Who did you think untied me and built the fire?" Virgil said.

Luther shuddered all over, like he'd been dunked in ice water. He remembered the prickling sensation of being watched on the top of the mountain, of being a target. Because he had been.

"I'll meet you back at the car. I'm going to get Adam a ginger ale," Virgil said, hands in his coat pockets, and strode toward the health food store.

Luther watched him go. He wanted to follow him, to go through every detail with the crazy fucker and figure out what the hell had happened up there on the mountain. But he couldn't. Not now. He couldn't afford to tip the balance with Virgil, couldn't risk him telling Adam the truth before this was over. Whatever that meant.

And he was a little bit afraid to learn more.

Instead Luther concentrated on where he had to be, on the outline of his vehicle, on the milky streaks on his windshield that absorbed the afternoon sun, on the ding on his bumper and the passenger's side mirror that was slightly off true.

And still, Luther's legs were shaking so badly, he stumbled and fell to one knee stepping over the curb.

54

The condition he was in, no way was JJ letting Harlan out of her sight. Grant proceeded to Dead Hollow, and JJ rode with Teddy and Harlan after she'd dropped the girls off at Dorothy's. The girls weren't crazy about staying behind. They'd heard much more than they should have this afternoon, but it was better that they'd heard it firsthand than in bits and pieces from less reliable sources later. At least, that's what JJ told herself. And Dorothy's house was the best place for them now. A co-worker had brought Otto home from the hospital an hour or so ago, so he would give the girls (and Dorothy) something else to focus on.

JJ sat between Harlan and Teddy. Teddy's hands were shaking so badly, JJ had almost insisted on driving, but he probably needed something else to focus on, too. The seat belt seemed to be the only thing holding Harlan upright—that and the passenger door. (She resisted the "mom urge" to check it was secure while the vehicle shuddered down the highway.) JJ grabbed Harlan's hand impulsively—it radiated heat—but tried to let go as soon as she realized what she'd done. Harlan held her fast.

"Whoever that is, it's not Iris," Harlan said, voice weak but certain. "I'd know if it was."

JJ nodded and blinked hard. Her mind could not comprehend Iris's heart, severed from her body, decomposing on a rock in the woods. And yet her mind kept trying to do so, no matter how much she begged it not to.

Still holding her hand, Harlan shut his eyes. His breath was audible but moved in and out evenly, as though he were practicing a relaxation exercise. His hand gradually cooled in hers, and JJ felt herself becoming calm. That is, until she noticed how rapidly—almost violently—his eyes flicked back and forth beneath his stained lids. She flinched at the sight, and Harlan gave her hand a last squeeze before releasing it and opening his eyes.

"It'll be okay," he said, closing his eyes again and resting his clasped hands on his lap. "I promise. But, stick close to me, if you don't mind."

It was the way an elderly person—say one who'd been in a coma for weeks—would ask for help if he were proud but not quite stupid. So why did JJ think there was more to it than that? A wry smile touched her lips.

Because Harlan's a tough, wily old bastard.

They turned off the highway onto a rutted gravel road with an abrupt downhill drop. JJ passed Dead Hollow nearly every day on her way to work, but she'd never been into Dead Hollow proper before. She wondered if anyone still camped there. It had never been popular, and had fallen completely out of favor for years after Danny was kidnapped. But memories were finite, even bad ones.

Teddy's hands appeared steadier now, perhaps because he had to hold the steering wheel so tightly to stay on the road. When Grant had described where to meet him, Teddy had known the way, and he hadn't shown a moment's hesitation so far. At least, not so far as navigation was concerned.

A groan escaped Harlan before he bit off the sound. "I'm fine," he said, anticipating her.

He didn't look fine. His face was as ghostly pale as the hair hidden beneath a borrowed baseball cap. He wore some of her father's old clothes, musty from storage, and one of Otto's coats, but JJ chastised herself for not getting him a scarf, too.

JJ found the number of seriously ill or injured men in her life to be oddly unsettling. Her ex-husband was currently hospitalized with a gunshot wound. Otto and Harlan had only gotten out today. Adam had been hospitalized twice in the past month. And which of them looked the healthiest? Her money was on Marcus. He was probably harassing the other nurses already. It was one of his gifts, rolling in shit and coming out smelling like a rose.

Several law enforcement vehicles, all SUVs or pickups, were parked ahead of them in an open area at the bottom of the slope. JJ braced herself against the dash, her teeth clacking painfully, as Teddy rushed a little too enthusiastically to join them. He pulled over onto the last remaining portion of level ground that wouldn't block in the other vehicles, and the engine stalled before he could park.

"Close enough," Teddy said. "Harlan, tell me you're not goddamn stupid enough to go out there."

"I am not goddamn stupid enough to go out there," Harlan confirmed, opening his eyes.

Harlan winced when Teddy threw open the driver's door, as if even the air of the place burned his skin. JJ watched Teddy tug his jeans up and shamble toward the milling uniforms in a stereotypical old man gait that she'd never associated with Harlan. Of course, Harlan could barely walk now.

"Did you notice a limp?" Harlan asked.

"No," JJ answered. "Was I supposed to?"

Harlan didn't reply.

JJ saw Grant weaving his way to meet the large, elderly man.

Releasing her seat belt, she slid across the seat toward the driver's door.

Harlan's seat belt clicked free, and he caught her arm. "Don't."

"Don't what?" she asked.

"Don't go out there."

JJ pulled free of Harlan (it didn't take much effort to do so) and gave him her best stink eye.

"Humor an old man," Harlan said. When she continued scowling, he said, "Fine. But you're not going to like what I have to say."

Harlan sighed and scooted forward until his knees struck the dashboard. Resting his head against the back, he said, "If you go out there, you will draw *attention*. Attention you don't want. And I don't mean from law enforcement. Take a good look around."

JJ wasn't sure where Teddy and Grant had run off to, but many of the officers—all men, that she could see—moved with purpose deeper into the woods. Even leafless, the trees were thick enough for them to quickly disappear in the shadows. It got dark so early and so fast in the hollows. The clock promised more than an hour of light left, but the sky was the deep, pervasive blue-gray that precedes a thunderstorm in summer.

The canopy couldn't account for the gloom. To their right, the only trees with any foliage at all were a few scattered pines, short and scraggly and thin-needled. To the left, the trees were clearly dead, not just riding out the winter. The ground lacked the hint of earthy almost-pink color that came with a fresh crop of fallen leaves. There were no birds, no squirrels, no clumps of mistletoe in the tree crowns. No signs of life. And yet, the trees weren't rotting in place, either.

The edges of the lifeless trunks blurred as JJ's eyes scanned the landscape. The longer she looked, the harder she stared, the more she thought the blurring was... what? Something more than eye fatigue. That it was movement, or rather the traces—the *wake*—left behind by something weaving through the branches and along the ground. It made her uneasy. Uneasy enough to humor an old man and stay put.

She and Harlan sat in silence as the sky edged toward dusk. The forest shifted from pale, recognizable trunks to silhouettes looming against the remaining light. JJ hugged her arms tightly as the truck grew chillier. Since Teddy had taken the keys with him, they couldn't turn on the heat. Assuming it worked. She stared at Harlan. Would she be able to sit here, calm as he was, if Grant had been kidnapped as Iris had? No way. But she couldn't forget how long Harlan had been hospitalized. The man shouldn't be sitting at all.

JJ reached for the door handle, thinking to track down Teddy.

"Please stay put," Harlan said, eyes still shut. "Teddy is on his way."

Half a minute later she saw flashlights bobbing toward the parked cars from the woods, and a single figure—no uniform— approached their truck. Harlan pulled himself upright and slipped off his cap to rub his head, his silver hair a luminous blur in the dim vehicle.

Teddy struggled to get in the pickup, bracing against the door, then supporting himself with the steering wheel as he dragged his other leg inside. Panting slightly, he said, "It's got Lawrence written all over it."

Both men were so pale and drawn in the artificial, overhead light that JJ wanted to check their pulses. Instead she asked, "What does that mean?"

"Do you want to go find him?" Teddy asked, looking past her at Harlan as though she were transparent.

"Yes," Harlan said, "but there are complications."

And now Teddy's eyes locked on JJ.

JJ's head swung back around to Harlan, who was nodding. "What the hell are you two talking about?" she asked. "Is Iris okay?"

"It wasn't Iris. They don't know who it was, but likely someone much younger," Teddy said. "I believe what happened here was a first step, and we need to find this man before he does hurt Iris. I'm not entirely sure how Adam fits into everything—"

"Let me try Luther again," JJ said, pulling out her cell phone. The dome light faded away as she squinted at its screen. No signal. "Shit."

"I tried," Harlan said, "but I can't get in touch with Adam either."

It took JJ a moment to comprehend that he meant get in touch with Adam without a cell phone. *With his mind.* Her own brain—and neck—ached, her attention swiveling between the two men. "What does that mean?" she asked.

"You're not in touch with Virgil lately, are you?" Harlan asked.

Teddy grunted a curse. "No. I don't suppose I am."

Was that why Harlan had asked JJ about seeing the limp? Frustration gave way to fear as she demanded, "What the hell is going on?"

Harlan rested a calming hand on her arm. "I think Virgil is blocking us from reaching him and Adam."

"Why would he do that?" JJ asked.

"I don't know," Harlan admitted. "He hates me, but Teddy—"

"He thinks he's protecting Adam," Teddy suggested. "From what, I can't guess. And whether he really is protecting Adam, or it's just another of Virgil's delusions... who knows?"

JJ recalled her earlier conversation with Teddy about his relationship with Virgil. "Wait—you said Virgil would drive Adam crazy if they were together."

Teddy let his silence speak for him.

JJ watched law enforcement vehicles switching on their headlights, providing harsh illumination to narrow sections of forest and plunging the rest into deeper darkness. What had Adam and Luther gotten into? Nothing the men out there would understand. So what the hell were *they* going to do about it?

"There's something else," Harlan said. "This is where I found Adam after his mother's accident."

No wonder Harlan had been certain whatever happened here was connected with the kidnapping. When Rachel was missing, JJ had thought Adam was the key to finding her. It seemed now that he was the key to everything, or at least his family was.

"He was sitting on Lawrence's altar," Harlan added.

Teddy's breath huffed. "And as a toddler, Adam damn well didn't find his way there on his own."

"Wait a minute," JJ cut in. "You keep saying altar. What do you mean—like, an *altar* altar?"

Harlan grimaced. "Afraid so. Over the years, people have identified hot spots of power and placed altars there. The one in Dead Hollow predates Lawrence, but he used it during his lifetime."

"The idea being that altars were like batteries," Teddy added. "Lawrence thought what he did there would store power he could draw upon later when he needed it."

JJ gasped when Harlan continued, "There was a bloody knife on the altar next to Adam. It wasn't Adam's blood."

"Virgil?" Teddy asked.

Harlan shrugged. "Charlotte's the one who led me to the boy."

Charlotte... Adam's dead mother? JJ shook her head. She didn't believe Harlan, but she didn't quite *disbelieve* him, either.

"So you think... what?" Teddy asked, apparently unable to articulate any theories of his own.

"That something was at work here, something bigger than Virgil and Charlotte. And that somehow, together, they shielded their son. They protected Adam."

JJ shook her head, having just hit the wall on the supernatural bullshit. Danny was crazy, and he had Iris. Virgil was crazy, and he was with Adam. Both Iris and Adam were in danger. Simple as that. But she wasn't about to argue philosophy or religion or whatever the hell this crap was with the two old men. It didn't matter, because the why didn't matter. They all wanted the same thing.

"How do we find Iris and Adam?" she asked.

"You're not going with us," Teddy said.

"Yes, I am," JJ said, grabbing the truck keys from his nerveless hand. "And I'm driving. You were scary enough on the way here, and now you look like you're ready to pass out."

Teddy slid out of the truck to trade places. "Fine," he said. "You can drive us to your house. But you're still not going with us."

The air outside felt strange, cold and... metallic? She struggled to identify a subtle odor. Harlan said nothing when she got back in and avoided looking at her. Or maybe he was avoiding the harsh, overhead light.

JJ maneuvered the unfamiliar truck carefully. She couldn't see the terrain in the growing darkness, especially reversing, and she hadn't driven a manual transmission regularly for years. She supposed she'd have to borrow one to teach Evie, when the time came. It was an important skill, even if stick was becoming the exception.

Three lurching pivots and a couple of curses later, she finally had the truck pointing in the right direction and crept past the other parked vehicles. Her peripheral vision caught streaking movement on one side, but she ignored it. Harlan and Teddy and all their goddamned woo-woo—

"JJ! Wait!" Grant yelled, suddenly appearing like a ghost in her headlights.

Grant stutter-stepped backwards as JJ slammed the brakes, stalling the truck. Her heart pounded in her chest, and Teddy gripped the dashboard next to her.

The Sheriff knocked on her window before she could catch her breath. "JJ, I need you to come with me."

She fumbled with the window, then gave up and opened her door. "What are you—"

"Now," Grant said.

55

Evie hoped her mom got back soon, because Rachel's mom was driving her crazy. And Evie didn't think she was alone. Mr. Nicholson had winked at her once, when Evie retreated against the couch as far as possible to avoid Mrs. Nicholson's obsessive hovering. Honestly, Mrs. Nicholson was nice enough, and Evie could understand why she was stressed out, but Evie preferred hanging out with Rachel's dad. He actually did stuff outside, and sometimes he let the girls help. Though obviously not with the chainsaw.

For now, Mr. Nicholson was wearing an old pair of work pants that Mrs. Nicholson had sliced up the middle and then pinned back together. His leg was so cool in a gross, skin-crawling way. Evie was surprised Rachel had watched with her while Rachel's mom changed the dressing. The stitches had looked more like staples than anything sewn into flesh. Definitely creepy cool.

Rachel had been very quiet this evening, and not just while Evie oohed and aahed over her dad's wound. She got that way sometimes if her mom was being particularly pushy, but Evie thought there was something else bothering Rachel, too. She hadn't had a chance to ask her about it because Rachel's mom wouldn't let the girls out of her sight after their little disappearing stunt. Evie was pretty sure she hadn't figured out that they'd escaped through the window, or she would have totally freaked out. The secret thought made Evie smile.

Suddenly she felt Mrs. Nicholson's wary eyes on her. That's what she got for smiling.

"Are you girls caught up on your homework?" Mrs. Nicholson asked.

Evie was, but she seized the opportunity. Her face fell. "I left my book in my room at home. Is it okay if I run over and get it?"

"Which book?" Mrs. Nicholson asked, but Evie was ready.

"The one I have to write a book report on for English," she said.

"That's not due for another week," Rachel said.

Evie glared at her friend. Just because she was stuck here... "I know," Evie improvised, "but I don't read as fast as you do, and I'm a few chapters behind."

Rachel's father coughed, and Mrs. Nicholson's attention swung quickly to him, as though she was all that stood between him and pneumonia. "Fine," she said, "but over and right back. And if you take Trooper, make sure you wipe his paws."

"Got it," Evie said, and raced from the living room.

It was nearly dark outside. Evie grabbed her jacket and a flashlight from a kitchen drawer, then gave Trooper a quick pat. He'd been exiled to the Nicholson kitchen and wore a hopeful going-outside look with his pleading eyes. Unfortunately, Evie had forgotten to bring a leash and didn't trust him not to chase after a raccoon. Besides, she wouldn't be gone long.

Evie pulled up her hood. She was wearing a black sweatshirt over black sweatpants, her favorite outfit for pretending like she was a ninja. She knew every inch of the woods between their houses almost as well as she knew every inch of her own bedroom. Which made sense, because she'd spent more time in the woods. She had a favorite, well-worn path through the brush on the Nicholson side, and likewise a favorite path through the interior trees. It carried her past a fungus growing from a stump in concentric circles. Mostly white with light tan accents, the fungus always looked the same. Of course, nothing stayed the same, and Evie was determined to see what happened when it changed.

But not tonight. She'd never admit it, but Evie regretted not bringing Trooper, or coming up with an excuse for Rachel's company. Since she was alone, she used a more direct route. She'd left the Nicholson porch light on, and her mother had left theirs on as well. All Evie had to do was make her way from one light source to the other. Her flashlight made the forest feel somehow creepy, so Evie didn't use it, relying upon memory and enough residual natural light to provide contrast between the tree trunks in her path.

Evie circled around back when she reached her house, the leaves gathered around its walls rustling incessantly. She hadn't brought a key, so she used the one tucked away by the basement entrance. It was hard to get the key in the lock (the basement light was out), but eventually she jammed it home and slammed herself against the sticky door, falling inside. Evie had a "bad habit" (her mother's words) of leaving the spare key inside the house when she'd used it, so she left it in the door to ensure she wouldn't forget it.

Evie barely spared a glance for the unfinished basement as she sprinted upstairs, emerging near the back of the house. The house was always quiet, but now it was eerily so, with only the occasional ticking buzz of a kitchen appliance to break the silence. The glare from the porch through the front windows was bright enough for Evie to navigate to the kitchen without turning on an interior light. She grabbed the step stool, retrieved a chocolate bar from her mom's cabinet stash, and shoved it in her jacket pocket. Rachel's mom could make really good food—even the bizarre stuff, with ingredients Evie had never heard of—but Mrs.

Nicholson rarely made real desserts. Sharing the chocolate with Rachel in secret would be a worthy challenge.

Hand on the front door knob, about to leave, Evie remembered the basement key. And the book, her whole excuse for coming over in the first place! Evie smacked her hand against her forehead, the way she'd seen adults do on TV, before grabbing the book from her desk and racing to the basement. If she didn't hurry, Mrs. Nicholson would be mad, and they'd never be able to sneak the chocolate bar.

Outside, Evie put the spare key away before realizing she'd left her borrowed flashlight inside. *Poop.* She wasn't about to go back, instead continuing around the side of the house closest to their other neighbors, which didn't seem as dark. She still tripped over something halfway to the front porch, falling to one knee. As she brushed the leaves off her pants, she noticed the sound of an idling engine. Maybe her mom had finally gotten home. But after listening for a moment, she knew, *That's not Mom's Bronco.* And she was pretty sure it wasn't the Sheriff, either.

Stalking toward the front of the house—toe-heel, along the side of her foot, the way her grandfather had taught her—made Evie less afraid. Maybe someone was trying to break into their house and steal something, even though her mom always claimed they had nothing worth stealing. She squatted low as she rounded the corner.

A man stood between Evie and the Nicholson house. He was trying to steal Trooper's doghouse. That made no sense at all. No, wait, he wasn't stealing Trooper's doghouse, but he was beating on it with a crowbar. Or maybe prying something from it? He squatted and peeked inside with a flashlight before going back to work. They hadn't used Trooper's tie-out since he'd almost died, so Evie couldn't imagine what was in there.

The vehicle parked in the driveway was an old pickup, but Evie couldn't make out the color, and Beecham County was thick with old pickups. She crept toward the driver's side of the truck, keeping its massive metal body between her and the man. The truck engine helped cover any sounds of Evie's footfalls on the driveway. It had a crew cab, with both doors open, but there was no light inside except for the instrument panel. Come to think of it, the headlights weren't on, either. She peered over its hood at the man. He was tall, about Adam's height but a little thicker, with short, dark hair. She couldn't see his face.

She'd have a better angle from the back of the truck.

Evie glanced inside as she passed the open doors, enough to confirm there were no passengers. She could barely see over the truck bed, and he'd turned again so she still couldn't see his face. There was something familiar about him, but only *slightly* familiar, not like someone she saw on a regular basis.

She couldn't get past the man to return to the Nicholson house. She didn't know the woods on this side of the property, and it didn't appear those neighbors were home yet. Evie couldn't even remember their names, she saw them so rarely. She might be able to sneak back to the basement, but she couldn't help remembering that's where her mom had shot a guy, so strangers could figure out where basements were, too. And she didn't fancy her chances of stealing the truck before the man got to her, idling or not. It was a stick shift and she wasn't sure she could reach the pedals.

What would Mom do?

The crescendoing squawk of a nail being ripped from wood rang out above the droning engine.

Maybe something in the truck would tell her who this guy was and why he was stealing pieces from their doghouse. Her eyes scanned until they caught a flash of contrasting stripes, visible even in the dim interior. The puddled fabric was just beyond her grasp, so she kneed up into the back seat of the truck.

It was Iris's scarf, she was sure of it. In better light, the stripes would be lime green, alternating with black. They'd joked it was her Harry Potter scarf. Had Iris been in this truck?

Grit worked its way under Evie's fingernails in no time as she ran her hands over the floor, searching for anything other than potato chip bags and a box that had held an air filter. The front seat was a high-backed, bench type. She squinched her face with distaste as she stretched beneath the driver's side. A snuff box. Maybe a tool? There was something heavy wrapped in cloth.

She pulled it free and peeled an edge of the dirty rag away—*it was a gun.* Like the kind her mom kept locked in the glovebox.

Evie's heart beat so fast it vibrated in her chest, like that rattling, purring noise some of the boys at school could make with their mouths but she never could.

She clutched the gun with one hand and reached under the seat again with the other, across the middle toward the passenger side. There was something else under there, paper, and maybe a bungee cord? She nearly coughed when her breath stirred the dirt on the floorboard.

And then she heard the screaming.

It wasn't very loud—not this far away—but it was unmistakable. Because it was Rachel. But why would Rachel be screaming like that?

Suddenly Evie knew who the man was.

Oh God, oh God, oh God...

"Shit!" the man said, his voice so near she knew it was already too late. He must've been circling the truck when Rachel screamed. Evie shoved the gun under the seat next to her, pulled her hood around her face and tucked her pale hands in her cuffs. She tried not to flinch as the back door slammed shut by her feet just before a heavy object landed on the floorboards in the front. *The crowbar?* She heard something lighter smack onto the front seat a moment later, followed by the bang of the driver's door.

The man shoved the truck roughly in gear and spun it around on the gravel, rocking Evie's head against the back seat. *Don't touch the front seat, don't touch the front seat...*

Her eyes were wide open behind her hood. Even though she

couldn't see, she daren't shut them. Every bump in the road rocked along the length of her body, and something was poking her hip.

She knew they'd arrived at the bottom of the driveway when the truck whipped around, ping-pong slamming her against both seats. The man didn't seem to notice.

"Sonuvabitch!" he said.

Did she hear another truck now? Rachel's dad must be chasing them. Mr. Nicholson, he could save her! Mr. Nicholson could kick this guy's butt, even if he did just get out of the hospital.

The truck slammed into a pothole, and Evie bit her lip hard enough to bring tears to her eyes. He was driving too fast, out of control. The vehicle veered all over the narrow road and sometimes off it, sliding or grinding across the changing surface. He was going to kill them.

The pickup swung wildly onto the main road. The truck's roar was so loud it hurt her chest, and she wondered which would explode first—the engine or her heart. Soon he made another turn, and the back end fishtailed across the pavement. Evie's stomach kept moving when the rest of her body stopped. She pressed one desperate hand over her mouth and the other against her stomach.

Disoriented, she had no idea where they were, but she was grateful when the rumbling, popping slowed. The man in the front seat whooped and laughed and said, "Goddamn! That was worth the trip."

So Mr. Nicholson wasn't saving her.

Please don't turn around, please don't look back here...

Now Evie did close her eyes, squeezing her hands together and pressing her hands against her hooded face.

She was all alone. With the man who kidnapped Rachel.

56

———

When Luther and Virgil returned to the car, Adam woke long enough to point out Luther's sandwich (Adam had gotten it from the server before leaving the cafe). The men were tense, and Adam felt certain they'd been arguing. But as soon as the vehicle was in motion, Adam was out again. His dreams were fractured and unrelenting, fleeting visions he could never quite grasp. Voices called his name, some threatening and some reassuring, but never clearly enough for him to follow or answer.

He bolted upright, heart pounding, when the SUV stopped. He couldn't remember the last image he'd seen in his mind, but he couldn't shake its influence either, like a bad hangover.

"Good timing," Luther said. "You need a Coke or something?"

Adam blinked and peered forward between the seats. They'd stopped at a chain convenience store, the kind where you could use a different gas pump every day of the week. Adam's tongue stuck to the roof of his mouth. "Sure. Thanks," he said.

Cold air rushed in as Luther rolled out, but Adam's father remained in the passenger seat. Adam rubbed his face, trying to focus.

"How do you feel?" Virgil asked.

"I'm fine," Adam said automatically.

"I asked how you feel," Virgil repeated, with a level of intensity that suggested he expected an honest answer.

Adam scooted to the center while he considered, reconnecting with the sensations he spent most of his time trying to block out. "Exhausted," he admitted. "Foggy. Confused. My horizon line seems off by about ten degrees and my ears feel full, kinda like an ear infection."

"You had bad ear infections all the time when you were little," Virgil said. "That's another reason they were worried about you not talking."

Adam had forgotten about Danny perforating his eardrum when they fought in the river in Watkins County. He'd taken a round of antibiotics, but even without infection, the injury itself could still be causing him some problems. Lately, he'd fallen from a normal if unambitious and meandering life into an episode of *The Twilight Zone*. Stacked up against the inexplicable or some mystical sort of explanation, he'd choose the diagnosable any day.

"So we're on our way to get Iris?" Adam asked, speaking to his father's profile.

"That's the idea."

What would it mean for them to "get Iris?" Adam struggled to rally a coherent stream of thought, but his brain seemed to be experiencing a flood season or drought, he wasn't sure which. "And Luther's okay with this? Us all gung-ho instead of sending in law enforcement?"

Virgil turned his head away, but not before Adam saw his mouth twist in distaste.

"What?" Adam asked. "What'd I miss between you and Luther?"

"We initially had a difference of opinion," Virgil conceded, "but now he agrees."

Adam winced as he rubbed the heel of his hand in circles across his forehead. "I'm not sure I do."

"Then you're wrong." Virgil's voice was calm, matter-of-fact.

Maybe he was wrong. Sure, they could call in an anonymous tip, saying they'd seen Iris wherever, but what kind of response would that garner, a state away from where she was last seen? An ambivalent one at best, the kind that got people hurt.

"We have any kind of plan?" Adam asked.

"First, make sure it's the right place. Then you and I try to suss things out, see if we can reach Danny from afar before moving in. You think you're up for that?"

"Sure," Adam said, in the same tone of voice he'd used to ask for a soda.

Virgil twisted toward him, so quickly Adam flinched. He took Adam's head in his hands, spread fingers pressing from the crown to the back of his head. His thumbs pressed against the broad bones of Adam's face below his eyes. The pressure was in the hurt-so-good category, inflicting mild pain for greater relief. Adam closed his eyes and, beyond the discomfort, he could feel some clarity returning to his mind.

"Whatever happens," Virgil said, "I want you to remember something. The boy you knew is thrice gone. He was never there to begin with, never who you thought he was. Then he became someone else when I took him, and now he's transformed into someone else again. Don't let your memories—or your guilt—make you hesitate. I won't."

Adam wondered how his father knew about his guilt, since he didn't seem to experience any himself. At least, not around Danny or Iris or Adam. But he probably had guilt around Adam's mother.

"And you don't owe Danny a thing," Virgil continued, still massaging Adam's skull. "You already saved him once."

Adam stiffened. "What? When?"

"You know damn well when," Virgil muttered.

Adam racked his brain. He couldn't mean recently, considering how near Adam had come to putting an end to his old friend. Maybe closer to Danny's kidnapping. But what could Adam have done as a child to help him? Then he remembered the dream he'd had at Iris's, when he'd told Iris that Danny was dead after screaming *Daddy, no!*

Adam's eyes flew open. "But I saw you kill him."

Virgil shook his head. "You saw me hit him with a... actually, I don't even know what it was. But your voice stopped me. Well, made me try to stop. And that was the difference between Danny being dead and just thinking he was."

Adam shut his eyes again, then murmured, "Why don't you know what you hit him with?"

"I wasn't completely..."

"In your right mind?" Adam suggested.

"In control of myself." Virgil sighed. "Lawrence never gives up. And you can't afford to forget that. My father is relentless. He will not let anything—even death—stand in his way. He will always try to find a way back. And once that happens..."

Virgil's fingers hesitated, and Adam tensed. He wasn't sure which he found more disturbing, the idea itself or Virgil's unwavering belief in it. After a moment, Virgil dug his fingers in deeper. He kept kneading until Adam felt his muscles—and his mind—release. Then Virgil's fingers relaxed as well.

Adam's head followed Virgil's retreating hands like a dog begging for more attention. When he opened his eyes, he saw his father's smile had spread to his eyes, crinkling the weathered skin that surrounded them. "Your mom would be proud of you. I know my mother is."

Virgil twisted to face front again as Luther emerged from the store, rushing through the cold toward the vehicle with a paper sack in hand.

"Iris'll be telling you that herself, soon enough," Virgil said. "I have no doubt."

Adam took a deep breath, and the tension that tugged his brows forward eased. The man's confidence was contagious.

They were going to save Iris.

TWENTY MINUTES LATER, Adam wasn't so sure. "You want to take another look at that map?" Luther asked.

"I told you, this is the right road," Virgil said, but kept rotating a couple of printed sheets in his hands.

Whatever their earlier "difference of opinion," Adam didn't think it had been resolved. Not completely. The men's voices were tight, but they were polite with each other, as they'd never been before. Neither Luther nor Virgil had the temperament to pretend an amiability he didn't feel. The only explanation Adam could come up with was that they were putting on a show for his benefit, that they were hiding something. Despite his earlier optimism, it made Adam uneasy.

"See, here," Virgil said, pointing at a gravel road that turned off the current poorly paved one. "Right here."

Luther slowed to a crawl for the turn. Adam, perched in the middle of the back seat, still braced a hand against the SUV as it rocked back and forth during the transition from asphalt to gravel. It was a cold, forbidding place, which contributed to Adam's uneasiness. Snowflakes blew in the air, but they were the dry kind that seemed more like dust than frozen water. The landscape was treeless, with no mountains on the horizon. Adam felt exposed. Flat as it was, the barren fields of brown grass had just enough rolling slope to hide what was immediately beyond them, before rising again into sight.

They drove for a few minutes in silence before Luther asked, "Any of this look familiar?"

"This is the place," Virgil said confidently.

"I know what *you* think," Luther snapped. His control was slipping. "I was talking to Adam."

Adam tugged on his seat belt to lean forward for a better look. "No," he said. "Not really."

Not until they crested the next rise.

"I'll be damned," Luther said. "There's a house up there."

The fading white structure was vaguely familiar, but it was a gnarled oak tree halfway across the field to their right that caught Adam's eye. "There! I remember that dead tree. I saw it right before Danny wrecked."

"Now do you believe me?" Virgil demanded.

Luther leaned over the steering wheel, trying to get a better view of something. The high grass had been disturbed at the edge of the road, but Adam couldn't tell how. He removed his seat belt (*bing, bing, bing*) and slid over to press against the side window. Luther slowed his vehicle even more, so much that Adam was tempted to get out and walk. Finally, he could see a shape pressing against the vegetation.

There was a car. Just off the edge of the road, nose down in the grasses.

Luther stopped his SUV but kept it idling as he pulled alongside the wreck. "Yes," he said, answering Virgil's long-ago question, "now I believe you. What do you say we take care of this asshole?"

57

JJ felt numb, but she didn't feel guilty.

Oh sure, she felt guilt on a regular basis about interactions with her daughter, things she could have done differently, but those were little, indulgent pangs, bits of her own mother's psychology she'd never been able to shake off. The core belief she'd gotten from her father was something JJ's mother had never understood: don't borrow guilt or sorrow; life will give you enough that's legitimately your own.

So JJ didn't feel guilty about being with Harlan—watching over Harlan—while her daughter was taken. Nor did she feel guilty leaving her daughter with Dorothy and Otto. She wasn't angry with Dorothy for letting Evie run next door. There was no point in it. She would have done the same. The person to be angry with was the man who'd taken her.

Iris, Adam, and Evie were in danger. She'd listed them in reverse order of priority, though Adam would have disagreed with her assessment. The martyr would have put his grandmother ahead of himself. Hell, he might have put Trooper ahead of himself.

JJ shook her head; she was thinking about Adam to avoid

thinking about her daughter. Thinking about what might be. She sat in Dorothy's living room, listening with half an ear while Grant and a man she didn't recognize interviewed the Nicholsons again. Rachel had become upset, Otto had gone outside, seen the vehicle and pursued him, but the other man had had too much of a head start. And Evie was gone. End of story. More people JJ didn't recognize—law enforcement from multiple agencies—pored over the Tulley property in the dark. Much as they had done with the Nicholsons last month.

Rachel huddled between her parents, eyes red and face puffy, knees hugged to her chest.

Rachel had come back alive. Evie would, too.

But JJ had found Rachel, not law enforcement. She and Adam. And Harlan. She glanced over at the elderly man, reclining in the nearest armchair with his legs outstretched, as close to lying down as he could be. While she stared, his head swiveled toward her, and he opened his eyes, giving her a slight nod.

"JJ?" Grant said, tapping her arm lightly.

The details of him breaking the news to her in Dead Hollow were a blur. She thought she'd collapsed. But eventually Grant had gotten her into his vehicle and driven her here. Just now, when he'd tapped her arm, that was the first time he'd touched her since then. Maybe he was afraid she'd fall apart again.

Except she wouldn't. She was done with that.

Maybe he was afraid *he* would fall apart.

"Yes," JJ said. She had no idea what she was affirming, but found it hard to believe it was anything important. No one would trust her with important decisions right now, not if they had any sense.

Grant and the other uniformed man moved toward their colleagues in the kitchen.

"Dorothy, honey, why don't you make everybody some coffee?" Otto suggested, voice strained.

His wife searched his face, then glanced at his leg in horror. His foot rested on an ottoman, and the thigh of his sliced pants was spotted with blood.

"Dorothy, it's nothing to worry about. But if you get me your first aid kit, I can look at it while you take care of our friends in the kitchen," JJ said, rising on numb legs.

Her friend hesitated, uncertain.

"Please, Dorothy," JJ said. "It'll give me something useful to do."

Dorothy acquiesced. The room was quiet, the only sound the murmur of voices from the kitchen, until she returned with a brightly marked pack. "Do you want to help me in the kitchen, Rachel?" she asked.

The girl shook her head and snuggled closer to her father.

"I'll help, Mom," said a young man's voice.

JJ wasn't sure when their son Jacob had returned home. Perhaps he'd been there when she arrived and she hadn't noticed him. She'd probably missed a lot. At fifteen, his dark head already bowed significantly to meet his mother's eyes. He put a solicitous hand against her back and walked with her to the kitchen.

"JJ?" Otto said softly.

She gloved up, undid the improvised closure on Otto's pant leg, and carefully peeled away his bandage. Gazing at the damage to skin and flesh, she considered whether to clean it or simply add a fresh bandage. "If you're too hardheaded to go in tonight, you need to keep an eye on this. When's your first follow-up scheduled?"

Otto grunted as he leaned forward to grasp her wrist. "JJ—"

"Don't say it," she warned. If he said he was sorry, she might start to unravel, despite her vows otherwise.

"What are we going to do?" Otto asked instead.

And that almost undid her, too.

"Adam's the only one who can tap into Danny to find him,"

Teddy said. "And Danny gets us your daughter and Iris. So Adam is our priority."

"Adam doesn't have a phone, and no one's been able to get in touch with Luther," JJ said, fumbling with the dressing, hands shaking so her voice didn't have to.

Was Iris with Danny when he took Evie? Was Iris with JJ's daughter now, watching over her as best she could? That gave her some measure of comfort. Unless Iris was already gone, beyond helping anyone. Surely Harlan would know, or at least suspect, if that were the case. Silent so far, maybe the man already knew the worst. Or maybe he was just fucking exhausted.

Rachel fidgeted with something on her tiny wrist, avoiding the adult scrutiny when she volunteered, "I could try to find Evie. The way Adam found me."

Her eyes briefly met JJ's before quickly flicking away. Hands slightly bloody, JJ pressed her forearm against her mouth at the glimmer of fearful hope in the girl.

Teddy inclined his head toward Rachel. The ends of his gray hair stuck out from a knit cap he'd never bothered to remove—purple and red with a poof ball on top—and he would have looked vaguely ridiculous, if not for the seriousness with which he regarded the child. "I don't know anyone else in the world who could have done what Adam did in finding you. So when I say you can't track down your friend that way, I'm not saying you're not strong or determined or even gifted. All I'm saying is you're not Adam."

Rachel gazed up at him, just as earnest. "Then maybe I can talk to Adam. I saw him last night."

"Where?" JJ asked. "Where did you see him?"

Her sudden interest startled the child, and Rachel tucked her arms around herself. "I saw him through your window, sitting under a tree. But the tree wasn't really here; I don't know where it was."

Harlan hitched up in his chair for the first time all evening.

"I'll bet *he* reached out to *her*," Teddy suggested. "Consciously or not."

"Whatever connection he forged with the child before was powerful enough to nearly kill him. That doesn't go away," Harlan said. He and Teddy exchanged a look.

"What?" JJ demanded.

But Harlan simply said, "It means there is a way to get through to him. We just have to figure it out."

JJ stared at Harlan, trying to decide if he was hiding something from her—he usually was—and what she was willing to do to the old man to find out. Before she could formulate a plan of torture, Dorothy returned to the living room with a tray of mugs in her hands. JJ decided it was time for another tack.

"What if Luther's been in touch with Beth?" JJ said. "I could ask her—"

"I already did," Grant interrupted, he and Jacob following on Dorothy's heels. "She ran some Virginia addresses for him, but he's already checked them out and reported back in to her. She has no idea where he is now."

JJ fastened Otto's pants leg again, as best she could, peeled her gloves from her hands and stood to throw them away. But she couldn't. She held the gloves away from her body and couldn't move from her spot, sure there was something else they should be doing, something else she could set in motion.

"What about Luther's phone? Is there some way to trace that?" JJ asked.

"I'm working on it," Grant said, then excused himself from the group as his radio crackled to life.

Once he was gone, Teddy sighed and rose slowly from his chair. "Harlan," he said, "perhaps you and I—"

Teddy stopped, much as JJ had done moments earlier, frozen in place. Except his eyes... JJ didn't know what they saw, if it was even on this earth, but she was certain it wasn't the Nicholson living room.

"Teddy?" she said.

"Don't touch him, JJ," Harlan said, but his face showed the same concern she felt. "Theodore," he said, "where are you?"

Teddy muttered something unintelligible before grabbing at his shoulder. His eyes were still elsewhere, but he winced, and his hand slid from his shoulder to his chest. His other hand snatched at the arm of his chair as he lost his balance. Jacob was nearest, and grabbed first the chair, then Teddy, as the piece of furniture began to flip on its side. The teen herded the old man back into the chair as JJ dropped her dirty gloves on the floor and rushed to him.

"Teddy?" JJ said.

"No," he whispered, air wheezing from his throat. "It can't be. Harlan, did you feel that?"

If Harlan responded, JJ didn't hear him.

Teddy's face was pale and sweaty. JJ took his wrist in her hands. His pulse was as slow as her own mind was racing (the mantra *my daughter, my daughter—please God, save my daughter* repeating for the past two hours). She couldn't control Teddy's heart, but JJ finally centered her own mind with the observation, *You have got to be kidding me.*

JJ glanced over her shoulder at Grant and waved for him to help her. "Goddammit, Teddy, you picked a helluva time to have a heart attack."

58

Adam watched Luther pull his gun from its holster and examine it in ways that meant nothing to Adam. When Luther nodded to himself and reached for the door with his free hand, Virgil said, "Wait."

Virgil looked over his shoulder at Adam and asked, "Ready?"

Adam closed his eyes and pressed his mother's key against his sternum. He breathed deeply, but found it more difficult to relax in the car than when sitting outside. As before, he concentrated on the crackling sound of the campfire the night Danny was kidnapped, feeling it transition to the gravel road that had crackled beneath their tires just moments ago, and then...

Then nothing. No connection.

Easy, Virgil whispered in Adam's mind.

He went deeper. There was a sense of the ground slowly dropping beneath him like an elevator, and his ever-present nausea, but that was all. No Danny. Except, he felt a tug—

Adam, let it go.

A force pulling him toward the abandoned car in the grass and something... *wrong*. Deeply, deeply wrong.

Walls appeared abruptly in Adam's mind, then a solid floor beneath them. There was nowhere left to go.

"Danny's not here," Virgil said aloud.

Adam opened his eyes.

"He used that car, but he's gone now. I don't know where," Virgil admitted. "And I don't know if Iris is with him."

Luther exited the car, moving cautiously around the back of the SUV. Adam followed, hand tracing the blue metal bulk next to him to counter a hint of light-headedness. Virgil used the passenger door for cover while Luther advanced on the abandoned car with his weapon drawn.

The little gray sedan wasn't all that different from Iris's, but not as well cared for, making it difficult to distinguish old damage from new. Adam's eyes were drawn to the neglected house instead. Even from a couple hundred yards away, areas of exposed wood stood out against the once white paint. A big, black SUV sat near the front steps, the vehicle incongruous parked in front of a modest farmhouse that could have fairly been described as old a generation ago.

"Car's clear," Luther said, having done a complete circuit.

"What do you think of the other one?" Adam asked, squinting in the dusky light, but it didn't help him distinguish any more detail.

"I don't like it," Luther said. "And I'm thinking there's a good chance *it* won't like *us*. If this car was Danny's, who the hell brought the fancy SUV?"

Virgil had already stuck his head in the abandoned car and appeared ready to climb in. Luther approached the trunk, but Adam hung back. Buckled in slightly on one side, the trunk wasn't securely shut. Luther holstered his weapon and, standing slightly uphill on the road side, lifted his leg and gave it a kick. The dull *thunk* of his strike surrounded them, prickling the hair on the back of Adam's neck. Adam's mind screamed, *Don't open it,* but before he could speak, Luther had planted another solid heel. The trunk lid came free, throwing Luther off-balance. He fell against Adam, but Adam held his ground and peered around the man.

"Luther," he said, "what is that?"

A white, roughly rectangular object practically glowed in the dim trunk.

"Looks like a cooler," Luther said, reaching toward it, then pausing. "Too bad I didn't think to bring any goddamn gloves."

He pushed the trunk lid higher and started to pull his hands inside his sleeves, but seemed to think better of it.

"Don't touch it," Adam warned, a hand straying to his rolling stomach.

"I don't need to," Luther said. "It's open."

He was right, or at least, it wasn't latched shut. A gas can sat next to the cooler, and a rag lay between them. Luther picked up the rag and used it to nudge the cooler closer to the front edge of the trunk, closer to the light. As he did, a stain on the rag itself caught Luther's eye. He held it gingerly toward the sky for a better look.

Meanwhile, Adam was transfixed by the cooler. By the isolated dark spatters on its exterior, and a smear next to the handle. His fingers were drawn to the surface like a magnet. Like a pulsing magnet.

"Hey!" Luther said, seizing his arm. "What happened to not being grabby?"

Luther still held the rag in his hand, and as the cloth brushed Adam's skin...

He felt the familiar slicing pressure against his esophagus, his lungs exploding. The dark touch of death. And then beyond death, something else. A knife, piercing the skin of his chest—

Adam staggered backward, bile rising in his throat, and pointed at the now-empty, bloody cooler. The high grass enveloped him like a shroud as he fell to his knees. He choked on vomit, trying to hold it in. Coughing, he was unable to distinguish where another man's suffocating death ended and his own suffering began. A drumming sensation in his head was akin to a rainstorm pounding a metal roof, obscuring the sights and sounds around him.

"Adam?" Luther said, then called out for Virgil.

The grass fought Adam's father as, linking an arm around his waist and grabbing his jacket, he dragged Adam free. Adam gagged, coughed, felt Virgil's arms around him, engulfing him as completely as the grass had, as though trying to shield him.

"Easy, son," Virgil said. "What happened?"

Luther said something Adam missed and moved back to the trunk, nudging the cooler open farther. Eyes tearing, Adam was wiping his mouth when Luther exclaimed, "Jesus Christ! What the hell did he have in there?"

Adam tried to look at Luther, but—suddenly—he couldn't move. Virgil froze above him, and not just Virgil. It felt as though the entire world held still. Adam heard Virgil say, *Remember, stick close to Luther*.

But his father hadn't spoken aloud.

Dad? Adam said.

Except his own jaws were still locked. Only his mind was free.

Then the world lurched forward again. Luther drew his gun and dropped low to the ground, using the car for cover. Adam lifted his head, attempting to rise, but Virgil shoved him back down.

Did Adam feel the impact or hear the sound first? He wasn't certain, but even with his wonky hearing, the rifle's echo was unmistakable. So was the shudder that ran through Virgil's body before his grip released Adam's shoulders.

Blood spattered Adam's face, but in the confusing kinetic blur he couldn't tell where it had come from. And yet, he could have counted the wrinkles on the knuckles of his father's hand as it tumbled past. Virgil slid from Adam, falling off to the right. He landed on his side on the ground, momentum carrying him over onto his back. Virgil's eyes stared at the sky, as did the red-rimmed wound in his head.

No... no, no, no...

59

L uther yanked Adam toward the abandoned car as the man reached for his father, for the hole—no, *holes*—in his skull.

"Adam!" Luther yelled, as he struggled against him.

The younger man elbowed Luther in the gut, but Luther grabbed him and slammed him against the car. The impact sent both of them to the ground, just as the next round shattered the car window above them.

Luther got to his knees and watched Adam do the same, shaking his head and sending little bits of safety glass flying. He looked dazedly at Virgil lying a few feet away and would have gone to him again.

Luther seized Adam's shoulders and shouted, "Stop!"

Adam placed a palm on the ground and extended the other toward his father, protesting, "I can fix this!"

"No, you can't! You can't fix Virgil." Luther gave Adam's shoulders a shake. "Look at me!"

Adam's eyes were slow to focus on Luther, so slow Luther had time to register the odors of sickness and the mechanical fluids leaking from the car next to them.

"I'm sorry, Adam. Virgil is dead, and if we don't figure out something fast, so are we."

Luther pressed him to sit, but Adam resisted until Luther added, "And Iris won't have a chance in hell, either."

Adam finally dropped to the ground, and Luther sat next to him. He dug a knuckle into his forehead. Virgil lying in front of them made it damn hard to concentrate on a way out of this clusterfuck alive.

"Okay," Luther said, thinking out loud. "We don't know how many people are in there, or if Iris is one of them, so I don't fancy firing blind. We don't know what their weaponry is like, but since all I have on me is a pistol with one extra magazine, we're obviously outgunned."

Adam's head turned slowly to Luther. He was wearing puke and blood and maybe a little brain matter, and his hollow eyes kept flicking to his father's body. Still, he said, "We drive through the front door."

"I like your spirit," Luther said, "but they'd pick us off before we got anywhere near it. And even if we were driving a tank, what happens when we get out?"

Adam brushed his arm against the ground next to him, trying to wipe off a vomit smear. "So we sit here and wait for help?"

"What help would that be?" Luther asked. "Look around—who's gonna call in a few rifle shots? And nobody knows we're here. My cell phone's in the car. If we can get to it, if we even have reception, I don't know what the response time will be."

"Sounds like you already have a plan," Adam said. "That you want to run."

Luther realized Adam was right; he had made up his mind. "The pressure's all on us. Whoever's in that house doesn't have to *do* anything except take their time picking us off. Unless they think we've called the law. But the longer we sit, waiting, the more likely they'll decide it's to their advantage to come get us, or take us out while they're hauling ass out of here."

"What if they just shoot out our tires?"

Luther nodded. "Not as easy as they make it out on TV shows, but they've got a marksman. We'd still have a little time though, and we could ride on the rims for a while. Plus, once we're stuck here, they still have to deal with us one way or another. It looks like they'd prefer to kill us outright now, but if that doesn't happen I'm hoping they'd rather be rid of us sooner than kill us later."

"Okay," Adam said, surprising Luther. "But I need help carrying my father to the car."

Luther shook his head.

"You can't expect me to leave him here!" Adam protested.

Luther stared at the dead man. He was lying so near—just a few yards—and yet they had no cover to reach him without getting shot. And there was no way they'd make it to the SUV with him in hand.

Watch over Adam.

Luther had heard those words, right before the shot that blew Virgil's brains out. But how the hell was he supposed to do that? They were fucked. Luther ran a hand over his exhausted face.

You didn't make it easy, you crazy bastard.

Luther placed a hand on Adam's shoulder and squeezed it hard. "Virgil's gone, and carrying his body around isn't going to change that. It'll just get us killed."

Adam lifted the vomit-free arm to his face, eyes red and lips trembling. "But I can't leave him. He was alone one way or another most of his life, and I can't do that to him."

Luther tried to ignore the spatter in Adam's hair as he leaned closer. "Fine. Which one do you want to be left alone? Your dead father, or a living Iris?"

Adam looked at Luther as if he could kick him in the nuts, but Luther could tell he'd gotten through. He continued. "We'll call someone as soon as we get clear of here and get him taken care of. I promise."

"I just, I never even..." Adam's voice trailed off. His shoulders hitched once, and he pressed his arm against his face harder. He swallowed, so hard Luther heard the gurgling lump in his throat, and said, "Okay. What do we do?"

Luther picked his baseball cap off the ground and tugged it down on his head securely. Adam wasn't wearing his, either. He must have taken it off while napping in the car. "We'll run to the back, get in that way and crawl through. Kinda wish I'd sprung for the power lift gate. Stay low. You ready?"

The two men rose to squatting positions. Luther watched Adam take a couple of deep breaths, filling his lungs completely before exhaling, then nodded.

Luther licked his lips, wiped his hands on his pants, and felt his heartbeat rock his frame. "Go!" he yelled.

It wasn't far to the rear of the vehicle—slightly more than the distance to Virgil's body—and they made it without incurring any more fire. Luther popped the back and slipped an arm inside to grab an interior strap while the two men crouched behind the vehicle.

"Make it quick," Luther said.

He raised the door high enough for Adam to slip into the cargo space, then immediately lowered it again. Luther waited a three-count before following, wedging his larger body through the narrow opening, only to mash against Adam in the small space. He pulled the door down until he heard it latch shut.

"The back seat lays down, but we need to release both sides at the same time," Luther said, wriggling for a better angle.

A shot rang out as Luther's head briefly tipped above the back seat. Tempered glass fragments rained on them as the window on Adam's side and the back glass shattered. Luther had a sudden flash of a young Les throwing handfuls of gravel at him in their driveway, abrading the skin from his chest.

"Sonuvabitch!" Luther yelled, as they released the seat and it fell forward, flat beneath them. "Stay down. I wouldn't count on that door to stop a bullet, but at least it'll keep the fucker from knowing where to shoot one."

"You think?" Adam faced away from Luther, cheek against the rough, fuzzy fabric of the seat back. The glass scattered throughout his dark hair caught the last of the day's light.

Now for the tricky part.

More glass pebbles crunched beneath Luther as he inched forward. The front had reclining bucket seats. The driver's side probably wouldn't lie completely flat with the back seat flipped forward, but it would come close. Luther's fear was that as soon as he lowered it, he'd come into sight, or at least be a helluva lot nearer to exposed. He'd have to move fast.

"I'm gonna jump up front and see if I can get us out of here. Stay put," Luther said. Scenarios raced through his mind, and he added, "Unless the asshole shoots me, too. Then climb over me and get us the hell out of here."

"Got it," Adam said.

Luther jerked the lever on the side of the seat. It hit him in the face as it dropped, and Luther had to get out of his own way to launch over it into the front. Another shot rang out as he landed across the two seats, and he nearly threw up when the gear shift hit him in the gut. The windshield didn't shatter, but something hit Luther in the forehead, and soon his left eye was burning beneath a stream of blood.

"Fuck!" he said, swiping at the stream and digging something deeper into his brow.

"You okay?" Adam called out.

"Fucking peachy," he said.

He heard Adam moving around in the back, but Luther couldn't worry about what he was up to.

Keeping low, Luther curled awkwardly around the gear shift and slid his legs down into the wheel well on the driver's side. He released the seat and pushed it back as far as it would go, but there was still barely enough space for Luther to breathe. The key was in the ignition, and the engine turned over on the first try. Had he parked the vehicle with its wheels straight? Probably, since the road was flat. He hoped so.

Luther released the emergency brake, put the vehicle in reverse, and waited. The idling speed didn't have enough torque to make the vehicle move. Maneuvering around the steering wheel to reach the pedals was a pain in the ass. He struggled to keep it straight as he pressed the gas gently with his hand. Slowly, the wheels began to turn.

"Left a little," Adam said.

Luther glanced back between the seats and saw that Adam had lifted the back and was hanging onto the strap as he watched their crawling progress. Luther turned the wheel slightly left.

"Sorry—other left!" Adam yelled.

Luther's breath grew short as he cursed and adjusted. It had been less stressful getting shot at. A minute or two later, their coordination had kept them on the road, but Luther doubted they'd progressed fifty yards.

"Fuck this," he said. "Adam, just let the door go."

He did. Luther took his hand from the gas, stretched out his legs and lay back on the seat. Almost flat, he twisted until he could barely reach the steering wheel while propping himself up on his other elbow, looking over his shoulder to see out the back with his one good eye.

Foot on the accelerator, Luther heard another gunshot, but no impact. The shooter had probably overshot, trying to compensate for the round's change in trajectory once it hit the windshield. Luther snorted. Like he had a fucking clue how to hit something half as far away as this guy had. Half as far away as Virgil had been.

Abs cramping, Luther was grateful when they finally came to a wide spot. He nearly ran off the road, wheels lurching over the edge of a steep incline, as he turned the vehicle to face the right way. Adam quickly shut the rear hatch, while Luther raised the seat back a few inches and slid the seat bottom forward a little as well. Then Luther drove with his head at dashboard level like a child stealing a truck for another mile.

"Can I get up now?" Adam asked, flat on his belly.

"Not yet," Luther said, but felt a moment's lightheadedness as he popped his seat up to normal height and hauled ass.

The battered SUV bounced and slid on the gravel road at forty miles per hour, trailing a dust cloud. When they made it to the next secondary road, Luther stopped at the intersection. His face was wet, and he was dizzy and sweaty. He started to say something, but forgot the words before they made it out his mouth. Forgot who he was talking to.

"Luther?" Adam said, scrambling into the front.

Adam. That's who he was talking to. "We need to keep moving," Luther said. "But I think I need you to drive."

He felt Adam's hands on his face. The one on the left side slipped.

"Frick," Adam said. "Move over."

And he grabbed Luther's shoulders, pulling him to the passenger seat and somehow climbing over him.

"You do know frick is just fuck with..." Luther couldn't work out the rest. "A frick," he finished, but that didn't sound right.

Adam adjusted his seat and pulled onto the road, back the way they had come. "Put your seat belt on," he said.

Luther did, gladly. Adam drove fast.

"Luther, where's your cell phone?"

Luther turned his head slowly. He felt like he was doing everything slowly. "I don't know. I don't remember," he said. Dusk had settled, and he couldn't open his left eye. "And I can't see very well."

So Luther closed his eyes.

60

———

It was full dark now. Lying on the floor, if Evie peeked from behind her hood, she could see a hint of glow cresting the front seat from the dash and the headlights. Evie was afraid to find out where they were going, afraid of what had happened to Miss Iris, afraid that the man driving the truck might find her and of what he would do to her. She was afraid her mom—and Rachel—would be freaking out right now.

But the thing that occupied her mind most was that she had to pee. There were some funky smells on the floor, but she was pretty sure if she peed her pants, the man would smell it. At least she was lying on her side instead of her belly.

She didn't know how long the man had been driving, but he was doing it at what felt like a reasonable speed. She hadn't been thrown around at all since he'd gotten clear of Mr. Nicholson, and a while back she'd felt the pickup slow before turning onto a smoother road—she was guessing the interstate. She'd considered trying to jump out then, but she thought the door locks had clicked automatically at her house and didn't want to give herself away if that was the case.

A cell phone rang. The springs in the front seat creaked as the man shifted and said, "Yeah."

Eyes shut tightly, Evie didn't dare breathe. They'd been traveling a straight road, and she felt the truck drift slightly.

"Dammit," the man said. The truck jerked on the road before he spoke again. "Rashid, listen, I got it but—"

He paused. Evie thought she heard the rise and fall of a voice on the other end of the line, but she might have imagined it.

"What do mean there was a problem at the safe house?" Pause. "Fine, that's why I called earlier. To tell you to meet me at the backup. But what happened?"

The pause was longer this time, and Evie heard the man breathing. "Is he dead?"

The truck jerked again, like maybe the man was adjusting his grip on the wheel.

"Describe him," he said. Pause. "If you got a good enough look to blow his goddamn brains out, you got a good enough look to fucking tell me how old he was, how long his hair was, something—"

Rachel had said there were two men that had taken her, or one that had taken her and one that watched over her later. Was he talking to the second man?

"All right. Fine. I'll see you when I get there."

She felt him slap the phone down on the seat, heard his breathing devolve to a shallow pant. Suddenly the truck was whipping across the road to the right, throwing Evie against the back seat. The road surface changed (*shoulder?*) and the truck wobbled back and forth, braking and sliding. It finally came to a stop, and the man bolted from the driver seat, slamming the door behind him.

Assuming he wasn't standing in the road, Evie scrambled toward the door by her feet. She'd just reached it when she heard the man scream—not words but noise, a shrieking howl that must have scraped his throat raw.

She fumbled with the door lock, pressing as hard as she could against the knob, but it wouldn't budge. A whimper snuck out her throat. She'd have to climb the seat and go out the front. But when Evie peeked over the seat back she saw him already crossing in front of the truck. The headlights washed the colors from his hunched form, making him seem strange and monstrous.

She was trapped.

She threw herself back on the floor, more forcefully than she'd intended, as the driver's door opened. Evie tucked her pale hands in her cuffs and held her fists in front of her mouth to muffle the sounds of her panicked breathing.

But the man probably couldn't hear it over his own. He began a series of deep inhales, like her mom did sometimes when she was trying to calm down. Evie timed her own breaths to coincide with his.

Suddenly he laughed, but it was a scary sound, with a crazy, high lilt at the end. "Fucker doesn't even realize he killed my father," the man said. He blew out his breath one last time and started the truck again. It took a couple of tries for the engine to catch. "So what are we going to do about that?"

Evie didn't know, but she had a feeling it wouldn't be good.

61

———

Adam's eyes kept tracking away from the road, following spidery cracks in the glass toward the bullet hole just off center of the windshield. The dim headlights barely reflecting off the highway caught in that tiny space. If the wind whistled through the opening, he couldn't hear it. Not over the roaring white noise of the missing windows.

Buffeted by the winds from outside, Adam was shivering with cold. He wasn't sure how much longer he could hold it together. His hand brushed his chest, feeling for the little bump beneath his shirt. When he found his mother's key, he pressed so hard the bones beneath it went numb. He felt like he had a bomb inside his body, and he was about to fly apart.

"Luther," he yelled. When was the last time the man had moved? "You still with me?"

Luther lifted his head without opening his bloody eye. "Yeah," he said, but his body slumped again a moment later.

The area Adam drove through was undeveloped, industrial, or simply abandoned. He hadn't seen any houses or businesses or signs indicating which. He hadn't seen anything at all, except the highway and empty fields. Adam thought he recalled passing a sign for a hospital a couple of hours ago (*when Virgil was still alive*), but since he'd only woken at the convenience store, he was none too well oriented. He didn't even know the name of the town, but its first lights were coming into view. Not surprisingly, it was a convenience store, though not the same one they'd stopped at earlier.

Adam swung into the parking lot too fast, slamming the brakes hard enough to make the SUV lurch but still bumping the curb. He left the vehicle idling and ran inside.

The fluorescent lights were bright, but short of blinding because it hadn't yet hit full dark outside. The cashier, a middle-aged man with red hair, chatted with a slightly younger man in a trucker cap who rested against the checkout counter. Both straightened as Adam burst through the glass doors, and the cashier's hand slipped under the counter.

"Hospital?" Adam asked, leaving a smear of blood on the glass and metal.

The cashier pointed his free hand and said, "Just keep going that way."

His other hand stayed next to the counter.

"Thanks," Adam said, and rushed back outside.

Luther roused, looking toward Adam when he opened the driver's door. Beneath the store's lights, the gore on Luther's face was striking, almost nauseating. Thank God he hadn't gone in with him. The cashier might have shot first and asked questions later.

Adam caught a glimpse of his own haggard, blood-streaked face in the rearview mirror before reversing out of the lot. Then again, maybe Luther wasn't that much worse.

He wished he'd looked for Luther's phone when he'd stopped. Except whoever was holding Iris at that house—if she'd even been there—would be long gone before Adam could convince the cops to respond. Or even tell them where the house was. The one who best knew where they'd been and how to get there was Virgil.

And he was still there.

Adam shuddered and rocked slightly in his seat, like a pressure cooker venting steam. But it wasn't enough. His head felt as though someone had pulled out all the bones and put them back in out of order. A jumbled skull Lego. It just felt *wrong*. He thought of Otto's uncle, and how Otto said he'd killed himself so he could *stop seeing*. Had he done it by putting his gun in his mouth?

Where was Luther's gun? Not in the mount by his knee. Back in the holster at his side? Adam leaned across the man to see...

The vehicle vibrated when it drifted off the road onto the gravel shoulder.

"Frick!" Adam jerked the wheel back toward the center.

What the hell's wrong with me?

He focused on the lights ahead as tangible goals, on getting from one (a car wash) to the next (a chain diner) to the next (streetlight), until he saw the red and white sign for the hospital entrance. The emergency room was the closest building to the road, with a vast, mostly deserted parking lot. Adam still didn't see much in the way of a town in the distance, so it probably served several rural counties.

The illumination left something to be desired in the outer fringes of the lot, and Adam missed a one-way turn. Luther stirred when he hit the brakes and reversed.

"Where are we?" he asked.

"An ER. Somewhere."

Adam was reluctant to attract attention doing the front door drop-off. He was also aware they needed to get their stories straight before going in. "If I park, can you make it inside?"

Luther's hands drifted toward the bloody side of his head in the dark. "Yeah."

Adam chose a spot a few rows from the front. His hands shook as he put the SUV in park. "Come on."

Stepping down from the vehicle, Adam noticed Luther's cell phone and grabbed it. It had been lying on the floor next to his feet all along.

"Here," Adam said. But as he approached Luther, he hesitated to touch the man, holding the device out so Luther could pluck it from his palm. He couldn't have said why.

"Thanks," Luther said, and stood, staring at the phone. The injury to his head had stopped bleeding, his irritated eye half-open and weepy, but Luther was none too steady on his feet.

Adam asked, "You got a story ready?"

"I don't think there's any point in reporting what happened to anyone here at the hospital. It's too late to catch the shooter, and we'll just get hung up dealing with people who don't know shit," he said. "I think I should call Grant first."

"Then call," Adam said. Luther had confirmed his own reasoning, but Adam wasn't sure how much longer he could wait, knowing his father's body was alone in the dark.

They crossed the broad drop-off area, now clear of vehicles. Luther stumbled stepping onto the sidewalk and dropped his cell phone.

"Goddammit," Luther muttered. He grabbed for the device, lost his balance, and sat down hard on the concrete.

Adam looked down at him. Unsteady himself, Adam wasn't sure he could get the bigger man to his feet.

"You do know I meant to do that," Luther said. "Think they'll send out some good-looking nurse to pick me up?"

The corner of Adam's mouth curled. "If they do, how much should I tell them he needs to be able to bench press?"

The deputy huffed a chuckle, and Adam extended an arm. When their hands met, both blood-stained, Adam gripped Luther's tightly, and felt... what? An odd, tingling pressure from their link, then a sudden pain shooting to his skull. Adam fell to one knee, then dropped to sit on the sidewalk, clutching his head, before he toppled the rest of the way.

Luther reached toward him, but Adam groaned and batted his hand away—the pain was coming from Luther. Adam lay back on the cold concrete, staring at the ever-darkening sky, the only visible clouds produced by his panting breath. There was something inside Luther, tickling at the surface, trying to get through... *someone* wanted Adam to see it. And the pain wouldn't stop until he did.

Adam gasped, "What did you and Virgil argue about?" Adam lifted his head, and one look at Luther's stricken face convinced him he was on the right track. He continued, "What did Virgil know that I don't?"

"No," Luther begged. "Nothing good can come of this kind of talk right now. Virgil just died—"

"You think I didn't notice my father getting his brains blown out next to me?" Adam snapped, shuddering as the image filled his mind and the pain in his head grew more intense.

His shudder grew to a shiver with a sudden wind gust. Or maybe it was the wake of a passing car. Its headlights blinded Adam, piercing his skull like an icepick. Adam curled into a ball and pressed his fingers to his brows.

"Adam, are you okay?" Luther asked. "Buddy, it looks like your nose is bleeding again."

He was right. Adam could feel it tickling his upper lip and the side of his face. The sensation made him shiver even more. A few dark drops dotted the sidewalk next to him. But it didn't mean anything; it was a distraction. Adam sat up, shouting, "I asked you a goddamn question!"

"Easy, Adam. I'm just saying, we need to focus on what's in front of us. On getting Iris back safe. And wading into the past isn't gonna do that."

"Tell me what you and my father argued about." Adam's jaw clenched. "I deserve to know."

Luther's hand went to his face. Blood smeared like paste as his body began slowly rocking. "I'm sorry. I wanted to tell you," he said. "I swear to God, if I could change it..."

"Change what, Luther?" Adam demanded, while his mind leaped ahead. What would strike his father so deeply? What was the thing Virgil cared about the most?

"It was me," Luther said, voice breaking. "The night your mother was killed, I was driving the other car."

No, it couldn't be. Memories, his and his father's, flashed through Adam's mind. His mother's screams lost in the shrieking brakes, the ripping impact of the guardrail. But before that, voices. Loud, upset voices in the car. And sudden, bright light. *Headlights on the wrong side of the center line.*

Luther.

It was true. Who would confess to something like that if they hadn't done it? But more than that, it felt true—*wrong, but true*—deep in Adam's bones.

Luther had killed Adam's mother. And Virgil had known, but hadn't told him. Adam squeezed his throbbing head.

"Adam," Luther pleaded. "Please say something."

Over the pounding of his pulse, Adam heard a voice whisper, *Where's Luther's gun now? Is he still wearing it?*

Adam stared at Luther.

"Come on, Adam..." Luther held out a hand.

But the voice said, *Take his gun.*

Adam slammed into Luther, climbing atop the larger man and searching the far side of his body. He felt the weave of the tough synthetic fabric beneath his hand, then the edge of the weapon it held, and struggled to pull the gun free.

Luther elbowed Adam in the face, not a square shot, but enough to knock him off, back onto the ground. Rising to one knee, the deputy protected his right side, hand resting on the still-holstered weapon.

"Adam! Look at me," he said.

But Adam couldn't. His head spun, and he shook it to clear it, tumbling back onto his side. His body stayed in frantic, fruitless motion, rising and falling, putting more distance between him and Luther and taking Adam toward the parking lot.

"Adam, wait!" Luther said.

Adam bumped against a low, solid object at the edge of a landscaped section. A statue or bench. He gripped it, supporting himself while he took a moment to catch his breath, then stepped off the sidewalk in front of a moving car.

The horn blared and the bumper stopped so close to his leg, Adam brushed it with his fingers to make sure it was real.

"Adam!" Luther called out, voice ragged.

He kept walking.

"Adam, please. We have to..."

But the rest of his words were lost to Adam as he made his skull-humming, buzzing, staggering way to Luther's SUV. He still held the keys in his pocket.

So Adam got in and drove away.

62

___

Luther cringed as his SUV, with Adam behind the wheel, nearly sideswiped a pickup. It settled for striking the vehicle's side mirror so it hung limply from the truck's door. Where the hell was Adam headed? What was he going to do, other than run up Luther's insurance deductible? And what the hell was Luther thinking, confessing to the man the way he had, before Virgil's body was even cold?

He couldn't find his cell phone. He must've dropped the damn thing. Luther finally saw the device on the ground, but nearly fell again and gave it a little kick, trying to pick it up. "Shit."

Bracing himself on one popping knee, Luther stretched out a hand for his phone and caught a glint of something else with his one good eye. A familiar, silver chain. He'd first seen it around Adam's neck the night he'd nearly died rescuing Rachel. It must have broken while Adam was trying to take Luther's gun. Luther picked it up, careful not to let the key slide off, and tucked it into his pocket.

Luther checked his weapon with the security guard upon entering the medical facility. Then he signed in and took a clipboard from reception. A shaking hand strayed to the sticky blood that coated his jaw. It left a smudge on the blank admission forms. Didn't matter. He couldn't see well enough to fill them out anyway. Luther was damn near wrung out.

But he couldn't stop now. Instead, he pulled out his phone to make the call he'd been dreading.

It was time to tell Grant he needed help.

63

Teddy was being a hard-headed dumbass, and it might just kill him. But with her own child missing, JJ didn't have the maternal energy to spare for the man.

He'd refused to see a doctor, assuring them he'd be fine in a little while. If he wasn't, *then* he'd get medical attention. Rather than calling bullshit, JJ and Grant had helped him to Dorothy's sewing room, which had a twin sized bed in one corner. There they'd removed his boots and jacket, loosened his collar, and settled him against a pile of frilly pillows.

Dorothy had finally left them alone so she could tend to her injured husband. JJ perched on the edge of the mattress, while Grant shifted a mannequin so he could lean against the wall unencumbered. Harlan pulled a metal folding chair over to sit next to the bed.

"It's Virgil, isn't it?" Harlan asked.

Teddy nodded. His eyes were red, and a thin sheen of sweat shone on his face.

"Meaning something's happened to him, while he was with Adam?" JJ asked, wiping his cheeks gently with a damp washcloth. He nodded again. "What about Iris and Evie?"

Teddy took her hand in his, the skin slightly cracked and feverish, and said, "I'm sorry. I can't make heads nor tails of what's going on here. But we will figure it out. And we will get your daughter back."

Harlan shut his eyes and sank lower in the metal chair. JJ was afraid he'd slide right off the seat.

Grant's cell phone broke the silence. He glanced at it and headed for the door, saying, "Excuse me."

JJ watched him leave, then said, "So, practically speaking, how is Danny watching over both Iris and Evie?"

"Maybe he has help," Harlan said.

For some reason, the idea of another person frightened JJ even more. Was that because she was in denial about her childhood friend's ability to harm her child? Or was it speculation about the other person's motivation? It was hard to come up with a non-financial reason to help someone kidnap a child that wasn't deviant.

"Even if he has help, if Danny's behind it, he'll be calling the shots, right?" she asked. No one replied, so she fumbled on. "Okay, maybe not. But if we go on that assumption, maybe we can use what we know about Danny to figure out where he'll take them. The way we used what we knew about Virgil to find Rachel, and you and Adam used it to find the Schofield boy."

"All we know about Danny is by way of his connection to Virgil," Harlan said. "Teddy, is Virgil dead?"

JJ's gaze whipped between the two men, Harlan still with closed eyes, Teddy fidgeting with his left side, stroking his arm.

"I believe so," Teddy said.

JJ squeezed his leg. No wonder the man had had a heart attack. Obviously he'd been close to his nephew, perhaps the only person who ever was. "I'm sorry," she said, a tear spilling onto her cheek as thoughts of her vulnerable daughter shoved their way to the front of her mind.

"What I don't understand," Harlan said, opening his eyes, "is why I still can't get through to Adam."

Teddy shifted against the pillows, adjusting his shoulder. "If he was there when Virgil died, however it happened, that's bound to be traumatic for him."

He paused for a shallow breath, giving JJ a moment to reflect. If Virgil had died, she was glad Luther was with Adam. That he wasn't alone.

Teddy went on. "And we suspected Virgil was shielding Adam, blocking you and everyone else, real or imagined. Maybe there's a residual *wall* there—for lack of a better word—persisting somehow even though Virgil is gone."

Harlan tented his hands against pursed lips. "Could be. If that's the case, hopefully it'll fade away sooner rather than later. But one other possibility worries me. I know he didn't mean to, but there's no doubt in my mind Virgil fucked up Adam's head but good. Depending on what kind of damage he did, I'm not sure Adam can recover, or even live with it."

JJ bowed her head and dug her fingers into her scalp, massaging, resisting the despair that threatened to drown her. "Back to Danny," she said. "If he took Evie, it had to be a crime of opportunity. I have no idea why he would've gone to my house, but it would have appeared empty, and there's no way he could have known Evie would be there."

"Agreed," Harlan said.

"But Danny had to have had a reason for taking Iris," JJ said.

"Iris is special," Harlan said, clearing his throat, "to Adam, to Virgil, and to me. Not that I matter to the man, but obviously Danny has issues with Adam and Virgil."

JJ shook her head. "Fine, but that's who she is *to other people*. What about who she is, herself, that makes her special?"

The men went quiet, and finally Harlan admitted, "I don't know. Not in any context that might relate back to Danny. She is the woman who's always done what she thought was right, and screw everyone else. She's the woman who survived that bastard of a husband, who raised her grandson and chose to save him over her son. What about that angle—is there anything you can think of from your childhood, from Danny's relationship with her?"

JJ shook her head. "Iris was like a mother to all of us, including Danny." She hastened to add, "The good kind. Not the kind that sends you to therapy or serial killing."

The intervening kidnapping of her daughter had pushed the scene at Dead Hollow, the event that had drawn her and the men from home, from JJ's mind. Now that she'd raised the serial killer specter, it returned. "What did you mean that what was done at Dead Hollow had Lawrence Rutledge written all over it?"

Harlan nodded at Teddy to prompt him. "You said it, and he was your brother."

Teddy wrinkled his nose at the man, for the first time looking his old, mildly cantankerous self. "Lawrence styled himself a Christian, but he had an unhealthy fascination not just with the Resurrection, but with the idea of transcending mortality generally. And that sometimes strayed into the occult."

"Not to mention being a big fan of all that Old Testament sacrificial bullshit," Harlan added. "Lawrence sacrificed animals at the Rutledge property where Teddy lives now, and I believe in Dead Hollow as well. He definitely made offerings there of things that were *formerly* alive."

JJ shivered, hugging her arms closer and pulling her shirt tight. "Did he ever kill any people?"

Harlan's face was grave but unreadable, staring at Teddy. Finally Teddy said, "I really don't know. But he did talk about the idea as a way to return from the dead."

"Seriously?" JJ asked.

Teddy looked to Harlan. "You know this is the way he would have done it, too."

"I know I didn't think you were as unhinged as your lunatic brother," Harlan replied.

Teddy's already pink face flushed even deeper. As always there was a subtext, a history between the men, that was beyond JJ and did nothing to help her find her daughter. "So if Lawrence believed this crap, who else would have? Who else did he have a relationship with who might copy that idea? Remember, you said maybe Danny was working with someone. Maybe that's who the other person is."

Harlan raised his dark brows, intrigued by the idea. Teddy seemed to be as well. "I don't know," Teddy admitted. "But if it were someone acting on Lawrence's behalf—"

Teddy raised a hand when Harlan started to object, and continued, "Or thinking they were, using his playbook so to speak, that might explain why they'd kidnap Lawrence's wife."

"Because she meant so much to him?" JJ asked, not convinced. She knew—from observation and personal experience—that abusers often claimed to care deeply for the women they abused. And yet, that didn't ring true to her about Lawrence.

She wasn't the only one.

"That sonuvabitch didn't give a shit about Iris," Harlan said, straightening quickly, his own face flushing. "He only wanted to win. He'd be more likely to kill her than kidnap her after what she did—"

The color vanished from Harlan's face as quickly as it had appeared. "No," he whispered, hand moving to cover his eyes.

JJ, tired of always being three steps behind the men on the rare occasion they shared something out loud, demanded, "What?"

"You think, if this is someone acting under Lawrence's delusions, that they'll have taken Iris to kill her?" Teddy asked. "To sacrifice her."

Harlan didn't bother answering.

Iris's body—or maybe just her organs—on an altar. And JJ's daughter would be there. JJ's mind skittered away from the possibility, tried to convince her they were wrong.

"What if this person doesn't really know Lawrence that well?" she countered. "Maybe he is crazy enough to think he's bringing Lawrence back, and that Lawrence will want his wife there to greet him."

Except that would mean they'd need to sacrifice someone else. Someone like her daughter. JJ's limbs began shaking. Teddy's hand on her back steadied her.

"JJ," he said, "remember, regardless of his intentions for Iris, we've already decided Evie was a crime of opportunity. She cannot have been part of his plan."

Harlan finally spoke, voice weary. "And it follows a kind of twisted logic to bring Lawrence back by killing Iris."

"Why is that?" Teddy asked.

"Because she's the one who killed him."

Teddy's mouth fell open, and JJ was afraid he'd suffer another cardiac event. He stammered, "But I thought you killed Lawrence."

Harlan shook his head. "Give me a little credit, Teddy. If I'd killed the man, do you think I'd cover it up, try to make it look like suicide?"

"Well, no," Teddy admitted. "Ideally, you'd do it on Main Street at high noon. But I figured it just happened, and Iris convinced you to cover it up."

Harlan's lip curled and he pointed at the man. "You got it half right. It was self-defense—hell, that would've been the case even if she'd killed him in his sleep—but the criminal justice system was even less enlightened about that sort of thing in those days than it is now. So Iris convinced me, and Sheriff Mason, to help her pass it off as suicide. "

"Sheriff Mason?" JJ exclaimed.

"The elder Sheriff Mason," he clarified. "Ulysses had a lot of guilt over all the shit Lawrence had gotten away with over the years. And Iris can be very persuasive."

JJ jumped as the door, not fully closed, opened wide to admit

Grant. His forehead was nearly as wrinkled as Harlan's borrowed shirt. "It didn't sit well with Dad, though," he said. "Things weren't right between the two of them for years."

"You knew?" Harlan asked. Grant shrugged, and this time Harlan's face showed a genuine smile. "I'll be damned. So what's the word, Sheriff?"

"That was Luther," he said. "I'm sorry, Teddy. Virgil is dead. He was shot at a house in Virginia, right about the time Evie was taken."

JJ still sat on the bed, and Grant kneeled next to her so they were nearly face to face. "Iris may have been held at that house. Since it looks like her abduction and Evie's are connected, I'm heading over there now."

JJ stared at him, at his lightly freckled face, at the mustache that—coupled with exhaustion—was the only thing anchoring his youthful appearance in the right decade. She wanted so much to burrow into his chest, to sleep next to him and wake to find everything was okay, everyone was safe. But she realized, consciously or not, he was asking her permission to leave. She nodded.

"You'll have people in and out," he said, "and the Command Center is staffed. If I'm not back by morning, Beth will come over. Okay?"

JJ nodded again, and he reached out to cup her cheek, thumb brushing the skin lightly. Then he rose, clothes and joints rustling and creaking. There was nothing she could say to him that would comfort either of them or make him work any harder to get her daughter back.

He was passing through the doorway when she called out, "Grant, what about Adam?"

Grant's hand fidgeted with the door. "He and Luther were there during the shooting, but they both got away. Adam is fine," he said, before retreating out of sight.

Too bad she could tell he was lying.

64

Evie didn't have to pee so badly anymore. She hadn't peed her pants. It was more like her thirsty body had reabsorbed the fluid. (She'd have to ask her mom if that was possible.) She was hungry, too, and her head ached like it had the last time she got the flu.

She kept trying to come up with scenarios to get away. Having confirmed the child locks, it seemed the only thing she could do was wait for them to stop long enough for the man to leave the vehicle. And then wait for him to walk far enough away that she could sneak out the front. It was a lot of waiting, and a lot of crossing her fingers. For example, hoping he didn't have to get something out of the back seat before he walked away.

And there was always the gun.

She wasn't afraid to shoot him, but she knew he was a heckuva lot better at shooting people than she was. After all, he'd probably shot her dad. She tried not to think about that, her dad bleeding on the floor. Except he was in the hospital now, probably yelling at her mom, blaming her for Evie being gone. Because he always blamed Evie's mom for everything. She loved her dad, but she didn't think that was fair.

Sometimes the man driving talked to himself, but he tended to mumble and she couldn't make out the words. The pickup's soporific engine drone vibrated throughout her body. The floor beneath her was cold, and she could almost feel the frigid air rushing past beneath them. Still, Evie spent so much energy trying not to think about certain things (her mom and dad, and Rachel, and Miss Iris, and wondering if the man's friend had shot someone she knew), she found herself dozing off. She slipped in and out of consciousness so seamlessly, she wasn't always sure whether she was awake or asleep.

When the vehicle finally slowed, she jerked back to awareness so abruptly she was afraid she'd emitted a snoring snort. If she had, the man didn't seem to hear it. The vehicle stopped, but she couldn't see any lights from the floor. So it wasn't a convenience store or restaurant or anywhere else that might have other people. The man hummed something low and tuneless and slightly spooky as he got out of the truck.

Evie held her breath and closed her eyes, grateful no light flashed from above. She heard and felt him rummaging around in the metallic bed of the truck behind her. *Stay put*, she told herself, even though her heart pounded and her legs itched to run. Then another soft noise, and nothing. She waited... counted to twenty, then counted to twenty again. *Where is he?*

Evie crawled toward the back window, but she'd gone numb lying in one position for so long. The numbness progressed to a needly tingling so intense she almost cried. But Mom wouldn't cry.

She forced herself up, a few more inches, just a few more, until she could peek out the back window.

Crap! She ducked back down immediately.

The man was standing by the rear bumper, filling the truck with gas from a plastic can.

Evie returned to the floor, fighting the painful sensations in her still-waking side. She'd tucked her elbow beneath her when she heard the gas can bang in the bed of the truck. She cringed as the man opened the driver's door a moment later and flopped in his seat.

"Goddamn. Almost there," he said, and sighed. "But I can keep going, run off the road in about three miles and kill myself... Or I can take a little break, and kill everybody else when I get there."

Suddenly the seat flew back, slamming into Evie. The grinding of metal runners covered her squeak. She opened her eyes and watched the back of the man's head tilt an inch or two past the top of the seat.

"Seems like a no-brainer to me," he said.

65

Adam didn't know where he was, but he didn't want to be there. He didn't want to be anywhere. He didn't want to be.

He lifted his head. Stared out at the dark.

Now he remembered.

After leaving the hospital, Adam had struggled to find his way back to Virgil—to Virgil's *body*—but he'd lost all sense of direction beyond the town's lights. Frustrated, he'd screamed himself hoarse. Not that it took much effort to do that. His throat hadn't entirely recovered from the phantom choking at Danny's hands.

But screaming wasn't enough of a release. A hot, obliterating rage had built in Adam's head until he couldn't take it anymore. He'd pressed the accelerator, watching the speedometer climb on a secondary road. But there were no trees to slam into, no banks to hurtle from, nothing but grassy flats. He'd finally given up, lifted his foot from the gas and let the SUV drift. It had bounced off-road hard enough to hurt his kidneys. The high, brown blades slapped the vehicle like a wildfire, ripping as they caught in the shattered windows. When he'd finally rolled to a stop, he'd thought of Luther's gun with longing, could almost feel the cold metal in his hands. Even pressing against the roof of his mouth.

And now here he was. Some time later. Had he slept? Passed out? The sky had a vague not-quite-light quality, with thick, high clouds nearly obliterating a partial moon. A single, gnarled tree stood about twenty yards from the vehicle's front grill, barely distinguishable. It was reminiscent of the one he'd seen in the field before Virgil was killed. Had he found his way to Virgil after all?

No, he couldn't have. His father would be surrounded by law enforcement now, poking and prodding and measuring. Or maybe he was already lying on a stainless steel table, suffering the same indignities.

But there was *someone* by the tree.

Two someones.

The air felt dry against his eyes as he stretched his lids wide, trying to take in more. More detail, more light, more clarity. Suddenly, the tree rushed at him, like ground rushing at a falling man. Or did he rush at the tree? Adam's breath caught. No, he still sat in Luther's SUV; he hadn't moved. The tree had. And the two figures.

Both were female, but one was taller—an adult and a child— and both were so pale beneath their long, dark hair as to be almost ghostly. Adam reached automatically for the key at his chest, but it wasn't there. His heart flew to his throat (*where is it?*), but he pushed the panic away. It didn't matter; he didn't need it. He knew it was her.

His mother stared at him and raised a hand. The one that wasn't entwined with the girl's. The girl—*is that Rachel?*—raised her free hand as well. He was afraid if he left the vehicle, they'd disappear, so Adam put his palms to the cold glass of the spidered windshield. His right hand crept toward the bullet hole, and his wonky thumb fidgeted at it, as if searching for a way through.

Mom? he whispered. But he didn't think either of them could hear him.

His mother (what was she wearing? Why could he not hold in his mind what she was wearing?) gestured toward the tree behind her. The landscape shifted as his eyes followed the path she'd indicated. Instead of grassy flats, he was racing down a road flanked by rows of conifers, a blur of dark, intense green with the occasional gray smear of stacked rocks.

No... Adam shook his head and shut his eyes, but the scene continued to pass through his mind. *Please, not there.*

Soon he came to a familiar fork in the road with a familiar sign. But this time, the ball of flame that marked the path to the right wasn't faded. It was so vivid, he felt certain it would consume the wood it was painted upon. He veered to the right and careened past the sign deeper into the forest and saw stone, stretching from the earth until it was capped at waist level like a table. The top stone was rough, not worked but naturally flat. But the stains that wound and rippled over it... Adam was wrenched toward the knobbly, porous surface. The rusty stains were anything but natural—

"No!" Adam screamed, jerking himself awake.

He threw the door to Luther's car open, fell to his knees, and nearly crawled beneath the vehicle, shivering with fear and cold. The ground was grassy, not forested. He lifted his gaze slowly, reluctantly. Nothing but fields, not even a single tree in the distance. But his heart still slammed against his ribs. He clutched his arms to his shuddering body and rocked.

Please, please don't make me go there.

But gradually the rocking diminished, and he realized why he'd been shown that awful place. *Because Iris will be there.* And with that certainty, his mind grew calm. He sat back on his heels, staring up at the dark sky. The cold air burned his lungs, even breathing through his nose.

Of course he would go. For Iris.

He stood, legs still a little unsteady, and climbed back into Luther's vehicle. Once he was close, he thought he could find the place, but he needed a map to get in the neighborhood. How many hours away was it?

Adam started the car. The gas gauge read below a quarter tank. So he needed a map and gas. He took a moment to get his bearings before turning on the headlights. He'd drive in reverse, follow his own crushed grass path back to the road.

And then back to his uncle Teddy's.

Adam twisted in his seat and looked over his shoulder, squinting at the dim, red illumination from his taillights.

A woman's voice whispered in his ear, *Don't worry—you won't be alone.*

66

JJ jumped when the phone rang, immediately triggering self-recriminations.

How the hell do you fall asleep when your daughter's been kidnapped?

Exhaustion, obviously. She shoved Trooper out of the way, hurrying to get from the bed to the phone in the living room. Lurching down the hallway, she was too late—the ringing stopped. Arm against the wall to steady herself, JJ realized the phone had stopped because someone had answered it. A man. But a man Trooper trusted, calmly loping down the hall ahead of her. So she followed.

"I know," Harlan said. Darkness still pressed against the windows, and he stood in the small pool of warm light cast by a lamp on an end table. "We're on our way," he added, and hung up.

He hardly spared a glance for her now-cold bare legs, visible beneath an oversized T-shirt. "That was Teddy," he said. "We need to go. Get dressed."

She didn't ask why, just did as he'd said. By the time she emerged again, still shoving her arms into a flannel shirt that fit snugly over a long-sleeved T-shirt, Harlan stood by the door. He'd folded the blankets he'd used and left them in a neat pile on the couch.

"Walking or driving?" she asked.

Dorothy had insisted Teddy spend the night at the Nicholson house when JJ took Harlan home with her.

"Driving," Harlan said, and opened the door, letting in a wall of cold air and her dog.

He must've sent Trooper out to do his business. JJ figured that meant they weren't coming right back. She filled Trooper's water bowl and gave him an early breakfast. He stared at her and the food, as though wondering if this deviation from routine was a trick.

Harlan was already waiting on the porch. She patted Trooper's head absently before locking him inside, asking, "What time is it?"

"Time to get Evie," he said simply.

She dropped her keys, fumbled trying to retrieve them from the floorboards of the porch. "What the hell's that supposed to mean?"

"I think Teddy can tell us where she is," he said. "Or where she's headed."

JJ unlocked the door and pushed past Trooper, back inside to retrieve her daddy's Mossberg and a box of shells. She struggled to lock up again, but told herself it was the weapon hanging awkwardly from its strap over her shoulder. Harlan was under no such illusions. He took the keys from JJ's palsied hand, secured the front door, and said, "I'll drive."

"Look," JJ said, confirming the shotgun wasn't loaded before setting it on the back seat and climbing in the unfamiliar passenger side. "I don't do this mysterious sensei, Jedi master— whatever the hell kind of bullshit."

"I know you don't," Harlan said, blowing on his hands and

rubbing them together before starting the engine. "But I told you all I know."

She bit her lip and rocked anxiously in her seat, and not only because he nearly sideswiped her poplar tree.

"I also know Evie's okay," Harlan said. "For now."

He leaned forward, gauging where the ditch was as he made the turn from her driveway to the Nicholsons. His silver hair reflected the meager light from the dash.

Otto met them, limping, at the front door. "They're in the sewing room," he said, standing aside to let Harlan and JJ enter.

Harlan led the way, as though he'd been there a million times before rather than once. Teddy sat upright with a stack of pillows supporting him and Rachel on the bed next to him. Her hair hung in a pair of braids and she wore the same pink, ruffled pajamas she'd worn in the hospital. JJ thought they were her favorites. The girl didn't look up, just kept fidgeting with the friendship bracelet on her tiny arm. The one that matched her gift to Evie.

"Otto," Dorothy called out as she shuffled down the stairs. "What's going on? Is Rachel still with Mr. Rutledge?"

Otto left to intercept Dorothy, and JJ's attention returned to Teddy.

"Rachel was keeping me company tonight." He pointed at a sleeping bag, balled up next to the bed. "A few minutes ago, she woke up and told me she had a dream."

"Let me guess... Adam was there?" Harlan asked.

"Thanks to this one," Teddy said, putting a hand on Rachel's shoulder and hugging her toward him. "A woman came to Rachel and said she needed her help."

"She was looking for Adam. She gave him something so she could always find him, but he lost it," Rachel said.

"The key?" Harlan asked.

Teddy raised an eyebrow.

Harlan mulled for a moment, then said, "So Adam lost Charlotte's focus, and without it, whatever residual crap Virgil left behind that's blocking us was blocking her, too. To get around it, Charlotte used her own power and tapped into Adam's link to Rachel."

"Sounds that way," Teddy agreed. "Tell them what you saw."

"We didn't get close—not, like, to talk or anything—but she showed Adam something," Rachel said. "A place out in the woods. But not here, somewhere else."

"They're going to the summer retreat," Teddy said, trying to smile at an idea that seemed to make him anything but happy.

Harlan nodded a grim acknowledgment of what must have been an inside joke.

"Where is that?" JJ asked.

"Teddy's house. Pennsylvania. And a long drive—we best get going," Harlan said. "I'll explain later."

Rachel looked up, her frank expression at odds with her delicate young appearance, and said, "They're going home."

The hairs on the back of JJ's neck prickled. Where had she heard that before?

Harlan stared at Teddy. "You said Danny only visited once, and he sure as hell never lived there."

"And you don't think it was home to Lawrence?" Teddy asked.

Harlan shook his head. "Don't start. I don't need to hear that crazy bull—"

He paused, reconsidered his words. Rachel was looking particularly innocent, angelic even.

"Crazy bullcrap," Harlan finished. But for once, he seemed more concerned with moving than winning an argument. "It doesn't matter. JJ and I'll prove you wrong when we get there."

JJ was surprised when Harlan extended bare fingers toward the man. The two men clasped hands, heads bowed. They were silent long enough for her to get antsy, if she hadn't felt something was happening, something was passing between them that she didn't want to interrupt.

Finally, they lifted their heads and shared a smile. JJ's skin tingled when the men released each other's hands.

"I'm sorry I thought you killed my brother," Teddy said.

"That's okay," Harlan replied, smile turning impish. "I'm still sorry I didn't do it."

Teddy snorted. Then he told JJ, "Keep an eye on him."

She nodded and kissed the man's cheek, then the top of Rachel's hair. "I'm bringing Evie home," she promised, but couldn't look at the child as she left the room.

Otto and Dorothy were arguing in the kitchen, so JJ and Harlan slipped past them. Outside, JJ took her keys back from Harlan and was just getting in the Bronco when Otto hobbled out of the house.

"JJ!" he yelled. "Wait!"

He didn't approach, bracing himself against the metal rail, but Dorothy appeared a few seconds later with a bulging paper bag. She carried it—jogging in her slippers—out to the car.

"I put Evie's favorite muffins in there," she said, giving JJ a surprisingly forceful hug before racing back inside.

And then JJ and Harlan were gone.

"Are you sure Teddy's right about where Danny's headed?" JJ asked.

"Yes," Harlan said, without hesitation.

That's all she needed to know, that he was sure. Merging onto the interstate, JJ said, "If you want to do something useful, you can pour me a cup of coffee."

Dorothy had tucked two thermoses into the bag, one with coffee and one with a thin, brothy soup. JJ struggled to keep the Bronco steady against sudden, heavy winds as Harlan poured carefully into a cup wedged between his knees. He held it patiently until it was safe for her to remove a hand from the wheel.

"Thanks. The soup should probably be okay for you, but don't overdo it. I wouldn't risk the muffins yet. And no coffee," JJ said, taking a sip. It was strong and almost hot enough to burn her lips. "How are you feeling?"

She heard the smile in his voice as he replied, "You mean for someone who just got out of a coma? I guess I can honestly say I've been worse. Of course, then I didn't miss having coffee."

"Do you remember anything about it?"

"Not much," was his answer. But his tone said, *Nothing I care to share.* The paper bag crackled as he removed an extra cup and poured himself some soup.

"They medevacked you to Morgantown, as soon as they could get to you," JJ said, as if the man might be interested in what happened during a period of time he was obviously trying to forget. "Iris and Adam basically lived there the past couple of weeks. And you were only transferred to Beecham County..."

JJ paused. Was it yesterday? It didn't matter. Harlan probably wasn't listening anyway. But it helped her to talk out loud, keeping her mind busy while her hands were occupied on the wheel.

"You suffered serious head trauma, but my understanding is that the brain injury wasn't nearly as bad as it could have been. You just wouldn't wake up. Adam did something for you, didn't he?" JJ asked. "Something to help heal you, the way he did Rachel."

"Yes," Harlan said, "I suppose he did."

JJ was pretty damn sure there was no supposing about it. "When he healed Rachel, it almost killed him. But after he helped you, Adam managed to chase Danny and apparently swim half the goddamn South Branch of the Potomac. Teddy says Virgil helped him do that somehow, fed him energy."

Harlan sighed next to her and muttered, "No wonder the boy's so fucked up."

"What do you mean?" she asked.

"It's complicated," Harlan said, waving a hand dismissively. "It makes sense that Virgil'd help Adam chase after Danny. But the man wouldn't have crossed the street to piss on me if I were on fire. So whatever Adam did for me, he did on his own."

"How?" JJ asked. "What changed from when he'd healed Rachel?"

Harlan's hand strayed to his head, touching it gently as though it might break. "I'd given Adam some instruction earlier that day—very limited, but more than what he'd had before."

JJ glanced at the upcoming sign automatically, reading it as they passed, but she knew they'd be on the interstate for hours. "That's it? You gave him the CliffNotes?"

Harlan considered. "Could be the place, too. Some places have more healing power than others, and proximity to water helps. At least, it always has for me. Earth and stone seem to need a little more encouragement to share their energy. Sometimes they require a sacrifice."

"You mean, kill someone to save someone else?" JJ asked, wide eyes drawn to him.

"No," Harlan said. "I'm sorry—poor word choice, but I'm not at my most articulate right now. Quid pro quo, maybe? It's not like they're taking sides, they're just collecting a toll to use the road."

But it was too late. JJ's brain had already started down paths it was better served avoiding. So of course, her mouth went there, too. "What do you remember about Danny? About what went on between the two of you while Adam was gone. What was he like?"

Harlan sighed and traced his dark eyebrows with a finger. "You do realize I haven't had a goddamn drop of booze to drink in... well, however long you tell me it's been. I'm sorry, but chicken broth is not cutting it to talk about all this shit."

JJ lifted her own beverage to her lips. The bitter brew had cooled quickly in the thin, plastic cup. She drank it all down before wedging the container into her cupholder. She needed to clean her car. Evie had complained about it last week when JJ had picked her and Rachel up from school. *Geez, Mom, this is embarrassing*, she'd said, moving a stack of mail from her seat and rolling her eyes at Rachel. Another eerie foreshadowing of her teenaged self.

JJ's chest grew tight, and she squeezed the steering wheel even tighter.

"JJ," Harlan said softly, "do you want me to drive?"

She shook her head, not trusting her voice.

"The man I met, the man who used to be Danny, was determined and ruthless," Harlan said.

JJ suddenly felt faint. Maybe she needed Harlan to drive after all.

"But," Harlan continued, "he struck me down without remorse because I was an obstacle. For Evie at least, that's not the case. I'm not saying she's not in danger. She definitely is. But with Evie, he might just hesitate."

67

———

D anny's eyes flew open, instantly awake. He'd always been that way, barring sickness or injury. It had served him well with the man who'd been his first father and his secret temper, and with Virgil, his second unstable father. Instant wakefulness was also useful as an adult, when Danny found himself surrounded by people who'd spent a lifetime making bad choices and might not think his life was a bad trade for a decent fix. His gaze strayed toward the package in the glovebox. His nest egg.

He scrubbed his face with his hands, elbowing the steering wheel. The sound and sensation of stubble friction helped stimulate his blood. The sun hadn't yet risen, but it was getting there. Danny could see his path back to the road. He should be at Uncle Teddy's in an hour or so. He'd only been there once, but Virgil had imprinted its location on his mind. During his paranoid spells, Virgil made Danny recite the directions for his only safe haven should something happen to Virgil.

Well, now it had. And it was Danny's fault. Danny's hand shook as he started the truck. He listened to the soft scrape of leafless brush against the tailgate as he pivoted in the tight space.

Stupid motherfucker. How far south had things gone for Rashid to have killed his father? He'd said there were three men. Assuming it was Adam with Virgil, who was the third man? Rashid had said a big guy with short, dark hair who carried a gun and moved like he had law enforcement training. But the man hadn't identified himself as a cop.

Danny waited for a pair of headlights to pass, then turned onto the secondary road, oversteering a little to straighten out. The truck's alignment was way off. That was the drawback of stealing a vehicle that blended in—the owner probably took shitty care of it. Yet another reason the little bit of time he might save taking the interstate wasn't worth the risk.

He had felt clearheaded when he woke, but now things were getting fuzzy again. He tried to remember why Rashid was involved. Because Danny was trying to get established somewhere else and stay in Victor's good graces by using his man. But then why wasn't Rashid with him?

Iris. Jesus, why did he keep forgetting about Iris? Probably because he must have been as crazy as Virgil when he took her. Rashid was watching over Iris, bringing her. And Rashid had only done what Danny had asked him to do out at that nasty safe house.

But you couldn't let a man kill your father and get away with it.

The sun was peeking over the mountains, far enough to his right that Danny wasn't blinded, but near enough to dead ahead that he didn't have to contort to see it. Goddamn, it was beautiful. The barest hint of gray-blue high above, with the dark silhouette of the mountains against a smear of bloody orange and crimson. *Red sky in the morning...* who was supposed to take warning?

Danny couldn't remember.

His mind returned to the men at the safe house. A cop who wasn't working as a cop... *sonuvabitch.* It must be Luther Beck. Granted, he'd killed the man's brother, but Danny hadn't thought the deputy would be the vengeance type. He should've killed the bastard when he had the chance. And Danny never thought they'd connect him to Leslie. What link had they found that Danny had missed?

It didn't matter now. Virgil was a crazy fucker, but it turned out he'd been right about a lot of spooky shit, including his talk about forces converging. Things were coming to a head. Danny could feel it. And he wasn't afraid to die, if need be. So long as he took Adam with him.

68

———

Evie had dozed off. Slept even. Where was she? Had the truck been moving again? It wasn't now. She opened her eyes and peeked from behind her hood to see powdered dirt and grit and the curling end from a roll of Lifesavers on the floor of the truck.

It was daylight.

Crap!

Evie held in a gasp and pushed down the urge to bolt as she pulled her hood back, turned her head slowly... and found a man staring down at her. He filled the open door. He was her mom's age, with dark brows and hair (what there was of it, being almost buzz cut) and equally dark brown eyes.

"Well, what have we here?" he asked, smiling, lips only. When he spoke, it was through nice, even teeth that a tiny voice in her head said he would eat her with. "Are you lost?"

Could he really not know who she was? Or rather, not know that she knew who *he* was? She opened her mouth, but her voice had taken flight along with her senses.

The man casually discarded his smile and inclined his head, looking at her as if she weren't quite human. Or rather, as if *he* weren't. Then something flickered in his eyes. Good, bad, or both, Evie couldn't tell. His smile returned, more genuine this time, but no less scary.

"I see it now—how could I have missed it! You're JJ's girl, Evelyn," he said.

"Evie," she said automatically, voice hoarse with thirst and fear.

Bits of sky flashed behind him as he nodded. "You're right—Evelyn doesn't fit you. Was that your grandmother's name?"

She shook her head and used the motion to inch her hand closer to the front seat. "Grandma's name is Joyce."

"Not that grandma," he said. "I knew Joyce. Kind of a dumb bitch. She left Max to marry the Dweeb."

Evie narrowed her eyes at him.

"Sorry," he said. "JJ probably didn't tell you. When she was your age, that was her secret name for the man your grandma married."

Apparently he didn't see anything wrong with calling her grandmother names. Of course, he didn't see anything wrong with shooting her dad, either. Evie's cheeks went warm and her breath came short. "Are you Danny?" she asked.

His eyebrow raised, and he stretched up to rest one arm at head level on the doorframe. The keys jingled slightly in his hand. "Your mom talk about me?" he asked.

"Not much," Evie said, and he flinched. Just a little. "Grandpa said she didn't like to talk about it. But he told me once, when she got snippy with me for running off somewhere on my own, that you were why."

Evie shifted, fighting numbness, bringing her legs toward her until she sat with her back against the locked door. And her hand next to the seat.

"I liked your Grandpa," the man said.

Evie wanted to yell at him, to say someone like him wasn't allowed to like her Grandpa, but she didn't. "He told me how she used to search for you in the woods. How for years she thought she'd find you."

The man's body still blocked her, but his eyes flicked away. His chin dropped, stretching his face and his full lips, and he looked almost sad. Evie continued, "She and Adam—"

His eyes shot back at her, and his voice was ugly when he interrupted. "Oh, I'll bet she and Adam had a good old time, alone in the woods."

She wasn't sure how, but Evie had taken a wrong step. The man's chest heaved as he breathed deeply through his nose, mouth pinched with anger. So much for pacifying him.

"Why did you kidnap Rachel Nicholson?" Evie demanded.

His lip curled, and in a flash he was back to staring at her like he wasn't human. Like he was some kind of... creature. A predator. Evie was so scared, she felt the pee she'd held in all night soaking her pants. And once she started to pee, she couldn't stop. And that made her want to cry. She pressed her back against the truck door, harder and harder. But of course it wouldn't budge.

"I took that girl," he said, wolfish face leaning into the cab, "because I thought she was you."

And now she really was crying.

She'd never been so scared. But as much as her brain was shrieking inside, it still had the sense to ask, *What would Momma do?*

Evie's hand reached beneath the seat. She nearly dropped the gun in her lap trying to free it from its wrapping. The rag still hung from the pistol's barrel as she raised it to point at him.

69

*D**ammit.* He ought to know by now not to underestimate the Tulley women. Where the hell had the girl gotten a gun? Danny flinched as she shook it to fling the rag free. The dirty cloth draped across her forearm as it fell.

Danny jerked backward, banging his head painfully against the truck's frame as he cleared the opening. He slammed the door after himself and dropped low, squatting by the driver's door and edging toward the engine.

"The last thing you want to do is fire that gun in the truck," he called out, pausing by the front wheel. She had pulled the gun quickly, but desperation did not equal expertise. "Good way to lose your hearing. Not to mention shooting yourself, with a ricochet or a bullet fragment. You never know what'll happen once you pull that trigger."

He wouldn't be able to lie his way into the girl's trust. Kids were smarter than most adults gave them credit.

"How'd you end up in my truck anyway?" he asked. He hadn't bothered to disable the truck's child locks, which explained why she hadn't run. He thought he could just open the door from the outside. If not, he had the key. But he'd have to unlock and open the door pretty damn fast.

"I guess you've been in there since JJ's house last night, huh?" he asked. "No wonder you peed your pants in my truck."

Her voice shook as she yelled, "It's not your truck!"

Danny smiled. He'd gotten to her. "Are you calling me a thief? What makes you think this vehicle doesn't belong to me?"

"Because," she said, as he crept around the front of the truck toward the door she leaned against. "If it was, you'd have known about the gun."

Smart kid. And if it were his truck, he'd also be sure about opening the goddamn doors.

Danny had parked near Rashid's monster SUV in a dirt area in front of Teddy's house. The gravel had been washed away long ago, which was good so far as being quiet was concerned. But it did not help him find a decent-sized rock. A discarded old quart of motor oil, label faded, would have to do. He stretched, cringing against the possibility of noise as he picked up the plastic container, still half full. He held the motor oil in his left hand while he adjusted the truck key in the fingers of his right, just in case.

Danny rose and threw the oil into the bed of the truck. It slammed hard into the tailgate, not where he'd been aiming but satisfyingly loud. He yanked the back open, dropping the unnecessary keys as he maneuvered awkwardly around the door. The child fell backward and he grabbed her gun arm first, stripping the weapon from her grasp easily.

That was where *easy* stopped.

The girl was a little hellcat, kicking and screeching and biting. Danny wasn't sure how to subdue her without seriously injuring or killing her, which would only make his life even more complicated. He shoved the gun in the back of his pants and dragged her away from the open truck. Her legs lashed out as he lifted her off the ground, a toe catching Rashid's bumper. Danny squeezed a grunt from the child and kept squeezing until her breath became a thin wheeze.

"If you don't settle down, I will kill you," he said.

She swung her head, but only smashed the top edge of his ear against his skull. He suppressed a powerful urge to bite her ear in retaliation, then remembered his ace card. "I'll kill Iris, too. And it'll be your fault."

The girl tensed, then relaxed in his arms, and he slowly lowered her to the ground. That's when he noticed Rashid standing in front of them, gun pointed at the child.

The big man inclined toward his vehicle, lowering his sunglasses. "If you scratched my paint, I'm blowing your goddamn brains out myself."

The child's legs went slack and for a moment Danny was supporting her weight. He had to admit, Rashid was a much more imposing figure than he was, especially for a child (unless Cold Springs had changed a lot) who rarely saw a black man outside of the bullshit on the news. And Rashid had a penchant for scary-ass, big guns.

Danny walked the girl slowly toward the truck, keeping a hand on her shoulder as he grabbed a scrap of rope from the bed. He tied the girls' hands in front, but not too tightly. The improvised restraint would hold until he got her inside and figured out something more long-term. What the hell was he going to do with her?

Rashid shook his head as he watched Danny tug a knot secure.

"Are you kidding me?" Rashid demanded. "My impression was that we had some serious work to do. We gonna be babysitting anybody else? Puppies, or paraplegics?"

Danny smiled, pretended like he didn't want to knock Rashid's teeth out. Because Rashid was absolutely right. Danny had royally fucked this up at almost every turn, though he couldn't quite figure out how or exactly where things had gone wrong.

Of course, Rashid killing his dad couldn't go unanswered. But not until everything—and everyone—was taken care of.

Danny nudged the girl forward, toward the old man's porch. "Let's go."

70

Luther sat outside the hospital, waiting.

He knew his body was all out of whack, but he couldn't help feeling it wasn't much colder outside than the air conditioning had been inside. The local anesthetic was wearing off, and air felt funny against his sutured forehead. He found himself wrinkling his brows to test out the skin, before the vague tug reminded him there was a reason it had been numbed.

Where the hell was Grant?

Evie kidnapped. JJ must be losing her goddamned mind. When they spoke, Grant had said the car Luther described, with its bloody but empty cooler, was consistent with the vehicle Marcus Brown had seen parked at Iris Rutledge's house. (Luther would not have grieved if Danny had been a better shot where Marcus was concerned.) He endeavored to make sense of the connections, but exhaustion was getting the best of him.

The dark sky had lightened to a dingy bedsheet gray and Luther's ass on the cement bench had gone almost as numb as his head when his cell phone rang. *Beth.* He noticed a red battery warning while checking the caller ID. Hopefully Grant had a phone charger that would fit. Assuming the man ever showed up.

"Yeah," he said.

"Is the Sheriff with you?" the not-suspended deputy asked.

"I'm just fine, in case you were wondering," Luther said. "Although when you've said you cut yourself on broken glass, a bullet fragment in your forehead is kinda hard to explain—"

"Have you seen him at all yet?" she interrupted.

"No."

"Dammit." She sighed. "JJ's not at her house, and her vehicle's gone."

If it had been anyone else, Luther might have assumed she'd gone for a drive, or to see friends or family, seeking comfort. "You check the Nicholsons next door?"

"That's where I am now," Beth said. "They said she and Harlan Miller took off, but they don't know where."

"Harlan Miller?" Luther asked. "I thought he was in a coma."

"Not anymore," Beth said.

"Well, shit." Not that Luther wasn't glad to hear the man was conscious. But Harlan had been up to his eyeballs in recovering Rachel and Aaron Schofield, so the chances of JJ leaving to clear her head had just gone from slim to none.

Luther stood and gave a wave as a familiar Beecham County cruiser entered the parking lot at the far end. "Grant's here. I'll have him call you in a minute."

The drop-off area had a small overhang. Luther rested against one of its metal supports while Grant approached and pulled to the sidewalk. Luther opened the cruiser's passenger door and leaned in.

"Am I still suspended?" he asked.

"You can sit in the front seat," the Sheriff said, not precisely answering.

Grant drove toward the exit, but parked at the back of the lot instead of leaving. His eyes were red and shadowed, and Luther guessed the man hadn't been to bed the previous night. Not that he had either, unless you counted a short period of time he believed he'd passed out in his car while Adam drove.

"I went to see the scene," Grant said. "And Virgil."

"Don't suppose Adam was there."

Grant shook his head. "You're lucky you weren't both still there, laying on the ground next to him. That was a helluva shot."

Luther shrugged. It was, but he knew people who could've made it. Local hunters. Hell, Les might've done, were he still alive. It wasn't the first shot that bothered Luther. It was the relentless ones that followed it, the ones that nearly killed them both, despite the adrenaline that had to have been racing through the shooter's veins. "They find anything at the house?"

"One set of recent tire tracks. Nothing obvious inside."

Luther hadn't expected there would be. "And Virgil's body's still waiting to be moved?"

Grant nodded. "I felt funny, leaving him."

"Me, too," Luther admitted. He didn't realize he was shimmying, back and forth, in his seat until the light squeak of the seat springs broke through his reverie. He pressed his fingers against the top of the car window frame, until the motion stilled. "Beth called," he said, and related what she'd told him.

Grant apparently reached the same conclusion as Luther, bowing his head briefly—almost to the steering wheel—before trying JJ. When she didn't answer, he returned the deputy's call. They spoke briefly before Grant said, "Put Teddy Rutledge on the line."

"Teddy Rutledge?" Luther asked. When the hell had that slippery bastard shown up?

Grant shook his head, which Luther took to mean he'd explain later, and his voice took on official lawman mode. "Mr. Rutledge, this is Sheriff Mason. I need you to tell me where JJ and Harlan went, and why."

Luther couldn't distinguish the man's words on the other end, but he didn't need to.

"Sir," Grant cut in, "a child's life is at stake, not to mention Iris Rutledge. If anything happens to them—or to JJ—and I could have prevented it, I will hold you personally responsible. And I believe you will, too."

Grant's brows drew together as he looked over at Luther. "Yes, sir, he is with me... Yes, sir... Okay, I'll tell him."

The Sheriff shrugged at Luther and started to tell him something, until his attention was drawn back to the phone. "Yeah, Beth, can you text me those directions? Thanks. We'll stay in touch."

Grant hung up the phone, then stared at the screen, ignoring Luther.

"Well?" Luther demanded.

Grant stared a little longer, then shook himself, as if realizing his expectations of instantaneous typing and transmission were unrealistic. "They think Danny's headed to Teddy Rutledge's place with Evie."

"Why?" Luther asked.

Grant rubbed his eyes. "Frankly, I'm not clear on that part. But whatever the reason, JJ felt compelled to head that way, and that's good enough for me."

"And Iris?" Luther asked.

"The feeling is she'll be there, too," Grant said, then added, "Presumably with our sharpshooter."

"So you think Iris really was in that house?"

"Luther, I wish I knew. Although I guess at this point it really doesn't matter."

Could they have been that close to Virgil's mother and left her there? Maybe they should've tried to drive through the front door after all. Except Luther knew he'd been right about their chances.

"Where do you think Adam's head is right now?" Grant asked.

"Nowhere good," Luther admitted.

"You could've reported your vehicle stolen." Grant's lip curled at Luther's dumbfounded expression, and he continued, "I didn't say it was a good idea, but it was an option."

Luther didn't respond.

The Sheriff looked away before asking, "Did you let him go because you think you owe something to my dad?"

"What do you mean?"

"I know he told you to keep an eye on Adam," Grant said. "I know, because he told me the same thing."

Now it was Luther's turn to look away, out over the parking lot, becoming slightly less empty.

Grant continued, "Dad's the one who convinced me to come back to Beecham County and run for Sheriff. He knew his mind was slipping. And there were things he wanted someone he trusted to know, so they wouldn't die with him."

Luther almost bolted for the ER again, where people were coughing up their lungs and bleeding out their eyes. There was only one person—other than Rudy—he'd confessed his secrets to. He cleared his throat. "Did the Sheriff tell you why he asked me to do that?"

"He didn't mean to," Grant said. "But he let enough slip, when he got confused about who I was or *when* we were, that I put two and two together. Is that why Adam took off, because he figured out you were there that night?"

Luther pressed a palm to his forehead, and felt the same pressure in his chest he'd felt at Les's hospital bed. "Yeah," he admitted. "And I was a helluva lot more than there."

"And knowing that, you don't think Adam would've shot you? You don't think he could be dangerous?" Grant pressed.

Luther sighed. "I'm telling you, if the man's dangerous to anybody, he's dangerous to himself."

Grant's phone finally pinged with their directions, and he blinked his tired eyes clear. "Damn," he said. "I thought he lived in Virginia, but that's all the way to Pennsylvania."

"Want me to drive?" Luther asked.

Grant raised a brow. "Can you see out of that eye?"

"Mostly," Luther lied. It hadn't been injured exactly, but they'd had to flush a lot of blood and debris. He'd refused the offer of a patch, but so far he wasn't getting much more than blurry light on his left side.

"Uh-huh," Grant said, handing his phone to Luther. "Then you can see to read me directions."

Luther held the phone to his face, closer, then farther away. He hadn't the slightest idea where his glasses were, and with one eye... "You'll catch Route 692 first," he guessed.

"Give me that," Grant said, grabbing his phone and shaking his head. He glanced at it quickly before setting the device to rest in the cupholder. Back on the highway, he crossed to the far turn lane before saying, "Teddy Rutledge had a message for you."

"Oh?" Luther couldn't recall ever meeting the man.

"He said you had something of Adam's." Grant turned left to eventually merge onto the interstate. He snuck a quick glance at Luther as he continued, "He said to make sure you gave it to Adam when we get there. I don't know how Adam's supposed to know where everybody is. He doesn't even have a phone."

Luther's hand went to the necklace in his pocket. "He'll be there," he said.

At the end. With Luther.

Just like crazy Virgil said.

71

Evie's legs shook so badly, she almost couldn't walk. She pointed her tied hands toward the ground and hugged her arms tightly to her body. Danny's fingers gripped her shoulder while they mounted the front steps of the old house, to steady her or keep her from running. Probably both.

She should've shot him. She should've shot Danny when she had the chance. *Why didn't I?* she accused herself, bottom lip trembling.

She couldn't see past the big, black man walking in front of her. She didn't understand why he was there, but he scared her. It wasn't that he was black. Old Mr. Llewelyn was black, and Evie wished he lived in their spare room so she could listen to his stories all the time. This man scared her because he reminded Evie of her grandmother tending her flower garden with her sprayer thing full of poison. Grandma never gave a second thought to all the bugs that didn't bother her roses, just sprayed indiscriminately because that was what she had to do to get the ones that did. To get the job done. Evie felt like she was a ladybug, and this man wouldn't care that she was caught in the crossfire, either.

His impersonal approach scared her, but Danny scared her more. He seemed to be in charge, but she had no idea why he was doing whatever he was doing, and she wasn't sure he knew, either. As if it changed from moment to moment.

The big man didn't bother looking at her as he held the screen door. The house appeared even older inside, like a great aunt's home Evie's mom took her to visit once in a while. It didn't have the same vinyl and metal kitchen chairs, or the same funky smell (this space smelled vaguely of grease and herbs), but it did seem faded and worn. Evie's gaze was drawn toward the living room and a tattered sofa with one occupant.

"Miss Iris!" Evie said, pushing past the man in front of her and throwing herself at the elderly woman on the couch. She hadn't meant to cry, but she was, chest heaving, and she wasn't sure she could stop.

"Easy, Evie," Iris said, stroking her hair awkwardly. "You're okay."

Evie's nose was running, about to drip on Iris's lap. She sucked draining gunk back into her head before looking up at the elderly woman. She was wearing handcuffs with pink fur. Danny must have done that. And one eye was blue-black with bruises and nearly swollen shut. Danny must have done that, too. Evie flashed stink eye at the man before turning back to Iris.

"Did they hurt you?" Evie asked, her voice softer than she intended. She'd wanted the angry parts to be bigger than the scared parts.

"I'm fine, sweetie. Better now that I've got you for company," Iris said. But Evie could tell she was lying, on the verge of tears herself because Evie had been dumb enough to end up stuck with her. "Come sit next to me."

"I can't," Evie whispered, eyes falling to her damp, stinking sweatpants. "I peed my pants."

Iris gave a little laugh. "Oh, honey, so did I. Twice. But you're not gonna hurt this old couch. Come on up here."

Evie edged carefully onto a cushion next to Iris, albeit reluctantly. The two men were watching them, waiting. Neither spoke, but they finally retreated a few steps to the kitchen table. They dropped their voices, and she couldn't really make sense of their conversation. But she figured that meant they couldn't hear her, either. She needed to tell Iris something she was sure was important, though she was less sure why.

"The man woke up yesterday," Evie said.

"What man?" Iris asked.

"I forget his name. The coma man," Evie whispered. "He's at our house."

Iris's uninjured eye was smudged nearly as dark as the bruised one. The creases in her face appeared deeper than usual, and a flake of dry skin stuck to the corner of her mouth. But all of this lifted as her cuffed hands flew to her mouth. She blinked, and even though she looked sad, she smiled. "Good. Thank you."

Meanwhile, Danny and the other man were arguing. They kept their voices low so she and Iris couldn't hear them, but it was something about their Business, whatever that was. The big man was calm—cold even—and became more so the longer they argued. Danny, on the other hand, became more short-tempered. There was something else too, some other way he was changing, but it was hard for Evie to put her finger on. He just seemed meaner.

"Sweetie," Iris said, leaning close but never taking her eyes from the men, "things could get crazy pretty soon. And when that happens, your job is to run if you can, hide if you can't. Got it?"

"What about you?" she asked.

Evie noticed a bruise and a couple of small cuts on Iris's hand when she reached out to stroke her hair. "I'll be doing the exact same thing. But it's easier for me to do that if I know you're safe. Promise?"

"Yes, ma'am," she said. "Whose house is this?"

"Nobody you know," Iris said, still watching the men. "It belongs to Adam's uncle. Well, technically his great-uncle."

"You mean Uncle Teddy?" Evie asked.

Iris flinched with surprise. "How do you know Teddy?"

"He brought the coma man to our house," Evie said. "And he broke our closet when the Sheriff came."

Iris opened her mouth, then shut it, seemingly unable to decide which part to respond to. Finally she said, "I've known Teddy for a very long time—longer than your parents have been alive—and he never was good at maintaining living quarters. Though I must admit, his home is an improvement over the last place they had me."

"Since it's Uncle Teddy's house, does that mean he knows we're here?" Evie asked.

"I don't know."

Evie fidgeted with her bracelet. "Maybe Rachel can find us. She sees stuff like Adam does."

Iris stared at her, and for an instant her expression reminded Evie of Rachel's mom. Then her face softened and she said, "There are so many people looking, someone will find us. I promise."

Evie let Iris pull her near, snuggling against the woman. It was going to be okay. Someone would save them.

Except, no matter how hard she squeezed Evie, Miss Iris's cuffed hands still trembled like desperate birds flying against the bars of a cage.

72

———

Luther tucked his hand beneath his leg when he noticed it creeping toward his brow. His forehead—hell, his whole skull—had begun a slow, insistent throb. He'd thrown the pain pill prescription the ER doc had given him in the trash, but he wouldn't say no to a bottle of Tylenol. Although it'd probably kill him on an empty stomach.

"Shot in the head, huh?" Grant asked.

"It was just a little piece of the bullet or the jacket or something—I thought it was glass—but yeah, I guess I was. Technically." Luther grinned. "Too bad I wasn't on duty."

He glanced over at the Sheriff, but the man's eyes stayed glued to the road and the cars ahead of them as if they were about to do something interesting. "About that..." Luther said.

Grant sighed. "Luther, I understand you want an answer about your suspension. But I can't give you one right now. You running off with Adam... A vigilante is a dangerous candidate for law enforcement."

"I wasn't a vigilante!" Luther snapped. The sudden flush in his face made his head hurt worse. "I wanted to help, and you wouldn't let me."

Grant's eyes swung toward him. "You were traveling with a fugitive."

Luther looked away. He had him there. What the hell had Luther been thinking, not turning Virgil in? Would the man still be alive if he had? Would Iris be safe at home? "I was trying to do the right thing," he said.

"I know, Luther." Grant squinted against the morning glare and slipped on his sunglasses. "But that's the problem. When you're a sworn officer, the right thing also has to be the lawful thing. That's how most dirty cops get that way. It's not that they're greedy or bad people. It's that they lose sight of the fact that they're not the arbiters of what's right. The law is."

The hills were mostly naked here (no trees and little scrub), and the interstate cut through the mountain rock the way a kid would do it—crudely, with no regard for aesthetics. It hurt to look at it. Luther's sunglasses were probably in his car with Adam, and he couldn't have put them on his face anyway. He lowered his visor and indulged in a fantasy of a dark, undisturbed bedroom with a good, solid mattress.

"You think being an outlaw is genetic?" Luther asked.

"I don't know," Grant said. "But a family reputation is a hard thing to get free of. To *stay* free of."

"That's supposed to be my line," Luther said.

"Fair enough," Grant said. "But I think I'm set on a good track to put a dent in the Mason reputation. Not to mention my position as Sheriff. Who knows? Maybe we'll be unemployed together."

That was something Luther hadn't considered. Goddamn, he was too tired for life to be this complicated.

"Could you give JJ a call?" Grant asked. "I saw a tower a little ways back and she might answer if you call, thinking it's Adam."

Luther had been using Grant's phone charger, plugged into the cigarette lighter. He tugged the cord free before dialing and putting his phone to the less swollen side of his face. "It's ringing."

And it kept ringing, with no answer. He hung up when JJ's voicemail picked up, then called again. Twice. Finally, JJ picked up, on an iffy line with the drone of static almost surpassing her voice.

"Luther?" she asked. "Are you there?"

"Barely. JJ, listen, the Sheriff and I are on our way to Teddy Rutledge's house," Luther said.

"Where?" JJ asked.

"Nice try," Luther said. "We know that's where you and Harlan are headed. Promise me you'll wait for us when you get there."

Her reply was a muffled buzz. By the time Luther realized she was talking to someone else with the receiver covered, her voice returned in his ear. "Why would I do that?"

"Because you think Evie is there, and so do we. And because you want your daughter home, safe and sound. We're trained professionals, JJ. We are the best shot she has. Do not throw that away."

Luther watched Grant trying not to watch him while they waited for JJ's answer.

"How long 'til you get here?" she asked.

He looked to Grant and mouthed, *how long?*

"Maybe ninety minutes," the Sheriff said, loud enough to carry.

"That's too long," JJ said.

Luther leaned toward Grant and checked the speedometer. "I can cut fifteen minutes off that," he said. "Come on, JJ. You know I'm right."

"Fine," she said. "We'll wait. As long as you're not late."

Luther let out the breath he didn't know he'd been holding. "Good. "

He was about to hang up when JJ asked, "Luther, where's Adam?"

"I don't know, but I think he's on his way. We'll see you soon." Luther hung up, then turned to Grant and asked, "Lights, no siren?"

Grant nodded, accelerating, and said, "And give the State Police a heads-up, so they don't think somebody bought a light bar off eBay."

Luther had just finished reassuring the locals that the rednecks were only passing through when their cruiser entered a half-hearted snow flurry at the crest of a mountain. The dry, swirling flakes looked more like post-apocalyptic ash than precipitation. "Sheriff, what do you think we'll find when we get there?"

"I wish I knew, Luther. But we've got about an hour to figure out how to deal with it."

73

———

J J hadn't admitted to Luther that, by Harlan's calculations, she was an hour away from Teddy's herself. She'd wanted Luther to feel like she was making a bigger concession than she was since she might not make one at all. Did he seriously think she could wait while her daughter was in danger?

They were on a private road now, having just passed a pair of stone cairns taller than JJ's Bronco, one made even higher by a raw, wooden cross perched on top. The road was flanked on both shoulders by rows of evergreens that made the prematurely dark sky seem even more ominous. She leaned over the steering wheel, staring up through the windshield, trying to catch a glimpse of blue. Hell, she'd settle for clouds that didn't look on the cusp of spawning a tornado.

"I know," Harlan said. "It's claustrophobic as hell. But for what it's worth, we're almost there. We'll stop at the fork in the road."

Her stomach was queasy, and JJ's heart raced like a cat's purr. "Do you think Adam's coming?"

"I hope so," Harlan said.

JJ sucked in air, as short of breath as if she'd been holding it on purpose. Maybe she had since that damn spooky cross. "Adam had a dream, while you were still in Morgantown."

"Oh?" Harlan said.

His voice sounded artificially matter-of-fact, and she found she couldn't look at him. "It was about Evie. He called me in the middle of the night from the hospital because he thought she was in danger."

"What did he see?"

How could the man's voice be so calm? It reminded her of Grant, and she suddenly wished he were with them. That she'd waited, or dragged him along. Not that it would have taken dragging.

"I don't know, because I didn't want to know. And he didn't really want to tell me," JJ said, and paused. It physically hurt to continue. "Her hands were covered in blood."

To Harlan's credit, he didn't talk about metaphors or try any of the stupid rationalizing shit she'd spouted at the time. But she wished he'd say something. She glanced over at him and saw his eyes were closed. One hand was braced against the dash, and his face twisted slightly as though he were in pain.

"Harlan, are you all right?" she asked, eyes returning to the road just in time to avoid a large, fallen branch.

"Evie's going to be okay," he said.

"You promise?" she asked, without looking. Because if he was lying she didn't want to know.

He squeezed her arm through her layers and said, "I promise."

And she believed him. Sort of. But she still felt like throwing up.

"Slow down," Harlan said.

JJ automatically looked at her speedometer as she eased off the gas. But she wasn't going too fast. As she raised her eyes, she saw they'd arrived at the crossroads.

The road forked, with simply painted, weathered signs

mounted on trees on either side. On the left, the symbol was a basic pyramid shape. To the right was a sign with a ball of flame.

And a battered blue SUV.

JJ's seat belt tugged tight across her chest as she slammed on the brakes.

In the V-shaped space between the two paths stood more conifers, and nearly at the point of the V was a stack of stones and a kneeling man. A lone, dark-haired man.

Adam.

74

———

The hours of driving were a blur to Adam. While parking Luther's SUV at the fork in the road, he'd noticed an empty bottle of water and granola bar wrapper on the seat next to him. He had no recollection of opening or consuming either of them. He'd stumbled from the vehicle, not quite sure why he'd stopped.

And then he'd found the stones.

A wall of rock drew his eye first, a massive boulder streaked with lichen and strewn with dead leaves. About the width of a generous living room and as high on one end, the other side sloped to almost join the ground. Time and weather were doing their best to separate the single boulder into boulders, as was a tree perched atop it. A root as thick as the tree's main trunk wrapped sinuously around the stone and disappeared into the earth. And next to the root, tucked in like a shadow, was a stack of stones. Just a few, the bottom one disappearing into the earth as the root did. Their surfaces were so flush, they could have been a single stone sliced into sections. They weren't a trail-marking cairn or the work of a bored hiker... these stones *meant something*.

Adam wasn't a religious man. Iris was in her own way, but churches had never really touched him. Not the way the stones did. So he'd knelt in front of them and rested his forehead upon the ground. Adam had been falling apart for a while, crumbling from the inside out. Now, finally, he could see why.

The last time Adam was at Uncle Teddy's, Adam had suffered a seizure, his mind crushed beneath the onslaught of craziness from an untethered Virgil. In the seizure's aftermath, he remembered waves of colors and light in his mind's eye, but the core of the craziness seemed embodied within intense indigo lines, silhouetted against a dull red background.

Now he saw them again. Though not nearly as vibrant as before, layers of indigo crazy and confusion overlay his mind, like frost on a window in a nuclear winter. But that wasn't all. Anchored within his psyche were remnants of blue walls constructed by Virgil, enduring like bombed fortifications in the aftermath of a battle. Shrouding the walls was a gauzy, sticky film, peeled away easily enough once Adam could see it. Part of Adam wanted to cling to these tatters of Virgil's misguided attempts to protect him. But that's exactly what his father had done, clung to illusions until they became real, until they became the foundation of his world. And Adam needed to see clearly to face whatever it was Danny had become.

So he chipped away. It wasn't something that could be accomplished in a day, this dismantling, and perhaps not by Adam alone. But the hours passed unnoticed as he stripped away layers. Waiting patiently for he knew not what.

Until JJ arrived. *With Harlan.*

Adam ran to the vehicle and opened the passenger door, gripping its heavy metal so hard his fingers ached, just to be sure he wasn't hallucinating. Harlan stepped down, eyes glistening. He was skinnier, and when they embraced, Adam thought the older man felt frail. Still, Adam wasn't certain who was holding up whom.

"I'm so sorry," Harlan said, voice husky in Adam's ear. "But it's good to see you, son."

Adam had no words, but Harlan didn't seem to expect any. Together, they turned to stare gravely down the path into the woods that neither wanted to travel.

"He's got Evie," JJ said.

Adam hadn't noticed JJ pass around the truck. He looked from her to Harlan, trying to make sense of what she'd said.

"Danny kidnapped Evie," she clarified, expression stoic but voice cracking the tiniest bit.

Adam's time with the stones had made him stronger, but an image from his dream of Evie—from his *vision* of her—shrieking in anguish and smeared with blood still took his breath away. Adam's knees buckled.

His mind babbled, *I should have stopped it. I could have stopped it. Why didn't I stop it?*

"Hey!" Harlan said, following him to the ground. He rested his forehead against Adam's, his unruly dark brows tickling Adam's skin, and the panic receded enough for Adam to breathe. "We *can't* stop it, no matter how much we want to. We can't stop what hasn't happened yet. It doesn't work that way."

And Iris... what about Iris? What about the man who'd killed his father?

"Easy." Harlan rested his hands on the back of Adam's head. "Just because we can't stop it ahead of time, doesn't mean we're powerless."

Harlan released him, and the two men rocked back on their heels to face each other. With hollow cheeks and sallow skin, Harlan looked nearly as ill as he had in the hospital. Except for his eyes. Even exhausted, an impish spirit resided in Harlan's eyes. But that mischievous twinkle was overshadowed—Harlan had seen something. Was it related to Adam's vision of Evie? Adam knew Harlan wouldn't tell him, but he didn't have to.

"Okay," Adam said. "So what do we do?"

"I knew you'd say that, and yet... you're always surprising me." Harlan bit his lip, then turned it into a half smile. "We have to split our forces, because that's what Danny will do. JJ and I will head for the house; you'll take the altar."

That's where Danny was taking Iris—to the altar. Adam didn't know how he knew it, but he did. But if Danny was splitting his forces, that meant the other guy would still be at the house with Evie.

"No," Adam said. "The two of you don't stand a chance against Danny's partner."

"Like you do?" JJ demanded.

"He's a professional—he killed Virgil with one shot—and I doubt that's where his skills end," Adam countered.

"Luther and Grant are on their way," JJ said.

"Good," Adam said, rising. "And I'll go with you."

"Son, Iris would prioritize the child's life over her own, just as you are. I have no quarrel with that," Harlan said, getting up more slowly than Adam had and pointing toward the other path. "But there's more at stake than Iris's life, I'm sure of it. Teddy thinks it's all tied to Lawrence. To him..." Harlan paused and dropped his head, as if reluctant to go on. Then the words tumbled out. "To Lawrence somehow coming back. I don't believe that, but I tend to have a blind spot where that bastard is concerned."

Adam blinked. *Coming back?* What did that even mean?

"If, God forbid, Teddy *isn't* out of his mind, you can't let Danny shed blood on that altar, especially not yours or Iris's. You both have considerable power. Iris denies hers, but she's still the most effective shielder I've ever met. And you're both intimately connected to Lawrence, his wife and his grandson. In the sacrifice business, that counts for a lot."

Adam couldn't quite process what Harlan was telling him— he was right, it did sound crazy—but more than that, Adam couldn't let go of his fear for JJ's daughter. Harlan currently wore every minute of his however-many decades. But if Adam went to Evie first, maybe Harlan could keep Danny busy until Adam returned, or someone else was free to help him.

"You're the one who has to stop Danny," Harlan said firmly. Then he continued, *And I have to stay with JJ.*

JJ didn't chime in. That's when Adam realized she hadn't heard Harlan's words; they were meant for him alone. *Frick.* What did Harlan know that he was unwilling to speak aloud? It didn't matter. There was no time for second-guessing. Adam had to trust him.

"Okay," Adam said.

"It's only about half a mile. You'll have to walk," Harlan said. "And when you get there... Don't believe everything you see, but don't discount anything, either. There's power tied to that altar. *Blood* power. But there's a barrier, too, that helps keep things contained. You'll see it. And you'll know what to do."

JJ stood rooted next to the Bronco, as though someone had pulled the plug on her higher brain function. She'd need to hold it together a little longer, but stalling out briefly might keep her from running off before backup arrived. Adam went to her, pulling her to him so tightly he could feel a mild tremble pulse throughout her body. She smelled of muffins and coffee and some indefinable JJ essence that hadn't changed since childhood.

"Please wait for Luther and Grant," he said. "And be safe."

"Always," she whispered.

And then he had to let go.

Adam felt like he was forever letting go.

Returning to Harlan, Adam rested his forehead against the other man's, surprised they were nearly the same height. And surprised he didn't feel anything unusual at the touch, except a peculiar sense of calm he tried to emulate.

"I'll bring her back," Adam said.

"I know you will," Harlan replied, patting Adam's shoulder. "See you on the other side."

Adam nodded and stepped back, away from Harlan and toward a place that scared him more than anything else ever had in his entire life. Alone.

75

"Mitch, man, I was willing to cut you some slack because we've collaborated before, and you've always been solid, but I don't know what the fuck is going on here," Rashid said. "And I damn well know Victor doesn't, either."

Danny heard something in the man's words that raised his hackles. "You mean, he won't know unless you tell him. You asking for more money?"

Sitting across from him at Teddy's kitchen table, Rashid grew so still it was spooky. "I'm asking for more fucking sanity. This is not the way to run a business."

His eyes were flat, almost as flat as his tone. Danny and Rashid had worked together enough for Danny to know that meant Rashid was close to losing control. Well, not losing control —he didn't do that. Close to committing to action. Usually violent action.

Like, say, shooting someone's father.

"I understand," Danny said, although it felt like pulling barbed wire through his intestines to say it. "Don't worry. We're finished with this tonight."

Rashid cocked his head to one side. "Why do you want to wait until nightfall? And waste another day."

Why, indeed? Danny shut his eyes and took a deep breath. He heard the whispering inside, tickling the backside of his eardrum. *He's right; it's time. I promise, he'll be waiting.* And the voice hadn't lied to him yet.

He opened his eyes and smiled. "Okay," Danny said. "I'll take care of the old woman now. We'll drop the kid somewhere on the way."

Rashid's eyes flicked toward the couch. "You think that's wise, if you're setting up shop somewhere near here? You want to be always looking over your shoulder?"

Like the man gave a shit. He was just pissed because the child had seen *his* face. Whatever. Danny would make his own decision about what to do with the kid after he killed Rashid. "Fine," Danny said, mouth straining with the same grimacing smile. "But I'll take care of this first."

Rising, Danny felt the exhaustion and sleep deprivation and whatever the hell else was fogging up his head fall away. "It's time, Iris," he said, moving toward the woman.

Iris wobbled a little standing and bent to whisper something in JJ's girl's ear. Goddamn, the kid really did look like JJ.

"Let's go, Iris."

The girl grabbed Iris's leg when she tried to leave. "No! You can't have her."

Iris attempted to reassure her—"It'll be okay, Evie"—but the child was having none of it. Danny could tell Iris was struggling to maintain her composure as she pushed at the girl's still-tied hands. Something about the action was strangely familiar to Danny; it made him uneasy. He glanced over his shoulder at the windows instead, at the woods beyond. When his eyes finally found their way back, Iris was peeling the girl's fingers away.

"Evie, stop," she said. "I'll be back."

"No, you won't," the girl said, face twisting as she started to cry. She climbed across a coffee table after Iris but fell, landing on her elbows and nearly busting her chin. The child stared straight at Danny, eyes fierce, and said, "I was there when you shot my dad."

So the guy at Iris's house was JJ's ex. Danny felt his mouth fall open, just far enough for air to caress the moist space between his lips. He felt like he should return the favor. "Really? Where were you when I poisoned your dog?" he asked.

It worked. Her mouth gaped. Danny carried the image with him, smiling as he led Iris to the front door. He passed Rashid on the way, also standing, weapon drawn lest he have to touch the venting child.

"I should've shot you when I had the chance," the girl yelled, somewhere between anger and grief.

"Yes," Danny said, throwing a simple canvas bag over his shoulder as he ushered Iris out the door. "You should have."

"I'M sure you're tired, but it's not that far," Danny said, taking Iris's elbow as they descended the front porch steps. "And I thought you might enjoy the walk. I guess you don't really need your coat. Because you know where we're going, don't you?"

She paused, gazing around the yard—the weathered outhouse, the fire pit with its ashes and char, the bits of trash scattered among the conifers—as though she'd never seen it before. Or knew she'd never see it again. "I think I have a pretty good idea," Iris said, then pointed toward Rashid's vehicle. "And I would like that jacket, if you don't mind."

Some part of Danny couldn't refuse her. But he didn't remove her handcuffs, just settled her coat over her shoulders before steering her away from the driveway.

"This way," he said, heading instead toward the forest to their left.

The air was cool but not frigid, or maybe he was impervious to the cold. Pale yellow light strobed through bare branches and gave green needles in the canopy a hint of glow. Danny wanted to drag his feet through the deep leaves, like he had when he was a child, pretending it was heavy snow or sand, sapping his strength. But he didn't.

Perhaps their path had once been recognizable, but now it appeared no more than fortuitous spacing among the trees. "They didn't actually process this way, did they?" he asked.

"No," Iris said, walking next to him. "Something about not wanting a direct line to the house."

He studied the woman who'd lived alongside Lawrence Rutledge for decades. "You thought it was bullshit, didn't you?"

She almost smiled as she replied, "I wouldn't use that language."

So if they hadn't processed this way as part of their rituals, who had used the path? Presumably Lawrence, doing things he didn't share. Or it may have predated him. "You've never been to the altar, have you?"

"Not during a ritual," Iris said.

"You always refused to go," Danny said. He heard a mocking edge creep into his voice. "You didn't want Virgil to go, either. You thought it wasn't good for him. But he went anyway."

Iris had been keeping pace with him, but she stopped. Her voice was surprisingly clear as she spoke of her son. "You do know that man killed Virgil?"

Danny couldn't meet her gaze. "Yes," he said, and nudged her forward. "He wasn't supposed to. Don't worry—I'll take care of him, too."

They lapsed into silence, save the soft panting of their breath and the rustling and occasional branch-snapping of their feet. Danny's mood had transformed since they set out—that happened often lately—but he couldn't make it out. He wasn't quite sure why he was here. There was a kind of numbness in his jaw. He rotated it back and forth and rubbed its scruffy surface, as if to reassure himself that it was his, that he was present.

A gap in the silvered trunks indicated a clearing ahead, but he didn't think she'd noticed it when she abruptly asked, "Did he hurt you?"

"Virgil, you mean? He almost killed me right after he took me. But he didn't mean to. " Or so Virgil had said, and at the last moment he'd hesitated. He'd still struck him hard, and Danny had thought he was dead. Until he woke and Virgil said they were leaving so he could get farther away from the voice. "Watch yourself here," Danny said, taking Iris's elbow as she stepped over a fallen log.

A few more yards, and there it was.

The altar.

A great slab of rock, looking as though it had sprung from the earth. Because it had. That's where rocks came from. Danny fought the impulse to giggle.

Iris halted as soon as they emerged from the ring of trees and shook her head. Virgil had always said his mother was impervious to the supernatural and to the things that walked between. But here she saw something that drained her face of color—except where Danny had punched her—and sapped her legs of strength. She dropped to her knees and whispered, "No."

"Sorry, Iris. But it's time," he said, and found himself singing under his breath, "*A faint, sickening scent of irises persists all morning...*"

She shrank from him, eyes wide. It was just a song—no, a poem—though he wasn't sure who'd written it or how he knew it. But it felt *right*.

"Let's go, Iris, dear," he said, seizing her cuffed wrists. "You had to know this day would come."

Iris's feet alternated between pumping to keep up and digging her heels into the ground as he dragged her toward the altar. She begged him, "No, Danny. Don't do this. Danny..."

He paused in a moment of—not indecision—*anticipation*, as they approached the rock, and he considered how best to proceed. Should he place her upon the altar? *Certainly*. That's what it was there for.

They passed a woodpile, mostly rotten now, before reaching a band of bare earth that surrounded the altar, twenty feet or so in all directions. Danny scraped a toe across the ground and found it black beneath the surface. *Burned by fire.*

The altar consisted of two stones, a tall base and broader top, roughly rectangular shaped and flat except for a slight angled depression in the center. Four heavy metal rings, two at each end, were mounted on thick wooden beams rather than attached directly to the stone. It resembled an implement a farm animal would tow. The beams weren't part of the "original construction"—Danny wasn't sure how he knew that, but he was certain. They rested just above the surface of the rock. Was that a metal plate beneath them? He wasn't sure how the beams were secured, but when he tugged at the one farthest from the woodpile (what he considered the head of the altar), it didn't budge from the slab.

Danny retrieved a cable bike lock from his bag. Iris was so light—all bird bones, really—that he swung her onto the slab easily with his free arm. The impact slowed the elderly woman's reactions enough for him to wrap the cable around her handcuff chain, then secure the cable through one of the metal rings.

"Danny, no..."

Iris recoiled from the surface beneath her and attempted to roll off it. But the stone was as broad as it was high, so instead of touching the ground her legs merely acted as an anchor. She cried out as the weight hung from her shoulders and desperately kicked her legs, unable to twist to the ground or pull them up.

"Oh, Iris. *You upon the dry, dead beech-leaves... burnt like a sacrifice*," Danny muttered, hooking an arm under Iris's calves and easily tossing them back onto the slab. Then he rummaged through his bag for a knife he'd found in the old Rutledge house.

The leather sheath had a funky smell, but the weapon it held was in good shape. The steel flashed weakly as he held it up to the sky's dying light, admiring the way the back of the fixed blade curved in slightly about a third of the way from the point. It probably wouldn't cut paper, but it wouldn't have to. Danny dragged his thumb along the blade and hissed, then wiped his thumb on his pants as he reconsidered his assessment.

"You don't have to do this, Danny," Iris said. She lay flat on her back, arms stretched overhead and legs still, her voice now almost calm. "You're not him. You can choose to not be him."

He should've built a fire—he wanted to—but he didn't really have that kind of time. He smiled, looming over her until Iris shut her eyes and turned away. The dim light stripped decades from her face.

"Iris," he said, "I'm afraid there's only one thing that can stop me, one thing I'd rather do than cut out your heart."

And the universe answered him.

"Danny!" Adam's voice rang out across the clearing. "I'm here."

Danny grinned. "And that's cut out his."

76

Luther sat with one hand braced against his seat and the other clutching the oh-shit bar as they rocketed down the private road, the cruiser occasionally bottoming out.

"Do you think she'll wait for us?" Grant asked.

Luther said, "She won't wait long. But I think we're close."

"Stupid damn woman," Grant muttered. A moment later, after cresting a modest rise, he slammed the brakes.

Ahead was a fork in the road, with JJ's Bronco pulled over on the left side. And to the right—

"I'll be damned," Luther said. "There's what's left of my car. Adam must have made it after all."

Harlan exited JJ's vehicle slowly and steadied himself against the side panel as he trudged toward the new arrivals, while JJ rushed at them so quickly Grant barely had time to get out of the car before she embraced him.

"Thank God—I was about to leave without you," JJ said, arms wrapped around the Sheriff's neck. "We think she's here."

"Evie?" Luther asked, rounding the cruiser.

JJ nodded, releasing Grant, and pointed up the road. "We think she's at the house. But Adam's gone to look for Iris."

And she filled the men in on what they thought they knew so far. It sounded to Luther like a lot of fanciful speculation with nothing solid to support it. But Luther had seen a lot of crazy shit lately, things he couldn't begin to explain. Ultimately, he'd back the Sheriff's play, whatever that was.

Having already wandered a state or two from their jurisdiction, they'd contacted Agent D'Antonio on the way. Thanks to Teddy's relationship with Virgil, it was simple enough for D'Antonio to send someone to check the property, but it wouldn't happen immediately. D'Antonio was standing by for their report, in the hopes they'd find evidence that would justify sending an entire team. No matter what they found, they'd be on their own for the immediate future.

Harlan was the only person who'd been to the house before, so they spent a few minutes debriefing him on the layout of the property, particularly the house and its relationship to the ritual area.

"You're sure there's no back door?" Grant asked.

Harlan's hand rocked from side to side, equivocating, "Technically, there's a back door. But they nailed it shut after the steps collapsed and one of Lawrence's loonies damn near broke his leg. The house is raised," he said, anticipating their next question, "so it's none too easy to get in and out the windows, either."

"So what do we do?" JJ asked, anxiously shifting from one foot to the other.

Grant held up a finger, the universal sign for *give me a minute*, then pressed it to his lips in thought. Luther figured he'd be lucky if JJ let him have the full sixty seconds.

About forty seconds in, Grant turned to Luther. "You have your vest? In your car, maybe."

That would have been nice, during their little shoot-out when Virgil was killed. Luther shook his head and wiped a bit of weeping goo from the corner of his irritated eye. "Remember, I'm on suspension."

Grant nodded, then grimaced, as if he were coming to terms with something he didn't like the taste of. "I assume, if I ask you to stay put in your vehicle, you're going to ignore me," he said to JJ.

"Of course I am," she said.

"And you?" Grant directed at Harlan.

"I go where she goes," he said.

Grant gazed up at the darkening sky.

"Oh law enforcement gods, forgive us for the dumbassery we're about to undertake," Luther muttered.

Grant cracked a sardonic smile in acknowledgment. They had too damn many civilians, too little firepower, and no backup. But also, no time.

"Harlan," Grant began, "you said the forest comes pretty near to the house. How close you think you can get JJ and Luther to the residence without being seen?"

Harlan considered. "They do what I say, we ought to be able to tap on the walls."

"Good. That's what I want you to do. Except for the tapping part. Get as close as you can, and be ready for whatever happens. Luther, you're carrying?"

"Yes, sir," he said.

"And so am I," JJ added.

Grant shook his head. "JJ, I really wish you wouldn't." She responded by crossing her arms and digging in. "Fine. Don't shoot anybody. Follow Luther's lead. Don't go anywhere until he gives you the okay. And if you can't do what he tells you, I'll lock you in the goddamn car."

"Where will you be?" Luther asked.

"I'll drive in closer, near enough to tip whomever off and hopefully give y'all a little cover, but not right on the doorstep. Then I'll walk the rest of the way and say I'm looking for Teddy. Just to talk."

"As law enforcement?" Luther asked.

Grant nodded. "If someone's inside holding Evie or Iris, hopefully that'll draw the man out and you can take him down."

"Are you goddamned crazy?" Luther demanded.

Grant thumbed toward the cruiser. "I'll wear my vest."

"What if they're both in there, Danny and his sharpshooter friend?"

"Then I guess you better make sure you take two pairs of cuffs," Grant said.

The man really was insane. Luther looked at JJ. She had no idea what Grant was up against, but it might not have mattered to her anyway. Not until it was too late. After all, it was her daughter they were talking about.

"Sheriff, can I have a word?" Luther said, walking toward the back of the cruiser without waiting for an answer.

Grant followed. "Luther, we really don't have time for this."

Lowering his voice, Luther said, "That man—Rashid or whoever the hell he is—killed Virgil with a head shot."

Grant sighed. "I know, Luther; I saw his body."

Luther's hands trembled as he put a finger in Grant's face. "You might've seen his body, but you weren't there. One shot. From way the hell away. And unless you've got one of those fancy fucking Kevlar helmets..."

His voice had gone gruff, and he let it trail off while he sat on the bumper of the car and felt the car shift slightly beneath him.

The Sheriff raised his auburn brows. "You got a better idea?"

Luther shut his eyes, resisting the urge to scratch at the one that was bothering him. "Fuck if I do," he admitted.

"Okay, then. I need you to keep an eye on JJ, and an eye out for Danny Carpenter." Grant indicated the direction Adam had gone. "Assuming he is where they say, if he finishes whatever the hell he's doing and gets past Adam, he and his buddy'll have us boxed in."

"Got it," Luther said, turning back toward JJ and Harlan.

"Hey," Grant said, grabbing his arm. He had an expression on his face that would only pass as a smile for someone who'd never seen one. "That's it? No smartass reply?"

Luther shook his head, grim. "Come see me if we make it out of this, and I promise, I'll be the funniest sonuvabitch you ever met."

77

Evie wanted to wipe her eyes and her snotty nose, but she couldn't. If she did, the man staring at her might notice her hands weren't really tied anymore.

Her tears had been real—she was terrified, for herself and Miss Iris—but while Evie made a scene, the elderly woman had loosened the ropes that bound Evie's wrists. Now what? The house didn't have a phone, so there was no way to call for help. She could ask to use the bathroom. That got her out of the house, but she'd been to the outhouse once (it wasn't as stinky as she'd expected) and hadn't seen any way to escape. It was basically a closet with a poop pit and no back door.

"I'm hungry," she said.

She wasn't. She'd shared her chocolate bar with Miss Iris, and they'd given her a piece of peanut butter bread and a glass of water earlier. But the man would have to put his gun down to make another. At least he'd have to stop staring at her. Evie was on the couch, and he sat in the armchair across from her, gun arm resting on his leg. He wasn't creepy like a pervert—she knew how those men stared—but he assessed her in a cold, calculating way that gave her the heebie-jeebies.

"You can have something when he gets back."

But by that time, either Iris would have escaped from Danny or (it made Evie shiver inside to think it) Iris would be dead. And Evie thought there was a good chance she'd be next. Especially if this guy had anything to say about it.

"Do you need to go to the bathroom?" the man asked.

But his voice didn't have any concern in it. He didn't sound annoyed, either, like her dad sometimes did about those things. He didn't sound anything.

Would he kill her before Danny got back? Is that why he wanted to take her outside?

"No, I'm fine," Evie said, and sat quietly, holding the rope together in her palms.

She scrunched into the corner of the couch and dropped her head, as though she were too scared to look at him, which wasn't far from the truth. She even closed her eyes. She didn't want to cause any trouble or draw any attention to herself.

Danny and Iris had been gone long enough for Evie to settle into a comfortable but dangerous state of denial (*I can just wait for them to get back; Iris will know what to do*) when Evie heard the armchair creak. She kept her head low and cracked her eyes enough to peek past her lashes, but didn't otherwise move. The man was looking over his shoulder toward the driveway, gun arm in the same position. He stood slowly and moved away from his chair.

Had Evie heard a vehicle approaching? She couldn't be sure. She hadn't seen anything, but she wouldn't have. She sat facing the man, with the bulk of the open living room and combination dining room and kitchen between them. The kitchen window was too high for her to see anything without standing. The front door lay to her right and overlooked the woods, not the driveway. Finally, the overcast sky was prematurely dark, but not so dark as to require headlights. Someone who didn't want to be seen wouldn't have used them anyway.

Someone like her Mom, or the Sheriff. She wished Trooper was with her. She'd like to see him take a chunk out of this guy's leg. Except he'd probably shoot Trooper before her dog had a chance.

The man had kept the gun pointed at her while he made his way out of the grouped furniture, but now he brought it into both hands and dropped his stance, creeping slowly toward the kitchen window.

"I see you," he muttered, chin extending for a better look from beside the glass. "You're just lucky I don't have a clear line."

Evie edged forward until her feet almost touched the floor. She figured he wouldn't forget she was there, and acting totally oblivious would be more suspicious than showing interest in what was happening.

The man looked at her, but kept his gun pointing outside. "You even try to move from that couch, they're gonna be cleaning your brains off it."

Evie swallowed and nodded, but he was already back to focusing on whatever was outside. *Run if you can, hide if you can't*, Miss Iris had said. The man was the same distance from the front door as she was, and he had longer legs and no furniture in the way. The hallway to her left was closer, and it must lead to bedrooms. Maybe she could escape through a window. She doubted she'd have time to hide.

But once she made a break for it, he had no reason not to kill her. Of course, he didn't have much reason not to right now anyway.

Evie inched her feet to the floor and leaned forward, eyes drawn to a rectangle of light in the hall, evidence of an open door. She stared at that light, poised on the balls of her feet. *It's just a race*, she told herself, so she would not think about being afraid.

Meanwhile, the man reached over the kitchen sink and slowly slid the top half of the double-hung window down, its wooden frame emitting a soft protest. Evie was surprised she didn't feel wind rush in from outside, but it was already so cold inside the old house she might not have noticed.

"Hello? Mr. Rutledge?" A familiar man's voice drifted in through the window from outside. "I was hoping to ask you some questions. Are you here, Mr. Rutledge?"

Was that the Sheriff? Evie smiled and fought the urge to stand. She'd hoped he'd save her, but she'd never actually thought he could. Maybe Mom was here, too.

But the man at the window with the gun... Too late, Evie realized he was going to shoot the Sheriff. And she couldn't stop him.

Run. Now Evie! Iris's voice echoed in her head.

But she couldn't let the Sheriff die. Her eyes skittered around the room, looking for something, anything to use as a weapon. Her water glass. Desperate, Evie grabbed it from the table and, rising, threw it toward the window. Water droplets arced through the air, and the sounds of breaking glass and a gunshot filled Evie's ears as she ran for the hallway.

78

Harlan had said it wasn't far to the residence, but at times JJ wasn't sure the man would make it. He leaned heavily on the cane he'd brought from JJ's house as the ground rose beneath them, quiet except for the soft wheeze of his breath. Quieter than Luther clomping behind her. But the house was now in sight, so much as anything was in sight in the darkening wood.

The house that held her daughter.

Her eyes—her heart—strained for a glimpse of Evie, though her mind knew better.

Only one story, but raised as Harlan had said, with a deep, covered porch. Set off to one side, far enough to be inconvenient but probably not quite far enough to avoid the odor in high summer, was an honest-to-God outhouse. She didn't see anything else manmade nearby other than the odd bit of trash in the woods and a couple of plastic chairs in the yard. There certainly weren't any abandoned vehicles or anything else large enough to use as cover.

Luther motioned them to a tight clump of trees and whispered, "What do you think?"

Harlan, his lips pale as the sky had been at midday, shrugged. "Up to you."

Luther's eyes, one still looking in need of medical attention, darted from one end of the structure to the other, then over his shoulder toward the road Grant would approach upon. "Well, since it's the only egress, let's see if we can get alongside the porch, right up next to that wall. Can you do that?"

Harlan raised a dark brow.

"Fine," Luther said, "do you think *I* can do that without getting us killed?"

Harlan's cracked lips curled in acknowledgment. He said, "The front door faces the woods, so as far as being seen through there goes, we're good until we hit the porch steps. If we approach from the rear of the house, he'd have to do a fair bit of contorting to see us from the kitchen window. But there is a decent view from Teddy's bedroom, which is why that bare section ahead worries me a little." Harlan indicated a patch of deadfall, with a few trunks still standing. "If we take it on all fours, I think we'll be mostly out of sight below the brush."

"Lead on, old man," Luther said.

Harlan used the natural rise and fall of the landscape and its attendant vegetation to conceal their approach. Crawling over the damp, cool ground, every motion exposed wet leaves, soaking the knees of JJ's pants in no time. She'd secured her shotgun across her back too loosely, and it kept threatening to brain her. But movement was good. Moving made it harder to think about the fact that almost everyone she cared about it in the world was gathered in this square mile or so of crazy. And she'd have to be very damn lucky for all of them to walk away.

Soon they were on their feet again, crouching at the edge of the woods mere yards from the house. Because the terrain sloped beneath it, the house's height above the ground increased from front to back. Wooden sheathing filled in the gap, an improvised afterthought. Harlan ducked low, tucking his cane beneath his arm, and hustled across the final stretch. Once he made it to the house, he waved JJ on, and then she did the same for Luther. Huddled against the moldy plywood, they were out of sight of anyone inside. They crept slowly through sparse leaves toward the front of the house, stopping several feet short of the porch.

Now all they had to do was wait.

JJ didn't do waiting well.

She glanced over her shoulder at the sheathing, more or less still attached but with warped and yawning edges, fighting an irrational fear that someone hiding beneath the house would squeeze through and grab her. She copied Harlan when he lowered to a kneeling squat, though Luther remained standing next to them. She'd already loaded her shotgun, but took the opportunity to chamber a round. Harlan narrowed his eyes at her, and she narrowed hers right back, pointing at the still-engaged safety. She didn't need to be told—even nonverbally—not to shoot him.

Harlan removed a glove and reached for her hand, she assumed in apology. He shut his eyes, and JJ felt a sense of calm spread through her body, trying to quiet her frantic need to do something. A moment later, he opened his eyes and wobbled off-balance as he leaned closer. She had pulled her hair back in a low ponytail, but Harlan's breath stirred strands that had slipped free as he whispered in her ear, "Stay with me."

His tickling breath alone couldn't account for the shiver that ran through her body. JJ stared at Harlan (his dark eyes seemed lit by something brighter inside) and he gripped her hand more tightly.

Then she heard Grant's voice, calling out like a fool as he walked up the driveway. It struck her, as it hadn't fully before, how vulnerable he was offering himself as bait. Sacrificing himself for her child. She tried to stand to see him, but Harlan held her hand fast. She didn't fight him, just closed her eyes, overwhelmed by the enormity of what was unfolding.

JJ flinched at the loud, abrupt sound of a gunshot, almost directly overhead.

Luther's arm pressed her shoulder, and he said, "Stay put," as he passed, gun drawn.

She shook her hand free of Harlan's.

Like hell she would.

79

Standing, Luther watched the Sheriff adjust his hat—the one that wasn't made of Kevlar—as he called out, "Are you here, Mr. Rutledge?"

Damn fool man, Luther thought, an instant before the gunshot. And an instant before Grant fell out of sight.

Shit! It seemed to have come from above them—through the kitchen window, not from the porch. Luther couldn't see the Sheriff from this angle and didn't know if Grant was even moving. But Luther had to. He had to get the girl.

"Stay put," he told JJ, praying she did as he maneuvered around her.

Luther hurried toward the porch. Assuming the shooter was still inside and was alone (dangerous assumptions), he wouldn't be exposed until he reached its front corner.

The entry faced forty-five degrees away from the driveway, as though a breeze had blown the house blueprints askew. Knees bent, Luther kept his muzzle high and crept up the steps, close to one rail, the weathered wood flexing beneath his weight. The front door was flanked by two windows. Luther crossed the porch quickly, flattening himself against the wall on the handle side of the door. Turning the knob, he flung the door open, but stayed where he was, waiting, heart hammering and fingers tingling.

Quick peek.

The living room and kitchen were empty, but Luther didn't get a decent look at the dim hallway, which lay in a straight line from the front door. Crossing the threshold, he glimpsed the shooter there, a large black man advancing down the hall. Luther quickly veered sideways and took cover in a seating area, unsure if the man had seen him. He kept to the far side of the living room as he approached the hall, pausing at the corner, struggling to hear anything else over his own ragged breath. He took a moment to wipe his weeping eye so he could see where the hell he was pointing his gun, then heard a loud, heavy *thump*. And then again—*thump*—this time with a crisp, almost splitting edge.

The man was breaking down a door.

Evie must be inside.

Luther filled his lungs with air, blew it out... and flashed his head around the corner.

The man still stood in the hall, pushing against the bedroom door with a shoulder. He glanced up, and Luther jerked back (was that movement near the front door?) as the man's gun arm rose. Two shots popped from the hallway, reverberating down the narrow space. Luther blinked, scanning the front of the house (living room, open doorway to the porch, kitchen), but saw no one else. No other threat. Luther whipped around the corner and, finger twitching, returned fire.

Retreating, Luther took a half step away from the corner for more cover. His back slammed against the wall so he was facing the front door again, and there was still no one else in sight. He must have imagined movement a moment before. Luther counted in his head how many times he had pulled the trigger— three? No, four. Center mass. His arms hummed and his ears rang. Panting, he braced himself for one last peek.

The man was down, not moving. Luther approached slowly. He was dead—Luther knew he was dead—but he went by the book. The guy was huge, well over six feet tall, and his bloody chest filled much of the narrow hall. Luther could see two wounds there, marring a fancy gray sweater, and another hit to his throat, eyes half-open above it. There were no sounds of raspy, gurgling breathing, and there wouldn't be.

Luther nudged the man's gun from his hand and kicked it out of the way. He stepped carefully over the man's sprawling limbs *(dead man hopscotch)* and noticed he had a dimple like Adam's. He remembered the girl's description at the drug dealer's dump—he'd killed Rashid.

The door next to the dead man was open. Sort of, about a foot. A piece of furniture blocked it from opening farther, and he'd hate to get shot by whoever was waiting on the other side.

"Evie, are you in there? It's me, Deputy Beck," he called out. He wasn't sure how loud he was speaking—his hearing hadn't recovered from the gunshots, and his own voice echoed strangely in his ears. "Evie? I'm coming in."

A desk scraped across the floor as he applied his bulk to the door. The room appeared empty. He strode to the open window, but she'd have broken her goddamn neck jumping out of it. Then he checked the wardrobe. Clothes, but no kid. Which left the old standby. He holstered his weapon.

"Evie?" he said, body protesting as he kneeled on the hard floor. He lifted the edge of a sheet, lowered his head—

And nearly lost an eye when the knob end of a wooden baseball bat came flying at his face. He felt a painful twinge in one of his fingers as he caught the bat, then pulled it toward him. And there she was, a shape under the bed.

"It's okay, Evie. I'm Deputy Beck, and I'm here with—" He caught himself before mentioning the Sheriff. The child had already seen her father shot; hopefully she wouldn't have to see Grant, too.

Luther heard her say something about his uniform. "I'm not wearing one, but you know me. Remember, last year on your field trip you asked me how to escape from the holding cell."

Evie began wriggling out. He stepped back to give her space, but as soon as she emerged, covered in dust and smelling of urine, the child threw herself at him.

"Shh," he cooed, stroking her lank hair. "You're okay. Everything's gonna be alright."

He ran through a list in his head while he held the child, trying to put everything in order of priority. Call in D'Antonio and the rest of the cavalry, find out what the hell was going on with Adam and Danny Carpenter... but first was returning the girl to her mom and finding out if—God forbid—there was a vacancy at the head of the Beecham County Sheriff's Department.

Evie didn't protest when Luther picked her up, just wrapped her arms around him and buried her face in his neck. She was a little big for carrying, but it'd be easier to get her past the dead man this way.

"Don't look," he said, high-stepping around the man again and tucking her head more tightly against him.

When he reached the end of the hallway, Luther realized he was making assumptions again, and he couldn't afford to do that with a child. "Evie," he said, setting her gently on her feet, "I need you to stand right here for me, just for a minute or two. Can you do that?"

His words sounded indistinct to his own ears, but the girl nodded. He drew his weapon and made his way toward the kitchen windows, much as Rashid must have done. Cool air brushed his face as he surveyed the world beyond the open window. There was the Sheriff's cruiser, parked a little way down the drive. But where was the Sheriff? And for that matter, where was—

"Mom!" Evie screamed.

Like her mother, the girl hadn't listened. Instead of standing in the hallway, Evie had continued to the front door.

Where she'd found JJ, bleeding and motionless on the floor, her shotgun lying next to her.

80

Harlan had been right. Adam heard and saw things—crazy things—as he hiked up the path toward the altar. It reminded him of when he'd found Rachel on the mountain, the confusion and swirling shapes and shadows and voices. But this time, they wanted *him*, not Rachel. And this time, he was ready for it. Most of them were like insects, no worse than annoying as they buzzed around, vying for his attention. But one voice—an insistent, menacing whisper—had power. And it was familiar, so familiar that Adam almost spoke to it aloud.

But acknowledging his dead grandfather was probably a bad idea.

What did it mean that he was hearing Lawrence, and for that matter, how did Adam even know it was him? Was his grandfather's voice a residue imprinted on this place, like a lingering odor? Or was it something Adam carried within himself, part of his DNA, or left behind in Adam's mind by Virgil, alongside the ruined walls? He'd have to talk to Harlan about it when they got out of this. *If* they got out of this...

Adam knew he was close when he saw a brighter spot in the woods ahead and felt a change in pressure that made him tilt his head automatically to protect his recently injured ear. The air somehow felt both dense and hollow and reminded him of the expectant stillness before an intense storm. He pressed a hand against the rough bark of the nearest oak tree to steady himself before continuing.

And there it was, a mass of stone in the center of the clearing like a poisonous mushroom. The altar's base was a single boulder approximately the size of a dining table, tapering slightly as it left the ground. A second stone sat atop it, longer and flat like the table's top. Adam couldn't imagine how it had gotten there. Nothing living stood in its vicinity, but there was a stack of split wood nearby. Adam shivered at a memory of flames.

Images of what had been overlaid the present so completely, Adam didn't initially see Iris lying on the altar or Danny standing over her holding a knife. Adam shouldn't have been surprised when he did—he knew that's why he was here—and yet a small part of him was. A small part of him always would be.

His chest felt tight as he called out, "Danny! I'm here."

Adam strode deliberately across the clearing, gathering himself as he did. He knew, now that he'd arrived, Danny wouldn't kill Iris yet. Danny had been waiting for Adam, for the chance to torture him and savor every moment. But the closer Adam got, the more the long blade threatening Iris made him want to rush at the man.

Danny waited until they stood little more than arms-length apart before observing, "You sound a little rough."

"Probably 'cause somebody tried to choke me to death a few days ago," Adam said. "Well, not me personally. My throat happened to get in the way."

"Don't sell yourself short. I'm sure people want to choke you all the time," Danny said, straight-faced. "So it's just you?"

Adam looked over his shoulder, a parody of someone being followed. "Afraid so."

Danny's grin was unexpected. With dark hair nearly as short

as the stubble on his jaw and sunken eyes staring from his haggard face, not to mention the knife in his hand, Danny should have looked sinister. But Adam couldn't stop seeing his mischievous childhood friend in that grin, couldn't stop thinking about what might have been. For all of them.

"Too bad you never saw JJ," Adam said. Of course, if JJ'd seen Danny first, she'd probably have shot him. Adam noticed, as Danny's smile faded, that one side of his face had a slightly shiny, pink hue.

"Her girl said y'all used to look for me, after I disappeared. That true?"

Adam nodded. "Yeah."

"I guess the two of you were knocking boots while you were at it."

Adam sighed. "No, Danny, we weren't. It was never like that between us."

"Really?" He sounded surprised, but also like he believed Adam. "Huh. From the time we were little, I thought she'd end up with one of us, and I always figured it would be you. Damn, but her girl looks like her!"

Adam gave a half smile, somehow pushing away the fact that Danny knew that because he'd kidnapped her.

"You know, Rashid will kill her."

Adam swallowed, needing more saliva to speak. "JJ or Evie?"

Danny leaned against the slab. "Probably both if he gets the chance," he admitted, clenching his jaw, "even though I told him not to hurt Evie. Just gives me another reason to kill him."

Adam kept his attention locked on Danny, avoiding the sight of Iris on the stone behind him. "Rashid—that's the man who shot Virgil?"

Danny nodded, confidence faltering for the first time. He rubbed the knife blade against his jeans, fidgeting. Along one side until it slid off, then the other, back and forth, with a subtle metallic ping every time it released. "Was it quick?"

"So quick he almost killed me and Luther, too," Adam said. And then he remembered his father's voice, *Stick close to Luther.* "But Virgil knew it was coming."

Danny's eyes darted at Adam with a cold expression that made the back of Adam's neck tingle. "Did he take a bullet for you?"

A jumble of images bombarded Adam: Luther pulling his gun and taking cover, Adam starting to rise and Virgil shoving him down, his body shuddering when the bullet hit. "Yes," he whispered.

"Of course he did. The first son," Danny snapped, standing so suddenly Adam stutter-stepped back. "When Virgil hated me, it was because he knew I wasn't you. When he loved me, it's because he thought I was. Do you know what that's like?"

"No, I don't," Adam said, now holding his ground. "I never had a father."

Danny squeezed the grip of his knife, now held next to his thigh, until his knuckles whitened. He shifted on his feet so subtly, Adam might have been imagining the movement, or projecting his own. Finally, Danny's mouth curled, and he let out a harsh laugh. "Listen to us! We sound like one of those bullshit daytime talk shows."

"My best friend's a serial killer," Adam agreed, deadpan.

Danny picked at his jeans with the tip of the knife. "Okay, here's the way this ends. I'm willing to let Iris go, if you take her place."

Danny edged around the corner of the stone slab to stand at its head. It was Adam's first time seeing the altar in person. Having seen it in visions, weeks ago with Harlan and again last night, he thought he knew it intimately—how rough the stone would feel against the pads of his fingers, where fissures criss-crossed its surface, and where rain had failed to wash the blood away. But somehow he'd forgotten the thick wooden beams, one at each end, with their heavy metal rings. Rings that now secured his grandmother.

Adam stepped closer to Danny, bringing himself back within the man's reach and alongside Iris. She had bent her elbows as much as possible, easing the pressure on her arms and neck and shoulders. Adam tilted his head to see around her nearest arm. She didn't speak, just gave a small shake of her head. Her face was bruised on one side, the purple and red eye nearly swollen shut. Blood or dirt or some combination smeared the area above it at her hairline. There were other marks, too, scratches on her face and her hands, probably chafe marks beneath the fuzz of the cuffs. But Adam couldn't stop staring at her eye.

That's from a punch.

Adam breathed through flared nostrils before telling her, "Harlan's okay."

Iris's lips squeezed together, as though she were trying not to cry. "So I heard."

From whom? *Evie.* Evie must be here after all. Adam prayed JJ had waited for Luther. He shifted his gaze back to Danny. "You didn't have to involve Iris."

"No," Danny agreed, "but I did anyway. So what do you say? Hop up there and strap in, and it's over."

"As far as Iris is concerned? Or all of it?" Adam shut his eyes and let the cold breeze, scented with pine and threatening weather and a hint of decay, wash over him. And the voices, a multitude prickling at his mind, seething around the altar. Then he opened his eyes slowly and challenged Danny, "All of it, meaning *everything* you've done to quiet the voices."

Danny blinked, stared back at him, jaw set.

"All those men you pretended were me—how many were there? But it didn't start with them, did it? It started with Sarah," Adam said.

"She wanted to kill Virgil," Danny said.

Adam raised a brow.

"It was her escape plan," Danny insisted, finger straying to the edge of his blade, scraping across it. Adam didn't think he was aware he was doing it. Danny continued, "And she wanted me to help her. She wanted to bash his head in with a rock while he was sleeping."

He wouldn't have blamed the child if it were true, but Danny was lying, and not even bothering to do it very well. Which meant he didn't care if Adam believed him.

"Bash his head in like you did to Harlan?" Adam said, the anger warming his body. "Except he wasn't asleep, just forty years older than you. How's that limp coming along, by the way?"

"You've turned into a snarky asshole in your old age," Danny said, grinning. He rested his hand on his hip, coiled around the knife handle like a poised fist. "I think I like it."

"And you're still the same little punk—" Adam broke off and went rigid as a gunshot echoed in the distance. Iris flinched next to him.

"Well, that makes life interesting," Danny said. "Now you've got no reason to stall anymore. The offer for Iris's life is still on the table. What's your answer?"

Danny was going to kill Iris, and go on killing. No matter what. Unless Adam stopped him.

"Okay," Adam said.

"Adam, no, I can't let you do this," Iris said, her words tumbling over each other. "I can't lose you and your father within a day of each other. I won't have anyone left. You can't."

"Shh," he said. His shoulder blades tingled, waiting for Danny's blade to enter between them, as he took his grandmother's face gently between his hands. "Yes, you will. Harlan needs you."

The stone pressed against his waist as he stretched to kiss her unbruised cheek. He'd intended to tell her, *Be ready*. But before he had a chance, she whispered, "He's not Danny."

Adam straightened. *Not* Danny? What was that supposed to

mean? He stared at the man, a couple of feet from Iris's head at the end of the altar. He looked like Danny. What had Virgil said when he'd asked if Danny would kill Iris? *It depends on who he is...* There was something there. But Adam was out of time.

Danny said, "Undo the bike lock and help her down."

Adam reached past Iris's hands for the flexible band and twisted the lock closer. "What's the combination?"

"No, no, no—you have to earn it. Put your hand down," Danny said, indicating a spot on the beam with his knife.

"What are we, eight years old?" Adam asked, remembering tiny dents on the floorboards in the corner of Iris's porch and torn-up dirt at the edge of the woods. Danny had brought the knives then, too. Toying with the possibility of maiming each other was one of the few things they'd never shared with JJ.

"My game, my rules," Danny said.

That's what it was to him, a game. He seemed like Danny to Adam.

Adam laid his palm flat on the beam and spread his fingers. It was a big piece of lumber, but he still had to twist his hand slightly to accommodate his finger span. Iris had closed her eyes, and Adam stared at a twig caught in her frizzy hair, no more than eighteen inches below his hand.

"Let's have a warm-up," Danny said.

He tapped the knife in the spaces next to and between Adam's fingers, starting with his pinky, toward the thumb and back, slowly first, then faster. Adam fought the magnetism of the sound and the flashing movement, but it was hard to think clearly. Could he hit Danny now, knock him backward (using his non-dominant hand) without being stabbed? Unlikely, without a weapon of his own.

Danny's gaze lifted to meet Adam's with a secretive, *I know what you're thinking* smile. His knife hand kept moving, and Adam held his breath and his position as the knife nicked his thumb, enough to draw a trickle of blood.

"Whoops," Danny said, pausing. "I guess you were right about that thumb after all."

Adam had once blamed his wonky thumb, incapable of resting flush on any surface, for losing a pocketknife race. Danny had said he was a slowpoke wuss, and the next round Adam had sliced his thumb. After that, they'd played in the dirt to avoid bleeding on Iris's porch.

It took a few seconds for the blood to flow to the base of Adam's thumb, and then touch the beam. When it did, Adam felt something shift, like a slumbering beast within the altar had awakened. A hungry, slumbering beast that wanted more. Adam pressed his other hand to the altar to steady himself. He thought he heard a hint of whimper from Iris, and glanced over to see her lips moving. Was she praying?

"Okay, I'm warmed up," Danny said. He didn't seem to have noticed the shift that prompted Adam's unsteadiness, but the glittering intensity of his eyes unnerved Adam even more as he added, "Count the rounds to get the number."

Adam watched the knife flick from pinky to ring finger to pinky, on and on all the way to his thumb and back. Once through, then twice... When Danny's hand finally stopped, Adam said, "Three?"

Danny shrugged. "If that's what you counted."

Adam pulled the lock toward him, smearing blood on his hand and the cable as he twisted the first tumbler. The altar surface seemed to shimmer slightly beneath his fumbling fingers, blurring the stone's coarse texture.

"Only three more," Danny said, grinning.

Adam bit back his anger. He felt an unnerving tingle cross his skin when he returned his palm to the wooden beam, along with the certainty that something—or someone—was coiled and waiting.

"Do you think the voices will stop when you kill me, Danny?" Adam asked. "Because I don't. I think there'll just be one more."

Danny stiffened.

"If you're lucky. Because someone—or *something*—" Adam stared significantly at the altar, "is using you. And when it's done, so are you."

Danny pointed his knife at Adam. "I guess we'll find out."

Before he could lower the knife to resume his tapping, the muffled pop of gunfire resounded again, twice. Adam looked in the direction of the house, as though he could see through the forest. After a brief, ringing silence, the sound repeated three— no, four—times.

As the fourth shot faded away, Danny stabbed Adam.

81

The knife went completely through Adam's hand, driving into the wood beneath it. Adam cried out, first in shock, and then in pain. Danny rotated the blade back and forth in Adam's hand, trying to free its sunken tip from the beam.

The pain was agonizing, but Adam feared if he yanked his hand away, the knife would slice through the rest of it. He heard Iris's screams, Danny's frustrated swearing, and a grinding moan that tore from his own throat as his knees buckled. But the lower he dropped, the more the blade tugged at his hand. Adam braced his knees against the stone to stop his descent.

The knife finally came free, sending Danny stumbling backward. Adam clutched his arm to his chest, staggered away from the altar, and ran toward the woodpile. Recovering his balance, Danny skirted the altar corner in pursuit. Iris kicked out from the slab as he passed, barely catching Danny's side, but slowing him enough for Adam to reach his destination.

Adam grabbed a log from the top of the stack with his good left fingers, swinging it backhand as he turned. Danny threw up his free arm to block, and the rotten wood smashed against him, chunks flying. Adam blinked bits out of his eyes and dropped the useless scrap from his hand as he rounded the woodpile, keeping it between him and Danny's knife.

"Gotcha," Danny said, panting and shaking out his thumped arm.

Adam glanced down to see his own arm slick with blood. He hadn't even felt the knife's slash.

Fighting panic and the powerful compulsion to look at his butchered hand, Adam edged farther around the woodpile. His leading foot knocked over something tucked into the mass of split wood—an axe, the handle dark with age. Adam may have been fairly useless with his fists, but he'd worked in enough bars to know how to wield a blunt object. He hefted the axe in his left hand. About the length of a baseball bat, it was heavier than he expected. Or he was weaker than he'd realized.

"Well, aren't you the bad-ass," Danny said, breath coming fast as he circled. "But hasn't anyone ever told you not to bring an axe to a knife fight?"

Adam ignored him, sliding his good hand halfway down the wooden axe handle, adjusting until he had the balance right. The fingers of his right hand wouldn't respond, but he positioned the handle in the wedge between his thumb and fingers for added stability.

Danny changed direction, bolting around the stack counter-clockwise, and Adam rushed to meet him. The axe gave Adam a reach advantage and, instead of swinging, Adam jabbed at Danny. The head struck Danny in the ribs hard enough to double him over, but he held onto his knife. Adam fumbled, trying to modify his grip to swing at Danny's knees, but the bloody handle slipped in Adam's hands. Momentum carried the axe away from him, and when it struck the ground, the steel head tumbled free of the wooden haft.

With no better option, Adam dove for Danny's knife while he still struggled to stand. Danny twisted away, and the blade nicked Adam's good hand as he grabbed for it. Adam slammed Danny in the ribs with his right elbow, then melded his body to Danny's, stretching for the knife until he felt its crossbar jab his palm. Adam dug his elbow in again and, clawing at Danny's hand, seized the handle of the knife—with Danny's fingers and all— and yanked it toward Danny.

Adam couldn't see the knife, but it stopped suddenly. Then something slammed into Adam's forehead, stunning him. He realized he'd been head-butted when he smelled a sour note and felt Danny's hot breath hit his face. Adam swayed, grasping Danny's shoulder to steady himself, and they both went over.

"Adam, get up!" Iris screamed.

Yes, Adam thought, lying on his back, staring up at a narrow section of sky through dark-rimmed tunnel vision. *She's right; I need to get up.*

But he couldn't.

He blinked hard. Again, two or three more times, then turned his head slowly. To his left, bare ground. The axe handle. To his right, Danny stirring. Danny, with the knife still in his hand, swinging his arm toward Adam.

Adam sucked in air, rolling away on the exhale, and the blade struck the ground he'd left behind. He scrambled on hands and elbows and knees, seized the axe haft in his left hand and swiveled. Adam swung with his entire body, falling as the handle cracked against Danny's arm.

"Fuck!" Danny dropped the knife and crumpled, cradling the arm.

Adam made it to his knees, gasping for air, and watched Danny grab for the knife with his other arm. He stopped mid-motion, shuddered, and looked toward Adam, but his eyes were unfocused and his face pale. Danny shook his head and licked his lips. He started to rise, then collapsed onto his side. A hand fumbled to his lower back and came away bloody.

"Sonuvabitch," he groaned from the ground.

Adam crawled toward him warily. Danny's gaze followed him,

but he made no further move. Adam's whole body was shaking so badly he could barely close his bloody fingers around the knife handle. He sat back on his feet and tossed the blade toward the altar.

"Where are the keys for Iris's handcuffs?" Adam panted.

"I just thought you punched me," Danny said. "But you killed me. I didn't think you had it in you."

"Where are the keys?" Adam shouted.

"I don't remember," Danny muttered, closing his eyes and shivering.

"Come on, Danny!"

Adam did his best to stand, but a wave of dizziness swept the world from beneath him. He braced his good hand against the ground, and the flesh of his palm prickled with static. Adam shut his eyes and saw what looked like a dark, shimmering mist spreading from the altar beneath Iris. It fluoresced where it touched the blood on Adam's hand, and coalesced into familiar indigo lines, ropy tendrils snaking through the earth toward Danny.

On his own, Danny posed a threat to Adam and the people he loved. But Teddy was right. He was also a pawn.

Adam opened his eyes to see Danny's wide with fear as he whispered, "He's coming for me."

Virgil had sworn Lawrence wouldn't let death stop him. His words echoed through Adam's mind, *He will always try to find a way back.*

"Adam, please," Danny pleaded, pain and terror making his voice sound decades younger. "Don't let him take me."

Harlan had warned him about the altar's power, but what else had he said? Something about containing it... the barrier. He must mean the circle of dead earth. *Frick.* He had to get Danny outside the circle.

Adam looped his arms, the right one barely bending at the elbow, under Danny's armpits. Danny's lower back and the ground beneath him were dark with blood. Adam had stabbed his kidney. Danny was right; he was dying.

"Oh, Jesus, there he is!" Danny screamed, raising one arm to point.

He just wasn't dying fast enough.

Adam couldn't see anything—at least, not with his open eyes, and he didn't dare close them now. Danny outweighed him by twenty pounds, and his desperate kicking made him worse than a dead weight. Adam grunted as he dragged him backwards, leaving an intermittent blood trail and the dark tracks of Danny's heels.

A few steps beyond the fire-charred ring, Adam stumbled, dropping Danny so he cascaded across Adam's legs as they fell. Adam's vision started to brown out. He was breathing—he could see his chest heave—but it felt like he breathed in a world without oxygen. Sitting awkwardly, Adam lifted his face toward the sky, stretching his neck as if it would let more air in. It didn't.

A sudden spasm rocked Danny's body. Adam rested his good hand on his shoulder until it passed. Then, not thinking, Adam leaned back and put his weight on his right hand. The pain was like being stabbed all over again. He fell, head impacting the ground hard enough to stun him, making him reluctant to move. He couldn't remember what he was supposed to be doing.

Then Adam heard the voice, so clearly it was as though his grandfather were lying next to him.

I'd be happy to take you instead, darling.

Legs still pinned beneath Danny, Adam twisted to see... No one. He shut his eyes and saw the tentacles of blue light being withdrawn, back to the altar.

The voice wasn't talking to Adam.

It was talking to Iris.

82

"**S**hit!" Luther nudged Evie aside and knelt next to her mother. He slid JJ's forgotten shotgun out of the way. "JJ? Can you hear me?"

JJ's face was the color of tissue paper, and the skin over her cheekbones appeared just as thin. Her jacket hung open, and one side of the flannel shirt beneath it was dark with blood. She was breathing fast, and her eyes fluttered at her name, but she didn't speak.

"Evie, sweetie, did you see a phone anywhere?" Luther asked.

The child sat rocking on her heels by her mother's head, crying, hand patting JJ's hair as if she were a pet.

"Evie?" Luther yelled (he wasn't sure how loudly), and the girl jumped. "Your mom's gonna be okay. But I need you to stay calm and focus. Is there a phone in the house?"

She sucked in a big, snotty breath and shook her head before glancing down the hallway. "But I'll bet he had one."

For that matter, so did Luther. He grabbed Evie's hand before she could race off to frisk a dead man. "I got it," he said.

The connection was iffy, occasionally warping like a bad record, but he finally reached a human. Staring at JJ, who seemed to be slipping in and out of consciousness, Luther struggled to arrange the words properly in his head.

"Yeah, this is Deputy Luther Beck—"

The front door was still standing open, and movement on the front steps caught his eye. Luther dropped his phone and drew his weapon...

Grant leaned against Harlan, but straightened and stumbled across the porch as soon as he saw JJ. Luther holstered his weapon and retrieved his phone, now disconnected. *Fuck.*

The Sheriff fell to his knees next to JJ and Evie huddled against him. Harlan caught Luther's gaze over them. The old man looked grim, but not surprised. He nodded to Luther; it was up to them.

"Sheriff, the shooter is dead. I can't hear for shit," Luther said, only slightly exaggerating. "You need to call it in. No word yet on anybody else, so backup might be good. Remember, this is Theodore Rutledge's place. Ask if there's a spot close by that a chopper could meet us."

Stunned, Grant was slow to respond, but eventually his training kicked in, and he stood.

Luther scooted to make room for Harlan as Grant backed out of the house. "You know anything about gunshot wounds?" Luther asked, watching his lips for his reply.

"A little. Evie, dear, get me one of those blankets off the couch." Harlan ran eyes and hands over JJ, checking her neck. She blinked, but didn't seem grounded in the world around her. Harlan slid her jacket away and lifted her torso slightly. He mumbled words at her chest, but they were lost in his grunts of effort.

"Say again?" Luther said.

Harlan stared at Luther and enunciated clearly. "I need scissors and tape from the junk drawer in the kitchen, and you'll find a clean garbage bag under the sink."

Luther found the items where Harlan had said he would and

returned to find him trying to tear a blanket with his bare hands. Harlan gratefully took the scissors and cut wide strips from the blanket.

"Evie, I need you to sit on that side and hold your momma's hand," Harlan said.

"She squeezed it!" Evie said.

"Of course she did. I told you, she's gonna be fine," Harlan said, but his eyes told Luther a different story.

Harlan unbuttoned and cut and peeled away layers on JJ's torso and handed Luther a folded bit of blanket. "Exit wound's underneath, below the ribs and off to the side. I need you to apply pressure."

Luther pressed the fabric against JJ's side and stared at the bloody entrance wound while Harlan cut a square from the garbage bag. Of course—her lung. *Shit*. Harlan was working on a sucking chest wound that Luther's blasted ears couldn't hear.

Harlan glanced toward the front door, before securing the plastic to JJ with tape. "As soon as Grant gets his ass in here, I need you to find Adam and bring him back. We may be outside by then."

Outside? Why the hell would they have her outside—to meet the EMTs? Luther didn't have time to ponder. The Sheriff moved quickly but gingerly through the door, and Luther found he could make out Grant's words well enough now for context to give him the rest.

"ETA is twenty-five minutes. There's a spot they can land just off the road a couple miles from here and take her to Pittsburgh. They'll let us know when they're close."

Harlan nodded. "Over here, please, Sheriff, and take your deputy's place. Luther, go."

"Keys," Luther said.

The Sheriff tossed them to Luther and he ran out the door.

83

Adam had to get to Iris before Lawrence did.

He wriggled from beneath Danny (unconscious, possibly dead) and staggered toward the altar. Lying on her belly, Iris had pulled on her handcuffs relentlessly, wrists weeping blood into the pink fuzz. Adam watched as blue light crackled around the cuffs. Iris gasped and jerked her hands higher, but the light shimmered and spread in a broad pool around her. It spilled over the altar and onto the ground, stopping at the bare earth edge. It nearly took his breath away when Adam stepped on the charred dirt and into the light.

"Any ideas?" he asked, leaning against the altar, skin tingling.

Iris's mouth trembled, but her voice was strong as she asked, "The number Danny gave you, was it a three?"

Adam couldn't make sense of the question, suddenly overcome by nausea. He looked at the stone beneath his elbows—the altar was triggering him—and stood. The number... the bike lock combination. "Yeah, three."

Iris fumbled the cable around and began spinning the tumblers. "Okay, now what?"

"Pull on it," Adam said, unable to do so one-handed.

Adam heaved a sigh of relief as the lock released.

"Your birthday," Iris explained.

Adam pulled the cable free. Iris, still handcuffed, lowered her legs to the ground. They buckled within a few steps, and she took Adam down with her.

Lawrence's voice whispered from the dead earth like a song, *You're always asking, do I remember?* The word *remember* repeated, until the syllables became sound without meaning. It grew to a painful buzz, prying between the molecules in Adam's body, making them vibrate out of sync. His chest hurt, his heart losing its rhythm and trying to compensate.

I remember, Iris. Do you? The things I used to do to you.

Iris's hand brushed past her swollen face to cup her forehead, and she curled onto her side.

It looks like someone reminded you. But not enough. Not like I would. A guttural laugh. *Not like I will.*

"Get out of here," she groaned.

Because I remember what I did to you. And I remember what you did to me, too.

"Now, Adam. Go!"

Your face is ash, Iris. Indistinguishable from the cold, deathless sky...

And it was. Her face was so gray. But Adam couldn't carry her. He wasn't sure he could stand. What strength he had was being siphoned off. His eyes drifted shut, and he could see the life being sucked from him, traveling through the barren soil and into the altar. Where a dark but iridescent cloud seemed to be coalescing into a form. A human figure.

Iris shifted next to him and roused Adam from his stupor. She rose to her knees and crawled in awkward, jerking motions, as though her limbs weren't under her control. Adam watched as she stretched out her cuffed hands—

For the knife. What was she doing with Danny's knife?

Her jaws clenched, but a grinding moan escaped from her,

like someone trying to endure the unbearable. The harsh sound crescendoed, then stopped, Adam's breath stopping with it.

Iris spoke, and Lawrence's voice joined hers in a harmony that made Adam's skin prickle and hair stand on end. "A faint, sickening scent of irises persists..."

And there it was, a hint of fragrance. Adam's head whipped around painfully, but he couldn't find the source. He rose slowly, surveying, as Iris crawled the remaining few feet to the altar. Knife in one hand, she used the other to grab the stone platform and stand.

It's time, Iris, came Lawrence's voice, as omnipresent yet sourceless as the scent of dying flowers. *Time for the open darkness to draw you in, and drink up your brimming cup.*

Iris gripped the hilt in both hands, turning the blade toward her own body. Adam's chest seized as her intent finally became clear to him through the fog of pain and Lawrence's influence. He dove for his grandmother, knocking them both against the stone platform.

"Iris, no!" Unable to use his right hand and afraid of hurting her, Adam squeezed Iris's arms to her sides with his own. He bent his mouth to her ear and pleaded, "Iris, remember who you are."

Lawrence's macabre laugh surrounded them, rippling through Adam's body like an icy wave. His words arose in Adam's mind, *So earnest. Far too earnest to be of use as anything except fuel for the fire.*

And with that, Adam began to feel heat, tongues lapping at his feet, at his ankles and knees like flames. Iris, still holding the knife, struggled in his arms as he staggered away from the altar with her. But the heat only intensified. Iris whimpered and Adam flinched, pressing his eyelids firmly against it. That's when he saw a ring of fire around them, more than head-high and too thick to pass through. He stumbled back toward the altar.

There was no escape.

If they couldn't pass through physically... Adam's mind raced.

Iris protected herself by shielding naturally, unconsciously, but she wasn't shielding now. But what if Lawrence hadn't breached her defenses after all? What if he'd kept them from triggering, essentially going *around* them rather than *through* them? If that were the case, Adam just needed to remind her what to do.

"Come on, Iris," he said, squeezing her tightly.

Adam shut his eyes and reached out to her with his mind, the woman who'd raised him and protected him, whose blood ran through his veins. Iris's body shuddered, her arms still straining against his, but her mind was absent, elusive. Finally, he glimpsed a small creature hiding in a dim corner, tucked in upon itself. Somehow Adam knew this was an embodiment of Iris's protector, a piece of her usually cut off from her conscious mind. But the wall that had separated it from her consciousness, that protected *it* so it could protect *her,* was gone. Adam gave the creature a gentle nudge. It coiled more tightly, its back displaying a dark, textured surface somewhere between needles and fur.

Don't worry, Lawrence said. *The good, dark fire burns on untroubled...* Heat pressed closer with his voice, and Adam's legs grew weak.

Iris, now, Adam whispered, and gave the creature a solid, psychic shove while he still had the strength to do so.

The beast wheeled, fangs flashing in the relative dark. Two sets of eyelids peeled back to reveal golden eyes, scanning its surroundings. It shook its head, hairy spines flexing like a demon's crown, and opened its mouth.

Adam heard a mighty blast, like a shock wave, but only after it had knocked them both flat. He found himself inside a solid sphere that pulsed with the same indigo energy as Virgil's tattered walls. Iris's arms relaxed beneath him and she dropped the knife. She'd done it.

Lawrence roared, and heat swept over Adam's body while stinking bits of charred soil swirled around him. He coughed and braced himself, curling over Iris to shield her physically as she had done for their minds.

But as quickly as the maelstrom had arisen, it was gone. *He* was gone.

Adam lifted his head, blinking grit, and flinched.

He wasn't gone.

A figure knelt next to Danny's body, then stood and walked quickly toward them. "Adam?" he called out.

Adam wiped at his eyes, but smeared dirt and blood across his face instead of clearing his vision.

Iris squirmed from his grasp, looked toward the approaching figure and said uncertainly, "Luther?"

Adam squinted, holding his breath, then nearly collapsed on Iris with relief. She was right. Iris slowly stood. Adam lacked the will or the strength—or both—to do so, or to watch her. He hunched over and rested his forearms on his thighs, trying to catch his breath, afraid to touch the ground.

"He's dead," Luther said, voice loud. "Or so damn close there's nothing anyone can do."

"We know," Adam muttered, lifting his head.

Luther's mouth fell open. "Goddamn, you don't look much better. Can you walk?"

"If you help me up," Adam said.

"The cruiser's just down the path a little ways. I drove it in as far as I—"

"Where's Evie?" Adam asked.

"She's safe," Luther said.

Adam could barely feel his lips, they'd gone so numb, when he muttered, "Then it was JJ."

"She's been shot," Luther said, and held out an arm. Adam hesitated, unable to decide what to do with it, so Luther reached for Adam's hand instead. He cringed when he saw the mangled mess Danny had made of it.

"Jesus," he said. "We gotta do something about that bleeding."

Iris appeared next to him, holding Danny's bag and the bloody knife in hands still restrained by pink fuzzy handcuffs. Luther was dumbfounded, staring at the three objects.

"You don't have the cuff keys," Luther said.

"No," she confirmed. "Help me cut the bag strap."

Adam watched as Luther took the knife from her and pulled the strap taut while she held the bag. He'd sawed about halfway through the heavy fiber when the blade slipped and Luther nearly stabbed himself in the thigh. He took a deep breath and wiped the hilt and his hand on his pants leg before finishing that section and cutting the strap free from the other end. Then he tossed the knife back on the ground.

Iris draped the strap over Adam's arm and tied a makeshift tourniquet below his right elbow. Adam winced, as much at the unavoidable sight of blood dripping from his gruesome hand as from the pain.

Luther had averted his eyes, but dutifully took Adam's arm when Iris nudged him. Adam's vision went dark as they got him to his feet and waited for him to stop swaying. As did he.

Come on, Rutledge, suck it up. JJ needs you.

He stepped forward, trusting that the ground would be there and that they would pick him up again if he fell. His vision had nearly settled (still a little wobbly around the edges) by the time they passed through the circle and drew even with Danny's body.

Luther stopped. "Let me check for those handcuff keys."

He released Adam's arm and squatted next to Danny's body. As he did, a cold breeze whispered through the trees, and the hairs on the back of Adam's neck stood at attention. *He's still here.*

Adam shut his eyes and surveyed the area around the altar. An iridescent line, patchy and broken in places, spanned the ring of dead earth and led to... Danny. *Danny's blood trail.* It crossed the circle. Adam gazed at Danny's body and saw someone else staring back at him from the skull. A shimmering, indistinct older man's face, but with the undeniable

Rutledge stamp. Cleft chin, bump on the nose. And it grinned at Adam.

Suddenly Danny's arm darted—as though it had never been injured—toward his foot and beneath his pants leg. Adam saw a glint of metal as Danny's body rose and lunged at Luther faster than seemed humanly possible. Luther recoiled from Danny's swinging arm, toppling as he drew his weapon. Danny dropped his knife and seized the gun, wrenching it from Luther as he fell.

Time stretched as Danny turned toward Adam and Iris. Adam stepped in front of Iris, but instead of firing, Danny slammed into them, knocking Iris to the ground. Adam only just stayed on his feet as Danny pushed him backward like a high school football drill. *Toward the circle*, Adam realized. *He needs me to be in the circle when he kills me, or he gets nothing from it.*

Adam dug in his heels, fell to one knee and dropped his head. His neck and knee twisted painfully as Danny smashed against him and they both went down. Adam rolled as they landed, coming out on top and straddling Danny. Adam grabbed for the gun as Danny raised it, then pressed the heel of his useless right hand to Danny's arm, pushing sideways with all his strength. But Adam overbalanced. His hand slipped and he collapsed, elbow spearing Danny's chest with his full weight. Danny grunted, and Adam twisted Danny's arm and gun hand until it pointed at Danny's head.

Danny's face was as gray as a blood-smeared, animated corpse. The only sign of life was in his eyes, an unnatural hint of indigo shimmer over clouding brown.

"You're as weak as your father was," Danny sneered. His voice, but not his words.

Adam shoved his index finger into the trigger guard to cover Danny's, jamming it painfully. For a moment, Danny's eyes flickered, and Adam thought he saw something breaking through from behind Lawrence, a softening in Danny's face.

The booming pop from Luther's gun was almost as unexpected as the hole that appeared in Danny's head. Like Adam's father. Did Adam feel blood and brain spray his face this time, or did he imagine it? He squeezed his eyes shut against the images and sensations that threatened to undo him.

With his eyes shut, Adam could see that there was no lingering energy, no phantom face. He felt Iris's hand on his shoulder and opened his eyes. Lawrence was gone, and Danny was dead.

"What the hell was that?" Luther asked. His voice shook, or maybe it was the residual echo of the gunshot in Adam's ears.

Adam dropped Danny's hand, still wrapped around the gun, and tried to find the strength to stand. He heard Iris say, with the same hint of tinniness, "Luther, help me with Adam."

"That bastard was dead. He sure as hell shouldn't have been—"

"Luther!" Iris shouted. "It doesn't matter." Adam felt each of them take an elbow, as Iris continued, "Come on. JJ needs us."

84

Luther's cruiser was close. He drove them back as far as the fork in the road, where Luther traded it for his roomier SUV. Adam and Iris swept lingering glass from their seats before Luther gunned the engine, spinning the wheels in the gravel.

Body humming with pain and a sense of urgency, Adam had difficulty focusing on anything except the *ding-ding-ding* of the vehicle's *hey dummies! you're not wearing your seat belts* warning. "Is Harlan with JJ?" he asked.

"Yeah," Luther said. "There's a chopper on the way."

Moments later, he whipped the vehicle around and backed in at the front of the house. Adam's door was open and he'd stepped to the ground almost before Luther had the transmission in park.

"Hey," Luther yelled over his shoulder, "the man who killed your dad is dead."

The pain in Adam's stabbed hand was excruciating and he struggled to process what Luther had said (*the man who killed your dad*) before something else staggered him.

Adam slammed the door and rounded the vehicle to see, through the house's open front door, Evie kneeling—no, *sitting on her heels.* Her hands were dark with blood, and he watched one touch her face, then shove her hair back, leaving a sinister streak. She opened her mouth... but this time she didn't scream. Adam was too far away to hear her words when she spoke.

It was Adam's dream from Harlan's hospital bedside, but it wasn't *quite* his dream. And that had ended with Evie's scream, so when she stood and backed out of the way, everything was new.

Or it would have been, if the world hadn't slid directly from Adam's dream into his nightmares, echoes of his recent trauma at this very spot.

Evie made way for Grant and Harlan (*instead of Teddy and Harlan*) to carry JJ on a sheet (*not Adam by the shoulders and calves*) out the front door and down the porch steps (*they didn't bang JJ's shin*). A vertiginous wave overtook Adam as he heard Harlan say, "Put her by that tree," and simultaneously, "Put *him* by that tree."

It wasn't as cold as it had been that day, but the sun was roughly the same position in the sky. Adam's mind was bleeding weeks ago courtesy of Virgil, and JJ's body was bleeding today, courtesy of a bullet.

His dream of Evie versus Evie's reality, his past versus JJ's present, all intersecting in this place and time.

Luther appeared next to Adam, his bulk steadying. "I almost forgot. You lost this dropping me off at the hospital," he said, pressing warmed metal into Adam's less injured hand. "Your uncle Teddy said to make sure I gave it to you."

"Thank you," Adam said, squeezing the chain with his mother's key tightly. He almost didn't feel the pain.

Of course. Grant wasn't here to take Teddy's place; *Adam* was.

Harlan looked up as Adam approached, expression somehow both apprehensive and relieved, like a terminal patient eying a final syringe of morphine. Grant was slipping a bloody hand beneath JJ, Adam assumed applying pressure.

Adam knelt next to the Sheriff and said, "Grant, I've got this."

"We've got twelve more minutes until the chopper gets here—"

"Understood," Adam cut him off. "So why don't you let Harlan and I see what we can do for the next ten?"

Grant yielded his spot, but seemed reluctant to leave. Adam wiped his hand on his pants, then rested it—still holding his mother's key—on JJ's forehead, above closed eyes that briefly fluttered. The skin was cool and clammy.

JJ was dying.

"Grant, Evie needs someone now, too," Adam said.

He had a sudden flash—*motherfucking Marcus*. A giddy, snorting laugh, the product of exhaustion and pain and blood loss and the tiniest bit of hope, escaped him. It might not be for long, but JJ was still in there.

"Promise you'll watch over Evie, no matter what," Adam said. "Don't let Marcus have her."

Momentarily speechless, Grant stammered, "I—of course, JJ. I promise."

Adam bent over JJ, feeling her quick, shallow breathing, and watched Grant leave in his peripheral vision. "You hear that, Janie? But don't get the wrong idea. I was the one lying under this tree not so long ago. And I thought I was done. Ready to let go. But I wasn't, and neither are you."

He sat back, looked at Harlan.

"You sure you're up for this, son?" Harlan asked. "I've seen you look better."

Adam made an effort to smile. "You've seen me look worse, too."

"That's debatable. Is the rest of it over?"

Adam nodded. "Iris is fine."

"I know," Harlan said. "She doesn't want to watch, so she's hiding."

For Adam's ears only, he added, *Wondering which one of us will die.*

"Which *one* of us?" Adam asked. "That's funny; I never thought of Iris as an optimist."

Harlan barked a laugh, wiped the corner of his eye, then rested a bare hand on JJ's wrist. "You have any questions?"

"I think I've got the general idea," Adam said. Except he had forgotten one practicality—his savaged hand, currently good for little except causing him pain. He'd need one for connecting with JJ, one for grounding. He asked Harlan, "Any suggestions?"

Harlan tsk'ed. "You got any mobility left in that hand at all?"

Adam tried to manipulate his fingers. He thought there was some slight movement, but the way the pain made the whole world swim, he could have imagined it.

Harlan grimaced. "In that case, use your better hand for grounding."

Adam nodded and stared at his mother's key. He couldn't hang it from his neck with the broken chain, and he was afraid it would work its way into the wound on his palm. Instead, he wrapped it around his lifeless fingers like a rosary. The tourniquet below his elbow caught his attention. *That shouldn't be there.* He couldn't say why exactly, but he believed it would interfere. He looked up to find Harlan's eyes on him, with a gentle, almost apologetic confirmation.

"Luther," Adam called out, knowing he would be near.

"What do you need?" he asked, squatting next to Adam.

"Take that off, please." Adam indicated the strap.

"Are you sure?"

"Yes."

Adam wanted to laugh at Luther's single-minded focus on the strap, features wrinkled at the blood and adjacent gore. "Please don't puke on me," Adam said.

"Why not? I figure I owe you a few," Luther said, voice distracted as he dug his nails into the knot until it came free with a final tug. Luther shook his head as he unraveled the strap, then backed away. "Wasn't tight enough anyway. You're still bleeding."

How could he tell? Adam wondered, with a shuddering shiver. There was so much blood. Everywhere. Feeling none too steady, he shifted to sit with legs crossed rather than on his heels. Then he rested his ruined hand on JJ's belly, not far from the entry wound, and lay JJ's crimson-smeared fingers in his, tucking them beneath the coiled silver chain to keep them secure. Finally, he shut his eyes and lay his left palm flat, wriggling it through the pine needles to the damp soil beneath.

The ground supporting his hand was like the skin on a fruit. It separated Adam from nourishment, but superficially—it wasn't impermeable. Adam reached out, extending beyond his flesh, deeper and deeper into the earth. He felt something he visualized as a handshake, and then a tickling buzz against his palm. Having penetrated his skin, a humming resonance crept into his hand, up his forearm, and passed through his body. It continued to Adam's far shoulder, then raced down his arm to his mangled hand. Something bubbled inside his flesh, rearranging the molecules. It was torture, far worse than when Danny had seesawed the knife within him, and his better left hand shook with the desire to rip it from the ground. Instead, he pushed the bubbling out, through his fingertips into JJ.

Her body shuddered, but Adam's violent, boiling energy immediately met something else—something from Harlan—and was transformed. He had an impression of green, warmth and spring and rejuvenation and hope. He could even smell it, not flowers and sweetness, but the peppery effort of life bursting through rich, loamy soil.

As remarkable as it was, it wasn't enough. This place was most recently Teddy's, not Lawrence's, so it wasn't hungry for pain and suffering like the stone altar had been. But neither was it content to bestow life gratis.

Quid pro quo.

Adam felt Harlan pushing him away—psychically, but was it also physically? If Adam opened his eyes, would he see Harlan peeling JJ's fingers from his senseless ones? Harlan had expected this to happen, just as he'd known JJ was in danger, and he'd had a plan all along. He meant to protect Adam by giving his own life for JJ's. But Adam couldn't bear the thought of losing both Harlan and Virgil. And what if Harlan's remaining years weren't enough to satisfy payment?

The older man wasn't the only one who'd expected trouble. Charlotte had planted a seed when she'd come to Adam last night, but it had come to fruition when Adam surrendered to the stones at the fork in the road. Discovering the defenses Virgil had built for him, *within* him, Adam knew those fragments must still be there for a reason. And then, helping resurrect Iris's impassable shields by the altar, Adam learned the why and the how.

Adam tapped into the remnants of Virgil's walls now, feeding energy to restore them. They raised in his mind, sweeping over him and JJ like a deep, blue sea, cutting off Harlan and everything else. It was peaceful, being submerged but supported. It reminded Adam of jumping in the river with Danny, of that moment on the bottom before your lungs began screaming.

He savored the feeling as long as he dared. And then Adam laid himself bare, letting the place take what it would. So it did. Beginning at the tips of his crimson fingers, it took his life.

85

"What the hell's going on?" Luther demanded.

He'd taken a moment to cut the chain to Iris's handcuffs before rearranging the seats in his SUV and sweeping out the worst of the glass in the back. His mind screamed the whole time, a low, wordless, droning screech. Luther wasn't sure which was tweaking him worse, killing a man or watching one rise from the dead to die again. Danny's eyes... When he had risen, lunging toward Luther with a knife in his hand, the light in the man's eyes had come from elsewhere, not from within.

Those eyes had persisted in Luther's mind, in his shaking limbs, when he returned to find Harlan frantic, climbing over JJ to reach Adam, who'd collapsed next to her.

"You sneaky sonuvabitch!" Harlan shouted, cupping his hands beneath Adam's neck. "Fuck! Teddy, what the hell am I supposed to do? How do I fix this?"

Luther's head shot around, half expecting Adam's fugitive-aiding uncle to materialize. Instead, Iris appeared next to him.

"He left the walls up," Harlan said. "The dumbass locked me

out and left them up, and now I can't do a goddamn thing to help him. I can't get in."

Iris blinked unevenly as tears streamed down her bruised face. "He made his choice."

"Well, it wasn't his to make," Harlan countered, and leaned against the trunk of the nearest tree, pressing his fist to his mouth and staring down at Adam.

Luther scrambled to Adam's side. Sure, he'd been bleeding badly, and his face was pale and sunken as a corpse, but Luther hadn't actually thought he was dying. Not imminently. But Adam's lips were blue, and his skin was cold. His disfigured hand, the flesh above it darker than it had been just minutes ago, was still entwined with JJ's. Luther grabbed the other hand and poked and squeezed and waited, but couldn't find a pulse. The Sheriff dropped down on JJ's other side as Luther checked Adam's carotid.

"Well?" Grant asked.

"I got nothing," Luther said, stunned.

"Jesus. How the hell did he..." Grant shook his head.

And without JJ's medical expertise, who had a clue? "Harlan!" Luther barked. "What do we do?"

But the old man looked lost. "It's not just the blood. It's everything else. The sacrifice."

"Luther," Grant said, looking at his watch, "it's time to take JJ to that chopper."

"There's got to be something—"

"Luther!" Grant gripped his arm. "You know he wouldn't want JJ to miss her only chance."

Iris had an arm around Evie; the child couldn't go with her mother. Comforting the girl was probably the only thing keeping Iris from losing her goddamn mind. Luther's could certainly use some help.

"Okay," he said.

"You drive JJ while I secure the scene—at least one of them—and wait for the locals and D'Antonio's people," Grant said.

"You sure?" Luther asked.

Grant's voice was rough as he stroked JJ's hair and said, "I promised I'd keep an eye on Evie, too."

JJ's breathing seemed more regular, or at least less labored. *Goddamn, this better not have been for nothing*, he thought, stretching to untangle Adam's mangled hand from JJ's. The neck chain was twisted around them both. Luther tugged carefully. He knew it was stupid, but he didn't want to hurt Adam's hand, what was left of it.

"Come on, Luther," the Sheriff said. "You've got less than five minutes."

"I know," he said, cringing as he pulled harder. But Adam's fingers were locked. "Grab JJ's hand, will ya?"

Grant did, and Luther slipped the chain from her fingers and slid it up over Adam's wrist. The wound was enough to turn his stomach, so he turned his face away as he peeled Adam's fingers from JJ.

And he felt... *resistance*. Like Adam didn't want to let go.

Had Luther imagined it?

No way. Like he hadn't imagined little Aaron Schofield's lolling head righting itself as he held the boy's limp body in Les's room. Luther said, "He's still alive." *For now.* "Let's move!"

They used the sheet to carry JJ to Luther's vehicle first. Grant was favoring one side—Kevlar or not, you didn't escape a shooting unscathed—so Luther scooped up Adam before the Sheriff could protest.

"You're a heavy, floppy sonuvabitch, for no fatter than you are," he grunted, lumbering to the SUV.

The two bodies barely fit side by side in the back, and then only with Adam's legs bent. Luther had scooted the passenger seat forward to make more compartment room, but Harlan squeezed in anyway. Luther had a view of the man's ass the whole short, bouncing way down the road as he leaned between the seats.

"I can't imagine he has any blood left, but if he does, let's keep it where it belongs," Harlan said, applying pressure to Adam's hand and the brachial artery in his upper arm.

He said something else Luther missed. It was hard to hear over the wind rushing through the missing windows, and Luther was concentrating on moving as fast as he could while avoiding the worst of the ruts.

"What's that?" Luther asked, but he was pretty sure the old man was just talking to hear his own voice now, keeping the spooks away.

"Did you know I'm the one who found Adam the night his mother died?" Harlan asked.

If there'd been a ditch, Luther might have driven into it.

"I'm the one who found him in the woods, in Dead Hollow," Harlan said, swiping a hand across his face and leaving a sticky trail.

So Luther had put Adam there, and Harlan had carried him out. It gave Luther an icy feeling up his spine, the three of them brought together again.

"Charlotte, darling, I'm afraid it's all up to you this time," Harlan said.

Luther told himself the man had blown a fuse, talking to Adam's dead mother. The woman Luther had killed. Otherwise, he really would plow into a tree, and that wouldn't do much for Adam or JJ. Either way, the crazy bastard must have had eyes in his ass. They'd finally passed through the creepy pine corridor and Luther was leaning over the steering wheel for a better view of the adjacent field through his bullet-marked windshield when Harlan said, "Slow down, Luther. The access point's gonna be right up here."

Luther pulled over at a wider spot in the road. With no fence, he might be able to go off-road in four-wheel drive, but he wanted a closer look first. Harlan stayed put while Luther got out. The field was a lurching step down from the road. He kicked at the vegetation around the edge, but before he could gauge the drop-off, Luther heard the helicopter. He glanced over his shoulder to see it low in the sky, backlit by the remaining fuzzy daylight and coming to ground. Luther waved, scrambled around to the rear of the SUV, popped the back hatch, and ran to meet the paramedic.

"You're not our GSW, are you?" asked a big, Latino man in a blue jumpsuit, yelling over the sound of the rotors with the slightest hint of an accent.

Luther was wearing a fair amount of Adam's and JJ's blood. "No. This way," he said. As they reached the vehicle, Luther pointed to the corresponding areas on his own torso as he designated, "Entry and exit, with a..."

But the word escaped him. He slapped his chest.

"Pneumothorax?" the paramedic prompted as he jogged to the back and was met with two unconscious passengers. "Which one is it?"

"Her. But we're hoping you've got room for two."

The man shook his head. "We were called out for *one*."

"Well, I know that. We fucking called it in. But he's not gonna make it either if he doesn't go with you." Luther's hand drifted to his holster, and his voice was grim. "You're not leaving without him."

"Easy, man," the paramedic said, raising his hands. "Just let me take a look."

The SUV rocked as he kneed up into it, filling the remaining space. Luther couldn't see what the man was doing as he quickly examined Adam, muttering about severity scores and hemorrhagic shock.

Stepping down, the paramedic said, "You're right; he needs to go. Despite his friend being an asshole. And he won't put us over weight."

He radioed his colleague. Within minutes, they had transferred both JJ and Adam, and Luther watched the helicopter lift off with a full patient load.

Luther staggered back, legs quivering, and sat behind the wheel of his vehicle. He was shaking so hard, his teeth chattered intermittently. Driving was not an option, even the short distance back to the house. He'd give it a few minutes. That's all he needed, a few minutes to work through the adrenaline. A few minutes to stop thinking and feeling.

He'd forgotten about Harlan until a ragged sob tore through the old man's throat next to him. Just one. Luther watched as Harlan stowed the rest inside, elbow propped on the doorframe and mouth pressed against his fist. His eyes were red, lips chapped and face weathered like an old boot—for God's sake, the man woke from a coma to nearly lose the love of his life and watch Adam die. Luther reached over impetuously and grabbed Harlan's free hand.

That was a mistake.

Luther's guts lurched, like he was falling from the rocky precipice where they'd found the Nicholson girl. His feet pushed involuntarily against the wheel well, anticipating the impact of hitting bottom. But when Luther landed, it wasn't on that mountain a month ago, but in Dead Hollow thirty years ago. He was standing on the edge of the road, looking down at the twisted metal while being yelled at by a man that was now dead.

It was only an instant. Harlan untangled his hand from Luther's, and Luther abruptly found himself sitting in the SUV again, shaking next to the old man.

Except now, Harlan knew what he'd done, too.

"Fuck," Luther said, rocking in his seat. His stomach cramped and he felt ill all over, feverish and clammy and...

"Luther," Harlan said, gripping his sleeve-covered forearm firmly.

Luther couldn't look at him, but he heard a great, juddering sigh.

"We were all there, son," Harlan said. "But we're not anymore."

Luther nodded, or maybe it was the rocking. It was hard to tell; his body seemed to be acting independently of him. He white-knuckled the steering wheel, squeezing and squeezing while his eyes remained transfixed by the bullet hole in the windshield.

"Staying there, living there—or even dying there—it won't change what happened."

Luther felt a humming in his belly, heard it work its way to his tight chest, getting louder as it crept toward his esophagus.

Harlan's rough velvet voice pierced Luther like nothing had since his mother died. "You're just like Adam," he said. "You've got to let it go."

Luther began to weep.

86

The helicopter rose quickly, leaving the Rutledge property behind on its way to a Pittsburgh trauma center. JJ and Adam remained unconscious while fluids were drained from JJ but given to Adam, who had lost nearly forty percent of his blood. Both were whisked away for surgery upon their arrival. JJ's doctors congratulated her on the path the bullet had taken and were pleasantly surprised by the condition of her chest wall. Adam's prognosis was guarded. His team did what they could to save his life but couldn't salvage his hand. His arm was amputated below the elbow in a subsequent surgery.

Adam's first word upon waking—for several days—was *JJ*; he couldn't remember what had happened at Teddy's house after he killed Danny. Much of what happened at the altar was fuzzy as well, though thankfully Adam never woke thinking Danny was still alive, panicking he was still out there. In fact, once he knew JJ was safe, Adam felt less anxious than he had in a long time. He still had nightmares. But Adam hadn't realized the weight he'd carried with him every day until it was gone.

Absences were a recurring theme in his recovery, one Adam confronted every time he regained consciousness. He didn't always remember he'd lost a limb, but did wake with pain and a sense of dissonance, the knowledge that something wasn't right. Nurses and therapists were constantly in and out of his room, dealing with tubes and rewrapping compression bandages before teaching him to do so, gently chastising him for reverting to strange positions that could shorten the muscles in his residual limb.

Adam couldn't avoid looking at the empty space below his elbow if he'd wanted to, but he also spent a lot of time looking at his remaining left hand. At least, what he could see of it peeking from beneath its own bandages. Bruised and abraded, he memorized virtually every mark. It became his model, the only way to recall what his severed hand had looked like. This one had a dark brown spot, a freckle or mole, near the wrist. Had his right hand as well? He doubted it. That hand's distinguishing feature had been his wonky thumb, with its square knuckle, its odd angle, and its inescapable history with his mother's death. Adam felt more grief at the loss of that thumb than the limb itself.

His limb wasn't the simplest, but perhaps the most straightforward loss Adam confronted. The most difficult was that Virgil was gone—truly gone—now. Adam tried not to think about it, about the horrifying way his father had died. Alive, then not *(stick close to Luther)*. He was mostly successful, but the sound of rifle shots occasionally woke him from his nightmares. That, and a sinister whispering in the dark.

Danny was gone, too. Danny the adult, as well as Adam's idea of Danny the child. And Adam had killed him. So much of what Adam thought he knew—about his family and about his mother's death, about Luther and about himself—had crumbled. These were the losses that threatened to make him go numb and retreat so deeply no one could reach him.

But Adam told himself he was done running away.

Iris helped. She was at the hospital most days, looking like a patient herself until her bruises faded. They didn't discuss what had happened in the woods, or her time with Danny. He'd ask her about it eventually, when he was ready to hear it and had the strength to drag the truth out of her.

She was back to her imperious self, the only chink appearing once after she'd been absent for a day. Iris eventually admitted she'd gone back to Cold Springs, where she and Teddy had buried Virgil alongside Charlotte. Adam understood they couldn't wait for him, but he wished he could have been there with them, the only people remaining who'd had a connection with his father.

Adam was not JJ's first word, but he was her second, after *Evie*.

Like Adam, JJ's recollection of the events at Teddy's house was fragmented at best. She didn't remember being an idiot and following Luther into the house, though it wasn't hard to imagine. She didn't remember much about being shot, except the pain in her chest as she struggled to breathe and a single image: lying on Teddy's floor, staring at the dingy ruffle that skirted one of the armchairs, hearing more gunshots and feeling oddly detached. Perhaps because she was certain she was going to die.

JJ's mother had rushed to Pittsburgh to be with her daughter and granddaughter. During JJ's recovery (shorter than Adam's, but still plenty long enough to drive JJ nuts), her mother alternated between sitting with JJ and taking Evie out—to eat, to shop, to do anything that did not involve a hospital.

Iris also stopped by from time to time. Iris had always been like a godmother to Evie, but now Evie sat next to Iris whenever she visited, leaning toward her, sometimes even brushing the arm of her sweater for reassurance. It was both touching and disconcerting. JJ chose to see Evie's attachment to the formidable woman as a positive sign, trusting in her daughter's resilience. If anything, she was more worried about Adam.

The hospital was like a small city, especially compared to the modest one in Beecham County where JJ worked. Adam and JJ were in different wings and didn't see each other until the day she was released. Even then, she'd felt a shaming, silent dread about visiting him, saving it until the last moment. She desperately wanted to see that he was okay, but equally feared seeing that he wasn't.

Their meeting was awkward, but no worse than might be expected. JJ was in a wheelchair, she and her mother waiting for her discharge paperwork to be finalized. Adam was in bed, slightly flushed and in obvious pain from recent—was it physical therapy? Some kind of procedure? The fact that she didn't know was indicative of JJ's mental state. His face was gaunt, yet gave an impression of slight puffiness, perhaps from all the blood transfusions. As difficult as it was to meet his eyes, she soon realized (with more shame) it was the best way to avoid looking at his stump. They spoke briefly, lightly, with JJ's mother and Iris taking up most of the conversational slack. It was so good to see him, alive if not entirely intact, and surely the next time would be easier. Wouldn't it?

87

"So, Deputy Beck, what've you got to say for yourself?" drawled Sheriff Brogan.

The Kirby County Sheriff was a big man, slightly bigger than his uniform. His hat, resting on the table in front of him, had left an impression on his forehead. When he leaned back and rested his folded hands on his belly, the fabric around the buttons gapped.

Luther's uniform fit better than it had in at least a year. Of course, it helped that he was standing at attention.

"Well, sir, Deputy Kilbourne—" Luther almost slipped up and said Kiss-Ass, "was directly responsible for a prisoner's escape. After which, he clearly exceeded his authority and acted in violation of Ms. Jennifer Jane Tulley's rights. The unfortunate shooting at Ms. Tulley's property was a direct result of his flagrant disregard for her safety and that of a fellow officer. Although he was not a member of our department, I feared Deputy Kilbourne's actions would not reflect well on us and may even open us to civil, if not criminal, liability. Finally, he disrespected Deputy Marshall, who, according to the agreement between you and Sheriff Mason, should have been in a supervisory position over him."

Luther paused. Grant's expression never changed, but Luther knew what was running through the Sheriff's mind—*Luther, you're not exactly helping yourself here.* But Grant needn't worry; Luther was getting to the boot-licking.

"However," Luther continued, "my own actions did no credit to the uniform, either. I failed to follow the proper administrative procedure to countermand Deputy Kilbourne's orders and report him to a higher authority. Instead, I lost my temper and acted completely unprofessionally in striking the man."

"Twice," Sheriff Brogan cut in.

Luther suppressed a smile at the memory. "Yes, sir. Twice. I regret my impetuous actions and the trouble they've caused both our departments."

All Luther really regretted was that he'd only struck the man twice. *Stupid sonuvabitch.* But he held his tongue and let his uniform and his upright posture speak for him.

The Sheriff nodded. He'd chosen a plastic chair over a rolling one, and it flexed as his back pressed against it. "Deputy, I appreciate that. When we assume the uniform, we have to leave our baser selves behind to answer a higher calling. We cannot succumb to the same temptations lesser men would."

Luther's fingers ached with the urge to squeeze into a baser self fist.

"And I understand you were under some considerable strain at the time," Sheriff Brogan said. "Both with the case and of a personal variety."

"Yes, sir," Luther said, feeling the warm lick of his temper in his guts. He had no intention of bringing Les into this, not even to save his job.

Sheriff Brogan turned his attention to his counterpart. "The man who escaped—he's no longer an issue, correct?"

His remark disturbed even Grant's calm facade. Sheriff

Mason's jaw tightened visibly before he answered, "Mr. Rutledge was subsequently murdered in Virginia."

"Well, then, there you go. Crazy times, but it sounds like we can put all this to bed," Sheriff Brogan said. He rose and set his hat on his thick head, tugging it down hard. "And between you and me, Kilbourne is an annoying little ass-licking prick. *My daddy is a congressman* only gets you so far. Since the Staties decided to take a pass on prosecuting the woman who shot him, I'm hoping the little shit has hung himself this time."

Grant started to escort the man out, but the elder lawman raised his hands. "No, stay put, Sheriff Mason. I can find my way out. And be sure and give your momma and daddy my best."

Luther and Grant were left staring at each other. The Sheriff had actually shaved and was starting to look human again. The regular drives to Pennsylvania had been wearing on him.

Luther broke first. "So how do you think the Sheriff really feels about Kiss-Ass?"

Grant shook his head. "You had me worried at first, but administrative procedures? And *civil liability*? Where the hell did you come up with that?"

Luther grinned. "I must have seen it on an old episode of *Law & Order*. So does this mean we're good?"

"I don't know, Luther. Are we?" Grant leaned back in his chair, but instead of looking like a pompous ass, he just looked like a tired man, trying his best to do the right thing. "Are you really committed to being a deputy here in Beecham County?"

Oddly, Luther found that he was. More so than he'd ever been. When the elder Sheriff Mason had hired him, Luther had been driven to the badge by guilt. Guilt could be a swift kick in the ass to turn your life around, but it was no way to live it once you had.

"Yes, sir," Luther said. "If you'll have me."

"Good. In that case, I'll see you back here in uniform on Monday."

Luther breathed an audible sigh of relief, and Grant stood and extended his hand for a firm shake.

"Thank you, sir," Luther said, a slow smile crossing his face.

As he headed for the door, Grant said, "Just remember to walk the straight and narrow, or I'll loan you out to Sheriff Brogan. Permanently."

88

___

A dam woke to the smell of... something. He wasn't sure what, but it didn't matter because Iris was cooking it.

He blinked widely, his eyelashes briefly adhering to each other at the corners. Adam stretched out his arm and threw back the window curtain above his bed. The sky was clear, but transitioning from pale blue toward late-day oranges and purples as sunset approached. Iris had sent him to bed soon after they arrived home from the hospital. He must have napped for a couple of hours.

Adam peeled the bedding aside and set his socked feet on the floor. He raised his residual limb (he'd been trying not to think of it as a *stump*) and examined the compression bandage. It could go another couple of hours before changing. He was wearing sweats and a short-sleeved T-shirt. His inclination was to throw on a flannel shirt, too, but if the smells were any indication, Iris's cooking would have warmed all of downstairs. And they weren't expecting company, so he needn't feel self-conscious.

He found Iris making enough food for an army. Or, if it were summer, a family reunion. She stood slicing something on a cutting board at the kitchen table, likely because her counters were already crowded. He meant to greet his grandmother first, but the array of food and his growling stomach drew him on a circuit around the space.

"You know, Harlan uses an apron when he cooks," Adam observed, on the prowl for items that could be instantly eaten.

Iris, not wearing one, snorted. "Of course he does."

"Deviled eggs," Adam crooned, before stuffing one in his mouth. A couple dozen remained, tucked into square, plastic containers. He waited for an admonishment from Iris. When it didn't come, he popped another one and continued his scavenging journey.

Biscuits sat on cooling racks next to a slow cooker, its glass lid opaque with steam and condensation. Adam hovered, wondering what was inside.

"Yes," Iris said, "that is a roast with all the fixings."

Adam lifted the lid and got a facial with the scents of potatoes and carrots and onions and venison. A pot of some kind of tomato-based, meaty stew simmered on the stove, and the oven was on. He flipped the light and squinted through the window.

"Ginger cake," she said.

"Wow." Adam made his way to the kitchen table, where she was slicing potato candy. When he settled his chin on her shoulder it didn't even throw off her form. "What's the occasion?"

He expected a sideways response that wasn't a real answer. Instead, he got the simple, honest reply, "I'm reclaiming my space."

He'd forgotten that Danny had taken Iris from her home. Adam lifted his chin and surveyed the space with new eyes. Did it look different, or feel different?

"The rug," he said. "In the front room."

Iris nodded and pushed her hair back from her face. "Jim Henderson helped me get rid of it. Marcus had bled all over it."

Adam's lip curled in distaste. He'd forgotten about JJ's ex, too. "Any word on him?"

Iris shrugged. "I don't know where the legal stuff stands—I think they're still working that out—but Marcus seems to be behaving himself now, for what it's worth. And I think I told you, they cleared JJ on shooting that deputy. You want to help me with this?"

She nudged a roll of wax paper and three thin, cardboard containers, the kind you'd find in a bakery, with the back of her hand.

"Who's it for?" he asked, resisting the urge to dive into the potato candy, too. The sugar might make his head explode.

"One for Deputy Beth, to thank her for seeing to it that the worst of the mess here was already cleaned up. Although I haven't yet had the courage to check the bolthole. And then one for Evie and one for Rachel. I thought we'd take it over tonight," Iris said, adding with a little heat, "and Dorothy can just get over herself with her sugar phobia."

Adam put a bottom layer of candy in each container, then stared at the wax paper. He'd always written left-handed because of his wonky thumb, so he had some dexterity to work with. But how did you tear wax paper with one hand? Eventually, he'd be able to use his residual limb if he didn't have a prosthetic handy *(ha, ha)*, but for now it was too sensitive. He scooted the box to the edge of the table, pinned it with his right elbow, and tore the paper with his left hand. Not bad. Except it was about four times as big as what he needed. He considered using his teeth to tear it, but Iris would probably slap him. He looked up to find her staring at him.

"What?" he asked, wondering if she'd read his mind.

She held out a hand for the paper, tore it in fourths and gave the pieces back. Her eyes were sad, but she smiled. "I do believe you'll be all right."

Adam scooted a chair with his foot and sat to finish filling the goodie boxes. "And what about you?"

"Better now that Teddy's out of my house," she said. Finished slicing, she took her knife to the sink and called over the sound of running water, "The man apparently does not know how to clean a skillet."

Teddy had been staying at Iris's while she spent time in Pennsylvania with Adam in the hospital, but he'd gone to stay with Harlan yesterday. Adam couldn't imagine that lasting long.

Adam smiled, realizing his grandmother had done her usual excellent job of dodging and distracting. She carried yet another square plastic container to the table for the remaining candy. A cheap, grocery store bouquet sat in a vase in the center. Iris loved flowers, from humble roadside buttercups to regal stalks of gladiolus.

A faint, sickening scent of irises persists...

But not her namesake.

"Gram," Adam said, reaching out to touch a pale, pink carnation with his faintly trembling hand, "why don't you ever grow irises?"

She froze, then closed her eyes for a moment before asking softly, "Did you smell them, too?"

"Yes," Adam admitted, voice just as soft.

Over the past weeks, Adam had recovered most of the pieces of what had happened at the altar. But like any good jigsaw puzzle, the pieces had been shuffled. Occasionally one popped up and wanted his attention. As this one had.

"Lawrence was partial to a poem when we were courting, *The Scent of Irises* by D.H. Lawrence. I found it a little twisted for a love poem, but Lawrence liked it and he'd read it to me." She gave a harsh laugh. "I figured he liked it because they shared a name."

Iris turned her attention back to the potato candy. Adam listened to the pinwheels *plink* softly as she arranged them in the container. Hands occupied, she continued. "He quoted bits of it, after he hit me the first time. He considered that an apology. On a similar, later occasion, I told him I thought it was a stupid poem. Which led to the first time he knocked me unconscious. From then on, he'd trot it out whenever he was being particularly sadistic. But he'd change the words to fit the occasion. Needless to say, it ruined me on the scent—or sight—of irises."

Adam considered his memory pieces. He knew there was a match somewhere, a piece that would slide in next to this one and find its way home. "That's why you said, *He's not Danny.* On the altar. He'd quoted the poem."

Iris didn't contradict him, but she'd said all she intended to. And more than he would have imagined. "As soon as I finish this, we'll have a little stew," she said, avoiding his eyes. "Then maybe I'll freeze the rest. The roast is for tomorrow, and I thought I'd take some to—"

Adam touched her perpetually moving arm gently with his fingertips, just enough to make it still. He wrapped his arm around her, nestling his chin onto her shoulder, and returned to the question she'd sidestepped several minutes and a world of emotions ago.

"And what about you, Iris?" he asked softly. "Will you be all right?"

Her breath hitched a little on a big inhale, but when she turned to him her eyes were clear, and the skin crinkled at their corners. "Day by day, sweetie. Day by day."

89

———

"Are you sure he's dead?" Rachel asked.

Evie glanced at Rachel, nose pink with cold, as they tramped through the woods toward Evie's house. It was edging toward dark, and if Rachel's mom knew they were still outside, she'd have a hissy fit.

They'd had this conversation before, but Rachel kept returning to it. She might have been annoyed, but Evie understood. Plus every time she asked, Rachel sounded stronger, like she was closer to believing it. And every time Evie said the same thing, she did, too.

"He's dead. They both are," Evie said, though her brain still got fuzzy when she tried to figure out the other man. "Are you sure the older one was Adam's dad?"

"That's what Mom said." Rachel's voice took on the whispery quality that anything like gossip required. "I think that's why she doesn't like Adam."

Well, that's just stupid, Evie thought but didn't say out loud, swatting half-heartedly at a tree trunk with a stick. Rachel probably agreed, but it was hard to hear stuff like that about a parent, even when it was true.

"How did he die?" Rachel asked.

She didn't specify which one, but she didn't have to. "The Sheriff wouldn't say, but Miss Iris told me Adam killed him."

Evie had been a little surprised when Miss Iris had shared that information, but Miss Iris pretty much said or did what she wanted, or at least what she thought was right. Evie hadn't asked her about the other man. If Rachel was right about him being Adam's dad, that meant he'd been Miss Iris's son, and there had to be limits even to Miss Iris's toughness. Even if there wasn't, it seemed rude.

"I wish Uncle Teddy would come to visit," Rachel said, "but something about him bothers my mom, too."

There's a lot that bothers your mom, Evie thought. Or she believed she only thought, but a moment later Rachel gave her stink eye.

"Sorry, but it's true," Evie said out loud.

She and Rachel had been spending a lot of time together, and usually that was okay, but even your best friend can become irritating when she's the only person you ever speak with. Maybe that's why Evie said, feeling a nasty little rush of anger and power as she did, "Why do you keep asking me if he's dead, anyway? Don't you believe me?"

Rachel's face cleared, her parental indignation forgotten while she considered the question. At first, Evie was disappointed she hadn't hurt Rachel's feelings. Hadn't a part of her said it for just that reason? But as she watched Rachel pull a few long hairs free from the corner of her mouth, her mind anywhere but on Evie's pettiness, Evie felt relieved. Mom said that, after experiencing the kinds of things she had, a lot of people got the mean snappiness that kept bursting from Evie. (Although, Evie wanted to point out, Rachel hadn't.) Evie needed to be aware of it when it happened, because knowing the why would help her decide whether the anger was worth it. And this time, it wasn't.

"It's not that I don't believe you," Rachel said. "It's just that I feel like I should have known when he died. I should have felt something."

Evie leaned against a person-sized oak trunk and rubbed an itchy spot on her chin. That actually made sense. It also felt wrong to her that she hadn't felt it when her father or when her mother was shot. Something so momentous should shake the earth, the way it eventually shook her.

"I still think I could have found you," Rachel said. "With Uncle Teddy's help."

Evie wasn't so sure.

A breeze ruffled the mostly leafless branches above them, lifting Evie's long, straight hair, too. She gathered it and pulled it free of her jacket, before twisting it and shoving it back inside.

"We could try that stuff again," Evie said. "Like we did before."

"Mom doesn't like us messing around with weird stuff," Rachel said.

Weird stuff was undoubtedly her mother's term for it. "Even though it saved both our lives?" Evie demanded, then belatedly tried to get her anger in check. Fortunately, this time, Rachel agreed with her.

"I know, right?" she said. "But Uncle Teddy said not to worry about it. He said I can learn more when I'm older, maybe in a few years. He said he'll make sure I can; I just need to tell Dad, because I guess Dad doesn't feel the same way."

"Tell dad, and wait a few years," Evie said, deadpan.

Rachel shrugged, as if the waiting didn't bother her so much.

They'd been meandering, with Evie kicking leaves and smacking things, but when they heard a vehicle turn onto the Tulley drive, they scrambled through the final stretch of forest in a hurry. Evie ducked behind a tree, sliding into her default spy/catch-the-bad-guy play, and motioned for Rachel to do the same. It was the time of evening when most cars looked the same color, and this one's headlights glared, too, but Evie recognized the shape.

"That's Miss Iris," she said, stepping from behind the tree.

"Adam's with her," Rachel said.

Evie heard the excitement in Rachel's voice, but squinting in the dusk, she couldn't imagine how Rachel had seen who was in the car. It didn't matter. She couldn't wait to see him, either.

Everything else forgotten, she practically skipped the rest of the way to the car.

90

"The welcoming committee is here," Iris said, eyes flicking toward movement at the edge of the woods before returning to peer over the hood of the car. The headlights weren't doing much, and Adam had reminded her of Evie's habit of leaving her bicycle in inconvenient places.

The car was barely in park when Rachel and Evie sprinted up to the passenger door, stopping just short of pressing their faces against the glass.

"Scratch that," Iris said, and Adam heard her amusement. "It's the Adam Rutledge Fan Club."

Adam swallowed, throat dry, and his hand strayed to the bump that was his mother's key. When Iris gave it back to him in the hospital, he hadn't thought to ask who had fixed the chain. "At least I can still sign autographs."

"Hey," Iris said, squeezing his arm. "It's only JJ and the kids. And JJ... well, I think she's still a little rough around the edges."

He nodded, took a deep breath, and opened the door.

"Do you need help with that?" Evie asked. She stepped clear and nearly pulled Adam from his feet by solicitously opening the door wider.

"Thanks, Evie," he said.

He tried to let her exuberant energy pass through him, warm him, instead of bouncing against him and knocking him flat.

"I could use some help over here," Iris said. "Carrying *goodies.*"

Evie ran around to the other side of the car to help Iris, but Rachel lingered by Adam. He shut the door and asked, "How have you been, Rachel?"

"Good," she said. "But I haven't seen the woman again."

"Which woman—" Adam stopped. A dizzying wave of realization sent him leaning against the car. He aspired to sound matter-of-fact as he said, "You probably won't. I think she got everything she needed, and she's moved on now."

"She seemed nice," Rachel said, as Evie yelled her name.

Rachel went to lend a hand, giving Adam a moment to recover himself and push the questions away. *How did she find you? What did she say? What did her hand feel like on yours?*

At least he knew the answer to the last one.

JJ opened the front door, Trooper at her heel, and the warm interior light beckoned.

"Come on, girls," Iris said, leading a food caravan with Adam bringing up the rear. She told JJ at the door, "Lift a finger, and I will break it."

Adam raised a brow at JJ. "I wouldn't try her."

Everyone else shuffled inside, Iris issuing orders, but Adam and JJ got stuck at the threshold. JJ put a hand to his face, fingers straying across his cheek to his mid-ear sideburns. "You need a haircut," she said.

"You're as bad as Iris," Adam said. "Probably a good idea, though. I swear I saw gray in there the last time I shaved."

"We're too young for gray," she said softly, as if it was expected of her, not as if she believed it.

They still stood in the doorway when Iris returned from the kitchen.

"You're letting the heat out," she said. "I left the food on your counter. I've got more in the car, and the girls and I are taking it to Dorothy and Otto."

"We could just walk it over," Evie said. Her eyes were drawn to Adam's hanging sleeve.

"If I never set foot in the woods again, it'll still be too soon," Iris said firmly. "We're driving."

Adam held the door for Iris and the girls, then followed JJ inside.

"I'm making hot tea," she said, heading for the stove. "Would you like some?"

"Sure," he said, wandering around the living and dining area. Trooper followed, as though scenting his trail. Something was different, but Adam couldn't put his finger on it. "You back at work yet?"

"No," JJ called out, "but soon. Honey?"

"Yes, sugar?" he answered.

"Ha, ha," she said, voice dry.

Adam smiled as he made his way around the kitchen table, bumping a child's backpack so it slid from a chair. "Honey would be good."

Except for the backpack, the area was remarkably tidy—no piled papers, no carelessly discarded clothing, no stray hair clips... "Was your mom staying with you?" he asked.

JJ approached with two steaming, minty mugs and a curling lip. "How did you ever guess? She went home yesterday. I swear, I didn't bury her in the backyard, although I was tempted. Here, or the living room?"

Adam wasn't sure his physical therapist would agree, but he preferred an armrest for his residual limb. "Living room's good."

JJ set his mug next to an armchair and took the neighboring seat, still favoring one side as she moved. Trooper settled on the rug between them. She met Adam's eyes briefly and smiled, then stared at her tea. He caught her looking again when he reached for his mug with the wrong arm—that is, his right arm because the end table was on his right side—before realizing, *that won't work*. But she quickly looked away.

That's when Adam lost his self-consciousness. Seeing her so... beyond simply insecure but not quite broken... helped him jettison his own issues. Temporarily.

"Should I ask how you're feeling," Adam said, taking a tiny, hot sip, "or are we not doing that?"

She raised an eyebrow in acknowledgment. "Good question. It mostly doesn't hurt, except when I do something I'm not supposed to. How's your rehab—"

"That's not what I meant," Adam interrupted, shifting to take off his jacket. Her eyes followed his arm. Iris had secured the end of his long shirt sleeve with a safety pin so it didn't hang. He pressed, "How are you *feeling*?"

Her face flushed—was she angry? Maybe a little, but Adam thought he saw a slight relaxing in her shoulder, heard a little more solidity in her voice. "Confused," she admitted.

"Go on."

JJ set her mug on the coffee table and tucked her feet beneath her, wincing slightly. "Danny," she said. "I don't know. I guess I shouldn't be surprised. He always was a punk—"

"Don't do that."

JJ glanced at him, surprised. "Why not? He was an asshole—"

"No, JJ, he was a kid," Adam said firmly. "We were all kids. I know it's easier for us if we can say he had it coming—"

"I didn't mean that," JJ protested, face flushing more deeply.

"Yes, you did, and I totally understand. I killed Danny," Adam said, suddenly choking up.

He didn't think he'd ever said the words aloud. Sure, he'd been interviewed by various law enforcement agencies about what had happened (always with Grant present), but he didn't think he'd ever said it so bluntly. Adam had killed Danny. Arguably twice.

He glanced down to find JJ's reassuring hand on his knee and wasn't sure how long it had been there.

Adam cleared his throat before continuing. "I killed Danny because I had to. He had become something..." Adam couldn't bring himself to utter the word *evil*, though it was the first one that sprang to mind for the serial killer. "...Something I don't think he wanted to be. But the Danny we knew had already lost everything once; he doesn't deserve to be rewritten in our minds, too."

JJ's lips were deep pink and puffy, and the lower one trembled as she said, "Okay." She took a deep breath, then tried to smile as she countered, "He did put gum in my hair."

"True," Adam admitted, "but who do you think put a dead squirrel in Leslie's backpack after he picked on you about your mom leaving?"

Her brows wrinkled briefly, then cleared as she said, "I'd forgotten about that."

"Or wrote on the blackboard that Mr. Sampson was a—"

Adam paused, Iris's upbringing kicking in.

"A dickless wonder," JJ supplied.

Adam nodded. "After he gave you detention. And who do you think pulled the fire alarm when those eighth graders had you pinned between the fire doors by the side exit?"

This time her mouth dropped and emitted an appreciative, whooping exhale. "No!"

Adam shrugged. "Actually, I did that, but it was Danny's idea."

JJ shook her head. "Little Mr. Angel."

Adam pointed at his dimple and grinned. "You always said no one could stay mad at this face."

She scooted back in her chair, and her smile slowly faded.

"But it's not just Danny, is it?" he asked.

JJ shook her head, but acknowledged, "You are entirely too perceptive, Mr. Rutledge."

"Some might even say psychic."

But she didn't bite.

"For some reason, everything that happened the past couple of months has gotten twisted up in my head with losing my dad. It was really hard watching him die," JJ said, picking at the piped edge on her chair. "It wasn't quick—I lied about that—but it was inevitable. It's not that I thought he'd live forever..."

Her voice trailed off, and Adam finished her thought. "But a little part of you did."

She smiled weakly, eyes now as red as her lips with tears threatening. "Yes, I guess it did. Then when you came back... we almost lost you, with Rachel. And I just, I couldn't stand to watch it. But you kept getting sucked into stupid shit, and eventually so did I."

JJ stopped, trying to get her emotions in check, but it was too late. Tears rolled down her cheeks. Trooper got up and rested his long nose on the corner of her seat cushion so she could stroke his head. Adam moved to the edge of his chair, maneuvering around the dog to take his turn at her knee.

"But we both made it back," he said. "So did Evie. And so did Iris."

"They almost didn't," she objected, squeezing the loose, furry skin on top of Trooper's head into a peak.

Adam's voice was calm as he reminded her, "But they did."

"And you—" JJ stared down at the space where half his right arm used to be. "You're not whole."

And there it was. The same thing he heard from the moment he woke up until the moment, if he was lucky, he captured sleep. *You're not whole.* But the voice grew quieter, less insistent, every day. And that voice didn't need to be whispering in JJ's ear, too.

She hadn't quite given in completely, but she'd given up on trying to hide her tears. Adam sat on the arm of her chair, took the hand that wasn't stroking the dog and said, "You're right, my body isn't the way it used to be. But *I'm* still whole in the ways that matter."

JJ looked down at his hand, at an angry red line of scar so fresh it barely warranted the name, then quickly away, toward the windows where the world had now gone full dark. She held her breath, gathering herself to speak.

"All the stupid things I've done in my life, all the times I wouldn't back down, it's because I always knew I'd be okay. But I almost died. I would have, if it hadn't been for you. And when I was lying there," she said, her voice quivering, "all I could think about was Evie. What would happen to her if…"

A sob shook her, and she gasped in reaction. "I'm not supposed to," she said, arm to her side, but couldn't stop.

"Shh," Adam said, rubbing her arm.

He didn't want JJ to panic and make her pain worse. When arm-rubbing wasn't consolation enough, he slid into her chair with her. Trooper appeared mildly offended.

"Shh," he repeated. "It's okay to cry. Just let it out, nice and easy. You're safe, and you've got time. Just let it go."

JJ turned to him and shifted in the chair, not built for two, until she was practically on his lap. Adam held her with both arms, rocking gently, and soon they were both crying. For Danny, and each other. For Virgil. For everyone.

Eventually, Adam's face started itching, and he realized he was no longer crying, or rocking. Also, his legs were numb. He twisted to look at JJ. She'd also stopped crying, and opened her eyes at his movement.

"Do you think about what happened?" she asked, then clarified, "At Teddy's?"

That still covered a lot of territory for Adam, but it didn't matter. The answer was the same for all of it. "I try not to."

"I don't remember much, but one thing I remember clearly doesn't make sense." JJ said, "Who was the woman in the back of Luther's car? The one who held our hands on the way to the medevac?"

Adam smiled. "I don't think you'd believe me if I told you."

She gave him a suspicious look, but before she'd decided whether to challenge him, they saw headlights in the driveway.

"Iris is back," he guessed.

Trooper went to the door, and Adam heard his tail thump on the floor twice.

"According to Trooper, it's Grant," JJ said. "He usually comes by after work."

Adam wriggled free of her weight and the chair's constraints. JJ grunted a protest.

"Sorry," Adam said. "I don't want him to get the wrong idea."

"Don't be ridiculous," she said, grabbing a box of tissues from the coffee table and offering them to him.

Adam shook his head, wiping beneath his eyes with the heel of his hand. Fortunately his nose hadn't gone runny; he'd always been a two-handed nose-blower and didn't fancy figuring out his new technique in front of someone else, not even JJ.

JJ seized Adam's collar, forcing him to look at her. "Hey, are you okay?"

Adam held his lips shut with his teeth, long enough for his head to clear and Grant to cut the engine on his vehicle. And he remembered Iris's words. "Day by day."

JJ carried her crumpled tissue to the kitchen. "I forgot to start his coffee."

Adam followed and watched through the front windows as the Sheriff got out of his cruiser, bare-headed.

He hadn't realized JJ was watching, too, until she said, with a hint of wonder, "I think he loves me."

Adam corralled her head with his arm—no hand necessary—and kissed the top of her head, grinning. "Of course he does, you doofus."

91

The town of Cold Springs had two cemeteries. The one by the school always felt gothic to Luther, with looming conifers and older, larger gravestones, and the river far below just visible at the rear of the property. The next day, he found himself driving past the other cemetery on his way back to the station after responding to a vandalism complaint. Someone had spray painted "ASSHOLE" on Mr. Filmore's tractor, and after spending twenty minutes with the man, Luther sympathized with the culprit. It was a cool but not frigid morning, with the sun having burned off all the frost. In no particular hurry, Luther decided to stop.

Most of the town's recently dead were buried in this cemetery. The space was sandwiched between a couple of fields with grazing horses, and it backed up to forest. A sizable portion was empty still, next to the road, though Luther supposed that would change over the coming years. Because of this buffer and how slowly the few cars passed on the secondary road, it tended to be quiet. The wooded mountains rising on all sides gave a cozy feeling of security despite there being no trees within the cemetery itself.

There was no parking lot, but a paved path looped in one side and out the other, making a half-circle. Luther pulled to the asphalt edge on the near side where his family rested. People must have gotten more poor or more practical over the years; the majority of markers from the past generation or so were plaques rather than standing headstones. Rudy had sprung for a rounded gray stone with fanciful vine engraving for Luther's mother. For Leslie, now lying next to her, Luther had stuck with a simple granite plaque that would be raised at a slight angle when it was installed. He figured Les wouldn't much care what the marker looked like, so long as he was being remembered.

Luther had only been to the cemetery twice since Les's funeral. Once he'd felt agitated and hadn't stayed long. The other time, unable to sleep, he'd brought a bottle to keep him company. He'd dozed off next to Les's grave and woke up shivering.

Standing next to his brother's grave today, staring at the bare spot on the ground, Luther was surprised to find a feeling of peace. He didn't speak, although he'd engaged in full conversations with his dead mother in the past. Instead, Luther was content to stand silently, hat in hand, and watch the trees sway gently in the distance before the breeze arrived to brush his skin, carrying the distinctive cold scent of winter, along with a hint of wood smoke and horses.

He was about to leave when a familiar gray sedan pulled in. Iris Rutledge's body blocked his view of the dark-haired head next to her until they rounded the loop.

Luther hadn't seen Adam since he was loaded on a helicopter (hospitals were hard for Luther, the way Les had passed), but he'd known this moment was coming.

Iris stopped her car, engine still idling, to let Adam out. Luther strode to meet them, and Iris rolled down her window as he approached.

"Luther, you still need a haircut," she called out.

He grinned and put his hat back on his head as he leaned down to speak with her. "Yes, ma'am, I do."

She surprised Luther by grabbing his nearest hand and giving it a squeeze. "Drop by the house sometime and I'll see if I can make you look respectable."

She gave his hand a pat before rolling up her window.

"I'm afraid I'm a lost cause," he muttered, waving at the receding car.

Adam squinted beneath a baseball cap, watching her leave. He wore baggy jeans and an open winter jacket over a flannel shirt, so it was hard to get a sense of his physique. His face was still on the lean side, cheeks and brows a little too prominent. But he looked a helluva lot better than Luther would have expected, clean-shaven with the dark smudges that had lived beneath his eyes mostly gone.

"She got me last night," Adam said, pulling his hat off long enough to rub his hand over his freshly shorn head.

"When did you get out?" Luther asked, then realized it sounded as though he meant prison instead of the hospital.

"Yesterday, but I'll probably be back and forth for a while," he said.

Adam shoved his left hand in his pants pocket before shaking his head and giving a rueful smile while staring at the other gaping sleeve. The fabric swung like a mischievous kid's stretched out shirt, but Adam wouldn't be popping anyone on the nose with a hidden fist. "I wonder how long it'll be before I stop wanting to put my hand in my pocket."

Luther shrugged. "The mind is a strange thing. I've still got a pair of pants from high school I try on once in a while, and they'll barely come up past my knees anymore."

Adam gave a wry huff.

"So what are you gonna get, a hook? Or one of those crazy robot arms that make you some kind of superhero? Personally, I'd go for the hook." Luther began ticking off items on his fingers. "It's simple. It's classic. You can dress it up or down."

"The little black dress of prosthetics?" Adam asked, mouth twitching.

"Hell, yes," Luther said enthusiastically. "And if you go back to bartending, I guarantee you'll get better tips with a hook. Especially if you work in some kind of theme bar. Pirates or Jimmy Buffett or some shit."

Adam laughed despite himself, which made Luther feel better than almost anything, except maybe getting his job back.

"Thanks, Luther. Most people—"

"Most people aren't jerks like me," Luther cut in. "And most people don't know what a goddamn miracle it is you're still walking the earth. That any of us are."

Luther indicated the grave a row beyond Adam, the only one fresher than his brother's. "Virgil saved both our asses."

Adam nodded, then looked away. "Even if he didn't mean to help you."

And here they were, not talking about the thing they weren't talking about. But Luther's anxiety around it was manageable now, nothing like the mountain that had been sitting on his chest. So he'd decided to stop not talking about it.

"About what happened..." No, that wasn't right, and Luther had to start right. "About *what I did* to your mom—hell, your whole family—"

"Don't, Luther," Adam said. "I've got that locked up in a little box, so I don't have to deal with it. Because I can't. Not now. Not with everything else."

"Are you sure that's healthy?"

"Yes, I am," Adam snapped, then clenched his fist before releasing it with a heavy exhalation. "Look, I will deal with it. Eventually. I will open that box, and then you can say whatever you have to say. Maybe we'll have some grand, kumbaya moment, or maybe we'll beat the crap out of each other and never speak again. But for now, I really need to keep it in that box."

"Okay," Luther said.

Adam clutched his right bicep with his left hand. Luther wondered if he was in pain, or maybe he was trying to comfort himself.

"You know, Adam, your dad was watching out for me, too. Despite what I'd done. He had this idea in his head that I had to be there at the end of it all. And I, uh..." Luther cleared his throat. Adam needed to hear the rest, even if it made Luther's skin crawl. "Right before he died, he told me to watch over you. It's like he spoke in my head."

Adam finally met Luther's gaze, but didn't seem surprised. "He told me to stick close to you."

Luther's eyes were drawn to Virgil's grave, almost as if he could hear him speaking. No wonder the man had been crazy, carrying that stuff around all the time. "He was right about me being there," Luther admitted, "but wrong that I'd help you. Directly anyway."

"I shot him, but it was your gun that killed Danny. Or Lawrence. Whoever—or *what*ever—that was."

Luther shivered and shook his head. "That's my little lockbox," he admitted. "And maybe someday I'll be able to open it without going batshit crazy..."

Or maybe not. Luther was content to never find out.

"Okay," Adam said. Then he grinned. It was so unexpected—and genuine—Luther was sure it had caught Adam off guard, too.

"Did you pull a gun on the helicopter pilot?" Adam asked.

"No! Harlan's been telling stories," Luther protested, straight-faced. "It was the paramedic."

Adam snickered.

"And I didn't *pull* the gun," Luther continued, matching Adam's grin with a mischievous one of his own. "I just reminded him it was there."

Their smiles faded, and a comfortable silence fell around them, much like the one Luther had experienced earlier by Les's grave. It made Luther glad they'd decided to let those boxes lie unopened. For now.

"So what are you going to do?" he asked.

Adam shrugged. "I've got a little while to figure it out."

Luther glanced over at the department cruiser. "Your car still running?"

"Stick shift," Adam said simply.

Luther winced. "Sorry."

Adam shrugged again. "Don't forget the dead battery and bald tires and everything else. Yours still running?" he asked, with a grin creeping back on his face.

Luther snorted. "As long as I don't mind freezing my nuts off and squinting through a bullet hole."

A pickup pulling in to the cemetery drew their attention. Luther recognized the silver hair as the truck drew near. "Is that your ride?"

"I guess so," Adam said, in a tone that suggested Harlan's arrival was unexpected, though not unwelcome.

"Well," Luther said, "I should be heading back to the Sheriff's Department. Beth has informed me that after all our shenanigans, I owe her—*a lot*—and I don't want to get on her bad side. Give me a call sometime, if you need a ride, or... whatever."

"Or Iris and I are ready to kill each other?" Adam suggested.

Luther laughed. "Well, if buying you a beer will help keep the homicide rate down in Beecham County, I'm happy to be a martyr to the job. Even off duty."

Harlan parked behind Luther's cruiser and rolled his window down when the deputy reached him. Luther hadn't seen the old man since they'd loaded Adam on a chopper and Luther had had his little... breakdown? Breakthrough? Either way, he was grateful to Harlan, but felt uncomfortable meeting him again. Like

Harlan hadn't just seen him naked, but pulled a splinter from his pasty ass, then applied ointment and a Band-Aid.

"Deputy Beck," Harlan said. "Good to see you back in uniform. That *might* help keep you out of trouble."

"Thank you, sir," Luther said. "Since I am on duty, I might ask if your neighbor Jim Henderson ever got his *borrowed* farm truck back."

Harlan grinned and pointed a finger at Luther. "You have a suspicious mind. He has not—Teddy is still driving it—but he will soon. I promise."

"Uh-huh," Luther said, answering his grin. He glanced over toward Adam, who had made his way to his parents' graves. Luther's grin faded as he watched Adam squat awkwardly, placing his remaining hand on the ground to balance, then drop to one knee. "How do you think he's really doing?"

Harlan's eyes followed Luther's. "He's alive."

That would have seemed like a low bar, if recent events hadn't made it downright astounding. Still... "And?" Luther pressed.

"And it'll take time. But Adam'll get there," Harlan said. He turned to Luther, and his voice was firm but gentle, reminiscent of the last time they'd spoken. "And so will you."

92

Surrounded by grave markers, Adam reflected that grief was like a nasty strain of flu. Just when you thought you were doing okay and started making plans to leave the house, suddenly you found yourself back in bed feeling like crap again.

Last night, he and Iris had spent a pleasant evening with JJ and Grant and the girls. Afterward, back in familiar surroundings and finally away from hospital lights and noises and prodding, he'd slept better than he had in a long time. But when Adam woke this morning, he'd lost all that contentment and wished he could have stayed asleep. Or never woken.

When Iris suggested a cemetery excursion, Adam had immediately agreed, trusting her almost spooky instinct for knowing what he needed. But she hadn't mentioned she'd be leaving Adam there. And he hadn't anticipated Luther. Over the past couple of months Adam had discovered, somewhat to his surprise, that he genuinely enjoyed spending time with Luther. But Adam had also found that in his darkest moments (which he seemed to have slid into again) he forgave and hated Luther in equal measures. Of course, he could say the same for himself. Except for the forgiving part.

And now Harlan was here.

Had Iris really wanted Adam to visit his parents' graves, or was this one of her circuitous ways to connect him with Harlan? Adam stood in front of his mother's headstone, the trench from his father's grave still fresh and naked next to him, and realized he was too tired to care. He sunk to both knees on the damp ground, felt it soak through his jeans, and realized he didn't care about that, either.

Eyes shut, he let his head sink to his chest. It wasn't simply grief. Virgil was gone—*his father was gone*—but he felt a bit like he had the final few weeks of Virgil's life when Adam's mind had been bombarded by sensations and images and noise all the time. He wasn't seeing vivid images, but Adam found himself blinking at shadows that weren't there, turning his head to follow ghosts in his peripheral vision. And while he couldn't identify a particular sound, there was a feeling of fullness in his head and ears reminiscent of the aftermath of loud, sustained noise. It was as if pressure were building in his skull, and he had no way to vent it.

Adam had sat with the muddled chaos in his head and tried to tease his way through it, the same way he had spent hours peeling away maleficent layers at the stones before confronting Danny and Lawrence. But he couldn't. He couldn't seem to find that place within himself again. He thought of Otto's uncle *(blew his brains out)*, and of struggling with Luther for his gun outside the emergency room. What would Adam have done with that gun? And now... he could write left-handed; could he shoot left-handed, too?

Adam's fingers brushed the engraved lettering on the headstone and an image flashed into his head. A baby sat on a floor, and in the way of dreams and visions, Adam was both *the child* and *watching* the child.

Something square was directly in front of him—a diaper bag?—between him and where he wanted to be. He grabbed a corner and tugged, but it wouldn't move. He would make it move. Leaning against the bag, he stood, but his bowed legs couldn't maintain standing yet. They collapsed and he thumped to the floor on his bottom. He blinked hard in surprise, but it didn't hurt. He tried again with the same result. But this time, he heard a giggle.

He lifted his head and a different world swam into focus. There she was, sitting on a sofa on the other side of the bag, long flowing hair swinging forward and back as her body swayed with laughter. That's where he wanted to be. With her.

So he faced the obstacle again. He'd go over it. He stood, clutched the sides of the bag and fought his traitorous buckling knees. He grunted with effort as he lifted one leg, then the other, but couldn't get either high enough.

A familiar man's voice said, amused, "It sounds like he's trying to poop."

"Don't you listen, Little Man," she said, reaching for him. Her hands were beneath his arms, and the floor and all his effort fell away as she said, "But you know, you could have just gone around it."

Her face became his world as they touched noses, then she settled him over her shoulder and he nestled his head into her neck. "Why do you make everything so difficult?" she asked.

Adam jerked and found himself caught somewhere between the child and his adult self, as her brown eyes bore into his blue ones and her voice repeated, intense and challenging and somehow present, *Adam, why do you make everything so difficult?*

His eyes flew open and he sucked in a gasp of air. Adam stared at his fingers, at bits of dusty grit they'd picked up from the stone. *What was that?* Was it a memory, or something more?

The dead turf had gone flat against the ground with approaching winter, like lawn bedhead. Adam worked his fingers through the grass to the earth, extended his consciousness, deeper and deeper...

And felt Harlan's hand on his shoulder.

"I wouldn't advise that, son."

The elderly man leaned heavily on his cane, as if it were a necessary support rather than a potential weapon. "I understand the inclination," he continued, "but you never know what you'll find still hanging around a cemetery."

"I saw Mom," Adam said.

Harlan inclined his head toward his truck and began slowly walking back. "I'm not surprised."

Adam wobbled when he stood, still retraining his old movement habits. A mass of puffy, pale gray clouds blew in as he followed Harlan, blocking the sun and making the chill more noticeable. It was cold inside the truck, too, but at least there was a seat. Adam stared at the dark, wet knees of his pants.

"JJ saw Mom, too," Adam said. "In Luther's car, on the way to the helicopter."

Harlan's mouth curled so slightly it would be an exaggeration to call it a smile. "I figured as much, though I'm a little surprised JJ saw her."

"So Mom was there? With us?"

"Well, not exactly," Harlan said, resting a hand on the steering wheel, staring straight ahead as though they were moving. "It's more like you were somewhere else, with her. Somewhere you couldn't stay."

And why couldn't he stay?

"*Somewhere?*" Adam snapped. "Please, don't blind me with technical terms."

Harlan glared at Adam, who took a deep breath before continuing, "I'm sorry, Harlan. I don't know if I can live like this, the way I feel now."

"May I?" Harlan asked, reaching toward Adam with a bare hand.

Harlan slid Adam's sleeve up, revealing his forearm and the trailing edge of another livid scar that extended almost to his shoulder. Adam braced himself, but nothing catastrophic happened at Harlan's touch. Warmth radiated from there, up Adam's arm to his skull where it tingled; it wasn't painful, but it felt active. Bony plates shifted and there was a tumbling sensation inside, like objects tipping over as a dog raced through an overcrowded room. Adam smiled at the image—suddenly he could see the dog, a rich, reddish-brown pit bull mix with white markings and a wide-tongued, goofy grin. Who was he running toward? Not Adam, or not *just* Adam...

The image vanished as quickly as it had appeared when Harlan released Adam's arm and asked, voice gruff, "Better?"

Adam opened his eyes. The sun was back, but his skin was cool. He had a sneaking suspicion they'd been sitting in the truck cab longer than the minute or two it seemed. And he didn't feel perfect by any means, but he did feel significantly better. "Yes, thanks," he said.

"Goddamn, son, why didn't you say something before?" Harlan blew out his breath next to him. "I guess because you have to make everything difficult."

"You heard that?" Adam asked.

Harlan nodded. "Only because there was so much energy behind it, like Charlotte was giving you a dope slap. You know, our connection hasn't been the same since—"

"Since Danny almost killed you?"

"That," Harlan acknowledged. "And when Virgil started shielding you. According to Teddy, your father was also using you, unintentionally, to balance himself. Draining your sanity like some kind of psychic vampire."

"Is that what's wrong with me?"

"Partially," Harlan said, and sighed. "I have a theory, but it's a little... *woo-woo*."

Adam almost chuckled as he recalled Harlan's reaction when Adam had used the term the first time they'd met and asked, "So now I'm the train?"

Harlan smiled. Adam suspected the remark had been a test to see how engaged Adam was, how well his mind was connecting the past and the present.

The older man continued, "Your father was nuttier than a fruitcake, but he wasn't all wrong. The remnants of Virgil's walls you saw in your mind, I believe they were broken because they'd been doing their job. That those—and Virgil—were all that stood between you and Lawrence. Unfortunately, Virgil was also the bridge that connected you."

Adam realized Harlan was right. He'd first heard his grandfather while dozing at Iris's after Luther and JJ had left. Through Virgil.

"He said, *I've been waiting.*" Adam's words were barely above a whisper, and he touched the smooth surface of the truck seat beneath him, reassuring himself when and where he was. "He wondered what I'd do when he showed me what was possible. Later he found me, or I found him, when I was looking for Virgil. But I didn't know…"

Who he was. Who to turn to. Who to trust and ask for help. And now Adam locked those old anxieties in his bursting box, along with Lawrence's later visitation in the hospital parking lot and his whispered command, *Take his gun.*

"I'm afraid I underestimated the sonuvabitch," Harlan admitted. "Which shouldn't be surprising. I had a bad habit of doing that while he was alive, too."

"Why didn't you tell Virgil the truth?" Adam asked. Iris had told him how his grandfather died while Adam was in the hospital. The fact that she'd killed her husband surprised Adam less than the fact she'd confessed it. He'd been unable to speak coherently at the time, but had squeezed her fingers with his remaining ones. They hadn't spoken of it since.

"And why would I do that?" Harlan asked, as usual not needing elaboration. "So he'd hate me less? He wouldn't have believed me. And if by some miracle he did, well, that'd be an even worse shitstorm. His relationship with Iris was already complicated enough. No, better the evil he knew."

Adam turned to look at Harlan, to watch his reaction as he asked Harlan the question he asked himself most nights. "Is he gone now?"

"Lawrence? I think so," Harlan said, his voice light, expression unconcerned. "I've learned not to take anything about that man or the way the world works for granted. But I think it is highly unlikely that he will ever be bothering us or anyone else again."

Harlan gave his head a quick shake. "But that's something we can discuss another time, at our leisure. Speaking of which... what I did today was not a cure, it was a start. And the effects won't last forever. You need to purge all that shit Virgil and Lawrence left behind. Not to mention cleaning up some of the mess *you* made. That shield of yours was about as subtle as nuking a house to get rid of rats."

"And that'll fix me?" Adam asked.

"I don't know; fixing you is a pretty tall order," Harlan said, but relented when he saw Adam's anxious expression. He gripped Adam's arm reassuringly. "Hey! It's okay. Teddy and I will help. But you need to learn how to do these things yourself, and how to protect yourself more... artfully."

Adam stared at the man, at the cheeks that had filled in a bit in the weeks since the showdown at Teddy's. His brows were transitioning from dark to gray, but his eyes shone like the silver hair above them. Harlan wasn't lying. He wasn't hiding some grand, elaborate plan. Although he did have a simple one.

"We could work here, at my cabin," Harlan said, "but the sad condition we're all in, it'll take a week to do it right..."

"And if Teddy spends another night under your roof, it might be his last?" Adam guessed.

Harlan threw his head back in exasperation. "That man! It's only been two days, and I'm already having sympathy for psycho Doreen. I might stab him, too."

"Except you're the one she stabbed," Adam said.

"Oh, yeah," Harlan said, and his levity faded. "Losing Virgil like that hit Teddy pretty hard. I worry about him being alone just yet. I was hoping you'd be up for one last road trip. Take Teddy home, get him situated. You think you could stay there, at his place?"

Adam knew Harlan wasn't asking about his aversion to using an outhouse. Could he sleep in the Rutledge home, or would he always be vigilant, so near the altar in the woods and the things that had happened there? Maybe. If he could, he'd certainly have no excuse for insomnia anywhere else.

"I'm willing to try," Adam said.

Harlan nodded. "And while we're there, we'll get you straightened out. It'd be good for Teddy to have a project."

Adam raised a brow, asking silently, *I'm a project now?*

Harlan laughed. "Is that a yes?"

"I've got appointments coming up," Adam said, glancing at his arm, which didn't ache as much as it had earlier. Harlan had helped, but the limb had its own daily cycles, too. "More rehab, and fitting a prosthetic—"

"I know," Harlan said. "But we'll be closer to where you were treated initially, and you can go to their outpatient facility instead of getting a referral here."

Adam saw his grandmother's hand at work. "So Iris is okay with this?"

Harlan started the truck and let the engine idle. "Son, you get on with her better than anyone else—including me—when it comes to sharing space, but I doubt she'll be disappointed to have the house to herself for a while. Although I did have to promise we'd be back by Christmas."

Christmas. Already. Adam had been a fugitive on Halloween and spent Thanksgiving in the hospital last week. (Turkey and gravy on his meal tray had tipped him off.) Most years, he'd called Iris from his current crappy apartment on Christmas morning. It'd be nice to spend the holiday with her in Cold Springs.

"Okay," Adam said. "As long as you're not feeding me ass tea every day."

Harlan grinned. "Not *every* day. But the things Teddy and I need to teach you—things you should've learned years ago—often go down easier with a cupful of ass tea."

"Did anyone teach my father?" Adam asked, though he was sure he knew the answer.

"The wrong person taught Virgil," Harlan said. But instead of the heat that usually tinged his voice when he spoke of Lawrence, Adam heard a hint of regret.

Adam leaned back as Harlan rolled out of the cemetery onto the back road. They passed a shaggy blonde horse, standing with its head hanging over the fence. Adam wondered if it was waiting for someone, hoping for a treat. He rested his temple on the cold window. Soon shadows of adjacent forest flickered across his eyes. Adam lifted his arm toward the glass out of habit, then tucked it next to him. He missed tracing patterns on the foggy window, even if it seemed an odd habit to lament. As Luther had said, the mind is a strange thing.

A strange and wonderful thing.

Adam's thoughts wandered to the dog he'd seen, bounding playfully, when Harlan had laid his hand on him.

"I've always wanted a dog," he said.

Harlan grunted, but didn't take the bait.

"I don't suppose you know when..."

"I told you, it doesn't work that way."

Adam smiled. Harlan had just confirmed his suspicions, that what he'd seen had tapped into Harlan's prescience. There'd been someone else with Adam, someone important to both him and the dog.

"Who is she?" Adam asked. "Where will I find her?"

Harlan laughed. "You never give up, do you? Well, it doesn't matter, because I don't know. That one's for you to figure out." Harlan's eyes sparkled as he turned to Adam. "But I can tell you this, son. I think it'll be exciting."

ACKNOWLEDGMENTS

Thank you as always to my excellent editors Alida Winternheimer (you were right about owning the woo-woo) and Calee Allen (my favorite seatbelt/seat belt wrestling partner), and to the bestest beta readers Sandy Mom and Paul. Special thanks to my husband for not breaking anything while helping choreograph action scenes, and for owning the role of Epiphanator.

Thanks also to the Writer's Detective Bureau community for keeping me honest on a couple of weapon issues. Any mistakes are my own, possibly on purpose. Besides, this book has psychics. How much realism do you expect?

I feel so fortunate that narrator Alex Knox joined the team while I was working on this final installment. He does a stupendous job on the Dead Hollow audiobooks, and the energy he brought to the project helped me when I was running on empty. I heard his voice(s) in my head while I wrote *Heir*. (I'm not supposed to talk about the voices I heard while writing *Prodigal* and *Founder*.)

I've noted before that this series is a departure from the Sydney Brennan Mysteries in almost every way—setting, genre, point of view, themes, you name it. But while wrapping up *Heir*, I finally realized the biggest difference between them: Sydney Brennan is the series of my *head*. Dead Hollow is the series of my *heart*. And finishing the trilogy breaks my heart just a little bit. Okay, maybe more than a little bit.

But don't worry. I can't say when, I can't say how, but Adam will be back. *And I think it'll be exciting.*

ABOUT THE AUTHOR

A recovering criminal attorney, Judy K. Walker writes from her home in Hawaii, where she is surrounded by husband, dogs, cat, and assorted geckos. Her life's journey may have taken her thousands of miles from her West Virginia origins, but she was thrilled to return to her roots in the *Dead Hollow Trilogy*.

She also writes the Sydney Brennan Mysteries, a private investigator series set in Tallahassee, Florida, another of her stops along the way.

Learn more about my books and connect with me online at:
www.judykwalker.com

ALSO BY JUDY K. WALKER

The Sydney Brennan Mysteries (In Order of Publication):

Back to Lazarus (A Sydney Brennan Novel)

Secrets in Stockbridge (A Sydney Brennan Novella)

The Perils of Panacea (A Sydney Brennan Novel)

No Safe Winterport (A Sydney Brennan Novella)

Braving the Boneyard (A Sydney Brennan Novel)

River Bound (A Sydney Brennan Novella)

The Dead Hollow Trilogy:

Prodigal

Founder

Heir